AMERICAN
DIRT

ALSO BY JEANINE CUMMINS

A Rip in Heaven: A Memoir of Murder and Its Aftermath

The Outside Boy

The Crooked Branch

AMERICAN DIRT

DIRT

Jeanine Cummins

FLATIRON
BOOKS
NEW YORK

AMERICAN DIRT. Copyright © 2019 by Jeanine Cummins. All rights reserved. Printed in the United States of America. For information, address Flatiron Books, 120 Broadway, New York, NY 10271.

www.flatironbooks.com

Endpaper map by Rhys Davies

Designed by Omar Chapa

Library of Congress Cataloging-in-Publication Data

Names: Cummins, Jeanine, author.
Title: American dirt : a novel / Jeanine Cummins.
Description: First edition. | New York : Flatiron Books, 2020.
Identifiers: LCCN 2019036052 | ISBN 9781250209764 (hardcover) |
    ISBN 9781250754080 (international, sold outside the U.S., subject to rights
    availability)| ISBN 9781250209771 (ebook)
Subjects: LCSH: Drug traffic—Mexico—Fiction. | Organized crime—Mexico—
    Fiction. | Immigrants—Mexican-American Border Region—Fiction. |
    GSAFD: Suspense fiction.
Classification: LCC PS3603.U663 A64 2020 | DDC 813/.6—dc23
LC record available at https://lccn.loc.gov/2019036052

Our books may be purchased in bulk for promotional, educational, or business use. Please contact your local bookseller or the Macmillan Corporate and Premium Sales Department at 1-800-221-7945, extension 5442, or by email at MacmillanSpecialMarkets@macmillan.com.

First U.S. Edition: January 2020
First International Edition: January 2020

10 9 8 7 6 5 4 3 2 1

For Joe

Era la sed y el hambre, y tú fuiste la fruta.
Era el duelo y las ruinas, y tú fuiste el milagro.

There were thirst and hunger, and you were the fruit.
There were grief and ruins, and you were the miracle.

—*Pablo Neruda,* "THE SONG OF DESPAIR"

AMERICAN
DIRT

CHAPTER ONE

One of the very first bullets comes in through the open window above the toilet where Luca is standing. He doesn't immediately understand that it's a bullet at all, and it's only luck that it doesn't strike him between the eyes. Luca hardly registers the mild noise it makes as it flies past and lodges into the tiled wall behind him. But the wash of bullets that follows is loud, booming, and thudding, *clack-clacking* with helicopter speed. There is a raft of screams, too, but that noise is short-lived, soon exterminated by the gunfire. Before Luca can zip his pants, lower the lid, climb up to look out, before he has time to verify the source of that terrible clamor, the bathroom door swings open and Mami is there.

"*Mijo, ven,*" she says, so quietly that Luca doesn't hear her.

Her hands are not gentle; she propels him toward the shower. He trips on the raised tile step and falls forward onto his hands. Mami lands on top of him and his teeth pierce his lip in the tumble. He tastes blood. One dark droplet makes a tiny circle of red against the bright green shower tile. Mami shoves Luca into the corner. There's no door on this shower, no curtain. It's only a corner of his *abuela*'s bathroom, with a third tiled wall built to suggest a stall. This wall is around five and a half feet high and three feet long—just large enough, with some luck, to shield Luca and his mother from sight. Luca's back is wedged, his small shoulders touching both walls. His knees are drawn up to his chin, and Mami is clinched around him like a tortoise's shell. The door of the bathroom remains open, which worries Luca, though he can't see it beyond the shield of his mother's body, behind the half barricade of his *abuela*'s shower wall. He'd like to wriggle out and tip that door lightly with his finger. He'd like to swing it shut. He doesn't know that his mother left it open on purpose. That a closed door only invites closer scrutiny.

The clatter of gunfire outside continues, joined by an odor of charcoal and burning meat. Papi is grilling carne asada out there and Luca's favorite chicken drumsticks. He likes them only a tiny bit blackened, the crispy tang of the skins. His mother pulls her head up long enough to look him in the eye. She puts her hands on both sides of his face and tries to cover his ears. Outside, the gunfire slows. It ceases and then returns in short bursts, mirroring, Luca thinks, the sporadic and wild rhythm of his heart. In between the racket, Luca can still hear the radio, a woman's voice announcing *¡La Mejor 100.1 FM Acapulco!* followed by Banda MS singing about how happy they are to be in love. Someone shoots the radio, and then there's laughter. Men's voices. Two or three, Luca can't tell. Hard bootsteps on Abuela's patio.

"Is he here?" One of the voices is just outside the window.

"Here."

"What about the kid?"

"*Mira,* there's a boy here. This him?"

Luca's cousin Adrián. He's wearing cleats and his Hernández jersey. Adrián can juggle a *balón de fútbol* on his knees forty-seven times without dropping it.

"I don't know. Looks the right age. Take a picture."

"Hey, chicken!" another voice says. "Man, this looks good. You want some chicken?"

Luca's head is beneath his *mami*'s chin, her body knotted tightly around him.

"Forget the chicken, *pendejo.* Check the house."

Luca's *mami* rocks in her squatting position, pushing Luca even harder into the tiled wall. She squeezes against him, and together they hear the squeak and bang of the back door. Footsteps in the kitchen. The intermittent rattle of bullets in the house. Mami turns her head and notices, vivid against the tile floor, the lone spot of Luca's blood, illuminated by the slant of light from the window. Luca feels her breath snag in her chest. The house is quiet now. The hallway that ends at the door of this bathroom is carpeted. Mami tugs her shirtsleeve over her hand, and Luca watches in horror as she leans away from him, toward that telltale splatter of blood. She runs her sleeve over it, leaving behind only a faint smear, and then pitches back to him just as the man in the hallway uses the butt of his AK-47 to nudge the door the rest of the way open.

There must be three of them because Luca can still hear two voices in the yard. On the other side of the shower wall, the third man unzips his pants and empties his bladder into Abuela's toilet. Luca does not breathe. Mami does not breathe. Their eyes are closed, their bodies motionless, even their adrenaline is suspended within the calcified will of their stillness. The man hiccups, flushes, washes his hands. He dries them on Abuela's good yellow towel, the one she puts out only for parties.

They don't move after the man leaves. Even after they hear the squeak and bang, once more, of the kitchen door. They stay there, fixed in their tight knot of arms and legs and knees and chins and clenched eyelids and locked fingers, even after they hear the man join his compatriots outside, after they hear him announce that the house is clear and he's going to eat some chicken now, because there's no excuse for letting good barbecue go to waste, not when there are children starving in Africa. The man is still close enough outside the window that Luca can hear the moist, rubbery smacking sounds his mouth makes with the chicken. Luca concentrates on breathing, in and out, without sound. He tells himself that this is just a bad dream, a terrible dream, but one he's had many times before. He always awakens, heart pounding, and finds himself flooded with relief. *It was just a dream.* Because these are the modern bogeymen of urban Mexico. Because even parents who take care not to discuss the violence in front of them, to change the radio station when there's news of another shooting, to conceal the worst of their own fears, cannot prevent their children from talking to other children. On the swings, at the *fútbol* field, in the boys' bathroom at school, the gruesome stories gather and swell. These kids, rich, poor, middle-class, have all seen bodies in the streets. Casual murder. And they know from talking to one another that there's a hierarchy of danger, that some families are at greater risk than others. So although Luca never saw the least scrap of evidence of that risk from his parents, even though they demonstrated their courage impeccably before their son, he knew—he knew this day would come. But that truth does nothing to soften its arrival. It's a long, long while before Luca's mother removes the clamp of her hand from the back of his neck, before she leans back far enough for him to notice that the angle of light falling through the bathroom window has changed.

There's a blessing in the moments after terror and before confirmation. When at last he moves his body, Luca experiences a brief, lurching exhilaration at the very fact of his being alive. For a moment he enjoys the ragged passage of breath through his chest. He places his palms flat to feel the cool press of tiles beneath his skin. Mami collapses against the wall across from him and works her jaw in a way that reveals the dimple in her left cheek. It's weird to see her good church shoes in the shower. Luca touches the cut on his lip. The blood has dried there, but he scratches it with his teeth, and it opens again. He understands that, were this a dream, he would not taste blood.

At length, Mami stands. "Stay here," she instructs him in a whisper. "Don't move until I come back for you. Don't make a sound, you understand?"

Luca lunges for her hand. "Mami, don't go."

"*Mijo,* I will be right back, okay? You stay here." Mami pries Luca's fingers from her hand. "Don't move," she says again. "Good boy."

Luca finds it easy to obey his mother's directive, not so much because he's an obedient child, but because he doesn't want to see. His whole family out there, in Abuela's backyard. Today is Saturday, April 7, his cousin Yénifer's *quinceañera,* her fifteenth birthday party. She's wearing a long white dress. Her father and mother are there, Tío Alex and Tía Yemi, and Yénifer's younger brother, Adrián, who, because he already turned nine, likes to say he's a year older than Luca, even though they're really only four months apart.

Before Luca had to pee, he and Adrián had been kicking the *balón* around with their other *primos.* The mothers had been sitting around the table at the patio, their iced *palomas* sweating on their napkins. The last time they were all together at Abuela's house, Yénifer had accidentally walked in on Luca in the bathroom, and Luca was so mortified that today he made Mami come with him and stand guard outside the door. Abuela didn't like it; she told Mami she was coddling him, that a boy his age should be able to go to the bathroom by himself, but Luca is an only child, so he gets away with things other kids don't.

In any case, Luca is alone in the bathroom now, and he tries not to think it, but the thought swarms up unbidden: those irritable words Mami and Abuela exchanged were perhaps the very last ones between them, ever. Luca had approached the table wriggling, whispered into Mami's ear, and Abuela, seeing this, had shaken her head, wagged an admonishing finger at them both, passed her remarks. She had a way of smiling when she criticized. But Mami was always on Luca's side. She rolled her eyes and pushed her chair back from the table anyway, ignoring her mother's disapproval. When was that—ten minutes ago? Two hours? Luca feels unmoored from the boundaries of time that have always existed.

Outside the window he hears Mami's tentative footsteps, the soft scuff of her shoe through the remnants of something broken. A solitary gasp, too windy to be called a sob. Then a quickening of sound as she crosses the patio with purpose, depresses the keys on her phone. When she speaks, her voice has a stretched quality that Luca has never heard before, high and tight in the back of her throat.

"Send help."

CHAPTER TWO

By the time Mami returns to pull Luca from the shower, he's curled into a tight ball and rocking himself. She tells him to stand, but he shakes his head and rolls himself up even tighter, his body flapping with panicked reluctance. As long as he stays here in this shower with his face lowered into the dark angles of his elbows, as long as he doesn't look Mami in the face, he can put off knowing what he already knows. He can prolong the moment of irrational hope that maybe some sliver of yesterday's world is still intact.

It might be better for him to go and look, to see the brilliant splatters of color on Yénifer's white dress, to see Adrián's eyes, open to the sky, to see Abuela's gray hair, matted with stuff that should never exist outside the neat encasement of a skull. It might be good, actually, for Luca to see the warm wreckage of his recent father, the spatula bent crooked beneath his fallen weight, his blood still leaching across the concrete patio. Because none of it, however horrific, is worse than the images Luca will conjure instead with the radiance of his own imagination.

When at last she gets him to stand, Mami takes Luca out the front door, which may or may not be the best idea. If *los sicarios* were to return, what would be worse—to be on the street in plain sight, or to be hidden inside where no one might witness their arrival? An impossible question. Nothing is better or worse than anything else now. They walk across Abuela's tidy courtyard and Mami opens the gate. Together they sit on the yellow-painted curb with their feet on the street. The far side is in shade, but it's bright here, and the sun is hot against Luca's forehead. After some brief swell of minutes, they hear sirens approaching. Mami, whose name is Lydia, becomes aware that her teeth are chattering. She's not cold. Her armpits are damp, and she has goose bumps across the flesh of her arms. Luca leans forward and retches once. He brings up a glob of potato salad, stained pink with fruit punch. It splats onto the asphalt between his feet, but he and his mother don't move away from it. They don't even seem to notice. Nor do they note the furtive rearrangement of curtains and blinds in nearby windows as the neighbors prepare their credible deniability.

What Luca does notice is the walls that line his *abuela*'s street. He's seen them countless times before, but today he perceives a difference: each house here is fronted by a small courtyard like Abuela's, hidden from the street by a wall like Abuela's, topped with razor wire or chicken wire or spiked fence posts like Abuela's, and accessible only through a locked gate like Abuela's. Acapulco is a dangerous city. The people take precautions here, even in nice neighborhoods like this one, especially in nice neighborhoods like this one. But what good are those protections when the men come? Luca leans his head against his mother's shoulder, and she puts an arm around him. She doesn't ask if he's okay, because from now on that question will carry a weight of painful absurdity. Lydia tries her best not to consider the many words that will never come out of her mouth now, the sudden monster void of words she will never get to say.

When they arrive, the police pull yellow *escena del crimen* tape across both ends of the block to discourage traffic and make room for the macabre motorcade of emergency vehicles. There are a lot of officers, a whole army of them, who move around and past Luca and Lydia with choreographed reverence. When the senior detective approaches and begins asking questions, Lydia hesitates for a moment, considering where to send Luca. He's too young to hear everything she needs to say. She should dispatch him to someone else for a few minutes, so she can give forthright answers to these dreadful questions. She should send him to his father. Her mother. Her sister, Yemi. But they are all dead in the backyard, their bodies as close as toppled dominoes. It's all meaningless anyway. The police aren't here to help. Lydia begins to sob. Luca stands and places the cold curve of his hand across the back of his mother's neck.

"Give her a minute," he says, like a grown man.

When the detective returns, there's a woman with him, the medical examiner, who addresses Luca directly. She puts a hand on his shoulder and asks if he'd like to sit in her truck. It says SEMEFO on the side, and the back doors are standing open. Mami nods at him, so Luca goes with the woman and sits inside, dangling his feet over the back bumper. She offers him a sweating can, a cold *refresco*.

Lydia's brain, which had been temporarily suspended by shock, begins working again, but it creeps like sludge. She's still sitting on the curb, and the detective stands between her and her son.

"Did you see the shooter?" he asks.

"Shooters, plural. I think there were three of them." She wishes the detective would step aside so she can keep Luca in her line of sight. He's only a dozen steps away.

"You saw them?"

"No, we heard them. We were hiding in the shower. One came in and took a piss while we were in there. Maybe you can get fingerprints from the faucet. He washed his hands. Can you believe that?" Lydia claps her hands loudly, as if to scare off the memory. "There were at least two more voices outside."

"Did they say or do anything that might help identify them?"

She shakes her head. "One ate the chicken."

The detective writes *pollo* in his notebook.

"One asked if *he* was here."

"A specific target? Did they say who *he* was? A name?"

"They didn't have to. It was my husband."

The detective stops writing and looks at her expectantly. "Your husband is?"

"Sebastián Pérez Delgado."

"The reporter?"

Lydia nods, and the detective whistles through his teeth.

"He's here?"

She nods again. "On the patio. With the spatula. With the sign."

"I'm sorry, señora. Your husband received many threats, yes?"

"Yes, but not recently."

"And what exactly was the nature of those threats?"

"They told him to stop writing about the cartels."

"Or?"

"Or they would kill his whole family." Her voice is flat.

The detective takes a deep breath and looks at Lydia with what might be interpreted as sympathy. "When was the last time he was threatened?"

Lydia shakes her head. "I don't know. A long time ago. This wasn't supposed to happen. It wasn't supposed to happen."

The detective folds his lips into a thin line and remains silent.

"They're going to kill me, too," she says, understanding only as these words emerge that they might be true.

The detective does not move to contradict her. Unlike many of his colleagues—he's not sure which ones, but it doesn't matter—he happens not to be on the cartel payroll. He trusts no one. In fact, of the more than two dozen law enforcement and medical personnel moving around Abuela's home and patio this very moment, marking the locations of shell casings, examining footprints, analyzing blood splatter, taking pictures, checking for pulses, making the sign of the cross over the corpses of Lydia's family, seven receive regular money from the local cartel. The illicit payment is three times more than what they earn from the government. In fact, one has already texted *el jefe* to report Lydia's and Luca's survival. The others do nothing, because that's precisely what the cartel pays them to do, to populate uniforms and perform the appearance of governance. Some of the personnel feel morally conflicted about this; others do not. None of them have a choice anyway, so their feelings are largely immaterial. The unsolved-crime rate in Mexico is well north of 90 percent. The costumed existence of *la policía* provides the necessary counterillusion to the fact of the cartel's actual impunity. Lydia knows this. Everyone knows this. She decides presently that she must get out of here. She stands up from her position on the curb and is surprised by the strength of her legs beneath her. The detective steps back to give her space.

"When he realizes I've survived they will return." And then the memory comes back to her like a throb: one of the voices in the yard asking, *What about the kid?* Lydia's joints feel like water. "He's going to murder my son."

"*He?*" the detective says. "You know specifically who did this?"

"Are you kidding me?" she asks. There's only one possible perpetrator

for a bloodbath of this magnitude in Acapulco, and everyone knows
who that man is. Javier Crespo Fuentes. Her friend. Why should she
say his name out loud? The detective's question is either a stage play or a
test. He writes more words in his notebook. He writes, *La Lechuza?* He
writes, *Los Jardineros?* And then shows the notebook to Lydia. "I can't do
this right now." She pushes past him.

"Please, just a few more questions."

"No. No more questions. Zero more questions."

There are sixteen bodies in the backyard, almost everyone Lydia loved
in the world, but she still feels on the precipice of this information—she
knows it to be factual because she heard them die, she saw their bodies.
She touched her mother's still-warm hand and felt the absence of her
husband's pulse when she lifted his wrist. But her mind is still trying to
rewind it, to undo it. Because it can't really be true. It's too horrific to be
actually true. Panic feels imminent, but it doesn't descend.

"Luca, come." She reaches out her hand, and Luca hops down from
the medical examiner's truck. He leaves the still-full *refresco* on the back
bumper.

Lydia grabs him, and together they walk down the street to where
Sebastián parked their car, near the end of the block. The detective follows, still trying to speak to her. He doesn't accept that she has quit the
conversation. Was she not clear enough? She stops walking so abruptly
he almost stumbles into her back. He draws up on his tiptoes to avoid a
collision. She spins on her foot.

"I need his keys," she says.

"Keys?"

"My husband's car keys."

The detective continues speaking as Lydia pushes past him again,
pulling Luca along behind her. She goes back through the gate into
Abuela's courtyard and tells Luca to wait. Then she thinks better of it and
brings him into the house. She sits him on Abuela's gold velveteen couch
with instructions not to move.

"Can you stay with him, please?"

The detective nods.

Lydia pauses momentarily at the back door, and then squares her
shoulders before pushing it open and stepping out. In the shade of the

backyard, there's the sweet odor of lime and sticky charred sauce, and Lydia knows she will never eat barbecue again. Some of her family members are covered now, and there are little bright yellow placards set up around the yard with black letters and numbers on them. The placards mark the locations of evidence that will never be used to seek a conviction. The placards make everything worse. Their presence means it's real. Lydia is aware of her lungs inside her body—they feel raw and raggedy, a sensation she's never experienced before. She steps toward Sebastián, who hasn't moved, his left arm still bent awkwardly beneath him, the spatula jutting out from beneath his hip. The way he's splayed there reminds Lydia of the shapes his body makes when he's at his most vividly animated, when he wrestles with Luca in the living room after dinner. They squeal. They roar. They bang into the furniture. Lydia runs soapy water into the kitchen sink and rolls her eyes at them. But all that heat is gone now. There's a ticking stillness beneath Sebastián's skin. She wants to talk to him before all his color is gone. She wants to tell him what happened, hurriedly, desperately. Some manic part of her believes that if she tells the story well enough, she can convince him not to be dead. She can convince him of her need for him, of the greatness of their son's need for him. There's a kind of paralyzed insanity in her throat.

Someone has removed the cardboard sign the gunmen left weighted to his chest with a simple rock. The sign in green marker said: TODA MI FAMILIA ESTÁ MUERTA POR MI CULPA (*My whole family is dead because of me*).

Lydia crouches at her husband's feet, but she doesn't want to feel the cooling of his pallid skin. Proof. She grabs the toe of one shoe, and closes her eyes. He's still mostly intact, and she feels grateful for that. She knows the cardboard sign could have been affixed to his heart with the blade of a machete. She knows that the relative neatness of his death is a sort of deformed kindness. She's seen other crime scenes, nightmarish scenes— bodies that are no longer bodies but only parts of bodies, *mutilados*. When the cartel murders, it does so to set an example, for exaggerated, grotesque illustration. One morning at work, as she opened her shop for the day, Lydia saw a boy she knew down the street kneeling to unlock the grate of his father's shoe store with a key dangling by a shoelace around his neck. He was sixteen years old. When the car pulled up, the kid couldn't run because the key snagged in the lock; it caught him by the neck. So *los sicarios* lifted the grate and hung the kid by the shoelace, by the neck, and then pummeled him until all he could do was twitch. Lydia had rushed inside and locked the door behind her, so she didn't see when they pulled down his pants and added the decoration, but she heard about it later. They all did. And every shop owner in the neighborhood knew that that kid's father had refused to pay the cartel's *mordidas*.

So yes, Lydia is grateful that sixteen of her loved ones were killed by the quick, clinical dispatch of bullets. The officers in the yard avert their eyes from her, and she feels grateful for that, too. The crime scene photographer sets his camera down on the table beside the drink that still bears a smudge of Lydia's truffle-colored lipstick on its rim. The ice cubes have melted inside, and there's a small puddle of condensation on the napkin around her glass. It's still wet, and that feels impossible to Lydia, that her life could be shattered so completely in less time than it takes for a ring of condensation to evaporate into the atmosphere. She's aware that a deferential hush has fallen over the patio. She moves to Sebastián's side without standing. She crawls on hands and knees, and then hesitates, staring at his one outstretched hand, the ridges and lines of his knuckles, the perfect half-moons of his nail beds. The fingers do not move. The wedding band is inert. His eyes are closed, and Lydia wonders, absurdly, if he closed them on purpose, for her, a final act of tenderness, so that when she found him, she wouldn't have to observe the vacancy there. She claps a hand over her mouth because she has a feeling the essential part of herself might fall out. She shoves the feeling down, tucks her fingers into the fold of that unresponsive hand, and allows herself to lean gently across his chest. He is cold already. He is cold. Sebastián is gone, and what's left is only the beloved, familiar shape of him, empty of breath.

She places her hand on his jaw, his chin. She closes her mouth very tightly and places her palm against the coolness of his forehead. The first time she ever saw him, he was slouched over a spiral notebook in a library in Mexico City, pen in hand. The tilt of his shoulders, the fullness of his mouth. He was wearing a purple T-shirt, some band she didn't know. She understands now that it wasn't the body but the way he animated it that had thrilled her. The flagstones press into her knees while she covers him with prayers. Her tears are spasmodic. The bent spatula sits in a puddle of congealed blood, and the flat part still bears a smudge of uncooked meat. Lydia fights a roll of nausea, slips her hand into her husband's pocket, and retrieves his keys. How many times during their life together has she slipped her hand into his pocket? *Don't think it, don't think it, don't think.* It's difficult to remove his wedding ring. The loose skin of his knuckle scrunches up beneath the band so she has to twist it, she has to use one hand to straighten his finger and the other to twist the ring, and in this way, at last, she has his wedding band, the one she placed on his finger at the Catedral de Nuestra Señora de la Soledad more than ten years ago. She slips it onto her thumb, places both hands on the crate of his chest, and pushes herself to her feet. She lurches away, waiting for someone to challenge her for the items she took. She almost wants someone to say she can't have them, that she can't tamper with evidence or some horseshit like that. How satisfying it might be, momentarily, to have a direct receptacle for some lashing belt of her rage. No one dares.

Lydia stands with her shoulders loose to the earth. Her mother. She moves toward Abuela, whose body is one of those now loosely covered with black plastic. An officer steps to intercept her.

"Señora, please," he says simply.

Lydia looks at him wildly. "I need a last moment with my mother."

He shakes his head once, the slightest movement. His voice is soft. "I assure you," he says, "that is not your mother."

Lydia blinks, unmoving, her husband's car keys gripped in the vise of her hand. He's right. She could spend more time in this landscape of carnage, but why? They are all gone. This is not what she wants to remember of them. She turns away from the sixteen horizontal shapes in the yard and, with a squeak and a bang, passes through the doorway into the kitchen. Outside, the officials resume their activities.

Lydia opens the closet in her mother's bedroom and withdraws Abuela's solitary piece of luggage: a small red overnight bag. Lydia unzips it and finds that it's full of smaller purses. It's a bag of bags. She dumps them on the bed, opens her mother's nightstand, pulls a rosary and a small prayer book from the drawer, and puts them in the overnight bag along with Sebastián's keys. Then she stoops down and sticks her arm beneath her mother's mattress. She sweeps it back and forth until her fingertips brush a fold of paper. Lydia pulls the wad out: almost 15,000 pesos. She puts them in the bag. She throws the pile of small purses back in her mother's closet, takes the bag to the bathroom, opens the medicine cabinet, and grabs what she can—a hairbrush, a toothbrush, toothpaste, moisturizer, a tube of lip balm, a pair of tweezers. They all go into the bag. She does all this without thinking, without really considering which items might be helpful or useless. She does it because she can't think of what else to do. Lydia and her mother are the same shoe size, a small blessing. Lydia takes the only pair of comfortable shoes from her mother's closet—quilted gold lamé sneakers with a zipper on one side that Abuela wore for gardening. In the kitchen, the raid continues: a sleeve of cookies, a tin of peanuts, two bags of chips, all surreptitiously stuffed into the bag. Her mother's purse hangs on a hook behind the kitchen door, alongside two other hooks that hold Abuela's apron and her favorite teal sweater. Lydia takes the purse down and looks inside. It feels like opening her mother's mouth. It's too personal in there. Lydia takes the whole thing, folds the softened brown leather into the end pocket of the overnight bag, and zips it in.

The detective is sitting beside Luca on the couch when Lydia returns, but he's not asking questions. His pad and pencil are resigned on the coffee table.

"We have to go," she says.

Luca stands without waiting to be told.

The detective stands, too. "I must caution you against returning home right now, señora," he says. "It may not be safe. If you wait here, perhaps one of my men can drive you. We might find a secure location for you and your son?"

Lydia smiles, and there's a brief astonishment that her face can still make those shapes. A small puff of laughter. "I like our chances better without your assistance."

The detective frowns at her but nods. "You have somewhere safe to go?"

"Please don't concern yourself with our well-being," she says. "Serve justice. Worry about that." She's aware that the words are leaving her mouth like tiny, unpoisoned darts, as futile as they are angry. She makes no effort to censor herself.

The detective stands with his hands in his pockets and frowns toward the floor. "I'm so sorry for your loss. Truly. I know how it must look, every murder going unsolved, but there are people who still care, who are horrified by this violence. Please know I will try." He, too, understands the uselessness of his words, but he feels compelled to tender them nonetheless. He reaches into his breast pocket and pulls out a card with his name and phone number on it. "We will need an official statement when you're feeling up to it. Take a few days if you need."

He proffers the card, but Lydia makes no move to take it, so Luca reaches up and grabs it. He's maneuvered himself in close beside his mother, laced one arm behind her through the strap of the red overnight bag.

This time, the detective doesn't follow them. Their shadows move as one lumpy beast along the sidewalk. Beneath the windshield wiper of their car, an instantly recognizable orange 1974 Volkswagen Beetle, there is a tiny slip of paper, so small that it doesn't even flit in the hot breeze that gusts up the street.

"*Carajo,*" Lydia curses, automatically pushing Luca behind her.

"What, Mami?"

"Stay here. No, go stand over there." She points back in the direction from which they came, and for once, Luca doesn't argue. He scuttles up the street, a dozen paces or more. Lydia drops the overnight bag at her feet on the sidewalk, takes a step back from the car, looks up and down the street. Her heart doesn't race; it feels leaden within her.

Her husband's parking permit is glued to the windshield, and there's a smattering of rust across the back bumper. She steps into the street, leans over to see if she can read the paper without lifting it. A news van is parked just beyond the yellow crime scene tape at the far end of the block, but its reporter and cameraman are busy with preparations and haven't noticed them. She turns her back and tugs the slip of paper free from the wiper. One word in green marker: BOO! Her quick intake of breath feels like a slice through the core of her body. She looks back at Luca, crumbles the paper in her fist, and jams it into her pocket.

They have to disappear. They have to get away from Acapulco, so far away that Javier Crespo Fuentes will never be able to find them. They cannot drive the car.

CHAPTER THREE

Lydia circles the orange Beetle twice, glancing through the windows, inspecting the tires, the gas tank, what she can see of the undercarriage by stooping down without touching anything. Nothing appears different from how they left it, not that she was paying much attention. She stands back and crosses her arms over her chest. She won't dare to drive it, but she must at least open it, to retrieve some of their belongings from inside. That need feels urgent, but her mind cannot reach beyond the immediate present, so she doesn't get as far as the word *keepsakes.*

She peers through the window and sees Sebastián's backpack on the passenger-side floor, her own sunglasses glinting on the dashboard, Luca's yellow-and-blue sweatshirt sprawled on the backseat. It's too dangerous to go home now, to the place where they all live together. She needs to be quick, to get Luca out of here. For a brief moment, Lydia considers that if there's a bomb in the car, it might be kinder to take Luca with her, to call him over here now before she opens the door, but her maternal instinct defeats this macabre idea.

So she approaches with the key shaking in her hand, using the other hand to steady it. She looks at Luca, who gives her a thumbs-up. *There won't be a bomb,* she tells herself. *A bomb would be overkill after all those bullets.* She pushes the key into the lock. One deep breath. Two. She turns the key. *Thunk.* The sound of the door unlocking is almost enough to finish her. But then silence. No ticking, no beeping, no whoosh of murderous air. She closes her eyes, pivots, returns Luca's thumbs-up. She swings the creaky door open and begins rummaging inside. What does she need? She stops short, her confusion momentarily paralyzing. *This cannot be real,* she thinks. Her mind feels stretched and warped. Lydia remembers her mother walking in circles for weeks after her *papi* died, from sink to fridge, sink to fridge. She'd stand with her hand on the tap and forget to turn it on. Lydia can't do a suspended loop like that; there is danger. They have to move.

Sebastián's backpack is here. She must pick it up. She needs to accomplish the tasks immediately before her. There will be time later to begin the work of comprehending how this could have happened, why it happened. She opens her husband's backpack, takes out a sloshing thermos, his glasses, the keys to his office, his headphones, three small notebooks and a fistful of cheap pens, a handheld tape recorder, and his press credentials, and places everything on the passenger seat. Her husband's Samsung Galaxy Tab and charger she keeps, though she powers the tablet all the way down before returning it into the now-empty backpack. She doesn't understand how GPS works in these devices, but she doesn't want to be trackable. She retrieves her sunglasses from the dashboard and shoves them onto her face, almost stabbing herself in the eye with one outstretched stem. She pushes the seat forward to see what's in back. Luca's church shoes are on the floor, where he left them when he changed into his sneakers to play *fútbol* with Adrián. *Oh my God, Adrián,* Lydia thinks, and the cleft feeling in her chest opens deeper, as if there's an ax hacked into her sternum. She squeezes her eyes closed for just a moment and forces a cycle of breath through her body. She lifts Luca's shoes and places them into the backpack. Sebastián's red New York Yankees hat is on the backseat, too. She grabs it, climbs out of the car, and tosses it to Luca, who puts it on. In the trunk, she finds Sebastián's good brown cardigan, which she shoves into the bag. There's also a basketball (which she leaves) and a dirty T-shirt, which she keeps. She slams the trunk, walks back to the front seat to select one of his notebooks, not yet allowing herself to consider the reason she does this—to retain a personal record of his extinct handwriting. She chooses one at random, places it in the backpack, and then locks the doors behind her.

Luca comes to stand beside her before she beckons him. *My son is fundamentally altered,* she thinks. The way he watches her and interprets her wishes without command.

"Where will we go, Mami?"

Lydia gives him a sideways glance. Eight years old. She must reach past this obliteration and find the strength to salvage what she can. She kisses the top of his head and they begin to walk, away from the reporters, away from the orange car, Abuela's house, their annihilated life.

"I don't know, *mijo,*" she says. "We'll see. We'll have an adventure."

"Like in the movies?"

"Yes, *mijo.* Just like in the movies."

She slings the backpack onto both shoulders and tightens the straps before hoisting the overnight bag, too. They walk several blocks north, then hang a left toward the beach, then turn south again, because Lydia can't decide if they should be somewhere crowded with tourists or if they should try to stay out of sight altogether. She frequently looks over her shoulder, studies the drivers of the passing cars, tightens her grip on Luca's hand. At an open gate, a mutt barks at them, lunging and nipping. A woman in a drab floral dress comes out of the house to correct the dog, but before she can get there, Lydia kicks it savagely and feels no guilt for having done so. The woman yells after her but Lydia keeps moving, holding Luca by the hand.

Luca adjusts the brim of his father's too-big Yankees hat. Papi's sweat is seeped into the hatband, so little currents of his scent puff out whenever Luca pulls it to one side or the other, which Luca does now at regular intervals so he can smell his father. Then he has the idea that perhaps the scent is finite, and he fears he might use it all up, so he stops touching it. At length, they spot a bus and decide to get on.

It's midafternoon on a Saturday, and the bus isn't crowded. Luca feels glad to sit, until he realizes that the movement of his legs beneath him, carrying the weight of his small frame through the streets of his city, had been the thing staving off the crush of horror that now threatens to descend. As soon as he's seated beside Mami on the blue plastic seat, his tired legs dangling down, he begins to think. He begins to shake. Mami puts her arm around him and squeezes tight.

"You cannot cry here, *mijito,*" Mami says. "Not yet."

Luca nods, and just like that, he stops trembling and the risk of tears evaporates. He leans his head against the warm glass of the bus window and looks out. He focuses on the cartoon colors of his city, the green of the palm fronds, the trunks of the trees painted white to discourage beetles, the vivid blare of signs advertising shops and hotels and shoes. At El Rollo, Luca looks at the children and teenagers in line for the ticket window. They wear flip-flops and have towels around their necks. Behind them, the red and yellow water slides swoop and soar. Luca puts one finger against the glass and squashes the children in line one by one. The bus squeaks its brakes at the curb, and three damp-haired teenage boys get on. They pass Luca and Lydia without a glance and sit in the back of the bus, elbows planted on knees, talking quietly across the aisle.

"Papi's going to take me in the summertime," Luca says.

"What?"

"To El Rollo. He said this summer we could go. He would take a day off work one time when I'm not in school."

Lydia sucks in her cheeks and bites down. A disloyal reflex: she's angry at her husband. The driver closes the door and the bus moves off with the traffic. Lydia unzips the overnight bag at her feet, kicks off her heels, and replaces them with her mother's quilted gold sneakers. She doesn't have a plan, which is unlike her, and she finds it difficult to form one because her mind feels unfamiliar, both frenetic and swampy. She does have the wherewithal to remember that every fifteen or twenty minutes, they should get off and change buses, which they do. Sometimes they change direction, sometimes they don't. One bus stops directly in front of a church, so they go briefly inside, but the part of Lydia that's usually available for prayer has shut down. She's experienced this numbness a few times before in her life—when she was seventeen and her father died of cancer, when she had a late-stage miscarriage two years after Luca, when the doctors told her she could never have more children—so she doesn't think of it as a crisis of faith. Instead she believes it's a divine kindness. Like a government furlough, God has deferred her nonessential agencies. Outside, Luca vomits on the pavement once more while they wait for the next bus.

Around her neck, Lydia wears a thin gold chain adorned only with three interlocking loops. It's a discreet piece of jewelry, and the only one she wears apart from the filigreed gold band around the fourth finger of her left hand. Sebastián gave her the necklace the first Christmas after Luca was born, and she loved it immediately—the symbolism of it. She's worn it every day since, and it's become so much a part of her that she's woven her mannerisms into it. When she's bored, she runs the delicate chain back and forth along the pad of her thumb. When she's nervous, she has a habit of looping the three interlocking circles together onto the tip of her pinky nail, where they make a faint tinkling sound. She doesn't touch those golden hoops now. Her hand moves absently toward her neck, but already she's aware of the gesture. Already she's training herself to disguise old habits. She must become entirely unrecognizable if she hopes to survive. She opens the clasp at the back of her neck and slips Sebastián's wedding ring from her thumb onto the chain. Then she refastens the clasp around her neck and drops the whole thing inside the collar of her blouse.

They must avoid drawing the attention of the bus drivers, who've been known to act as *halcones,* lookouts for the cartel. Lydia understands that her appearance as a moderately attractive but not beautiful woman of indeterminate age, traveling the city with an unremarkable-looking boy, can provide a kind of natural camouflage if she takes care to promote the impression that they're simply out for a day's shopping or a visit to friends across the city. Indeed, Luca and Lydia could easily change places with many of their fellow passengers, which Lydia thinks of as truly absurd—that the people around them cannot see plainly what abomination they've just endured. It feels as evident to Lydia as if she were carrying a flashing neon sign. She fights at every moment against the scream that pulses inside her like a living thing. It stretches and kicks in her gut like Luca did when he was a baby in there. With tremendous self-control, she strangles and suppresses it.

When a plan finally does begin to emerge from the violent fog of chaos in her mind, Lydia feels uncertain whether it's a good one, but she commits herself to it because she has no other. At a quarter to four o'clock, just before closing time in Playa Caletilla, Lydia and Luca disembark from the bus, go into an unfamiliar branch of their bank, and wait in line. Lydia turns on her cell phone to check her balance, and then powers it all the way off again before filling out a withdrawal slip for almost the full amount: 219,803 pesos, or about $12,500, almost all of it an inheritance from Sebastián's godfather, who'd owned a bottling company, and who'd never had children of his own. She asks for the money in large bills.

A few minutes later, Luca and Lydia are back on the bus, their life savings in cash stuffed into three envelopes at the bottom of Abuela's overnight bag. Three buses and more than an hour later, they get out at the Walmart in Diamante. They buy a backpack for Luca, two packets of underwear, two pairs of jeans, two packets of three plain white T-shirts, socks, two hooded sweatshirts, two warm jackets, two more toothbrushes, disposable wipes, Band-Aids, sunscreen, Blistex, a first aid kit, two canteens, two flashlights, some batteries, and a map of Mexico. Lydia takes a long time selecting a machete at the counter in the home goods department, eventually choosing a small one with a retractable blade and a tidy black holster she can strap to her leg. It's not a gun, but it's better than nothing. They pay in cash, and then walk beneath the highway overpass toward the beach hotels, Luca wearing Papi's baseball cap and Lydia not touching her gold necklace. She watches everyone as they walk, other pedestrians, drivers in passing cars, even skinny boys on their skateboards, because she knows *halcones* are everywhere. They hurry on. Lydia chooses the Hotel Duquesa Imperial because of its size. It's big enough to provide a measure of anonymity, but not new enough to attract much in the way of trendy social attention. She requests a room facing the street and pays, again, in cash.

"And now I just need a credit card on file for incidentals," the desk clerk says as he tucks two card keys into a paper sleeve.

Lydia looks at the keys and considers snatching them, bolting for the elevator. Then she opens the overnight bag and pretends to rummage for her credit card. "Shoot, I must have left it in the car," she says. "How much is the hold?"

"Four thousand pesos." He gives her a clinical smile. "Fully refundable, of course."

"Of course," Lydia says. She props the overnight bag up on her knee and flips open one of the envelopes. She withdraws the 4,000 pesos without taking the envelope out of the bag. "Cash is okay?"

"Oh." The clerk looks mildly alarmed and darts his eyes toward his manager, who's busy with another customer.

"Cash is fine," the manager says without looking up from his task.

The clerk nods at Lydia, who presses the four pink bills into his hand. He puts them into an envelope and seals it.

"And your name, please?" His black pen hovers over the front of the envelope.

Lydia hesitates for a moment. "Fermina Daza," she says, the first name that comes to mind.

He hands her the room key. "Enjoy your stay, Ms. Daza."

The ride in the elevator to the tenth floor feels like the longest minute and a half of Luca's life. His feet hurt, his back hurts, his neck hurts, and he still hasn't cried. A family gets on at the fourth floor and then realizes the elevator is going up, so they get off again. The parents are laughing with each other, holding hands while their kids bicker. The boy looks at Luca and sticks his tongue out as the elevator doors close. Luca knows by instinct and by Mami's subtle cues that he must behave as if everything's normal, and he's managed that behemoth task so far. But there's an elegant older woman in the elevator, too, and she's admiring Mami's quilted gold shoes. Abuela's shoes. Luca blinks rapidly.

"How beautiful, your shoes—so unusual," the woman says, touching Lydia lightly on the arm. "Where did you buy them?"

Lydia looks down at her feet instead of turning to engage with the woman. "Oh, I don't remember," she says. "They're so old." And then she stabs the ten button repeatedly with her finger, which doesn't speed up the elevator but does have the intended effect of silencing any further attempts at conversation. The woman gets off on the sixth floor, and after she does so, Mami hits numbers fourteen, eighteen, and nineteen as well. They get off at ten and walk three flights down to the seventh floor.

A surprising thing happens to Luca after Mami finally opens the door of their hotel room with her card key, after she looks both ways up and down the carpeted corridor and ushers him quickly inside, after she dead-bolts and chain-locks the door, dragging the desk chair across the tiled floor and wedging it beneath the doorknob. The surprising thing that happens to him is: nothing. The cloudburst of anguish he's been struggling against does not come. Neither does it go. It remains there, pent up like a held breath, hovering just on the periphery of his mind.

He has the sense that, were he to turn his head, were he to poke at the globular nightmare ever so gently with his finger, it would unleash a torrent so colossal he would be swept away forever. Luca takes care to hold himself quite still. Then he kicks off his shoes and climbs up on the edge of the lone bed. A towel has been placed there, folded into the shape of a swan, which Luca takes by the long neck and thrashes to the floor. He clutches the remote control like it's a life preserver and clicks the television on.

Mami moves their Walmart bags, backpacks, and Abuela's overnight bag to the small table, and dumps everything out. She begins removing tags, organizing items into piles, and then quite suddenly she sits down hard in one of the chairs and doesn't move for at least ten minutes. Luca doesn't look at her. He glues his eyes to Nickelodeon, turns *Henry Danger* up loud. When at last she begins to move again, Mami comes to him and kisses his forehead roughly. She crosses the room and slides open the door to the balcony. She doubts there's any amount of fresh air that could succeed in clearing her head, but she has to try. She leaves it open and steps outside.

If there's one good thing about terror, Lydia now understands, it's that it's more immediate than grief. She knows that she will soon have to contend with what's happened, but for now, the possibility of what might still happen serves to anesthetize her from the worst of the anguish. She peers over the edge of the balcony and surveys the street below. She tells herself there's no one out there. She tells herself they are safe.

Downstairs in the lobby, the front desk clerk excuses himself from his post and heads for the employee breakroom. In the second stall of the bathroom, he removes the burner phone from his interior suit jacket pocket and sends the following text: Two special guests just checked in to the Hotel Duquesa Imperial.

CHAPTER FOUR

On the occasion of their first encounter, Javier Crespo Fuentes arrived alone at Lydia's shop on a Tuesday morning just as she was setting her chalkboard on the sidewalk outside. That week, she'd selected ten books from faraway places to promote with a hand-chalked sign that read BOOKS: CHEAPER THAN AIRLINE TICKETS. She was holding the door open with one leg as she lifted the sign through, and then he appeared, approaching quickly to help with the door. The bell above them jangled like a pronouncement.

"Thank you," Lydia said.

He nodded. "But far more dangerous."

She frowned and propped open the easel. "I'm sorry?"

"The sign." He gestured, and she stood back to assess her lettering. "Books *are* cheaper than traveling, but they're also more dangerous."

Lydia smiled. "Well, I suppose that depends on where you travel."

They went inside, and she left him to his own counsel while he browsed the stacks, but when at last he approached the counter and set his books beside the register, she was startled by his selections.

Lydia had owned this store for almost ten years, and she'd stocked it with both books she loved and books she wasn't crazy about but knew would sell. She also kept a healthy inventory of notecards, pens, calendars, toys, games, reading glasses, magnets, and key chains, and it was that kind of merchandise, along with the splashy best sellers, that made her shop profitable. So it had long been a secret pleasure of Lydia's that, hidden among all the more popular goods, she was able to make a home for some of her best-loved secret treasures, gems that had blown open her mind and changed her life, books that in some cases had never even been translated into Spanish but that she stocked anyway, not because she expected she'd ever sell them, but simply because it made her happy to know they were there. There were perhaps a dozen of these books, stashed away on their ever-changing shelves, enduring among a cast of evolving neighbors. Now and again when a book moved her, when a book opened a previously undiscovered window in her mind and forever altered her perception of the world, she would add it to those secret ranks. Once in a great while, she'd even try to recommend one of those books to a customer. She did this only when the customer was someone she knew and liked, someone she trusted to appreciate the value of the treasure being offered; she was almost always disappointed. In the ten years she'd been doing this, only twice had Lydia experienced the pleasure of a customer approaching her counter with one of those books in hand, unsolicited. Twice in ten years there'd been a wild spark of wonder in the shop, when the bell above the door was like mistletoe—a possibility of something magical.

So when Javier approached Lydia as she stood behind the register perusing catalogs, when she lifted his selections from the counter to ring them up, she was astonished to find not one, but two of her secret treasures among them: *Heart, You Bully, You Punk* by Leah Hager Cohen and *The Whereabouts of Eneas McNulty* by Sebastian Barry.

"Oh my God," Lydia whispered.

"Is something wrong?"

She looked up at him, realizing she hadn't actually looked at him yet, despite their cheerful banter earlier. He was fancily dressed for a Tuesday morning, in dark blue trousers and a white guayabera, an outfit more suitable for Sunday Mass than a regular workday, and his thick, black hair was parted sharply and combed to one side in an old-fashioned style. The heavy, black plastic frames of his glasses were similarly outdated, so retro they were almost chic again. His eyes swam hugely behind the thick lenses and his mustache quivered as she considered him.

"These books," she said. "They're two of my favorites." It was an insufficient explanation, but all she could muster.

"Mine, too," the man across from her said. The mustache hitched ever so slightly with his hesitant smile.

"You've read them before?" She was holding *Heart, You Bully, You Punk* with both hands.

"Well, only this one." He gestured to the one she was clutching.

She looked down at its cover. "You read in English?" she asked, in English.

"I try, yes," he said. "My English isn't fluent, but it's close. And this story is so delicate. I'm sure there were things I missed the first time around. I wanted to try again."

"Yes." She smiled at him, feeling slightly crazy. She ignored this feeling and plowed recklessly ahead. "When you're finished you could come back, we could discuss it."

"Oh." He nodded eagerly. "You have a book club here?"

Her mouth opened slightly. "No." She laughed. "Just me!"

"All the better."

He smiled and Lydia frowned, eager to preserve the sanctity of this moment. Was he flirting? Whenever a man's behavior was inscrutable, the answer was typically yes. She placed the book on the counter and her palm flat against its cover.

He read the caution in her gesture and endeavored to correct himself. "I only meant because sometimes the experience of reading can be corrupted by too many opinions." He looked at the book beneath her hand. "A remarkable book. Remarkable."

She conceded a smile, lifting her scanner from its cradle and pointing it toward the book.

When he returned the following Monday, he went directly to the counter, even though Lydia was busy with another customer. He waited to one side, hands clasped in front of him, and when the customer left, they smiled broadly at each other.

"Well?" she said.

"Even more incredible the second time."

"Yes!" Lydia clapped her hands.

One of the book's main characters had a condition where she couldn't prevent herself from jumping off high things. She didn't want to die, but she was constantly hurting herself because of this dangerous impulse.

"I have this same condition," Javier confessed suddenly.

"What? No!"

The condition was fictional.

And yet, Lydia had it, too. Anytime she stood too close to the balcony railing at home, she had to dig her fingers in. She had to press her heels to the floor. She was afraid that one day she would leap over without thinking, without purpose. She would splatter on the pavement below and the Acapulco traffic would screech and blare, swerving needlessly around her. The ambulance would be too late. Luca would be orphaned, and everyone would misinterpret the act as suicide. Lydia had run the scenario through her brain a thousand times as an attempted antidote. *I must not jump.*

"I thought I was the only one in the world," Javier confessed. "I thought it was a crazy fabrication of my mind. And then there it was, in the book."

Lydia didn't realize her mouth was hanging open until she closed it. She sat back onto her stool with a bump.

"But I thought *I* was the only one," she said.

Javier straightened his body away from the counter. "You also?"

Lydia nodded.

"Well, my God," he said in English. And then he laughed. "We will start a support group."

And then he stood there, talking with her for so long that she eventually offered him a cup of coffee, which he accepted. She pulled a stool around to the far side of the counter so he could drink it in comfort. He was careful not to get foam on his mustache. They talked about literature and poetry and economics and politics and the music they both adored, and he stayed for nearly two hours, until she began to worry that he'd be missed somewhere, but he waved his hand dismissively.

"There is nothing out there more important than this."

It was just as Lydia had always hoped life in her bookstore would be one day. In between the workaday drudgery of running a business, that she might entertain customers who were as lively and engaging as the books around them.

"If I had three more customers like you, I'd be set for life," she said, taking her last sip of coffee.

He placed a hand across his chest and bowed slightly. "I shall try to be enough." And then he said casually, softly, "If I had met you in a different life, I would ask you to marry me."

Lydia stood abruptly from her stool and shook her head.

"I'm sorry," Javier said. "I didn't mean to make you uncomfortable."

She gathered the cups in silence. The treachery wasn't in receiving his confession. The treachery was in her unspoken response: in a different life, she might've said yes.

"I should get back to work," she said instead. "I have to place an order this afternoon. I have to prepare some parcels for the mail."

He took seven new books with him that day, three of which were Lydia's recommendations.

On the following Friday morning a summer shower washed down the street, and two large, worrisome men crowded themselves in beneath the awning that hung above Lydia's bookshop door. Moments later, Javier appeared, and Lydia felt a strong measure of happiness. There would be new books to discuss! She tried to behave naturally, but as she watched those men in the doorway, her breath constricted in her chest.

"They make you nervous," Javier observed.

"I just don't know what they want." Lydia paced from her usual position, emerging from behind the register. She, like all the other shop owners on this street, already paid the monthly *mordidas* imposed by the cartel. She couldn't afford to pay more.

"I will send them off," Javier said.

Lydia protested, grabbing his arm, growing louder even as Javier's voice dropped to a comforting hush. He stepped around her when she tried to block his path.

"They will hurt you," she whispered as severely as she could without raising alarm.

He smiled at her in a way that made his mustache twitch and assured her, "They will not."

Lydia ducked behind the counter, lowering her head as Javier opened the door and stepped outside. She watched in astonishment as he spoke to the two bulky thugs beneath her awning. Both men gestured to the rain, but Javier pointed a finger, made a shooing gesture with his hand, and the men trotted off into the downpour.

Lydia was reluctant to understand. Even as his visits continued and lengthened, as their conversations deepened into more personal matters, as she caught fleeting glimpses of the men on two other occasions, Lydia willfully forgot the power Javier had wielded on that rainy morning. When eventually he spoke adoringly about his wife, whom he called *la reina de mi corazón,* the queen of my heart, Lydia felt her defenses relax. Those shields dropped further still when he revealed the existence of a young mistress, whom he called *la reina de mis pantalones,* the queen of my pants.

"Disgusting," she said, but she surprised herself by laughing, too.

It was hardly unusual for a man to have an affair, but talking so openly about it with another woman was something else. For that reason, the confession served both to cure Lydia of any flattered wisp of attachment and, as Javier revealed more and more of his secret self, to turn the key in the intimate lock of their friendship. They became confidants, sharing jokes and observations and disappointments. They even spoke at times about the irritating things their spouses did.

"If you were married to me, I would never behave that way," Javier said when she complained about Sebastián leaving his dirty socks on the kitchen counter.

"Of course not." She laughed. "You'd be an ideal husband."

"I'd wash every sock in the house."

"Sure."

"I'd burn all the socks and buy new ones each week."

"Mm-hmm."

"I'd forgo socks altogether, if it would make you happy."

Lydia laughed in spite of herself. She'd learned to roll her eyes at these proclamations because, in the weather of their friendship, his flirtation was only a passing cloud. There were far more important storms between them. They discovered, for example, that both of their fathers had died young from cancer, a fact that would've bonded them all by itself. They'd both had good dads, and then lost them.

"It's like being a member of the shittiest club in the world," Javier said to her.

For Lydia, it had been nearly fifteen years, and though her sorrow was now irregular, when she did stumble into it, her grief was still as acute as the day her father had died.

"I know," Javier said, even though she didn't say these things out loud.

So she endured his intense flattery, and he, in turn, accepted, perhaps even relished, her wholesale rejection of his flirtation. She came to think of it as part of his charm.

"But, Lydia," he told her reverently, placing both hands on his heart, "my other loves notwithstanding, you truly are *la reina de mi alma.*" The queen of my soul.

"And what would your poor wife say about that?" she countered.

"My magnificent wife only wants me to be happy."

"She's a saint!"

He spoke frequently of his only child, a sixteen-year-old daughter who was at boarding school in Barcelona. Everything about him changed when he talked about her—his voice, his face, his manner. His love for her was so earnest that he handled even the subject of her with tremendous care. Her name was like a fine glass bauble he was afraid of dropping.

"I joke about my many loves, but in truth, there is only one." He smiled at Lydia. "Marta. *Es mi cielo, mi luna, y todas mis estrellas.*"

"I am a mother." Lydia nodded. "I know this love."

He sat across from her on the stool she'd come to think of as his. "That love is so vast I sometimes fear it," he said. "I can never hope to earn it, so I fear it will disappear, it will consume me. And at the same time, it's the only good thing I've ever done in my life."

"Oh, Javier—that can't be true," Lydia said.

The subject made him morose. He shook his head, rubbed his eyes roughly beneath the glasses.

"It's just that my life hasn't turned out as I intended," he said. "You know how it is."

But she didn't. After weeks of learning about each other, this was where their common language faltered. With the exception of having only one child, Lydia's life had turned out precisely as she'd always wished it might. She'd given up hoping for the daughter she could no longer have; she'd accepted that absence because she'd worked at it. She was content with her choices, more than content. Lydia was happy. But Javier looked at her through the warp of his lenses, and she could see the yearning on his face, to be understood. She pressed her lips together. "Tell me," she said.

He removed the glasses and folded the stems. He placed them in his breast pocket and blinked, his eyes small and raw without their accustomed shield. "I thought I would be a poet!" He laughed. "Ridiculous, right? In this day and age?"

She put her hand on top of his.

"I thought I would be a scholar. A quiet life. I'd do quite well with poverty, I think."

She twisted her mouth, touching the elegant watch on his wrist. "I'm dubious."

He shrugged. "I guess I do like shoes."

"And steak," she reminded him.

He laughed. "Yes, steak. Who doesn't like steak?"

"Your book habit alone would bankrupt most people."

"*Dios mío,* you're right, Lydia. I'd be a terrible pauper."

"The worst," she agreed. After a beat she said, "It's never too late, Javier. If you're truly unhappy? You're still a young man."

"I'm fifty-one!"

Younger than she thought, even. "Practically a baby. And what have you got to be so unhappy about anyway?"

He looked down at the counter and Lydia was surprised to see genuine torment cross his features.

She lowered her voice and leaned in. "Then you could choose a different path, Javier. You can. You're such a gifted person, such a capable person. What's stopping you?"

"Ah." He shook his head, replacing his glasses. She watched him pushing his face back into its customary shapes. "It's all a romantic dream now. It's over. I made my choices long ago, and this is where they've led me."

She squeezed his hand. "It's not so bad, right?" It was something she'd say to Luca, to shepherd him toward optimism.

Javier blinked slowly, tipped his head to one side. An ambiguous gesture. "It will have to do."

She straightened up behind the counter and took a sip of her luke-warm coffee. "Your choices yielded Marta."

His eyes shined. "Yes, Marta," he said. "And you."

The next time he came, he brought a box of *conchas* and sat in his usual place. There were several customers in the shop, so he opened the box and placed two of the sweet treats on napkins while Lydia walked the aisles helping people with their requests. When they approached the counter to pay for their goods, Javier greeted them as if he worked there. He offered them *conchas*. When at last Lydia and Javier were alone, he withdrew a small Moleskine notebook from the interior pocket of his jacket and set it on the counter as well.

"What's this?" Lydia asked.

Javier swallowed nervously. "My poetry."

Lydia's eyes grew wide with delight.

"I've never shared it with anyone except Marta," he said. "She's studying poetry in school. And French and mathematics. She's much more gifted than her old *papá*."

"Oh, Javier."

He touched the corner of the book nervously. "I've been writing poems all my life. Since I was a child. I thought you might like to hear one."

Lydia pulled her stool closer to the counter and leaned toward him, her chin resting on her propped and folded hands. Between them, the *conchas* stained their napkins with grease. Javier opened the book, its pages soft from wear. He leafed carefully through them until he came to the page he had in mind. He cleared his throat before he began.

Oh, the poem was terrible. It was both grave and frivolous, so bad that it made Lydia love him much, much more, because of how vulnerable he was in sharing it with her. When he finished reading and looked up for her reaction, his face was a twist of worry. But her eyes were bright and reassuring, and she genuinely meant the words she gave him in that moment.

"How beautiful. How very beautiful."

The maturing friendship with Javier was surprising in its swiftness and intensity. The flirtation had mostly ceased, and in its place, she discovered an intimacy she'd seldom experienced outside of family. There was no feeling of romance on Lydia's end, but their bond was refreshing.

Javier reminded her, in the middle of her mothering years, that life was exciting, that there was always the possibility of something, or someone, previously undiscovered.

On her birthday, a day Lydia did not recall revealing to him, Javier arrived with a silver parcel the size of a book. The ribbon said, JACQUES GENIN.

"The principal chocolatier in Paris," Javier explained.

Lydia demurred, but not convincingly. (She loved chocolate.) And she accidentally ate every last one of the tiny masterpieces before Sebastián and Luca arrived at her shop that evening to take her out for her birthday dinner.

Because of an eruption of violence between rival cartels in Acapulco, Lydia and her family, indeed most families in the city, no longer frequented their favorite neighborhood cafés. The challenger to the establishment was a new cartel that called itself Los Jardineros, a name that failed, initially, to evoke the appropriate fear in the populace. That problem had been transitory. Shortly after their formation, everyone in the city knew that "The Gardeners" used guns only when they didn't have time to indulge their creativity. Their preferred tools were more intimate: spade, ax, sickle, hook, machete. The simple instruments of hacking and trenching. With these, Los Jardineros moved the earth; with these, they unseated and buried their rivals. A few of the dethroned survivors managed to join the ranks of their conquerors; most fled the city. The result was a recent decrease in bloodshed as the emergent winner flung a shroud of uneasy calm across the shoulders of Acapulco. Nearly four months of relative quiet followed, and the citizens of Acapulco cautiously returned to the streets, to the restaurants and shops. They were eager to repair the damage to their economy. They were ready for a cocktail. So, in the safest district, where tourist money had always encouraged some restraint, in a restaurant selected more for its security than for its menu, and surrounded by the shining faces of her family, Lydia blew out the candle on her thirty-second birthday cake.

Later that night, after Luca went to bed, and Sebastián opened a bottle of wine on the couch, their conversation turned inevitably to the condition of life in Acapulco. Lydia stood at the open counter, leaning across it with a glass of wine at her elbow.

"It was nice to be able to go out to dinner tonight," she said.

"It felt almost normal, right?" Sebastián was in the living room, his legs propped on the coffee table, crossed at the ankles.

"There were a lot of people out."

It was the first time they'd taken Luca out for a meal since last summer.

"Next we have to get the tourists back," Sebastián said.

Lydia took a deep breath. Tourism had always been the lifeblood of Acapulco, and the violence had scared most of those tourists away. She didn't know how long she'd be able to keep the shop afloat if they didn't return. It was tempting to hope the recent peace signaled a sea change.

"Do you think things might really get better now?"

She asked because Sebastián's knowledge of the cartels was exhaustive, which both impressed and discomfited her. He knew things. Most people were like Lydia; they didn't want to know. They tried to insulate themselves from the ugliness of the narco violence because they couldn't handle it. But Sebastián was ravenous for it. A free press was the last line of defense, he said, the only thing left standing between the people of Mexico and complete annihilation. It was his vocation, and when they were young, she'd admired that idealism. She'd imagined that any child of Sebastián's would come out of her womb honorably, with a fully formed, unimpeachable morality. She wouldn't even have to teach their babies right from wrong. But now the cartels murdered a Mexican journalist every few weeks, and Lydia recoiled from her husband's integrity. It felt sanctimonious, selfish. She wanted Sebastián alive more than she wanted his strong principles. She wished he would quit, do something simpler, safer. She tried to be supportive, but sometimes it made her so angry that he chose this danger. When that anger flared up and intruded, they moved around it like a piece of furniture too big for the room it occupied.

"It's already better," Sebastián said thoughtfully, from behind his wineglass.

"I mean, it's quieter," Lydia said. "But is it really *better*?"

"That depends on your criteria, I guess." He looked up at her. "If you like to go out to dinner, then yes, things are better."

Lydia frowned. She really did like to go out to dinner. Was she that superficial?

"The new *jefe* is smart," Sebastián said. "He knows stability is the key, and he wants peace. So we'll see, maybe things will get better under Los Jardineros than they were before."

"Better how? You think he can fix the economy? Bring back tourism?"

"I don't know, maybe." Sebastián shrugged. "If he can really stanch the violence long-term. For now, at least it's limited to other narcos. They're not running around murdering innocents for fun."

"What about that kid on the beach last week?"

"Collateral damage."

Lydia cringed and took a gulp of wine. Her husband wasn't a callous man. She hated when he talked like this. Sebastián saw her flinch and stood up to reach across the counter. He squeezed her hands.

"I know it's awful," he said. "But that kid on the beach was an accident. He was caught in the crossfire, that's all I meant. They weren't gunning for him." He tugged lightly on her hand. "Come sit with me?"

Lydia rounded the counter and joined him on the couch.

"I know you don't like to think of it like this, but at the end of the day, these guys are businessmen, and this one is smarter than most." He put his arm around her. "He's not your typical narco. In a different life, he could've been Bill Gates or something. An entrepreneur."

"Great," she said, threading one arm across his midsection and resting her head on his chest. "Maybe he should run for mayor."

"I think he's more of a chamber of commerce kinda guy." Sebastián laughed, but Lydia couldn't. They were quiet for a moment, and then Sebastián said, "La Lechuza."

"What?"

"That's his name." *The Owl.*

Now she was able to laugh. "Are you serious?" She sat up to look him in the face, to determine if he was messing with her. Sometimes he fed her nonsense just to test how gullible she was. This time, his face was innocent. "The Owl? That's a terrible name!" She laughed again. "Owls aren't scary."

"What do you mean? Owls are terrifying," Sebastián said.

She shook her head.

"Hoo," he said.

"Oh my God, stop it."

He worked his fingers into her hair, and she felt content there, leaning against his chest. She could smell the sweet red wine on his breath.

"I love you, Sebastián."

"Hoo," he said again.

They both laughed. They kissed. They left their wine on the table.

It wasn't until much later that night, when Lydia sat trying to read in the circle of lamplight that illumined only her side of the bed, when Sebastián had long since fallen asleep, his head resting on the bare skin of his arm, his snore a soft veil of familiarity in the room, that Lydia felt a dart of something worrisome pierce her consciousness. Something Sebastián had said. *In a different life, he could've been Bill Gates.* She folded her book closed and set it on her nightstand.

In a different life. The words echoed uncomfortably through her mind.

She pulled off the covers and swung her legs over the edge of the bed. Sebastián stirred but didn't wake. Her baggy T-shirt barely covered her backside and her feet were cold against the moonlit tiles of the hallway. She padded toward the kitchen, to the table where the three of them often ate dinner together. His backpack was there, not entirely zipped shut. She pulled out his laptop and turned on the light over the stove. There were notebooks in the backpack, too, and several file folders stuffed with photos and documents.

Lydia hoped she was wrong, but she knew, somehow, what she would find before she found it. Near the bottom of a stack of pictures in the second folder: there, sitting at a table on a veranda with several other men, the face that was now dear to her. The wide mustache, the recognizable glasses. There was no question who La Lechuza was. Behind the wine and the cake and the dinner, she could still taste his chocolates on her tongue.

CHAPTER FIVE

At home, Luca's little room has a night-light in the shape of Noah's ark. It's not a very bright one, but it makes enough light that when he has a nightmare and shoves back the covers to run in to Papi, he's able to see where his bare feet meet the tiled floor. So he's disoriented when he wakes up in the darkened room at the Hotel Duquesa Imperial. He can't make out a single shape in the blackness. He sits up in the unfamiliar bed, thrusting his legs over the edge.

"Papi?" It's always Papi he calls for first. Papi whose side of the bed he approaches, Papi he taps on the shoulder, who tucks him into the fold of his arm, who doesn't make him go back to his own room. Papi's pillow smells faintly of the amber liquid he drinks at bedtime. Mami is great for the daytime things, but Papi is better, infinitely better, at tolerating disruptions to his sleep. "Papi," Luca calls a second time, and his voice sounds strange without the close walls to contain it.

Luca clutches the edge of the puffy blanket. "Mami?" he tries then. There's breathing nearby, which ceases, then rearranges itself.

"I'm here, *mi amor*. Come here."

Mami. Luca draws his legs back beneath the covers and leans against the wall of pillows behind him, and that's when it returns, all at once. The memory of what happened. The truth of where they are. The breath squeezes out of Luca's small body, and his knees curl up to his face. He covers his head with his arms and screams without intending to—the sound escapes from him. Mami sits up quickly on her knees and reaches for the lamp, groping for the switch. Now the room is illuminated, but Luca can sense that only through the clamped shutters of his eyelids. Mami pulls him close and folds him up, gets her legs beneath him so the knot of him is on her lap, and they stay like that for a long time. She doesn't try to stop him from screaming or crying, she just hangs on and wraps herself around him as best she can. It's as if they are riding out a hurricane. When the worst of it has passed, perhaps fifteen minutes later, Luca's eyes feel like sandpaper and he still can't find a way to loosen the joints of his body, but at least he's breathing again. In and out, in and out. His face is swollen.

Lydia gets out of bed, wearing one of the long T-shirts she bought at Walmart, and Luca writhes. There's a physical pain to their minor separation. She grabs a bottle of water from the dresser and then darts back to him.

"I'm right here," she says. "I'm not going anywhere."

Luca lies on his side, curled up. She twists the cap off the bottle and takes a drink, then hands it to him. Her black hair is a wild tumble. He shakes his head, but she insists.

"Sit up. Drink."

He drags his body upright, and she holds the bottle to his lips, tips it in for him like she did when he was a baby.

"Someone once told me that the only good advice for grief is to stay hydrated. Because everything else is just *chingaderas*."

Mami cursed again! That's the second time since yesterday. Luca closes his lips, forcing the bottle out, but she hands it to him.

"Have some more," she says.

Her face is splotchy but dry, and there are dark circles beneath her eyes. Her expression is one Luca has never seen before, and he fears it might be permanent. It's as if seven fishermen have cast their hooks into her from different directions and they're all pulling at once. One from the eyebrow, one from the lip, another at the nose, one from the cheek. Mami is contorted. She turns the alarm clock face so she can see it. When she leans over the nightstand, the weight of Papi's wedding ring drags at the gold chain she wears around her neck, dwarfing the three little loops that have always lived there. She tucks it back inside the collar of her T-shirt.

"Four forty-eight," she says. "No more sleep for us, right?"

Luca doesn't answer. He drinks from the water bottle. She gathers her tumultuous hair into a ponytail, stands up from the bed again, and turns on the television. She finds an English-language cartoon. "Here," she says. "Practice," even though he doesn't need practice. His English is excellent.

She orders room service: eggs and toast and fruit. The thought of eating makes Luca's stomach churn, so he stops thinking about it. He lets his eyes hook into the television, and his body soften. His head feels like a cinder block, his nose stuffed. He opens his mouth to breathe gently, but when Mami steps into the bathroom and turns the shower on, Luca gets up from the bed and pads across the room to join her. She's sitting on the toilet, so he perches on the edge of the tub until she's finished. Then he takes a turn. Not because he has to go, but because he doesn't want to be alone in the other room. He sits there with his underwear around his ankles until he hears the handle squeak and the water stop. He stands and flushes just as she pulls back the curtain.

"You should take a shower, too," she says, stepping out, wrapping herself in a towel. "It might be a few days before you have another chance."

Luca looks at her in the mirror and shakes his head once. It's impossible for him to shower. To be alone there, wedged between the tiled walls with the sound of gunfire raking across Abuela's back patio. He shakes his head again, and shuts his eyes tightly, but it's no use. He's reliving it again, his body frantic, his breath a whip of panic. The sound that comes out of him this time is something between a whimper and a screech. He tries to be louder than the gunfire in his head.

"It's okay, it's okay, it's okay," Mami says, holding him. And even though Luca knows those words are not strictly true, he clings to them regardless.

She washes him instead in the sink with sudsy water and a washcloth, like she used to do when he was a baby. Neck, ears, armpits, tummy, back, bottom, undercarriage, legs, and feet. She swabs off the grime, the spots of dried blood, the clinging flecks of vomit. She makes him clean and dry. She pats him down with a white towel, fluffy and warm against his skin.

Even though they're expecting the room service delivery, the knock at the door, when it comes, startles them both. They are jittery from grief, and there's a thinness in the air that amplifies every sound. He doesn't want to, but Luca waits in the bathroom with the door locked while his mother answers the delivery. He hums softly to himself as soon as he's alone, but it's not music. There's no melody in it. Lydia hesitates between the two locked doors. Behind the bathroom one, she can hear the tuneless humming. Behind the other, a man's voice repeats the announcement of their breakfast delivery. She is barefoot on the carpet, and her hands shake as she lugs the desk chair out of the way and reaches for the doorknob. She wants to stretch up on her bare toes and look out the peephole to make sure, but how can she? How can she, when all she can imagine is seeing the dark tunnel of a gun barrel on the other side and then immediately seeing nothing at all ever again? But if that's the fate that awaits her, she tells herself, then no, at least she won't unlock the door and invite it in. She holds her breath as she reaches out silently and plants her hands on either side of the peephole. The young man outside pushes a cart laden with silver trays. He wears a uniform. His face is scarred with acne. His name tag says IKAL. None of it means anything about their safety. She returns to the flats of her feet, pads over to the dresser, and removes her machete from the top drawer.

"Be right there, just a second!" she says.

She's wearing the thick bathrobe she found in the closet, and she slips the machete into its baggy pocket. She keeps her hand in there and grips the handle tightly. She says the word "okay" out loud to herself. And then she opens the door.

Ikal, it is immediately obvious, is not a *sicario*. He's barely even a room service delivery boy. He ducks his head and clears his throat and seems embarrassed to be in a hotel room with a woman wearing a bathrobe. He averts his eyes as he steps past her and places their tray almost apologetically on the desk. Then he returns to his waiting cart in the doorway and hands her the billfold for her signature. Lydia feels confident enough to leave the machete in her pocket momentarily while she signs it. She thanks him and hands it back and then, just as the door is about to swing closed, he says, "Wait, I almost forgot," and Lydia's hand darts back into her pocket. But he only hands her some cutlery wrapped in two cloth napkins.

"And this," he says, producing a padded envelope from a lower shelf. "The front desk asked me to bring it up."

Lydia takes a small step back. "What is it?"

"A delivery," he says. "Arrived for you last night."

Lydia shakes her head. *No one knows we're here, no one knows we're here.* A panic refrain.

He's holding the parcel out between them but Lydia makes no move to reach for it. She stares at the brown paper. She can't see any markings on it, not even her name.

"Shall I put it on the desk with the food?" he asks. He gestures inside but seems reluctant to step back into the room without an invitation.

"No," Lydia says. She knows she's acting crazy. She doesn't care. "I don't want it."

"Señora?"

She shakes her head again. "I don't want it," she repeats. "Just get rid of it."

Ikal attempts to suppress the confusion from his face with a firm nod. He replaces the parcel on his cart, and it's not until its muffled rattle has almost reached the elevators at the end of the corridor that Lydia changes her mind. She opens the door and chases after him.

"Wait!"

When she returns to the room, Luca has already emerged from the bathroom and is standing over the tray of food, removing the covers from the plates. Lydia holds the small parcel away from her body as she carries it into the bathroom and places it carefully on a towel in the bottom of the tub. She steps out and shuts the door, closing the parcel inside. She fixes her coffee from the tray, drinks it in one long guzzle, and then dresses quickly, hitching her scratchy new jeans up beneath the hotel robe.

Luca eats standing up, wearing only his underwear. He is starving, and that hunger feels like a betrayal. How can his body want food? He jams a slice of toast into his mouth. How can the butter taste so good? Luca chews it into a paste before swallowing. He watches his mother

sideways without turning his head away from the television. He sees the
way Mami screws her lips up to one side, and he decides he's going to take
care of her. He won't be a baby anymore. He decides this very matter-of-
factly, in a single instant, and he knows it to be immediately true.

"We should go to *el norte*," he says, because he suspects that's her
plan anyway, and he wants to confirm that it's a good one, the only one,
to get to a planet where no one can reach them.

"Yes." Mami stands beside the bed in her jeans and robe. She seems
to have lost track of what she was doing halfway through getting dressed.
She seems both hurried and unable to move. "We'll go to Denver," she
says after a moment.

She has an uncle there. Lydia slips a plain white T-shirt over her head
and steps out from inside the puddle of robe around her feet. She feels so
prickly and raw that even the cotton of the T-shirt brushing against her
skin sends goose bumps racing down her arms. She rubs them off and
tells Luca to hurry up and get dressed when he's finished eating.

Back in the bathroom, she stares down at the padded brown envelope in the bottom of the tub, and can't decide whether she made the right
decision by bringing it into the room. Maybe it doesn't matter. Someone
knows they're here, so now they have to leave immediately, regardless
of what's inside. It wasn't curiosity that made her run after that food
delivery kid. She's not curious. She doesn't want to know what's inside.
But she knows that disinterest is a luxury she can no longer afford to indulge. If she hopes to survive this ordeal with Luca, then she needs to
pay attention to every single detail. She needs to be alert to every scrap of
available information. She lifts the envelope carefully by one corner and
examines the back seal. There's nothing out of the ordinary. She's going
to have to open it. In here, in the bathroom? Or should she take it out on
the balcony in case it explodes?

"*Carajo*," she says out loud.

"You talking to me, Mami?" Luca says through the door.

"No, *mijo*. Get dressed!"

She puts the parcel to her ear but can hear nothing inside. No ticking. No beeping. She lifts the parcel to her nose and smells it, but there's
no discernible odor. She carefully slides one finger beneath the sealed
edge, closes her eyes, and gently pulls her finger along the loosening flap.

In her head, the pounding of her own fear is louder than the ripping paper, but now here it is, opened in her hands. An ordinary brown envelope. No dreadful toxic powder spills out. No poisonous cloud of doom ascends.

Inside, tied with a pale blue ribbon, is an English-language copy of *Love in the Time of Cholera*. A book she once discussed with Javier, one of their many shared favorites. There's something tucked between its pages. She tugs on the ribbon, which gives way and falls to the floor at her bare feet. Her body feels like an arrow that's been launched from its bow but hasn't yet found its target. She's suspended, arcing, accountable to the laws of gravity. She opens to the page where an unsealed envelope is wedged into the spine. Of course she knows, she knew from the very first sound of mayhem in the yard, that Javier is responsible for the massacre of her family. It feels as impossible as it is true. But until this moment, she's protected herself from fully acknowledging that fact. Because once she accepts that incontrovertible truth, she must also acknowledge her own guilt. She knew this man. She *knew* him. And yet she'd failed to appreciate the danger he presented; she'd failed to protect her family. Lydia can't think about any of this yet; she isn't ready. She must find a way to delay her despair. Luca is the only thing that matters now. Luca. He is still in danger.

"Get dressed!" she calls again, her voice pitching out at an unfamiliar angle.

She looks down at the book in her hand. A passage is highlighted there, the moment when the widowed heroine, Fermina Daza, reeling in the aftermath of her husband's death, encounters the man, Florentino Ariza, whom she rejected fifty years earlier:

"Fermina," he said, "I have waited for this opportunity for more than half a century, to repeat to you once again my vow of eternal fidelity and everlasting love."

Lydia thrusts the book away from her and it somersaults into the tub. The envelope remains in her hand. She considers dropping it, too, and leaving it there, but she needs to know what it says. Her stomach plunges. She pulls the card out of its thick envelope and sees white lilies on the front. *Mi más sentido pésame.* Inside, the handwriting is immediately familiar.

> *Lydia,*
> *Hay sangre en tus manos también. Lo siento por tu dolor y el mío. Ahora estamos destinados a permanecer eternamente unidos por este pesar. Jamás imaginé este capítulo para nosotros. Pero no te preocupes, mi reina del alma—tu sufrimiento será breve.*
>   *Javier*

> *There is blood on your hands as well. I'm sorry for your pain and mine. Now we are bound forever in this grief. I never imagined this chapter for us. But do not worry, Queen of my Soul—your suffering will be brief.*

She drops the card and it lands in the toilet, where it darkens at once. Lydia's not sure what she'd been expecting when she opened it. There's nothing he could've written there that would make any difference. No quiet slashing of ink on paper can resuscitate her dead mother, her husband. No apology or explanation can reanimate Yénifer's brain, pin her soul back into her body. That girl smelled like grapefruit and sugar, and now she's gone. Lydia beats back a sob using an English word she's never liked: "Fuck!" It works, so she says it again and again. Perhaps she'd hoped the card might illuminate something. She reads it once more, floating, the ink beginning to bleed, and she's haunted by the familiarity of the handwriting. What had she missed? How can this be real? She tries, but she can't force it to make sense, and the effort makes her dizzy.

Only one thing is clear: Javier knows where they are. She doesn't have time to panic or reflect. She has to get Luca out of there. Now. They have to run. She bangs open the bathroom door and hisses at Luca once more to get dressed. He doesn't answer, and when she looks up, she sees that he's already dressed in fresh jeans and his father's red hat, that he's sitting on the chair beside the desk, wriggling his feet into his new socks. "Oh, *ándale,*" she says. "Good." But then he reaches out for the tray of food, to cram in a bite before tackling the other sock, and Lydia lunges toward him. She smacks the toast from his hand and it skids to the floor.

"Mami!" Luca is shocked.

She only shakes her head. "Don't eat it. Don't eat any more food." Luca is silent. "I don't know if it's safe."

She thinks about dragging him into the bathroom and sticking a finger down his throat, but there's no time. She crams all their belongings into her mother's overnight bag and the two backpacks. She hasn't even put on her bra yet. No time. Her hair is wet; it's leaving a damp ring around the shoulders of her T-shirt. She jams her bare feet into her mother's quilted sneakers, straps the backpack on herself, and grabs her mother's bag.

"You ready?"

Luca nods and picks up the second backpack, the one they bought at Walmart.

"Super quiet," she says. "No noise."

Luca seals his mouth.

Lydia pauses at the door to lean her ear against the wood and listen before she dares to open it. She pins Luca to the wall beside her and then cracks the door. The hallway is empty, the only sound coming from a television in the room across the hall. She takes Luca's hand and tugs him out, wedging a towel into the door so it won't even click as it closes. They run silently to the service stairs, and when Lydia hears the ding of the elevator at the other end of the hall, she shoves Luca through the door. Seven flights down, Luca flies in front of her. Lydia's feet touch every third or fourth step along the way.

CHAPTER SIX

They emerge from the stairwell into a small parking lot behind the kitchen and the stink of hot dumpster garbage. Lydia tells Luca they're going to be fine, but they must be both calm and quick now. They have to keep their heads. There's a wall of hedges to hide the work of tourism from the tourists, and together they shove through it, out onto a manicured path that winds among the sparkling pools before reaching the beach. Lydia listens all the time for the sounds of pursuit behind them, but so far there's nothing but the hushy voice of the ocean greeting the shore. The towel hut isn't open yet, but a man on the pool deck is pushing a cart of clean, folded towels, and he offers one to Lydia, who smiles and slings it around her neck.

"Thank you," she says, and takes one for Luca, too.

On the sand, they take off their shoes and try to make their silhouettes appear like casual morning beachcombers. In minutes, they arrive safely at the adjacent hotel property. They put their shoes back on and walk briskly through the lobby from back to front, discarding the towels on a lounger as they go. They pass potted palms and waiters carrying trays of orange juice, and the aroma of fresh coffee, and Lydia takes two muffins from an unattended tray of food on a stand. When they arrive at the hotel's front door, there's a shuttle bus waiting. They get on. Soon they're driving past the entry of the Hotel Duquesa Imperial, and Lydia can see three black SUVs lurking in the parking lot. She clutches at Sebastián's wedding band hanging from the gold chain around her neck, and feels for the three interlocking loops.

She doesn't know how Javier found them. Or why. Did he mean only to scare the shit out of her? To spike her grief with terror? Or to warn her, to soil the purity of her anguish with his weird, revolting compassion? His motives are messy; Lydia cannot begin to understand them. That highlighted passage he chose—the dead husband, the vulgar proclamation of love. Does Javier not remember what happens next? That Fermina Daza is repulsed by the declaration, that she curses his name and throws him out onto the street, that she wishes him dead and orders him never to return? Lydia understands nothing.

For an instant—only an instant—she considers telling the driver to stop. She imagines walking over to those SUVs and knocking on one of the drivers' windows. She thinks of going to Javier, wherever he is, meeting him outside the confines of the bookstore for the first time. She might embrace him, throw herself on his mercy, demand an explanation. She might beg him just to get it over with. She might punch and kick him, pull the machete from her pant leg, slash his face, slash his throat. And then she looks over at Luca, and it all evaporates. She's in a stuffy shuttle bus and there's something sticky on the seat. The ghost of some child's melted candy. She is here with Luca and she will protect him at all costs. This is the only thing left that matters. Ahead of them, a black SUV rolls slowly across the intersection.

"Can you take us to the bus depot?" Lydia asks the driver.

"I'm not supposed to deviate from my route."

"But there are no other passengers, it's only a few extra blocks. Who's going to know?"

"GPS." The driver points to a screen strapped onto his dash. "There's a different shuttle that goes to the bus terminal. This one's for the shopping district. You want to go back to the hotel, you can take the other shuttle."

"Please," Lydia says. "I can pay you."

In response, the driver brakes and opens the door. Lydia shoots him a hateful look but gathers her things and prompts Luca off the bus in front of her. It's too early for shopping, and the streets of the district are deserted. The driver closes the door behind them and rolls away. The boulevard is wide and open. It's only half a mile's walk from here to the bus station, but it feels an impossible, exposed distance to cover, like walking across a battlefield without armor or weaponry. She hides her fear well, but Luca can sense it anyway, in the cold slick of his mother's hand.

Getting to the bus depot feels like some deranged version of the game Crossy Road, where, instead of dodging taxis and trucks and trains, Luca and Mami have to duck and lurch between the possibility of concealed narcos in their tinted SUVs. The ever-present threat of gunfire screams through Luca's mind like the unexpected train.

"Don't worry," he tells Mami. "If anyone was looking for us, they'd go to the central terminal downtown, right? They wouldn't expect us to be all the way out here in Diamante." Luca doesn't know about the parcel, but his logic is enough to make Lydia smile for a moment.

"That's what I thought, too. Smart kid." She tugs the brim of Papi's red baseball cap lower on Luca's face. He walks too fast. "We have to walk like normal," she says. "Slow down."

"Normal people are sometimes late for a bus." Luca's limbs feel twitchy.

"There's always another bus," she says.

It's seven minutes past six in the morning when Mami purchases their one-way tickets to Mexico City, so they have thirteen minutes to kill before the bus leaves. The terminal is a modern structure, mostly glass, and even though the sun isn't up yet, the sky has begun to lighten, and Luca can make out the shapes of the cars in the parking lot. There's only one SUV, and it appears to be empty, lights off. But someone could be inside waiting, seat reclined, asleep on the job. Luca studies the SUV while Mami collects her change from the lady behind the counter. It's Sunday, so the buses back to Mexico City will be crowded with families heading home from their minivacations. Luca and Mami can look like one of those families. There's a handful of energetic children in the terminal already, chattering and skipping circles around their bleary-eyed, coffee-sipping parents.

Mami herds Luca into the handicapped stall in the ladies' bathroom and makes him stand on the toilet seat inside. It's the sort of thing she usually wouldn't tolerate. Luca doesn't think anyone in the terminal noticed them, and he feels pretty sure because he was studying the faces, but if there is someone looking for them here, if they do track them first to the bus terminal, then to the women's bathroom, and finally to the handicapped stall, well, then standing on a toilet with your back against a wall doesn't seem like a very effective way to survive. Luca leans his hands down on his knees and tries not to shake. He watches Mami remove her backpack and prop it in the corner before hanging the overnight bag from the hook on the back of the door. She has to dig nearly to the bottom of it to find a pair of socks. They're still attached by a plastic barb, which Mami snaps before putting them on. He doesn't know how she does that. Luca always has to cut them with scissors. Mami doesn't look that strong, but he knows she's really powerful, because she can always snap that plastic barb like it's nothing. She digs out a bra, too, and wriggles into it beneath her shirt. Then she zips up Abuela's gold sneakers and turns her back to Luca so her feet are pointing in the right direction in case anyone looks under the stall. They're alone in the bathroom, but he speaks to her very quietly anyway, so they can hear if the door opens, if anyone comes in.

"So we're going to Colorado?"

Lydia nods, and Luca wraps his arms around her neck.

He leans his chin on her shoulder. "Good plan."

"No one would ever think of Colorado." Lydia stares at the bag hanging in front of them and tries to remember if she ever mentioned Denver to Javier. Why would she have? She's never been there and hasn't seen her uncle since she was a kid.

"Plus, it's far," Luca says.

"Yes," Mami says. "Very far away from here."

In fact, Luca knows with some degree of precision just how far Denver is from Acapulco (almost two thousand miles by car). He knows this because Luca has perfect direction the way some prodigies have perfect pitch. He was born with it, an intrinsic sense of his position on the globe, like a human GPS, pinging his way through the universe. When he sees something on a map, it lodges in his memory forever.

"I'm going to miss the geography bee," he says. He's been studying for months. In September, his school paid six hundred pesos for him to take the international qualifying exam because his teacher was convinced he would bring home the $10,000 grand prize.

"I'm sorry, *mijo*," Lydia says, kissing his arm.

Luca shrugs. "It doesn't matter."

Before yesterday, that geography bee had seemed so important to all of them; now it feels like the most trivial thing in the world, along with everything else on the running to-do list Lydia kept beside the register in the bookshop: Fill out the church paperwork for Luca's communion. Pay the water bill. Take Abuela to her cardiology appointment. Buy a gift for Yénifer's *quinceañera*. What a waste of time it had all been. Lydia feels annoyed that her niece won't get to see the music box she purchased for her special day. How expensive it was! She realizes, even as this thought occurs to her, how bizarre and awful it is, but she can't stop it from crashing in. She doesn't rebuke herself for thinking it; she does herself the small kindness of forgiving her malfunctioning logic.

Luca whispers in her ear, "With a population of almost seven hundred thousand, Denver, nicknamed the Mile High City because of its elevation, is located just east of the Rocky Mountain foothills." Reciting from the memory of flash cards. "It is the state capital of Colorado and one quarter of its population claims Mexican heritage."

Lydia squeezes his arm, reaches up, and runs a hand through his black hair. The summer before last, when Luca's enduring interest in maps began to shift from fascination to obsession, Lydia kept him busy at the bookstore with guidebooks and atlases. It seems impossible that back then, just so recently, Acapulco was bright with tourists and music and the shops and the sea. Rock pigeons strutted across the sand. Vast foreign cruise ships disgorged their sneakered passengers onto the streets, their pockets fat with dollars, their skin glistening from coconut-scented sunscreen. The dollars filled the bars and restaurants. In Lydia's bookshop, they filled the register. Those tourists bought the guidebooks and atlases, along with serious novels and frivolous novels and souvenir key chains and tiny tubes of sand corked with tiny stoppers that Lydia kept in a big fishbowl beside the register. And, *ay, Dios mío*, those tourists couldn't get enough of Luca. Lydia set him up like a puppet on a stool, and he'd tell them, in precise English, about the places where they came from. He was six years old. A wunderkind.

"With a population of six hundred and forty thousand, Portland is located at the confluence of the Columbia and Willamette Rivers and is the largest city in the state of Oregon. The city was incorporated in 1851, sixty-five years after its eastern namesake in coastal Maine."

Henry from Portland, Oregon, stood in front of Luca with his mouth hanging open. "Marge, come here, you've gotta see this! Do it again." Marge joined her husband, and Luca repeated his spiel. "Incredible. Kid, you are just incredible. Marge, give the kid some money."

"Did you make all that up?" Marge asked skeptically, digging in her purse for some money regardless.

"Nah, he knew the rivers," Henry defended him. "How could he make that up?"

"It's real," Luca said. "I just remember things. Especially about maps and places."

"Well, Henry's right, it's incredible." Marge gave him a dollar. "And in perfect English! Where did you learn such perfect English?"

"Acapulco," Luca said simply. "And YouTube."

Lydia watched in silence and felt obscenely proud. Smug, even. Her boy was perfect—so smart and accomplished, so *guapo* and happy. She'd been teaching him English for almost as long as he'd been speaking Spanish. It was a skill that she knew would serve him well, growing up in a tourist town. But he quickly outstripped her knowledge of the language, and then they proceeded to learn together, mostly on her phone or computer. YouTube lessons, Rosetta Stone, soap operas. They often spoke English to each other when Sebastián wasn't around, or when they pretended to have a secret in front of him. Sometimes they tried out slang on each other. She called Luca *dude* and he called her *shorty*. Marge and Henry laughed at Luca's pragmatic charm and then gathered their friends from the cruise ship and returned to watch him perform. They offered him a dollar for every city he could tell them about. He made thirty-seven dollars that day and could've kept going, except the tourists had to get back to their ship.

So, yes, this geography bee has been almost two years coming. But Lydia cannot think of details right now, the annulled logistics of her life. Her brain can't hold them. Even the biggest, most fundamental facts seem impossible to comprehend. Outside the stall, the bathroom door swings open. There's no squeak, but they can tell someone has come in because suddenly the sounds beyond the door are temporarily louder, and then softer again as the door swings shut. They both hold their breath. Luca is still draped over Mami's back, and she grips his arms where they encircle her neck. The pads of his fingers turn yellow as they dig into the bones of Mami's wrist. She doesn't move. He squeezes his eyes shut. But soon there's the sound of the door latching on the neighboring stall. An older woman loudly clearing her throat. Luca can feel Mami let go of her breath like the air leaving a deflated balloon. He puts his lips against her neck.

After the lady in the stall next door finishes her business and washes her hands and compliments herself out loud in the bathroom mirror, it's time for them to venture back out. He knows they can't stay in this bathroom forever, but his heart beats in a clamorous thud when Mami opens the door. It's time to get on the bus. When they cross the lobby, Luca registers the faces of the people who remain in the terminal: the immaculate lady behind the counter with her lips outlined a shade darker than the lips themselves, the man in his paper hat selling coffee, the couple with the fussy baby who are waiting until the last minute to board. On the television affixed to the wall, Luca sees a prim newscaster and then, starkly, Abuela's little house. The yellow crime scene tape flutters and sags. The camera focuses on the courtyard gate hanging open, and then the back patio, the tented shapes of Luca's family covered by plastic tarps, the grim faces of *los policías* as they walk, stoop, stand, scratch, breathe, as they do the things living people do when they walk among corpses. Luca squeezes his mother's hand, not to get her attention, but to prevent himself from crying out. She doesn't look up. She pulls him along the shiny, tiled floor, but he feels as if he's walking in a sucking sand at high tide. Luca waits for the crack of a bullet to strike the front wall of the terminal. He waits for the shower of raining glass. But now his feet are on the pavement outside, and the pavement is a shadowy purple in the growing cast of daylight. His sneakers are blue there. Only two people wait in front of them to board the bus. Only one. Mami pushes him on ahead of her, and then she's there, too, glued to his backpack, propelling him down the aisle past extruding knees and elbows. And when he collapses into the seat, against the soft fabric of the cushions, and Mami plops down next to him, he feels more grateful and relieved than he ever has in his entire life.

"We made it," he says quietly.

Mami opens her lips without moving her teeth. She doesn't look relieved. "Okay, *mijo,*" she says. She pulls his head onto her lap and strokes his hair until, as their bus rambles north onto the Viaducto Diamante and gathers speed, he falls asleep.

CHAPTER SEVEN

It's a victory to get out of Acapulco alive, Lydia knows this. Yes, they've cleared the first significant hurdle. She'd like to feel her son's surge of relieved optimism, but she knows too much about the reach and determination of Los Jardineros and their *jefe* to experience any real respite from her fear. She stares out the window and keeps her head low.

In the early days of their marriage, Lydia and Sebastián took frequent weekend trips to Mexico City, trading cities with the tourists. They'd both gone to college there. It was where they met, and though neither of them had any desire to live in the capital, they enjoyed being close enough to visit. In those days, the state of Guerrero felt safe, insulated. Their country had its share of *narcotraficantes* back then, but they felt as distant as Hollywood or Al Qaeda. The violence would erupt in concentrated, faraway bursts: first Ciudad Juárez, then Sinaloa, then Michoacán. Acapulco, ringed by mountains and sea, retained its sunny bubble of protective tourism. The salty ocean air, the wheeling calls of the seagulls, the big sunglasses, the wind whipping down the boulevard to toss the ladies' hair around their sun-browned faces, it all intensified that swollen illusion of immunity.

It typically took Lydia and Sebastián just over four hours to drive from Acapulco to Mexico City in their orange Beetle because Sebastián sped like a lunatic around the gentle mountain curves, up and down the scenic slopes of the highway. Even though his driving was questionable, the road was broad and smooth. Lydia looked out over the landscape, at the sunshine leaning between the distant peaks, the terraces of clouds stepping down toward the irregular earth, the rooftops and steeples of the fleeting villages, and she felt safe with her new husband in their little orange car. At Chilpancingo they often stopped for a coffee or a sandwich. Sometimes they met with friends—Sebastián's college roommate lived there with his wife and the baby who became Sebastián's godson. And then a couple hours later, in Mexico City, they'd find a cheap hotel and walk the city for hours. Museums, shows, restaurants, dancing, window-shopping, the Bosque de Chapultepec. Or sometimes they wouldn't leave their hotel room at all, and Sebastián, sweaty, laughing, tangled in the sheets, would whisper into his wife's hair that they could have stayed in Acapulco and saved some money.

Lydia tips her head back against the bus seat behind her. It's inconceivable that those memories are from ten years ago, inconceivable that Sebastián is really gone. She feels a monstrous lurch inside her, so she reaches out to touch the soft curve of Luca's sleeping ear. Everything devolved so rapidly in recent years. Acapulco always had a heart for extravagance, so when at last she made her fall from grace, she did so with all the spectacular pageantry the world had come to expect of her. The cartels painted the town red.

As their bus passes the crooked shoulders of trees and a scar of blasted rock face where the road cuts through the countryside, Lydia notes that they've already reached Ocotito. She prays there will be no roadblock between here and Mexico City, but she knows that's impossible. Even before Acapulco fell, the roadblocks around Guerrero, as in much of the country, had become a menace. They are manned by gangs or *narcotraficantes* or police (who may also be *narcotraficantes*) or soldiers (who may also be *narcotraficantes*) or, in recent years, by *autodefensas*—armed militias formed by the inhabitants of certain towns to protect their communities from cartels. And these *autodefensas* may also, of course, be *narcotraficantes*.

In character, the roadblocks range from inconvenient to life threatening. It's because of the existence of the more serious ones that Lydia and Sebastián stopped traveling regularly to the capital shortly after Luca was born, the reason Luca has been to Mexico City only once before, when he was too young to remember it, and the reason Lydia allowed her driver's license to expire almost two years ago. They seldom left Acapulco now, and Lydia, like most women in Mexico's more precarious states, never travels alone by car anymore. This truth has felt like a growing, but theoretical, irritation to Lydia over the last couple of years, an affront to her contemporary feminine autonomy. But today it feels like a very real noose around her neck. She may have managed their escape from Acapulco for now, but she knows they're still trapped in Guerrero state, and she can feel the roadblocks all around the periphery of her mind, closing in on them.

Without waking Luca, Lydia spreads out the map and pins it with one hand to the seat in front of her. She studies the spreading veins of the roadways and feels the ticking futility of that action. If only their bodies could pass unimpeded along these highways as quickly and safely as her finger traces the route along the map. If the roadblocks were represented on the map key, their icon might be a tiny AK-47. But they're not on the map, because they're always moving, to maintain the element of surprise. Lydia knows that every road between here and Mexico City will have at least one roadblock occupied by Los Jardineros. She knows that the boys manning those roadblocks will be looking specifically for her and for Luca. She imagines that some of those boys are both ambitious and violent, that they'll be eager to recognize her. She wonders what reward they might receive for delivering her, either whole or in pieces, to her friend.

Lydia tries to refold the map along its previous creases, but her patience is flimsy, and she shoves it into the pocket of the seat in front of her. She tries to think clearly, to review their options. Most people she would ordinarily turn to for help are dead, and even if they weren't, asking for help is akin to walking into a friend's kitchen wearing a suicide vest. The risk of her very presence seems too selfish to consider. Although she's aware that Chilpancingo is crawling with Jardineros, she also knows that if they hope to avoid a roadblock, they will have to get off there. Boarding this bus felt like a tremendous victory only a few minutes ago, but maybe it was a mistake. Maybe they're speeding into a trap. She watches Luca, the rise and fall of his chest as he sleeps, and she attempts to match the rhythm of his breath.

When she was a kid, Lydia loved the *Choose Your Own Adventure* books. At the end of each chapter, you'd have to decide what to do next. Ride your bike to the park, flip to page twenty-three. Follow the mysterious stranger, flip to page forty-two. Whenever Lydia didn't like the outcome of her plot, or sometimes even when she did, she would backtrack and make a different choice. She liked being able to revise her own decisions, liked knowing that nothing was permanent, that she could always start over and try again. But it was also true that sometimes it didn't matter, the maze of the book seemed to funnel her back to the same result, no matter what she decided. This morning she and Luca had selected the 6:20 a.m. bus from Diamante, and now it's traveling north without delay. She closes her eyes and prays it was the right choice.

Luca wakes up as the bus approaches Chilpancingo. Lydia can't see much from their seats halfway back, but she tries. She leans into the aisle and looks for a roadblock ahead. Luca leans his forehead against the window, and presses his finger against the smudgy glass.

"Mami, look!" He yawns. "What are they?" On a ridge above them, rows of colorful houses snake up the hillside, all in matching clusters: red, blue, green, purple.

"Oh, they're just houses, *amorcito*."

"Only houses?" It's turned into a bright young morning. They've been on the road almost two hours.

"Why are they so colorful like that?"

"Just for decoration, I think."

"They look like LEGOs."

Lydia's breath hitches in her chest every time the bus jerks or turns or changes its speed, but there's no stopping. No armed men standing in the road. And soon, buildings line both sides of the narrow street and they've made it. They're in Chilpancingo. She makes the sign of the cross over herself and traces a smaller version on Luca's forehead. They pull up in front of a familiar building, a miniature of the station they embarked from in Acapulco this morning. The driver stops the bus and there's the loud hiccupping noise as he engages the brakes. He stands and announces past his mustache, "Five-minute stop."

A couple passengers stand up from their seats to stretch. At the front, someone gets off for a cigarette, but Lydia and Luca are the only ones who begin gathering their things to disembark. Everyone on board is heading to the capital.

"Are we getting out, Mami?"

"Yes, *mi amor*."

But then she stands next to her seat in the narrow aisle with her back-pack strapped to her shoulders and looks down at her sleepy son, at the top of his tousled black head, and she wishes they could make a run for it. She wishes they could hunker down in here, camouflaged among the travelers on this bus, and hold their breath all the way to Mexico City. Maybe they'd make it. Maybe the roadblock between here and there would be innocuous. A brief stop, a fistful of bills, a languorous waving through. *Thump thump*, two slaps on the side of the bus as it rolls on its merry way. Lydia imagines it all with a quiver of hope. The bus driver emerges from the terminal now and gets back on the bus. New passen-gers begin to board, and the driver takes their tickets one by one.

"Mami?"

"Come on."

As the shadow of the bus pulls away from the sidewalk, Lydia and Luca emerge into the blinking daylight of Chilpancingo. She feels both relieved and disheartened to be off the bus. But she takes a moment to remind herself that she's managed to get them this far: nineteen hours and sixty-eight miles away from the epicenter of calamity. With each minute and mile that passes, Lydia knows she's increased their chances of survival. She needs to take encouragement where she can find it. She mustn't despair at the enormity of the task yet ahead. She should focus only on the immediate next steps. Find Sebastián's college roommate.

On the sidewalk, she tightens the straps on Luca's backpack, which are drooping too far from his small shoulders. He looks like a turtle with an inadequate shell, yet somehow he's managed to draw his most vulner-able parts tightly within himself. She wonders about the lasting effects of that retraction.

"What's next, Mami?" Luca asks her, in the flat tone of voice that seems to be his only inflection now.

"Let's find an internet café," she says.

"But you have Papi's tablet, right?"

It's powered off in her backpack, and she's not going to turn it back on. She also left the SIM card of her own cell phone in a garbage can outside the bank in Playa Caletilla. She felt marginally crazy, paranoid, as she pried the thing out with her fingernail, but she didn't want to be a blue dot flashing on some remote, hostile screen. She adjusts the brim of Sebastián's Yankees cap slightly lower on her son's forehead. She should buy one for herself, too, she thinks.

"Let's go," she says.

El Cascabelito Internet Café is just opening for the day when Lydia purchases a coffee and fifteen minutes to look more closely at maps online. She buys Luca a bag of *platanitos,* too, but the green foil package sits unopened on the desk. Lydia chooses a computer in the back corner, one that has two chairs and a privacy partition so they're hidden from view of the door. Luca draws his heels up to the seat of the chair and rests his chin on his knees, but his eyes remain unfocused on the *platanitos* while Lydia studies the screen. From Chilpancingo there are only two viable routes to Mexico City, and both are virtually guaranteed to have roadblocks. Lydia chews the inside of her mouth, and her knee undertakes a jittery hop beneath the desk. They can't exactly walk to Mexico City from here. Lydia's never been claustrophobic, but today she feels so trapped. She can feel it in her limbs, a panicky longing to stretch. She can't see any way out. *Dismay will not help.*

She opens Facebook and finds Sebastián's friend. He's an attorney, and his profile shows the name of his law firm, but it's Sunday and it won't be open. She checks his About tab, and scrolls down to his *likes:* a local newspaper, a couple nonprofits, his alma mater, a fan page for Adidas sneakers, so much *fútbol.* But then, there. Bingo: a Pentecostal church here in Chilpancingo. A worship service at nine o'clock. She looks it up and finds it's about two miles away. There's a bus down the main thoroughfare, and twenty minutes later, Luca and Lydia are on it.

Lydia worries she wrote the address down wrong, because when they get off the bus, the street is lined with shops, all closed on a Sunday morning. They find the number they're looking for sandwiched between an electronics store and a jeweler. But just as she's double-checking the address on the scrap of paper in her hand, a young man pushing a baby carriage approaches and opens the door for his pregnant wife. Lydia peeks inside before the door swings closed, and she sees rows of folding chairs facing a stage. Luca tugs on her sleeve and directs her attention to a sign she hadn't noticed, propped in the window: IGLESIA PENTECOSTAL TABERNÁCULO DE LA VICTORIA. There's no steeple or stained glass, but this is the place.

Inside, it's bigger than she imagined, with low ceilings, and fans attached to the walls. There's a full drum kit, an amplifier, and some huge speakers set up behind the pulpit. There's no cross, no font of holy water at the entrance, but Lydia blesses herself out of habit, and Luca follows her example. She waits for some bubble of feeling to follow—a whisper from her legion of newborn angels, or perhaps a low-down rage at God instead. But nothing comes; it's spiritual tumbleweed. *Un desierto del alma* because she has room only for fear.

They sit in the last row, near the wall, and Lydia stows their backpacks under their folding chairs. She covers her face with her hands and instructs Luca to do the same, but it's not veneration. It's only for concealment, in case any of Los Jardineros are Pentecostal Christians, in case they traffic drugs on a Monday, stab people on a Thursday, and then come here seeking forgiveness on a Sunday. It doesn't seem more outlandish than anything else that's happened.

Through the screen of her interlaced fingers, Lydia watches the square of stark sunlight on the tiled floor grow brighter every time someone opens the glass door to come in. A few of the congregants notice them in the back row, and give them a welcoming nod or a smile, but most walk right past and find their usual seats.

The church is almost half-full by the time Carlos appears behind his wife and children. The wife greets everyone with hugs, and has the sharp voice of a *gabacha* above the hum of reverent conversation in the room. Lydia half stands from her seat and lifts a hand in greeting, but Carlos doesn't see her. The youngest son alerts him, points to Lydia in the corner, and Carlos turns.

"Lydia, oh my goodness, what are you doing here?" His voice arrives before he does, but soon he maneuvers himself between the rows of chairs to where she's standing. He embraces her. "It's so lovely to see you, *guau*, what a surprise!"

Luca watches while this man, Carlos, kisses Mami on both cheeks and holds both her hands in his.

"This must be Luca," the man says, bending toward him where he's still seated on the folding chair. "You look so much like your *papi*." He straightens up. "Where's Sebastián, did he come with you?"

"You haven't heard the news." Mami's voice sounds far away. Luca can tell without having to look that Carlos's face has suddenly shifted, that it's drained to a sickly gray, that he's already building the internal fortifications he'll need in order to hold the horrific story Mami's about to tell him.

"Come," Carlos says, "we can talk upstairs."

There's an office there, and it's not quite accurate to say that Luca zones out while his mother and Carlos talk, because that description would indicate some active participation of abstention on his part. Instead, his consciousness, like a helium balloon fastened to his person by some taut and fragile string, momentarily floats away. His body sits at a table with his backpack at his feet, his legs swivel the chair beneath his weight, his hands play with a nearby dish of paper clips, hooking them together into long strands, but his internal mappings are on vacation. The grown-ups glance at him now and again, past the barricades of their warbled voices and ashen faces, and his body responds to their questions with the appropriate nods or shrugs. A paper cup of water is set on the table before him, and he takes a dutiful sip. Downstairs, someone is playing the drums. An electric guitar. Luca can feel the bass vibrating through the floor. Then they're in Carlos's car, and they're driving through the streets of the city to Carlos's house. Mami sits in the backseat and tries to hold Luca's hand. He sees this, sees Mami's hand covering his own, and it's the warmth and press of her fingers that bring him back.

Once they pass out of *la zona centro*, Luca sees that Chilpancingo isn't so different from Acapulco. There are no seagulls here, no tourists, and the streets aren't as broad. But there are many colorful shops and taxis, people wearing their church clothes in the sunshine. There are ladies with handbags slung over their shoulders, boys with slipshod tattoos. Plenty of bright, foamy graffiti. The houses are all painted in vivid colors. Luca watches them flip by like cards in a deck. After three and a half songs have played on the radio, Carlos turns onto a street that's slightly wider than the others. There's an arching canopy of shade trees that creates the sense of entering a secret place, a hushy hideout. In the middle of the block stands a handsome white church with modest twin bell towers at the front. It's the kind they're used to. *Católica*. The other buildings on the crowded street stand back from the little church, giving it room. Carlos pulls into a parking spot.

Carlos's house is turquoise—the exact color of the middle stripe of ocean in Acapulco, in between the light sandy stripe near the shore and the darker blue at the horizon when you stand on the steps at Plaza España and look out on a sunny day. The house feels big and modern even though it's attached to an identical purple one on the right and an identical peach-colored one on the left. Carlos carries their bags inside.

Carlos's wife is named Meredith, and she's white. She's from Estados Unidos, and that's a fact Luca could've gathered without being told, just from the quick glimpse he got of her in church before Carlos took them upstairs. Her voice, her clothes. Her way of holding people by the shoulders and shaking them slightly while she speaks to them. Luca investigates the empty house, the family photographs, a closer look at the three boys, who all have Meredith's pink complexion and Carlos's dimples. The middle one looks about the same age as Luca. Meredith eventually arrives home without those boys (who stayed behind for even more church), and with her comes Luca's first experience of proprietary grief.

Proprietary is a word Luca knows (in Spanish, but not in English) because he knows lots of words other eight-year-olds don't, like *viscous* and *bombastic* and *serendipity*. But he's never truly understood the meaning of the word *propietario* until now. He's never felt the feeling before. It rumbles through him like a steamroller with a broad, flattening crush. Because who is this woman, crying for Papi? Who is this lady with her quivering features and her leaking eyes and her trembling hands and her need to be consoled? It surprises Luca—his ungenerous interpretation of such raw emotion. After all, she'd been Papi's friend at one time. Or at least she'd married Papi's friend. And she'd liked Papi well enough to make him the godfather to her eldest son. So why shouldn't she be saddened, even traumatized, by the news of his unexpected and violent death? Why shouldn't she weep and lament and exhibit her devastation? Luca cannot, therefore, explain why the display of it irritates him so. When she tries to hug him, he can't endure it, and Mami doesn't make him. She intercepts him and takes him to the bathroom and splashes water on his face, and when they return, Meredith has composed herself.

She urges Mami to sit while she makes tea for everyone. The tea doesn't move from the cups, but the conversation goes on for a long time regardless, and Luca lets most of it pass him without landing.

Meredith met Carlos when she was a college-aged missionary from Indiana, and she's still involved with that faraway cornfield church. That summer she first came here, she fell in love with Carlos and with his country. She liked the way Mexicans were easy in their faith. She liked the sense of being in a country where it wasn't controversial or weird to talk openly about God. In Mexico, prayer was normal then, public. Expected. To Meredith, those cultural conventions felt miraculous. So she and Carlos married young, and then she made it her life's work to preserve the link between Chilpancingo and that Indiana church community, to share the experience of this place with others.

In fact, right now there are fourteen Indiana missionaries visiting here for spring break. Those missionaries are being hosted in Chilpancingo by the church Carlos and Meredith attend. Meredith is the chief coordinator of this annual visit, and two additional ones each summer. It's a nonstop wheel of blond Indiana missionaries, cogging their way through Guerrero. The current group will fly home to Estados Unidos Wednesday afternoon, so the church's three passenger vans are scheduled to depart for Mexico City at seven o'clock Wednesday morning. This is where the conversation takes on amplified urgency. Luca sits up in his chair and fiddles with the handle of Mami's teacup.

Carlos says, "They can go in the shuttle, of course. It's perfect."

Meredith says nothing with her mouth, but conveys plenty with her eyes, and none of it is very accommodating.

And then Mami says, "We'd be safe getting through the roadblocks, if we were on the church shuttle."

"They'd never expect you to be with the missionaries," Carlos says.

Mami shakes her head. "They wouldn't even look."

And then Meredith uses her mouth. "Safe for who? Maybe safer for you, but I'm sorry, I can't put all those kids at risk." She shakes her head, and Luca has the notion that she looks nothing like the woman who was crying for Papi just a few minutes ago. She's different colors entirely, and her spongy features have hardened into new shapes.

Mami opens her mouth but manages to close it again without speaking. She fidgets with the loops of gold at her neck.

Carlos taps his pointer finger on the table between them. They all look at that finger. "Meredith, there's no other option for them. I understand your concern, but this is the only way to get them safely out of Guerrero. If we don't help them, they could die."

"*Could* is an understatement," Mami says.

But Meredith crosses her arms and shakes her head some more. Her hair is some color between brown and gold, and it's pushed back from her face with a black headband. Her nose is red, cheeks red, eyes hard blue. Mami lifts her teacup and tries a sip, but when she sets it back down, Luca can tell she didn't swallow any.

"I'm sorry, it's too risky," Meredith says. "It's not fair to do that to the kids, to their parents in Indiana. This is exactly the kind of thing those families fear, sending their kids down here to Mexico. Do you have any idea what it takes to placate those fears? We give them our word their kids will be safe. I personally guarantee their safety. I tell them this kind of thing will never happen."

Mami clears her throat and her face looks like a *bomba* about to go off, but she breathes through it. "This *kind of thing*?"

Meredith presses her eyes closed. "I'm sorry. I don't mean. I don't even know what to say."

"Sebastián is dead, Meredith," Carlos says. "My friend, your friend. He's gone. And fifteen more besides. This is not the kind of thing that happens, ever. Not even here. Do you know anyone else who's lost sixteen family members in one day?" Meredith glares at him, but he plows ahead. "We have to help them. If the suffering of our friends means nothing, if those kids can't be allowed to see us, to see Mexico as it really is, then what are they even doing here? Are they just drive-by Samaritans?"

"Carlos, don't," Meredith says, and Luca has the feeling this is a very old conversation between them.

"They just want to make pancakes and take selfies with skinny brown children?" Carlos asks.

Meredith slaps her hand against the table, and the tea ripples in the cups. But Mami intercepts the rising anger between them. She speaks like a void, like she's left the conversation entirely, and only her voice remains behind. She chants without any expression. "Sebastián, Yemi, Alex, Yénifer, Adrián, Paula, Arturo, Estéfani, Nico, Joaquín, Diana, Vicente, Rafael, Lucía, and Rafaelito. Mamá. They are gone. All gone."

A lump rises in Luca's throat and grows one size with each name that leaves Mami's mouth. He looks at Meredith to see how she'll respond, but her face is an unreadable smear of pink and blue. Instead it's Carlos who replies, placing his hands flat on the table. "We will help you," he whispers. "Of course we will."

Meredith stands to pace behind her chair, her arms crossed in front of her. "Lydia, I can't pretend to know what you're going through. It's unimaginable. And yes, of course we'll do everything in our power to help. But please try to understand, I also have to weigh my moral responsibility here. Sometimes there are no easy answers."

Mami tents her hands over her forehead. "I don't want to cause trouble for anyone. I just want to get Luca out of here. I have to." For the first time since all this started, Luca thinks she might unravel. He watches intensely, and her voice cracks. "Please. We're desperate."

Carlos looks up at his wife. "Honey, listen. I understand your resistance, I do. But sometimes there *are* easy answers. This is an easy answer: If we don't help them, if they get on a bus alone, if they get stopped at a roadblock and killed because we didn't have the courage to save them, can you live with that? Can we?"

Meredith sighs and leans over the back of her chair. "I don't know, I don't know."

"Just pray on it," he says. "Give it up to God."

She turns and clicks on the electric kettle, even though no one has yet managed to choke down the first cup of tea. With her back to the table she says, "Are you sure they're even looking for you now?" She faces the table again and leans against the counter. "Wasn't Sebastián the example they wanted? They got him, so maybe it's over now."

Luca looks from Meredith back to Mami, and she meets his gaze, and pauses, as if weighing how much to say in front of him. Perhaps she remembers that fear is good for him now. He should be afraid.

"No," Mami says quietly. "He won't stop until he finds us."

CHAPTER EIGHT

In bed, on the night she discovered that Javier and La Lechuza
were the same person, Lydia turned off the lamp but did not close her
eyes. She and Sebastián had always agreed that married people were entitled to a certain measure of privacy, that they needn't tell each other
everything. It was one of the reasons she'd fallen in love with him; he
didn't press her on personal matters, he was seldom jealous, and he had
no interest in annexing or directing her friendships with other men.

"You're a person, an adult," he said to her before they were engaged.
"And I am your lover. If we get married, you choose me. I hope you'll
continue to choose me every day." Lydia had laughed at his unfash-
ionable use of the word *lover,* but the sentiment thrilled her. Before
Sebastián, she'd always presumed that marriage would entail a sacrifice of
her liberty. That it had not, delighted her. They were both trustworthy,
and they fancied themselves quite modern. They kept nothing of import
from each other, but Lydia liked having a sacred cupboard within herself, to which only she was allowed access.

So there'd been nothing untoward in her failure to mention the
name Javier to her husband before, but, of course, that night, everything
changed. When Sebastián got up in the morning and kissed her forehead
on his way to the bathroom, she was still awake. She sat up in bed, her
stomach lurching with the movement.

"Sebastián," she said. She thought about not telling him, about asking questions instead. She knew that once the words were out of her mouth, her friendship with Javier would come to an end, and beneath everything else, there was a foundation of grief to that impending loss. She wanted her discovery to be untrue, a misunderstanding.

Her husband turned toward her in the gray light of the bedroom. "What's wrong?" He knew instantly, from the pitch of her voice. He crossed the space between them and sat beside her on the bed.

"He's my friend," she confessed.

Sebastián didn't go to work that morning. He called his editor and left a message that he was following a lead and wouldn't be in until later. He and Lydia sat together on the unmade bed and talked for hours, while outside the light shifted from gray to pink to broad, sunny yellow. When it was time to wake Luca and take him to school, they managed the routine in a distracted haze.

"I'll take him today," Sebastián insisted. "You wait here."

Lydia cried in the shower.

When Sebastián returned they continued their discussion at the kitchen table. Lydia's wet hair was knotted on top of her head and her face felt blotchy.

"Is there any chance you're mistaken?" she asked, her arms folded in front of her. She already knew the answer, but it made no sense. She was floundering.

Sebastian locked his eyes on her and answered in the most deliberate possible tone. "No."

She nodded. "The piece you're working on about Los Jardineros— does it specifically mention him?"

"Yes, it's all about him, his big debut. The whole *Hello, World, I'm a Major Kingpin* exposé."

Lydia tilted her head to one side, placed her hand against her forehead. "I don't know what to do," she whispered. "It seems impossible."

"There's nothing to *do*, Lydia."

"But I just can't understand it. I *know* him."

"I know, Lydia, I know. How charming he can be, how erudite. But he's also incredibly dangerous."

She pictured Javier's eyes, how exposed they looked whenever he removed his glasses. That word *dangerous* seemed so incompatible.

"I know it's difficult to get your head around it," Sebastián said. "I can see you're struggling, and I'm sorry." He paused before he shifted gears. "But he's a murderer, Lydia. Many times over. This guy is made of blood."

This guy. She shook her head again. Sebastián stood up and placed his hands on the back of his chair. He pushed it under the table. "He's not who you thought he was."

"But you said yourself, just last night, that he, that Los Jardineros, they aren't as violent as the other cartels."

He had said that, dammit. Lydia opened the kitchen window to the noise of traffic below.

"Lydia, I love you. I love your loyalty and your goodness. But we are talking degrees of murderers here. Less violent or not, he's still a major narco. And when you've killed that many people, killing becomes conventional. Does it matter that he's killed *fewer* children than other murderers have? It's not a moderation born of virtue. It's a *pinche* business decision. That guy would kill *anyone* if he thought it was the smart thing to do."

"Not anyone." Her voice was a weakening plea. "He has a daughter."

Sebastián dropped his head between his outstretched arms.

"Sebastián, listen," she said. "I know it all sounds absurd but I'm not naïve. I'm not an idiot, right?"

"You're the smartest woman I know."

"So I'm just, I'm trying to take it all in, to reconcile everything you're telling me, and to make it match up with the person I know Javier to be."

"I know, I know."

"It's difficult."

"I can't imagine."

"Because I do, Sebastián, I know him. And like you say, he *is* smart. In a different life he could've been someone good—"

"But it's not a different life, Lydia. He's not someone good."

"But maybe he still could be. That's what I'm telling you. Because people are complex and whatever you say he is, he's also this other person. This tortured, poetic soul, full of remorse. He's funny. He's kind. Maybe things could still be different."

"Wait." Sebastian surveyed his wife, who was now leaning against the kitchen windowsill. Outside a horn blared, and a breeze moved past a drying tendril of her hair. "Wait a second, Lydia. Are you in love with him?"

"What?"

"Are you?"

"Sebastián, don't be ridiculous. This is no time for histrionics."

He shook his head. "But do you have feelings for him?"

"No, not like that. I do love him—"

"You *love* him?"

"He's my friend! A real friend, someone who's become very important to me!" She leaned her hands on her knees and looked up at him. The coffeemaker gurgled and sighed. "His father died of cancer, too."

Her husband pulled the chair back out and sat down again. "Oh, Lydia."

Sebastián had never met Lydia's father, but his death was such a defining loss in Lydia's life, and indeed in Sebastián and Lydia's early courtship, that he felt a strong kinship to his deceased father-in-law, nonetheless. He knew all the stories. How, when Lydia was twelve years old (slightly too old for teddy bears), her lifelong favorite developed a gash in its nose. Lydia was heartbroken and embarrassed. The bear hemorrhaged his stuffing all over the house. Lydia's father went quietly to the pharmacy and returned with a bag that he placed on their kitchen table beneath a swing-arm lamp. He instructed her to bring the bear from her room. She transported the bear with great care, and when she returned to the kitchen, it had been transformed into an operating room. There was a sheet of plastic spread out across the table. Her father wore a mask and rubber gloves. His surgical tools were spread out beneath the lamp: needle, thread, a gleaming swatch of new leather. Lydia's father crafted an entirely new leather nose for her bear. Sebastián knew, too, that the only green vegetable his father-in-law ate was lima beans, that he had a three-inch scar on his leg from a childhood boating accident, that he sang loudly at concerts and sometimes in mortifying harmony with whatever act was onstage. Sebastián knew that the only time Lydia had ever seen her father cry was when Oscar De La Hoya won the gold medal round at the 1992 Olympics in Barcelona. Sebastián felt such a fondness for his father-in-law that he wondered if he knew the man better in death than he would have in life. They'd been dating only eight weeks, and were at the Estadio Azul in Mexico City attending a *fútbol* match when Lydia got that terrible phone call. Though the cancer had been slow, the end had been fast, unexpected. It was October 24, 2003, exactly one week before *el Día de los Muertos*. Reportedly his last words had been, "There's a party. I have to prepare."

Lydia and Sebastián left the stadium immediately, and he drove her first to her apartment and then, through the night, back to Acapulco. Her clothes were in heaps in the backseat. She couldn't think what she was supposed to bring, so she brought everything. She packed in a laundry basket. Sebastián held her hand in the dark and stopped on the side of the road near Cuernavaca when she thought she might throw up. He drove back and forth to Mexico City three more times that week: the next day, to retrieve his own clothes, two days later, to inform Lydia's professors and his own about their absences, and finally to bring some of her friends down for the funeral, and to join Lydia's mother in convincing Lydia to return to college.

In some way, Sebastián always credited that tragedy with being the thing that cemented their relationship. They had already known they were falling in love, and then the gravity of that heartbreak acted like a measuring stick for Lydia. It calculated the depth of Sebastián's character. The death aroused an unfamiliar stability in Sebastián. He found himself expanding in an effort to plug the holes in Lydia's life. So he understood, when she said this simple thing about Javier—that his father died of cancer, too—Sebastián understood the scope of what that shared experience really meant to his wife.

"How old was he," Sebastián asked, "when his father died?"

"Eleven," she said.

Sebastián grimaced. "Terrible."

Lydia went to the cupboard and took down two mugs, which she filled with coffee. She set one in front of her husband and sat down beside him once again. She drew her knees up and wrapped her arms around her legs.

"Sebastián, I think he's in love with me."

Sebastián filled his cheeks with air before letting it all loose into the room. "*Maldita sea,*" he said. "Of course he is."

In the short term, the only real change was that Sebastián began calling and coming to the shop more frequently than he had before. Four or five times a day he texted, and even if she was busy, she made sure to respond, to reassure him. All was well. Lydia was intensely nervous when Javier came the following week. She texted Sebastián beneath the counter. He's here. I'll call u after.

Javier carried a small parcel and his eyes were brighter than usual. He seemed eager for the other customers to withdraw, but Lydia took her time, reluctant to be alone with him. When the last couple wandered toward the exit without any purchases, she called after them, "Did you find everything okay?" They didn't answer her. The man only nodded, and the bell above the door startled as they left. Lydia's hands trembled as she spooned sugar into Javier's cup.

He smiled broadly at her from his stool. "I brought a gift." He prodded the paper-wrapped bundle across the counter to her.

It was plain brown paper, taped and devoid of ribbons, but the austerity of the wrapping didn't diminish the intimacy of an unwarranted gift on a Wednesday morning. Lydia opened it anyway. Inside was a wooden nesting doll, peanut shaped and about the length of Lydia's forearm, with a barely visible seam running around her middle. She was painted in festive colors: black hair, pink cheeks, yellow apron, red roses. Lydia pulled her apart at the seam and, inside, found her identical, smaller sister. She pulled her apart again, and again, and each time she discovered in miniature the shell of the doll before her.

"They're Russian nesting dolls," she said.

"Yes." Javier watched her face. "But really they're me. Keep going."

She pulled apart the last severed doll, no taller than her thumb, and inside she found the tiniest sister. This one was bright turquoise, and more beautiful, more exquisite and detailed than all the sisters before her. Lydia pinched her between finger and thumb. She held her up and studied the intricate silver filigree of her paintwork.

"And that's you." Javier tapped his chest with his fist. "*Muy dentro de mí.*"

Lydia blinked rapidly, but it was too late to conceal the tears that came to the corners of her eyes. Javier mistook them, and his smile broadened.

"You like them?"

She sniffed. "Very much, thank you." She hastened to pack the dolls back into one another while he watched.

He noticed the way she didn't take care to line up their tops with their bottoms. This was his first indication that something was truly askew. "What's the matter, *mi reina*?"

When the dolls were reassembled, Lydia rolled them back into their brown paper and placed them beneath the counter with her phone. There was no easy way to say it. She might as well be direct.

"I received some bad news last week," she said. He leaned forward, frowning. "About you."

He leaned back, frowning deeper. A very long silence grew between them, and then a customer came in, jangling the bell above the door. The woman bought three notebooks, three fancy pens, and a birthday card, and Lydia found herself unable to smile while she rang the woman up. She felt Javier's anxiety like a malediction in the room. It rattled into her chest. His shoulders were curled in, and he squeezed his flattened hands between his thighs. When the customer left, Lydia went to the door and locked it. She flipped the sign to CERRADO.

They studied each other across the counter. She stared into his eyes, and neither of them shifted their gaze.

At length, he spoke. "I presumed you knew." His voice was strained, raspy.

She shook her head without removing her eyes from his. "How would I know? Why would I know?"

His eyes swam even larger than usual behind the glasses. His mouth trembled as he spoke. "It feels as though almost everyone knows. I thought . . . somehow, I hoped it didn't matter to you. I thought it didn't matter because you knew me, you could see the person I really am."

"I can, I still can," she said. "But, Javier, that other part of you, the part I don't know . . . it's irreconcilable. That person is real, too, yes?"

Finally, he dropped his gaze from hers. He blinked his eyes repeatedly, removed his glasses, and cleaned them on the tail of his shirt.

"I love you," he said.

"I know."

"No, you don't."

Lydia pressed her lips together.

"I'm in love with you. I am *in* love with you."

She shook her head.

"Lydia, you're the only real friend I have. The only person in my life who wants nothing from me except the joy between us."

"That's not true."

"It is true! And when I'm not with you, I'm lonely for you. You have no idea the light you provide. You and Marta, you're all I really have. Nothing else matters. I would leave it all if I could."

"Then do!" She slapped her hand against the counter. "Leave it!"

He smiled sadly at her. "It doesn't work that way."

"It works whatever way you say it works! You're the *jefe*, right?"

"Yes, and if I leave, what then? What will become of Acapulco if I leave? How many people will die while they fight over who takes my place?" His elbows were up on the counter. He tugged at his hair in distress. "You know I never wanted this. It was an accident of fate that I ended up here."

Quite near the surface of her consciousness, Lydia knew that couldn't really be true. If it was a lottery ticket, it was one he had selected and purchased with his own money. She knew this, that he must have committed specific evils to have attained this rank. How many? Of what nature? Some combination of fear and sadness prevented her from asking. She didn't dare to contradict his justifications.

"But here we are, here I am." His eyes were pleading. "There's no getting out of it, Lydia, not for me. But it doesn't define who I am."

She could feel the dissonance throbbing through her brain like an erratic pulse. *Of course it defines who you are,* she did not say. She squeezed her eyes shut and felt him take her hand.

"Please understand," he said. "Try."

When Lydia had found Javier's picture in Sebastián's folder the previous week, she'd been riven with real anguish. Seldom had she experienced such profound and authentic friendship in her life. The prospect of losing that attachment grieved her. But now that Javier sat before her, clasping her hand in his, now that the thing had been spoken between them and confirmed to be true, all that was left for Lydia was autopsy. What love had been there was already slipping away. She could still sense it like a ghost in the room, vague and inanimate, but she could no longer feel it. Her affection had gone, leached out, like blood from a cadaver. When he squeezed her fingers, she caught the scent of formaldehyde. When he hooked his sad gaze into hers, she saw the glass of his lenses, spattered with blood.

CHAPTER NINE

In Carlos and Meredith's house in Chilpancingo, there are new ghosts to contend with. Trauma waits for stillness. Lydia feels like a cracked egg, and she doesn't know if she's the shell or the yolk or the white. She is scrambled. During the three days that follow, she and Luca are often alone in the house while the boys are at school, Carlos is at work, and Meredith prepares the Indiana missionaries for their return home. There is no temporary suspension of living as there usually is with death, because a public pause would arouse suspicion. Lydia and Luca have to stay hidden. The family has to carry on in their typical fashion. The sons have well-stocked bookshelves in their rooms, *gracias a Dios,* so while they're out living their regular lives, Luca reads two or three books a day. Lydia tries to read as well, but her mind can't hold the words. She doesn't have the reservoir of space to take anything else into her brain. So instead she tries to keep her body occupied. She cooks food that neither she nor Luca feels like eating. She cleans sinks and laundry and rugs that aren't dirty. She watches as Luca grows silent.

The afternoons feel a thousand hours long. Luca barely even changes positions on the couch as he reads. He moves when he finishes a book; he gets up to retrieve another from the shelf. Whenever he rises to use the bathroom, Lydia tries to coax him into eating. The rest of her time she spends at the old IBM desktop computer that sits on a small cart in one corner of the living room. She checks the headlines coming out of

Acapulco. There have been beautiful tributes to Sebastián by his colleagues, but Lydia can't read the reflective pieces. The word *héroe* makes her angry, as if he chose his death courageously, as if it means something. For God's sake, he died with a spatula in his hand. Instead she skims the news for emerging facts about the investigation, and it's as she expected: nothing. Because fear and corruption work in tandem to censor the people who might otherwise discover the clues that would point to justice. There will be no evidence, no due process, no vindication. So Lydia checks for other stories, new violence, any hint of what's happening among Los Jardineros. A tourist was accidentally killed in a shootout near the beach huts at Playa Hornos yesterday afternoon. A burned-out car with two bodies inside, one large, one small, was found outside Colonia Loma Larga this morning.

The mouse pointer trembles on the screen, but she manages to click out of the news and shift gears. Carlos will get them as far as Mexico City, but what then? She must try to make plans. She researches the buses, and yes, there are reports of increased roadblocks across the area, an uptick in disappearances. Travel within cities is relatively safe, but between cities it is strongly discouraged. Authorities advise deferring nonessential trips on regional highways in Guerrero, Colima, and Michoacán. Lydia feels a new wave of despair threatening to descend, but she doesn't have time for it. The roads are not an option. Even if her driver's license were current, she wouldn't risk driving with Luca right now, and the buses are no better. The roadblocks are too dangerous. So what's left? She checks airline tickets, although she doesn't love the idea of her name being on a flight manifest. Everything is digital now, and what good will it do to run a thousand miles away if her name raises a red flag in some online database? Tijuana is about as far as you can get without a passport, and that flight is three hours and forty minutes. Plenty of time for Javier to send a *sicario* to greet them when they deplane. Lydia imagines carnage at the baggage claim. She can see the headlines. There are no long-distance passenger trains in Mexico, so as a last resort, Lydia studies the freight trains the Central American migrants ride across the length of the country. All the way from Chiapas to Chihuahua, they cling to the tops of the cars. The train has earned the name La Bestia because that journey is a mission of terror in every way imaginable. Violence and kidnapping are endemic along the tracks, and apart from the criminal dangers, migrants are also maimed or killed every day when they fall from the tops of the trains. Only the poorest and most destitute of people attempt to travel this way. Lydia shudders at the YouTube stories, the photographs, the grim warnings delivered by recent amputees. She starts over, researches everything again from the beginning. Buses, planes, trains. There has to be something she hasn't considered. There has to be a way out. She clicks and scrolls and hours pass like sludge, while Luca turns page after page.

At the dinner table with Carlos and Meredith's three boys, Luca wears his father's hat, and Lydia doesn't demand that he take it off, even when Meredith tells her youngest "no hats at the table." The older boy wipes his milk mustache and grins at Luca, still wearing the Yankees cap.

"You like baseball?" the boy asks.

Luca only shrugs.

He was always a quiet child. As a toddler, Luca never babbled. In fact, he didn't speak at all until he was four years old, and by then Lydia had been panicking for two years. She began the practice of reading to him well before she suspected any problem, only because she was a book lover who enjoyed reading aloud to her baby. She liked the idea that, even before he understood them, he might begin with the most beautiful words, that he'd build language from a foundation of literature and poetry. So she started with Márquez and Tolstoy and the Brontës, and eventually, as a result of her growing alarm, she read to him not in the typical way that parents read fairy tales and bedtime stories to their children, but in a frenetic and urgent manner intended to save him. When her fears bloomed and the habit became more concerted, she called upon Paz and Fuentes, Twain and Castellanos. She was fluent in English, too (it had been her minor in college), so sometimes she read Yeats, rendering the lush green of Ireland in her Mexican accent.

When Luca was an infant, she brought him to work tucked into a sling across her chest, and they read together between orders and customers and cleaning and stocking the shelves. Sometimes it was a long while between customers, so the two of them could submerge vividly into their stories. As he grew, he'd sit in a bouncy rocker or on a little play mat she set up for him in the corner behind the register. Eventually he was free to toddle around the shop, but when it was time to read, he always sat without prompting, cross-legged and silent, head angled to one side, as if creating a funnel of his ear for the words she'd give to him. She tried books with and without pictures. Colorful books, tactile books, poetry, photography, art. Children's books, cookbooks, the Bible. Her son ran his hands carefully along the glossy or filmy pages, but still he did not speak. Sometimes she read until her voice gave out, and other days she quickly grew depressed by the solitary sound of herself in the shop, but whenever she wanted to quit, Luca would push the day's book toward her insistently. He'd open it and press it back into her lap.

The week before his fourth birthday, as they sat eating pozole at the kitchen table, Lydia lamented their boy's silence for the hundredth time. Sebastián balanced his spoon on the edge of his bowl and studied Luca's face. Luca studied him back.

"Maybe you don't speak Spanish," Sebastián said in Spanish.

Luca, mimicking his father, balanced his spoon on his bowl, too.

"That's it, isn't it," Sebastián said. "*¿Cuál idioma hablas, mijo?* English? Are you a *gabacho*? Wait!" Sebastián snapped his fingers. "You're Haitian. No—Arabic! Tagalog?"

Lydia blinked slowly at her husband, but Luca smiled and tried to snap his fingers, too. Sebastián showed him how. *Click click click.* Lydia was alone in her desperation. She reasoned that Sebastián must be concerned, also, but his dogged optimism prevented him from revealing it. The doctors could find nothing wrong. Lydia felt like screaming.

Instead, she patiently continued her efforts. Allende, Borges, Cervantes. She read so that the words she treasured might penetrate her son's solitude. And then one day, as she turned the last, unsatisfying page of a short novel by some pretentious young writer, Luca sat up and shook his head. He brushed his hands across his knees. Lydia closed the book and set it on the table beside the rocker where they were seated together. Luca picked it up and opened it to the first page.

"Let's read that one again, please, Mami, except this time let's make it a more agreeable ending."

Perfectly. As if simply continuing a conversation they'd been having his whole life. Lydia was so startled she nearly hurled him across the room. She pushed him off her lap onto his feet. She turned him around and stared at him. "What?" Luca pressed his lips together. "What did you say?" She gripped his arms at his sides, too roughly perhaps, in her fear that she was coming unhinged. "You spoke! Luca! You spoke?"

After a brief and petrifying pause, he nodded.

"What did you say?" she whispered.

"I would like to read it again."

She clapped both hands onto his cheeks, laughing and crying at once. "*Ay*, oh my God! Luca!"

"With a better ending."

She crushed him into her chest and squeezed him there, and then she jumped up and took his hands and spun him in a circle.

"Say it again. Say something else."

"What shall I say?"

"Exactly that," she'd said. "My boy. He speaks!"

Lydia closed the shop early that day and took Luca home to perform for his father. She remembers it so clearly, but she doesn't trust that memory now, because the further she gets away from it, the more fanciful it seems. How could he have been so silent for all those years? And then, how could he have started talking like that, like a news anchor, like a college professor, in those beautiful, complex sentences all at once? It's impossible. A miracle of syntax.

But now, in Carlos's turquoise house, after more than four years of talking beautifully in two languages, Luca's voice retreats, and the erstwhile silence returns. Lydia sees it happening, and there's nothing either of them can do to prevent it. It settles over him lightly at first, but soon, like a shellac, it hardens. By Wednesday morning, his muteness is pronounced. He responds to direct questions only with his face, his body. He perfects, once again, the art of the blank stare, and Lydia feels inside her some last, clinging boulder of sanity slipping.

During these days of calcifying quiet, the dreadful wheel of Lydia's mind never slows, no matter how she tries to arrest it. She keeps herself steady in front of Luca, but there are times when she has to excuse herself quickly. She slips into the bathroom and opens the tap so the running water will disguise the muffled, wrenching noises of her grief. Her body is a cramp of misery, and the physical sensation is so elemental that it makes her feel like a wild animal, a mammal bereft of her pack. At night, as she lies next to Luca in Sebastián's godson's narrow bed, she directs her thoughts toward blankness. She does this exercise with authority, and her mind obeys. She repeats this over and over: *don't think, don't think, don't think*. And because of this self-control, she moves mercifully toward sleep. The flashbacks dump adrenaline into her bloodstream a hundred times a day, so her body is helpfully exhausted. Her eyelids drop. But then there's the moment after letting go, the momentary drift after casting off from the shore and before being caught by the current, and in that lapse, she plummets. Her limbs jerk, her heart clobbers, and her brain provides the memory once again of clacking gunfire, the odor of burning meat, the sixteen beautiful faces, scrubbed blank of their animation and turned vacant toward the sky. She sits up in bed, steadies her pitching breath, and tries not to wake Luca beside her. Every night, this hurdle between wake and sleep. This one patch she can't cross. What kind of person does not bury her family? How could she leave them there in the backyard with their eyes and their mouths open, the blood cooling in their veins? Lydia has seen outspoken widows before, widows made brave by their anguish. She's watched them talk into the cameras, refusing to be silenced, placing blame where it belongs, scorning the violence of cowardly men. Naming names. Those women get gunned down at funerals. *Don't think, don't think, don't think.*

On Wednesday, Carlos takes the day off work to drive the third church van to Mexico City. Lydia leaves Abuela's red overnight bag on the end of the bed where they've spent the last three nights. Inside are her heels and Luca's dress shoes. She's crammed everything else into the two backpacks, and that's all they will carry now. They will fly north from Mexico City, she's decided. It's their only option. They will go with only these two backpacks so they'll be nimble, so they won't have to stand gazing at the baggage carousel waiting for what they don't need anyway. Lydia doesn't know what, if anything, Carlos and Meredith have told the Indiana missionaries about their two extra passengers, but no one asks her any questions when they get in. The teenagers flash their gooey smiles and try to talk to her about their Savior, but Lydia pretends not to speak English. She keeps one arm around Luca in the backseat and tries to act the way a normal person would act. She has difficulty remembering. The missionaries have duffel bags and fancy backpacks, and every single one of the girls wears her hair (curly or straight, coarse or silky) in two French braids. It's a missionary code, Lydia realizes, and she reaches up to touch her ponytail. The girl on the bench seat beside her notices.

"You want me to do yours?" She smiles at Lydia. "We all do each other's."

Lydia hesitates, because the most impeccable French braids in the world wouldn't cause anyone to mistake her for a teenage missionary from Indiana. But even ludicrous armor is better than nothing. The girl mistakes Lydia's reticence for a language barrier, so she points to her own braids, the braids of the two girls in the row ahead, and then to Lydia's hair. "You like? French braids?"

Lydia nods, pulling the ponytail holder out of her thick, black hair, and turning her back to the girl, who begins crawling her fingers along Lydia's scalp. It's hot in the van. When the girl is finished, she asks if anybody has a mirror. There are five teenage girls in this van, and not one of them is vain enough to carry a pocket mirror. Finally, one of the girls opens the camera app on her iPhone, switches it to selfie mode, and hands it to Lydia. "They're so pretty on you!" she says loudly, pointing to the braids. *"¡Me gusta!"*

Lydia looks at herself on the screen, twisting her head slightly to inspect the braids. She looks younger, she thinks, a little. She smiles and hands the phone back. Relief washes over Lydia when the singing starts, because the clamor of it fills the van and leaves no room for thinking. All the missionaries sing, and Carlos, too, loudly and cheerfully.

"You should nap," she says quietly into Luca's ear as they approach Axaxacualco. He looks at her without blinking. "I see traffic ahead. You should nap on the floor, here. Cozy." Lydia reaches beneath the bench seat and makes a space between two of the larger duffel bags. Luca slips into it and makes himself small. A stuffed backpack makes a pillow. He closes his eyes as the traffic begins to snag, and with it, the breath in Lydia's chest. The girls sing "Jesus, Take the Wheel" louder. Carlos catches Lydia's eye in the rearview mirror. He blinks once, because it's all the reassurance he can offer her. The line of cars in front of them has come to a stop. Theirs is the second of the three vans. Meredith is driving the one in front.

In the road ahead, two young men, two teenage boys, really, tote AR15s. Perhaps it's precisely because that make of gun isn't quite as pro-lific or as sexy as the ubiquitous AK-47 here that Lydia finds it all the more terrifying. Ridiculous, she knows. One gun will make you as dead as another. But there's something so utilitarian about the sleek, black AR15, like it can't be bothered to put on a show.

Sometimes the muzzle of one of those guns makes it inside the rolled-down window of a waiting car, but generally they remain outside, point-ing skyward. The boys hold their weapons with both hands. Mostly the drivers don't flinch. Mostly the drivers defer to the boys' exaggerated egos, go along with their pretend swagger, because although no one expects the boys to open fire, they all know that the only road to genuine bra-vado runs through faking it first. It's only a matter of time, and no one wants to find out if today is the day these boys finally mean it. One by one, the drivers reach carefully into their wallets or purses or glove com-partments to extract the *mordidas*. They hand over the money without complaint, and with genuine *bendiciones,* because these boys could be anyone, they could be the drivers' brothers or children or grandchildren. Certainly, they are someone's.

Carlos rolls and brakes, rolls and brakes. Luca keeps his eyes closed, and the missionaries sing. Lydia prays for the unlikely possibility that the boys on the road ahead are uncorrupted *autodefensas.*

The singing missionaries are conducting their own brand of bravado, too, because even though the roadblock is exciting to them, even though their pastor, who's in the van behind, explained that roadblocks are quite common here and nothing to be alarmed by, that they're almost like passing through a toll gate, the girls know that toll booth operators in Indiana don't carry automatic weapons. Secretly, in the sinful hidden chambers of their hearts, most of these girls had looked forward to ex-periencing a roadblock—the exotic thrill of it, the wash of adrenaline, the stories they'd get to tell when they returned home to Indiana! But on the way down from Mexico City, they'd been waved right through without stopping. A guilty disappointment. Still, now that the moment is actually upon them, now that they can see the boys in the road ahead, close in age to themselves and brandishing unthinkable weapons, now that their inexperienced missionary nervous systems are flooding their bloodstreams with chaotic hormones, every one of those braided girls feels sick with fright. Some of them wish for the courage to witness to the boys, to save them by reminding them of Jesus. But mostly they just want to go home. One of the girls in the front seat, the one with the iPhone, tries to start another round of singing, but no one joins her and the effort falters after a couple of bars. Carlos rolls down his window.

The boys stand on either side of the van ahead. Lydia can make out Meredith's silhouette in the driver's seat, talking to the boy at her window. He must be the one in charge. Meredith gestures with a finger to the other two vans behind, and both boys look back. Lydia freezes in her seat. There's no way they can notice her here, in the backseat of the van's darkened interior. The boy *jefe* on the driver's side of the van wears a plain blue ball cap with no insignia. He directs his colleague to investigate the other vans. The boy passes between the bumpers of the idling vehicles and approaches Carlos's window, the business end of his AR15 tracing the dotted white lines of the road. Lydia glances down at Luca on the floor and sees that his eyes are wide open, as round as soupspoons. She shifts mildly in her seat so her legs mostly cover him.

"Where are you heading today?" the boy asks Carlos, to make sure he tells the same story as Meredith.

"Only to the airport in Mexico City. Our visitors are flying home today."

"*¿De dónde eres?*" he says to the girl directly behind Carlos.

"They don't speak much Spanish," Carlos says in Spanish. "They're from Indiana."

The boy tips his head slightly inside the rolled-down window and surveys the silent, smiling girls. If he's susceptible to their pheromones, he's getting bombarded. His eyes land on Lydia, and he scrunches up his mouth.

"Who's the woman?"

"One of our counselors."

"*¿Estadounidense también?*" The boy has a handsome, skeptical face.

"No, she's from here. She's one of ours."

"Why's she sitting in back?"

Lydia knows not to glance at Luca, but he's her only anchor left in the world, and her eyes want to go to him. She glues her gaze to the back of Carlos's seat.

"One of the girls was carsick," Carlos says. "She went back there to help."

Lydia lifts her hand and places it maternally, mechanically, between the shoulder blades of the girl beside her, the girl who braided her hair. Lydia rubs a circle on the girl's upper back, and the girl wonders how Lydia can tell she's scared. The girl is grateful for the small demonstration of comfort, and gives Lydia a watery smile. The boy at the window wraps the fingers of one hand over the edge of the door and speaks directly to Lydia.

"¿Cómo se llama, Doña?"

"Mariana," Lydia lies.

"She still sick, Mariana?" He points to the girl beside her with his chin.

"She's feeling a little better, I think," Lydia says, still rubbing the girl's back. "Not great."

The unwitting girl supports the story by going quite pale in the face. She leans slightly forward and Lydia thinks perhaps she really is about to vomit.

The boy lingers, his AR15 hovering just outside the window, his eyes scrutinizing the lines of her face. He leans his head slightly inside the window again. "Only girls in this van? No boys?" he asks.

On the floor beneath Mami's feet, Luca's eyes gape and his mouth stays clamped shut. He doesn't even breathe. He's become an expert at hiding, perfectly still inside his body.

"All the boys are in the van behind," Carlos says.

The boy taps on the open window with the flat of his hand. Carlos hands him a thin fold of bills.

"Ten cuidado, y que Dios te bendiga," Carlos says.

The boy nods, folds the bills into the back pocket of his jeans, and trots past Lydia's window to the van behind. As he passes her window, Lydia sees the small, uncomplicated tattoo of a machete high on his neck behind his left ear. Confirmation: these are Javier's boys, Los Jardineros. There's the collective sound of breath being released into the van, but not

Lydia's. She allows her eyes to travel briefly to Luca's little upturned face. The eyes are closed now, and she presses hers closed as well, for a moment of suspended relief. She can feel her pulse in her eyelids.

"Everybody good?" Carlos asks in English, turning in his seat to look each of the girls in the face.

They giggle their replies. Lydia nods, dropping her hand back to her lap. It feels like a very long time before the boy completes his interview at the window of the third van. He waves when he passes again to rejoin his compatriot at the front of the queue. Both boys let go of their guns long enough to sling them onto their backs so they can lug the large log of their makeshift gate off the roadway. They open just enough space to allow the cavalcade of missionary vans to pass through.

A half hour later as they cross over *el puente* Mezcala Solidaridad above *el río* Balsas, the girls gasp and point their cameras out the windows and into the lush green canyons below. When Luca climbs out from his nest to snuggle in beneath her arm, Lydia finally begins to breathe.

CHAPTER TEN

They've survived long enough to see the sun-clogged streets and throttling colors of Mexico City. That is no small thing. They are now four days and 236 miles removed from their doom. But it's more than that, Lydia knows. Because the anonymity of the capital represents the fragile passage to their future. From here, she can feel a measure of hope; it may be possible to disappear. Lydia has determined that the least harrowing of their options is to fly. Something like superstition caused her to delay selecting a destination, but she did research all the northern border cities and compile a short list of the leading possibilities. From west to east: Tijuana, Mexicali, Nogales, Ciudad Juárez, Nuevo Laredo. Any one of those airports will do, like a back-porch screen door, hidden and intimate. From any one of those cities you can smell the fresh-baked pies on the windowsills of *el norte*.

When Carlos rolls open the back door of that church passenger van and the braided girls and their crammed backpacks spill out onto the bright tarmac, Luca and Lydia follow.

Beside the open back door of the van, Carlos grips Lydia's hands and whispers intensely into her ear. "He's still with you," he says. "I can feel it. He'll watch over you and your son. You will be okay."

Lydia envies his certainty. They embrace without tears while the braided girls and their adolescent male counterparts from the other vans avert their scandalized faces. Meredith stands beside Luca, awkwardly trying to adjust his backpack for him while he subtly dodges her efforts. When Carlos lets go of Lydia, Meredith steps forward to hug her, too, but whatever warmth once existed between the two women, mostly because of their husbands' bond, has been extinguished. Still, Lydia's gratitude is authentic. She looks Meredith in the eye.

"I know how problematic this was for you," she says. "To undertake this risk for us." Meredith shakes her head, but as a gesture of repudiation it's feeble. "I'm very grateful, Meredith. You probably saved our lives. Thank you."

"God be with you," Meredith says, and then the swell of noisy jabber from the gathered teenagers comparing roadblock stories consumes all other conversation, and both women are relieved to part ways. The automatic terminal doors yawn open with a rumble as the first few teenage missionaries amble through. While Carlos and Meredith say their goodbyes to the Indiana pastor-and-wife team, Lydia and Luca duck beneath the shade of an awning and make their way toward the tram that will deliver them to the terminal for domestic flights.

Luca has never been on a tram before. He tries not to feel interested in it, but it's amazing the way the slick, glassy thing arrives soundlessly and disgorges its people onto the platform. Luca grips his mother's hand, and steps out of the way while the people and their luggage jostle past them. He watches his feet as he and his mother navigate the tiny gap between fixed and moveable. Mami pulls him onto the tram without resistance, and they're in the front car, so how can Luca help but press his hands and forehead against the angled glass? Any kid would feel a little thrill in his tummy, watching the increasing speed of the track slip beneath his feet and vanish. It's like a roller coaster, gliding silently above the crisscrossing cars and buses, the taxis and lampposts, the aprons of runway dotted with waiting aircrafts, and trucks with crazy staircases on their backs. A plane swoops down in front of them, huge in the window, and Luca springs back from the glass with a gasp.

"Mami!" he says.

It's the first word he's spoken in three days, and he immediately regrets the sound of it, the plain, disloyal happiness of it. Mami smiles at him, but it's not her regular smile, and there's no mistaking the endeavor of it for actual joy. So why isn't he broken like that? What's wrong with him, that he can behave so normally? Mami runs her fingers across the top of his head and he pushes his face back toward the glass. He watches the tram swallow the track beneath them.

Inside the terminal, the mechanical hum of air-conditioning is like a sheen behind all the other noises: a little girl holds her mother's hand and rolls her dog-shaped suitcase behind her by the leash, a man shouts into his cell phone in a throaty, unfamiliar language, a woman clacks hurriedly along on her angry heels. There is the smell of lemon and freon. Luca follows Mami to a little kiosk with a screen on it, and he watches while she clicks around on there for a few minutes. Then he thinks he shouldn't be watching her, but he should be watching other people, to make sure nobody's noticing them, so he turns and looks, and no one is watching them except that little girl with the dog-shaped suitcase. She's standing in line with her mother, or rather sitting on the back of her suitcase. When her mother moves forward, she pushes with her feet to keep up. Luca would like a suitcase like that.

"We can't book from here." Mami interrupts his thoughts. "It won't let you buy a same-day ticket. We have to get in line." Mami picks up her backpack, which she'd set down on top of her feet, and Luca follows her over to get in line. He's happy to have a closer look at the dog suitcase, which, he can now see, also has a furry tail and ears.

The girl sees him admiring it and she smiles. She's about the same age as Luca, maybe a year younger. "You can pet him if you want to," she says. "He doesn't bite."

Luca takes a step back and hides his face behind Mami. But then a moment later, he reaches out and brushes the tip of the dog's tail with his fingers. The girl laughs and then her mother says, "Let's go, Naya," and the girl waves, pushing with her sneakers, all the way up to the ticket counter.

Luca and Mami are next, and soon they're standing in front of a lady wearing a blue suit and a red silk scarf. Her round face is repeated in miniature on the plastic name tag hanging from her neck. She smiles at Luca.

"Hello, little jet-setter!" she says to him. "First time flying?"

He looks up at Mami, and she nods, so he nods, too. Flying! He can't believe they're going to fly. He's not sure he wants to fly, but it's possible he *really* wants to fly. It's hard to tell.

"We're taking a little spontaneous vacation," Mami says to the ticket agent.

The woman's hands are poised over her keyboard. "Okay. Where to?"

"I was thinking of Nuevo Laredo?"

The woman clacks around on her keyboard at a comical speed. She can't really be typing that fast, Luca thinks. She's pretending. She frowns.

"No flights until Friday. Are you hoping to leave today?"

"Yes." Mami leans her elbows up on the ticket counter. "What about Ciudad Juárez?"

Clack clack clack. "Yes, that would work, there's a three o'clock flight, stopping over in Guadalajara. Arrives in Juárez at 7:04 p.m."

Mami bites her lip. "Nothing direct?"

Clack clack. "There's a nonstop at 11:10 tomorrow morning."

Mami shakes her head. "Okay, let's try Tijuana."

This time the woman covers up the sound of her typing with chatter. She doesn't even look at the screen or at her hands. They move in front of her as if they're two animals, independent of her body. She turns her round face toward Mami.

"Fun town. Ever been there?"

Mami shakes her head.

"I used to fly. I was a flight attendant before I had the babies. Did the Tijuana route, so once in a while we got to stay overnight." She winks at Luca. "Hope you like to party!"

Luca digs his fingernails into the palms of his hands to stop himself from thinking about parties, and the woman returns her round face and her round eyes to the screen in front of her.

"There's a direct flight to Tijuana at 3:27 p.m. Gets in at 5:13 p.m. They're two hours behind us."

"Perfect," Mami says. "Two seats?"

"Sure. And when do you want to return?"

Mami looks down at her gold sneakers against the terrazzo floor. Luca doesn't understand her hesitation, that she's attempting to perform an algorithm of calamity in her mind. Lydia knows they have exactly 226,243 pesos left because she counted it on the floor in Carlos's bathroom in Chilpancingo. They've already spent more than 8,000 pesos on the hotel and supplies and bus tickets. She also has her mother's purse, with a bank card she's afraid to use. Abuela had a savings account, and however much there is, they're going to need it. They'll have to pay a coyote when they get to the border, and if they're lucky, there will be a small sum left over to sustain them until she figures out what's next. They can scarcely afford to throw money away on a return airplane ticket they're not going to use. But neither can they afford to tell this friendly woman, this stranger, this potential *halcón,* that they're traveling only one way. Luca squeezes Mami's hand. "Returning next week, same day," she says.

"Very good," the woman says brightly, but Luca worries that her smile has turned a little stale. "We can get you on a return flight, let's see, how about 12:55 p.m. Gets in here at 6:28 p.m., nonstop."

Mami nods. "Good, yes, good. What's the price?"

The woman adjusts her red scarf as she scrolls down. Her fingernails are square and they're painted the color of concrete. They click when she taps on the screen. "Three thousand six hundred ten pesos each."

Mami nods again, and swings her backpack around to balance it on her knee. She takes out her wallet from the side pocket while the woman continues clacking on the keyboard.

"I can pay in cash?"

"Yes, of course," the woman says. "I just need photo ID."

Mami has separated their money into various places, keeping around 10,000 pesos in the wallet. Luca watches while she counts out the bills for the tickets, seven pink, two orange, one blue. She stacks the notes on the counter, and the woman picks them up to begin counting. Mami digs into the sleeve of the wallet then and retrieves her voter ID card, which makes a little snap when she places it on the counter. The ticket agent sets the money across her keyboard and picks up Mami's ID. She holds it in one hand and types with the other.

"Thank you." She hands the card back to Mami and looks at Luca.

"And what about you?" She smiles. "Did you bring your voter registration card?"

Luca wags his head. He obviously can't vote.

She returns her attention to Mami. "So I just need a birth certificate or some documentation to verify legal custody."

"Of my son?" Mami asks.

"Yes."

Mami shakes her head, and the skin around her eyes flushes pink. Luca thinks she might cry. "I don't have," she says. "I don't have that."

"Oh." The woman clasps her hands together and leans back from her keyboard. "I'm afraid he can't fly without it."

"Surely you can make an exception? He's obviously my son."

Luca nods.

"I'm sorry," the ticket agent says. "It's not our policy—it's the law. Every airline is the same." She's neatening the colorful money back into its stack. She's handing the stack back to Mami, but Mami won't take it, so she sets it on the counter between them.

"Please," Mami says, dropping her voice low and leaning in. "Please, we are desperate. We have to get out of the city. This is the only way, please."

"Señora, I'm sorry. I wish I could help you. You'll have to visit the Oficina Central del Registro Civil and request a copy of the birth certificate or you won't be able to fly. There's nothing I can do. Even if I could give you a ticket, you wouldn't make it past security."

Mami snatches the money and jams it into the back pocket of her jeans along with her ID. Her face is still changing colors, and now it looks whitened, washed-out.

"I'm sorry," the woman says again, but Mami has already turned to go. Luca follows and he doesn't ask where they're going, and soon they're on the metro. When they emerge at Isabel la Católica station, Luca's conflicted feelings only intensify, because being in Mexico City is a bona fide adventure. Everything is different here from Acapulco, and Luca struggles to take in all the color: the whipping flags, the fruit vendors, the baroque colonial buildings sitting shoulder to shoulder with their blocky modern neighbors. Music spills from wrought iron balconies, vendors hawk rows of luminous *refrescos,* and everywhere there is art, art, art. Murals, paintings, sculptures, graffiti. On one street corner, a colorful statue of tall Jesus—that's how Luca thinks of it because it's small for a statue but very tall for an adult human—stands with one fold of his bright green robe slung jauntily over his arm. Beneath this genuine onslaught of sensory stimulation, Luca manages to temporarily bury his guilt. His mouth hangs slightly open as he walks beside Mami, gulping in the scenery.

At a stall, Mami buys tamales and a bag of cut cucumbers. It's almost two o'clock, and Luca's hungry, so they sit beneath an umbrella to eat. He considers how strange it is that certain things haven't changed. The salted cucumbers taste just as they did before everyone died. His knuckles haven't changed. His fingernails. The width of Mami's shoulders. He chews without speaking. When their lunch is finished, Mami takes him to a square, concrete building with a statue of naked dancers in front, where the man behind the counter tells them that in order to get a copy of Luca's birth certificate, they have to go to the registration office in the state where he was born.

"Was he born in Mexico City?"

"No."

"In the state of Mexico?"

"No, Guerrero."

"Can't help you," he says. There's a sandwich sitting on his side of the counter, and he seems eager to get back to it.

On the sidewalk outside, Luca and Mami take a little break from moving so she can think. They squat down together in the shade of that square building. They lean against the wall, and after a few moments, Mami stands up. "Okay," she says, and her face has returned to its normal hue, and her hands are firm at her sides. She holds them in fists. "Okay." She says it again.

Next they walk a few blocks to a huge brick building with once-white stonework that's been discolored by time and weather and pollution. It has a gargantuan, arched wooden door, studded with massive golden buttons. Luca stares up and feels almost frightened by the scale of it, ten times taller than he is. But Mami is holding his hand, and together they pass beneath the bright purple flowers of the jacaranda trees. They walk through a smaller door cut into the gigantic door and enter the cool hush of the interior.

It's the Biblioteca Miguel Lerdo de Tejada, and even though this library specializes in economics, it's so absurdly beautiful that it was Lydia's favorite place to study when she was a literature and English student in college. It's also the place where she and Sebastián first met, mistaking each other for economics majors. As their romance evolved, they developed a mutual joke that they'd both been in the market for a more economically reliable mate than the one they accidentally ended up with.

With the exception of the new computers on the tables along the back wall, the library's *sala principal* looks exactly as Lydia remembers it. The ceilings are cathedral high, the cavernous space is saturated with natural light from above, and the walls are completely wrapped by the color-drenched murals of Vlady. Sebastián had once warned Lydia that she'd fail her exams if she persisted in doing her studying here; she squandered most of her time staring at those walls. She's long dreamed of bringing Luca to see this astonishing place, but she never imagined it would happen like this. She always thought she'd tell him the stories, but now that they're here, with the brutal weight of their departure from real life, she finds herself unable to call forth the memories onto her lips: Sebastián sneaking her contraband snacks while she studied for her finals. Sebastián once making her laugh so hard the librarian asked them to leave. Sebastián slumped in that study carrel right over there, struggling through *El laberinto de la soledad* only because he knew it was her father's favorite, and he wanted to know some of the same things her father knew, to get to know him.

How monumental Lydia's grief had been when her father died! It terrifies her now, to think of it, how deeply formative that single loss was in her earlier life. Now there are sixteen more. When she thinks of this, she feels as tatty as a scrap of lace, defined not so much by what she's made of, but more by the shapes of what's missing. She can't even imagine how this loss will shape the person Luca becomes. They need to do a funeral ceremony as soon as they're safe. Luca will need a ritual, a method of fashioning his grief into a thing he can exert some small control over. The sweep of it bows over her, but she returns to her mantra, *don't think, don't think, don't think.* She watches her son assess the magnitude of this place, the way his head tips back and his eyes swoop over every surface, the way he tries to chase the accidental smile from his face.

"It's okay, *mijo,* go look," she says. But Luca clings only more tightly to her hand. "Okay, then let's sit." She steers him to an empty computer table and they sit.

When the idea first occurred to her as she squatted in the shade of the Oficina Central del Registro Civil, it occurred as camouflage: they could disguise themselves as migrants. But now that she's sitting in this quiet library with her son and their stuffed backpacks, like a thunderclap, Lydia understands that it's not a disguise at all. She and Luca are actual migrants. That is what they are. And that simple fact, among all the other severe new realities of her life, knocks the breath clean out of her lungs. All her life she's pitied those poor people. She's donated money. She's wondered with the sort of detached fascination of the comfortable elite how dire the conditions of their lives must be wherever they come from, that this is the better option. That these people would leave their homes, their cultures, their families, even their languages, and venture into tremendous peril, risking their very lives, all for the chance to get to the dream of some faraway country that doesn't even want them.

Lydia sits back in her chair and looks at her boy, who's staring at a reclining fuchsia figure hovering on the wall above his head. *Migrante.* She can't make the word fit him. But that's what they are now. This is how it happens. They're not the first to go—Acapulco is emptying of its people. How many of her neighbors have fled in the last year? How many have disappeared? After all those years of watching it happen elsewhere, of indulging their remote pity, of shaking their heads as the stream of migrants flowed past them at a distance, from south to north. Acapulco has joined the procession, she realizes. No one can stay in a brutal, bloodstained place.

Lydia pulls her eyes away from Luca and focuses on the screen in front of her. Her search now is borne not only of panic, but of true desperation. There are no other options left for them. She opens a browser and finds the route that brings La Bestia closest to Mexico City. She lifts the headphones from their hook beside the computer and plugs them in. She checks YouTube first, and it's all horrible. So much more horrible than she even imagined. But it's better to know, to be prepared. She makes herself watch, and she pays no mind to the quickening of her breath or the racing of her pulse while she absorbs the stories.

The possible manners of death available on La Bestia are all grue-some: You can be crushed between two moving cars when the train rounds a bend. You can fall asleep, roll off the edge, get sucked beneath the wheels, have your legs sliced off. (When that happens, if the mi-grant isn't killed instantly, he usually bleeds to death in a remote corner of some farmer's field before anyone finds him.) And finally, there's the ubiquity of ordinary human violence: You can die by beating or stab-bing or shooting. Robbery is a foregone conclusion. Mass abductions for ransom are commonplace. Often, kidnappers torture their victims to help persuade their families to pay. On the trains, a uniform seldom represents what it purports to represent. Half the people pretending to be migrants or coyotes or train engineers or police or *la migra* are working for the cartel. Everybody's on the take. Here's a Guatemalan man—twenty-two years old—who lost both legs three days before his interview. He's missing a front tooth as well. "Somebody told me, before we got on the train," he says, "if you fall, if you see your arm or your leg getting sucked under there, you have a split second to decide whether or not to put your head in there too." The young man blinks into the cam-era. "I made the wrong choice," he says.

When she's seen enough of the horror stories, Lydia bows her head for a moment to assess her state of mind. Because despite everything she's just seen, she also knows that, like all criminal enterprises in Mexico, La Bestia is controlled by the cartels. Or rather, by a specific cartel, the mother of all cartels, an organization so nightmarish that people won't utter its name, and in this moment that's the key factor for Lydia. Because that cartel is not Los Jardineros. She knows from Sebastián's research that Javier's influence now extends well beyond the borders of Guerrero, that he has established alliances with cartels that stretch the length of Mex-ico. That he controls *plazas* as far away as Coahuila along the Texas bor-der. But if that reach extends to La Bestia, she knows it must be limited there. Javier is not the *jefe* on the trains. So her choice, then, is whether to escape one monster by running into the den of another.

Half a million people survive this journey every year, she tells herself. *This will provide anonymity.* No one will be looking for them on La Bes-tia. Javier would never imagine her traveling this way; she can scarcely imagine it herself. So perhaps she and Luca will have the same chance as anybody else at surviving the beast. Perhaps their chances will be better, in fact, because they have the means to prepare for the journey, and they've already proven themselves to be survivors. So it comes down to this: her fears of La Bestia, the prevalence of violence, kidnapping, death, those fears feel theoretical. They don't measure up against her new blood-cold fear of Javier, the memory of her mother's green-tiled shower, that *sicario* eating Sebastián's chicken drumsticks as he stepped among the corpses of her family.

Lydia decides that her plan, though shocking, is sound. She opens a clean browser to carefully research the route. In Mexico City, it looks like migrants gather at Lechería, within the limits of the city's northern sprawl. From there, the line travels a hundred miles north before diverging in three separate directions. There's a commuter train to Lechería not far from here, in Buenavista. Lydia's stomach does an acrobatic tumble.

"This is madness," she says out loud.

Luca snaps his eyes at her but utters nothing. She replaces the headphones on their hook beside the computer and stands up to gather their things.

"No." She heaves her backpack onto her shoulders, and gestures for Luca to follow. "No," she says again. Because she, the sensible, bookstore-owning, devoted mother-and-wife Lydia, the one from last week, is fighting with this new Lydia, the deranged Lydia, the one who thinks dragging her eight-year-old son onto the top of a moving freight train is a good idea. Neither Lydia has a better plan. "No," she says one last time. And then they're back outside in the riotous sunshine with nothing left to do.

In the market at La Ciudadela, Lydia buys a blanket and four canvas belts. They set out to find the commuter train to Lechería.

CHAPTER ELEVEN

*The commuter rail station is located at one end of a vast shop-*ping mall with a Sephora and a Panda Express and even an ice rink. The street in front is crowded with pink taxis and red buses. The shoppers and vendors wear fancier clothes than you usually see in Acapulco. Everyone has clean sneakers. At the bookstore window, Lydia pauses briefly to gaze at the tiered rainbow of gleaming books on display: the season's new releases, some of which are featured in her own window at home. She thinks of the driver who makes her deliveries stopping outside her shop, tenting his hands above his eyes while he peers through the grate and darkened glass. She thinks of her two part-time employees: bespectacled Kiki, who can never be trusted to stock shelves because she stops to read every book that passes through her hands, and Gloria, who's never read a grown-up book in her life but has great taste in children's literature, and is a diligent worker. She wonders how they'll manage now, without the bookshop income both their families rely on. Lydia thinks of her stockroom gathering dust, her undelivered parcels. When she steps back from the bookstore window, her hand leaves a ghost print on the glass.

Lydia and Luca have to wait in line at the Banamex on the third floor, and a girl nearby is hawking postcards from a large canvas bag. The Zócalo at sunset, the Palacio de Bellas Artes lit up like Christmas. Lydia thinks about buying one and addressing it to Javier. What would she write

there in the blank space? Would she appeal to his abandoned humanity, acknowledge his weird condolences, plead for their lives? Would she
make some futile attempt to articulate her hatred and grief? For all her
love of words, at times they're entirely insufficient.

In the bottom of her backpack, folded carefully into a compartment
she hasn't unzipped since they left Acapulco, is her mother's purse. Inside that purse, tucked into a slit in her wallet, is her mother's bank card.
Lydia knows her mother's PIN because she's the one who helped set it
up, who taught her how to use it. The small, brown handbag is the same
one her mother has carried for literally as long as Lydia can remember.
The leather is thick and was stiff when Lydia was younger, but it's grown
soft from years of use. The clasp broke long ago, so it's only the flap
folded over the opening that keeps whatever's inside from falling out.
Lydia does not pause to reminisce. She leans her backpack against the
glass wall beside her and opens her mother's purse. Luca doesn't watch.
He stands beside her, picking at the corner of a large sticker affixed to
the glass, advertising low-interest loans. Not long ago Lydia would have
corrected this behavior, would have told her son that someone paid good
money for that sticker and it's not his to pick from the window. Not now.
She stares into her mother's purse. There's a particular smell, or rather a
conglomeration of smells. It assails her, even here, between McDonald's
and the Crepe Factory. The aroma evokes immediate memories that Lydia
refuses to indulge. It's old leather and Kleenex (both used and unused)
and the cinnamon gum her mother always buys, and the black licorice
drops she likes, wrapped in a small white paper bag, and a miniature tube
of hand lotion with apricot extract, and the clean, babylike smell of her
pressed powder compact, all combined into the intimate, unmistakable
scent of Lydia's childhood. *Mamá.*

Luca smells it, too. He mouths her name without turning his face
away from the glass, "Abuela," and renews his attack on the sticker.

Lydia breathes through her mouth. When it's their turn she stands
at the ATM with the detritus of her life spilling out of the backpack around
her feet. A young woman using the adjacent ATM is careful not to look
at them. Lydia is embarrassed by the woman's caution. In addition to
fending off her memories, Lydia is also frightened. She worries that this
single electronic transaction will be like shooting up a flare to mark her

location. Her hand trembles as she jams her mother's ATM card into the machine and punches in the code. The machine beeps loudly and spits the card back out.

"*¡Me lleva la chingada!*" she says. Luca turns to look at her. "It's fine," she lies. And inserts the card into the machine a second time. She takes greater care now, watches the way her fingers shake as she punches in the code. She knows it. It's Luca's birthday. It has to work.

It works. *Gracias a Dios.*

It's unusual in a culture where adult children take care of their aging parents that Lydia's mother even had a savings account. Indeed, owning an ATM card made Abuela something of an anomaly among her peers, even in a robust urban economy like Acapulco's, even among Mexico's solid and growing middle class. But then, Lydia's mother had always been something of an anomaly. She'd always done things a little out of step with her generation. She refused the first two boys who asked to marry her, for example. And much to her mother's consternation, when she finally did deign to get married, well past her prime at the age of twenty-four, she did not immediately quit her job as a bookkeeper at a local hospital but instead returned to school to further her education. She was already three years a missus when she was certified as a public accountant and got a job working for the city. Her parents and peers sometimes raised their eyebrows at Abuela's choices, but Lydia's father loved being married to a trailblazer, even after their two daughters were born and he had to do more diaper changing than he meant to sign up for. So Lydia grew up with a mother who emphasized the importance of being independent and saving for the future. A mother who had loaned her the money to open her bookstore. Though Lydia had been grateful, she'd never imagined that her mother's eccentricity might one day save her life.

The number pops up on the screen in front of her, and it's more money than Lydia had dared to hope for: 212,871 pesos; more than $10,000. Lydia breathes a fragment that might just be relief, but feels like joy. This is a lot of money. The women in Abuela's gardening club would be scandalized by the amount. Lydia retracts the card and replaces it reverently in her mother's purse without making a withdrawal. It's safer to leave it in the bank until they need it. If money could solve all their problems, she and Luca would be saved. And yet there's still no way for them to buy their way out of Mexico City, and now, with this single electronic transaction, she knows she may have dropped a pin on Javier's map. She'd known that the vastness of Mexico City would be her only chance to make this transaction without immediately revealing themselves, and now that she's done it, they have to move. They order tacos at the food court, and Luca asks for extra sour cream, which Lydia finds remarkably comforting. They eat them on the 6:32 p.m. commuter train to Lechería.

It's still light out, with long shadows reclining across the pavements, by the time Luca and Mami arrive at the address she found at the library, but the doors of the Casa del Migrante are locked and the windows are darkened. Mami shields her eyes against the glass, and Luca follows suit. He can see nothing inside. A woman walks past them on the sidewalk, pulling a rolling metal cart full of groceries.

"*Está cerrado,*" she says.

"Closed?" Mami turns to look at her. "For the night?"

"No, closed for good. A few months ago. The neighbors complained. It was too many problems for the community. Look here." The lady lets go of her cart and opens the metal mailbox hanging beside the door. She draws out a pamphlet and hands it to Lydia.

"*Amigo migrante,*" Lydia reads aloud. "The neighbors of Lechería invite you to continue your journey to the Casa del Migrante in its new location at Huehuetoca." Lydia snorts. "How hospitable of them."

The lady throws her hands up in the air. "It's not the fault of the migrants, you poor people, but where you go, the problems follow." She returns to her cart, tips it onto its wheels.

"But wait," Lydia says, "where is Huehuetoca?"

The woman starts walking. "North," she says, waving back over her shoulder. Lydia looks at Luca, who only shrugs. He could tell her that Huehuetoca is about seventeen miles away, because he saw it on the map when Mami was looking up Lechería on the computer in the library, but his tongue lacks the capacity to formulate the words *Mami, it's too far to walk tonight,* so he follows his mother the wrong way down the street for three blocks, back toward the train station and the setting sun, before she spots a group of men wearing backpacks and baseball caps. Luca can tell her anxiety is growing with the length of their shadows. Soon it will be dark. The men turn to look at them as they approach, and they greet Mami immediately.

"*Saludos, señora. ¿Cómo va?*"

"Good, thank you. Can you tell us how to get to Huehuetoca?" she asks. "We just found this message—the migrant shelter is closed."

"Yes, it's closed. It's a hike up there to that other place, señora," the youngest man says. There's something sour on his breath.

"How far?"

"A distance. It has to be ten, fifteen miles from here."

"Wow."

The men all nod. One has a toothpick in his mouth. He's leaning on a low wall.

"Is there a bus?"

"No bus, but you can take the train from here to the end of the line at Cuautitlán. That gets you a little closer. You can walk from there, maybe four, five hours." Only the youngest man talks. The other two watch the conversation like it's a tennis match. Luca watches them watch the tennis.

"That's too far tonight," Mami says.

"You can camp with us." The man grins. "Go in the morning, señora." His body moves like a noodle, and the offer feels abrupt and dubious. Luca steps in between the men and his mother, not from any real sense of martyrdom, but because he's observed that, on occasion, the presence of children serves to inhibit people's bad behavior. He tugs on Mami's hand, and together they get moving.

At Lechería station once again, they take the next northern-bound train to the end of the line at Cuautitlán, where Mami splurges on a cheap motel room. She tells Luca it's their last stay in a hotel for a very long time.

In the morning, she wakes him at first light, and they set out north toward Huehuetoca, not necessarily because they need to find the migrant shelter, but because they need to find the migrants.

Cuautitlán is the last stop on the commuter railway line, but the tracks continue north. A new million-dollar fence separates the street from the tracks; it's part of the Mexican government's Programa Frontera Sur, which is funded largely by the United States, and aims to clear migrants from the trains. Migrants can't jump onto the trains here because the fence keeps them out, but about a mile north of the station that fence ends abruptly, so Luca and Lydia walk up the grassy little berm and stay beside the tracks.

Luca doesn't understand why they have to walk. He knows they have enough money to buy a ticket. He'd like to ask Mami about it, but his voice stays sealed inside. He hops from tie to tie on the outside of the track, and Lydia watches their backs to make sure there's no train coming. He still has the ticket card from yesterday in his pocket—the one they bought from Lechería to Cuautitlán. Mami trusted him to be in charge of his own ticket, even though they had to swipe it twice—once getting on the train and then again getting off. He digs into his pocket now and pulls out the card. He tugs on Mami's sleeve, and she turns to look at him. He waves the card at her, and she understands what he wants to know, because she understands everything.

"You can't buy tickets for these trains," she explains. "That was the last stop."

Luca frowns, and a small groove appears in his forehead. He tilts his head up and squints. He can see the tracks. He crawls his fingers upward through the air, tracing the railway lines he can see on the map in his memory.

"Those tracks beneath your feet keep going and going," Mami confirms. "All the way to *el norte*."

Luca's gaze expands and he can nearly feel the tracks beneath him, trundling through the miles ahead, stretching beneath the daytime and nighttime skies, all the way to Texas. So then why can't they buy a ticket?

"The trains that run north from here are only for cargo," Mami says. "Not for people."

With effort, Luca manages a single word. "Why?"

She shakes her head. "I don't know, *amorcito*."

It seems so simple when he asks it. *Why?* Didn't there used to be passenger trains in Mexico, along with the freights? Lydia has a vague childhood memory of trains ferrying more than just cargo across the landscape. She remembers people standing on platforms holding luggage, the cheerful peal of a steam whistle. But the railways stopped carrying passengers a lifetime ago, and Lydia searches her gauzy memories, but it's no use. She can't remember why, and it doesn't matter anyway.

Beside her, Luca continues stepping from tie to tie. He watches the toe of his blue sneakers press against the wood. Sometimes he asks *why* only because he's programmed to ask it, she realizes. He doesn't really care that she doesn't have an answer, as long as she gives him something.

"Some people ride the trains anyway," she says, glancing sideways at him. "Even without a ticket, even without seats."

Luca looks up from his feet and studies her face. He says nothing, but his eyes are round.

"They climb on top," she says. "Can you imagine that?"

Luca cannot.

Lydia feels encouraged by their progress. It feels good to grow the distance between Javier and them, but it's also frightening to venture out from the vastness of Mexico City and back into the modest districts, where Lydia can feel the urban fog of invisibility begin to dissipate. It's hard to feel inconspicuous when you're a stranger in a small place. So Lydia keeps her head down and stays vigilant. They walk quickly, and Luca doesn't complain, even when they pass a little bike repair shop and he longs to grab the handlebars of a bike leaning against the wall outside. It's green with a golden bell, and Luca thinks it's small enough for him. But they keep walking, and less than an hour later they happen upon a group of young migrants beside the tracks. They are all men, perhaps two dozen of them, gathered in a clearing behind a warehouse, just where the urban sprawl begins to diminish and the landscape begins to prickle and pop. A place between places.

Most of the migrants have backpacks and grim faces. They're a thousand miles into their journeys already, weeks from Tegucigalpa or San Salvador or the mountains of Guatemala. They're from cities or villages or *el campo*. Some speak the languages of K'iché or Ixil or Mam or Nahuatl. Luca likes to listen to the foreign sounds, the peaks and rolls of the words he doesn't understand. He likes the way voices sound the same in every language, the way, if you train your ear to listen just outside the words, to only the shifting inflections, you can attach your own meaning to the sounds. Many of the men speak English, too. But here, as they wait for the northbound train outside Mexico City, they all speak Spanish. Most are Catholic and have placed their lives in God's hands; they call on him with frequency and conviction. They invoke the blessings of his son and all the saints. It's been two days since the last train, and the men have grown weary of waiting.

Nearby, a woman sells food from a cart. She takes tortillas from one pail and fills them with beans from a second pail. She serves them without smiling or speaking. Luca and Mami buy breakfast and find a shady place in a bald spot beneath a tree. Mami flings out the brightly colored blanket she bought at La Ciudadela after they left the library, and they sit. Nearby, two young men are reclining with their heads on their backpacks. One leans up on his elbow facing them.

"*Buen día, hermana, y que Dios la bendiga en su camino,*" he greets them.

"Thank you," Lydia says. "And may God bless you on your travels as well."

He leans back with his head on his pack while Luca and Mami eat. Then he says, "You seem fresh on your journey. You have strong energy. My brother and I have already been traveling for fourteen days."

"Where did you begin?" she asks.

"Honduras. My name is Nando."

"Hello, Nando," she says, without offering a name in return. He doesn't ask.

"Nando, can I ask you something?" He props up again on his elbow. "Where is everyone?" she asks.

"Hah?"

"Where are all the migrants? I expected there would be so many people here, waiting for the trains."

"Well, with the migrant shelter gone from Lechería and now the new fences, I guess a lot of migrants don't stop here anymore. That's why it's only young men here now, *hermana,*" he says. "The athletes."

"*¡Los olímpicos!*" his brother says without raising his head or opening his eyes.

The brother is skinny except for his little potbelly, and Luca doesn't think he looks much like an Olympian at all. His hat covers his face from the sun.

"Really? The fence keeps people from stopping?" Lydia asks. It seems such an unlikely deterrent.

"Not only this fence," he says. "All the fences at all the train stations."

"They're everywhere?"

The man shrugs. "Most places now, at least in the south."

"And all those expensive fences, they're just to stop people from riding the trains?"

"Yeah, they're supposed to be for safety," he says. "But, see, they put the fence only where the train stops." He gestures back down the tracks, the way they came, and Lydia remembers the spot where the metal caging fell away and the track opened up. *La migra* had trucks there, watching the parade of foot traffic passing by. "By the time the train arrives here, it's already picking up speed. So you have to jump on while it's moving."

Luca gasps, causing Lydia and Nando both to look over at him, so he returns his attention to his stuffed tortilla.

"Haven't you seen the government signs attached to the fences? *Safety First!*" Nando laughs. "You going to jump onto a moving train, *hermana*?"

"Maybe not." Lydia frowns. "Or maybe."

The man draws his legs in and crosses them, looking at Luca. "What about you, *chiquito*? You going to jump onto La Bestia? Like a cowboy riding a bull at the rodeo?"

Luca's never seen a rodeo, and he's not even sure if he's seen a real-life cowboy. He shrugs.

"So that's it? They put up some fences, and just like that, people stop coming?"

"Who said they stopped coming? From my country, there are more people than ever, more and more all the time."

"So then if they're not on the train, where are they?"

Nando shrugs. "Most go with coyotes now, all the way from my country. One safe house to the next, to the next. A whole network all the way to *el norte*. But it's expensive, and sometimes those coyotes are no better than *los criminales*. So it's the people who can't afford that passage or who don't trust the coyotes—they come to La Bestia."

"And when they get here, and find the fence? What do they do if they can't get on the train?"

Nando plucks a blade of dry grass and hangs it from the corner of his mouth. "*Ay, hermanita mía,* I hate to tell you," he says. "They are walking."

Lydia is dubious. "They walk all the way to Estados Unidos from Honduras?"

Luca makes some calculations in his head. Even if these *hondureños* go only to the southernmost point on the northern border, their total journey must be close to sixteen hundred miles. He wonders if it's really possible for a human being to walk that far.

"Unless *la migra* gets to them first and sends them back," Nando says. "Then they get some rest. An air-conditioned bus in the wrong direction. Then they start all over from scratch."

Lydia takes the last bite of her food. "But you're not worried about *la migra*?" She wipes crumbs from the corners of her mouth.

"Nah." He smiles. "You don't have to outrun *la migra*. You only have to be faster than your brother. I got it covered."

"In your dreams, *gordo,*" the brother says.

"What about you, *hermana*? And your son? What will you do if *la migra* comes?"

Now it's Lydia's turn to lie back on her pack. Technically, *la migra* can't send them anywhere, because they're Mexican, and unlike Nando and many of the other migrants, they're traveling in their own country; they can't be deported. But Lydia knows that technicality won't help them at all if *la migra* here happens to work for Los Jardineros. She shudders. "We'll manage," she says.

Nando nods and smiles encouragingly at Luca. "Of course you will," he says.

At length, the migrants sitting or lying on the rails stand up and make the announcement to the others—they can feel reverberations in the track. The train is coming. Luca goes and puts his hand on the rail, but feels nothing.

"It's stopped down the line somewhere, *chiquito,*" Nando says. "It'll be along shortly."

When a few minutes have passed, another man calls Luca over. "Feel now," he says, and Luca obeys, placing his hand on the hot metal.

He can feel the energy of the train percussing through the waiting steel. He draws his hand instinctively in, and backs away from the rails to return to Mami's side. In the clearing, there's a flurry of activity among the migrants, who will now attempt to board. Everyone gathers their belongings and scatters across the area. They lay claim to their own patches of ground, spreading out, giving one another space to run alongside the train. They watch also for *la migra,* which tends to time its raids to coincide with the train's arrival. After two days of undercover waiting, more migrants are suddenly visible, emerging from their hiding places to attempt the perilous flying start.

Lydia quickly rolls up the blanket and straps it to the bottom of her pack. Then she turns to make the straps on Luca's shoulders as tight as possible. The tails hang down his legs. She ties them in a knot and tucks the loose ends into his waistband. She shifts her weight nervously from foot to foot.

"You want to do this, *mijo*?" she asks him. She hopes he'll say no. She hopes he says, "Mami, this is crazy, I don't want to die, I'm scared." But Luca just looks at her. He doesn't respond at all. "Maybe we'll try," she says. "Let's just watch first. We'll see what happens." She feels sick with dread.

When the train rounds the distant bend and comes into view, when Lydia can look down the track at its approaching nose, it appears to advance in slow motion. *We can do this,* she says to herself. *It's not going that fast.* It's loud as it pulls into the clearing; she can feel the chug in her bones, in her sternum, and many of the men step into a trot alongside. It's a challenge of competing details, all equally important, and Lydia finds herself rapt as she watches, trying to learn the techniques. You must match your speed to the train's speed, she sees, adjusting as you go. You must find the ideal point of access, a protrusion, a ladder, a spot with plenty of grip and some way to quickly get to the roof of the car. You must fully commit to your position once you've chosen it. You must defend it from other migrants whose urgency matches your own. Under no circumstances can you attempt to change course once you're under way. But you must also be mindful of tree limbs and other fixed hazards that threaten your track. You must pay close attention to what's ahead of you on the ground. You must take care not to step in a hole or trip over a rock while you run, not to stumble beneath the grinding wheels of the beast. You must never, ever forget the power of those churning, groaning, clattering, rumbling wheels. They shriek as a reminder.

"*¡Qué Dios los bendiga!*" their new friend calls out as he leaves them and begins to run alongside the train.

His brother trots along behind him, their pace more than a jog, less than a sprint. Nando runs, oscillating his head to both watch where he's going and assess the train cars behind for a good spot to climb on. He sees a ladder coming, two cars away. He slows down. One car away, he picks up his pace, glances in front of him, ducks beneath the slapping limb of a leafy shrub. He reaches for the ladder, wraps his fingers around the third rung. He takes two strides, three, four, with only his right hand on the ribs of La Bestia, and then all at once he swings his full weight from that arm. He reaches his left arm up now as well, his hand in a brief panic until his fingers find their target and seize. Now his body is caught, suspended. This. This is the moment of paramount risk. The arms attached, clinging, hauling. The body draped like a flag. The legs hanging low, not yet clear of the wheels.

"Get up," the potbellied brother shouts. "Get your feet up!" He runs.

And the instinct is to reach with those feet, to feel for what's beneath, to scrabble for purchase, to find some way to boost your weight from below. But no. You must curl. Bring the feet up. Up. Up! Nando's feet find the bottom rung. His arms stretch up to the next and now he's climbing. Strong. Solid. A few more seconds—slap!—a passing tree branch threatens his grasp, scratches his side, but now he's safe, he's over the lip, and he lies down on top, offering a hand over the edge toward his brother, who is running now, below.

Lydia's eyes are wide and now the brothers are gone, the other migrants around them dwindling in numbers as they board, one by one, two by two. She crushes Luca's hand in her viselike grip, but doesn't notice how hard she's squeezing it and he doesn't protest. They are rooted in place, unmoving, until all at once, every echo of the train is gone.

They walk.

There's a new reverence to having seen it with their own eyes, the unfeeling crush of the wheels along their rails, the men clinging to the exoskeleton like beetles on a window screen.

In the backseat of Papi's orange Volkswagen Beetle in Acapulco, Luca had his own little safety harness system. A bright blue cushion with monkeys on it that Papi had unfolded and somehow permanently affixed to the seat. When he was little, Luca liked the monkeys, the cushioned straps that went over his head and then around his waist. He felt snug in there. But last summer he started begging to be rid of the thing. It was babyish, he insisted. He was big enough to wear a regular seat belt now, he said. Luca watches the last hip of the now-silent train disappear around a distant bend, and cannot make sense of anything.

CHAPTER TWELVE

Even if they knew how long it might be before the next train, they cannot conceive of boarding La Bestia now that they've seen how it's done. Lydia thinks it over while they walk the seven miles to Huehuetoca. Would she put Luca on the ladder first? She would have to; there's no way she could jump on and leave him standing beneath the train without her. Could she run and climb on if he held on to her neck, his legs wrapped tightly around her waist? It seems physically impossible. Each time she tries to picture it, the fantasy ends the same way. Butchery.

Luca distracts himself from how tired his legs are becoming by looking at the unusual sights. They pass a place that's full of every kind of statue: bears, lions, cowboys, dolphins, angels, crocodiles. They pass some men who are laying bricks to build a wall. They pass a woman who's vacuuming instead of sweeping her front step, which makes Luca squeeze Mami's hand so she'll see it, too. When they pass a school and Luca sees some kids playing *fútbol* in the yard, he realizes it's Thursday, and that he should be in school in Acapulco, and Papi should be picking him up this afternoon because Thursday is Papi's day to pick him up, and sometimes Papi buys him *galletas* and they eat them on the way home if he promises not to tell Mami. After that, Luca doesn't look at the sights anymore. He watches his feet even though the sun feels hot on the back of his neck, and it takes them almost three hours to walk to Huehuetoca.

When they arrive, they easily find the place they're looking for, as it sits neatly beside the railroad tracks behind a wind-whipped green fence. The Casa del Migrante is a gathering of tents and simple structures on a large, flat parcel of land that's saved from being beautiful only by the utilitarian character of its buildings. The wide road that separates the *casa* from the railroad tracks is of dirt and rubble, and it's empty as far as Luca can see. It's flat here for a long stretch, but in the distance, when he allows his eyes to follow the tracks to the horizon, Luca can see the landscape erupt upward on both sides. The clouds, puffy and brilliant, come down to meet it. There are bald fields all around and behind the *casa*, and on the far side of the tracks as well, but Luca can see that the soil has been tended, turned, striped with darker bands of earth where the farmers will sow their crops at the right season. There's a rich mineral scent on the wind.

Luca and Lydia cross the parched road hand in hand and approach the chain link fence that's been woven through with strips of green plastic so it's no longer transparent. Three strings of barbed wire cut through the air atop the fence, and two signs hang beneath it. The first is a cloudy, sunstruck blue, and has a painting of Jesus and Mary, so Luca expects it to be a blessing, but it says: *Brother Migrant, we will watch over you and protect you from polleros, guides, and coyotes so that you may enjoy a happy stay here with our hospitality. Anyone found to be in transgression of these specifications will be handed over to the appropriate authorities. May God protect you on your journey!*

The second sign is much less flowery, a list of rules written in a plain black font, so long that its only decoration, a red banner at the very bottom, sits in direct contact with the dirt below: WELCOME, BROTHER AND SISTER TRAVELERS! Luca reads some of the rules at random.

- Persons requesting admission to the casa must be migrants. From this country or other countries, or deportees from the United States.
- Drugs and alcohol are prohibited. Anyone presenting symptoms of their use will be denied entry.
- Please remember that this is a place of sanctuary. Here you may rest while God restores your strength for the journey yet ahead of you. Your stay here must, therefore, be transitory, and limited to a maximum of three nights.

Before he can finish reading the list, two men greet them from the far side of the fence. Only their heads are visible above the green plastic stripping. One is an older man with dark glasses and gray hair, and he does the talking.

"*¡Bienvenida, hermana!*" he says. He steps closer to the fence so now Luca can see his shoulders as well, between the strings of barbed wire. He's wearing a dark blue cardigan and he smiles at them. "You're in need of shelter?"

Luca nods.

"You are migrants?"

Lydia nods, reluctantly claiming the word.

"Here," the man says kindly, gesturing to his stocky younger companion to open a gate a few feet away. "Please come in."

Inside the fence sits an unpainted cinder block building with open-air windows covered in sheets of black tarpaulin. It's ugly, and its bleak shadow steals into Luca and thieves the relief right out of him.

The older man folds his hands and speaks softly. "Are you in any immediate danger?"

Lydia thinks before she answers. "No, I don't think so. Not right now."

"Do you have any immediate medical needs?"

"No, we are healthy."

"*Gracias a Dios,*" the man says.

"Thank God," Lydia agrees.

"Are you thirsty?" He turns to walk, indicating that they should follow.

"Yes, a little."

They round the corner of the ugly gray building, and suddenly the space opens around them. Luca's lungs fill up with the rush he'd been waiting for. The chain link fence that surrounds the entire compound is opaque only at the front, so he can see now, beyond its boundaries in the back, across the bare cornfields to the town of Huehuetoca nearby, its houses clustering merrily up the hillside. Large prickly pear plants gather in clumps just outside the fence, their wide paddles cartoonishly green in the golden afternoon. The compound is much bigger than it looked from the road. There's one white van, a small house, a chapel, a string of Porta Potties, and two gigantic warehouses.

"Welcome to the Casa del Migrante, San Marco D'Aviano. I am Padre Rey. This is one of my helpers, Néstor."

Néstor raises one hand in salute but doesn't look at them. He keeps his eyes on Padre Rey's black sandals.

"We will get you something to drink right away, and you can freshen up for a few minutes."

Luca tucks his thumbs nervously beneath the straps of his backpack.

"Hermana Cecilia will get you registered after you've had a little rest."

"Thank you, Padre," Lydia says. "God bless you for your kindness."

They step inside the first of the two warehouse buildings, and even though it's well lit, it takes Luca's eyes a few minutes to adjust. It's the first time he's been out of the stark sunshine all day. At a table, a boy and a girl, both younger than Luca, are coloring. The girl turns her head this way and that, admiring her artwork. A group of men and women sit at another table, some cleaning and sorting beans, others peeling carrots. Bright orange shreds collect in piles on the table. In the farthest corner of the large room, more men are watching *fútbol*. Luca and Lydia choose an empty table and sit on lime-green plastic chairs. A lady with a red coverall apron brings them two glasses of cold lemonade. It has an umber tint, but Luca gulps it gratefully anyway.

"Dinner is at seven," the woman explains apologetically. "We can't make any exceptions unless it's a medical emergency."

It's after three o'clock in the afternoon, and they haven't eaten since the tortillas beside the tracks early this morning. But "No, it's okay, we're fine," Lydia says. "Thank you."

As the woman returns to the kitchen, Lydia is swamped with emotion. She swallows it with the lemonade. She examines the faces of the people at the other tables, but no one looks at her. Hermana Cecilia soon appears and brings them to her small office. She's a tidy little woman, and her office is papered with children's artwork. A pot on her desk holds a pink plastic flower. There are green chairs just like the ones in the big room. Hermana Cecilia's voice is the most soothing sound Luca has ever heard, a peaceful, uninflected hum of determined protection, so that no matter what words she says, the words Luca hears are *You are safe here, you are safe here, you are safe.* From a shelf behind her desk, she produces a tub of crayons and a small stack of clean, white paper.

"Would you like to stay here and draw?" she asks Luca with her hum-voice. "Or sit in the big room with the other children?"

Luca's hand shoots out and grabs Mami's.

"It's okay," Hermana Cecilia says. "You can stay with your *mami.*"

Lydia stands to pluck the backpack from his shoulders. She encourages Luca to sit at the other desk, beside the door.

"This way you can color," she says. "You won't have to hold the paper on your lap."

Luca sits, and Lydia returns to sit across from the nun, who has some paperwork and a file folder in front of her.

"Before we begin, I want you to know that you don't have to answer anything that makes you uncomfortable. I ask that you try, because the answers you give will help us assist more people in the future, to prepare for new patterns of arrivals. But all the information we gather here is anonymous. You needn't give your real name unless you want to."

Lydia nods her consent, the nun lifts the cap off her pen, and they begin.

"Names and ages?"

Lydia gives a little twist of her neck before she responds. "I'm thirty-two and my son is eight."

Hermana Cecilia writes down: *María, 32, y José, 8.*

"Where are you traveling from?"

She hesitates, then asks a question of her own. "No one has access to these files?"

Hermana Cecilia folds her hands and leans slightly forward. "I assure you, *hermana,* whatever, whoever you're worried about will never see these files. The only copy is kept locked in that filing cabinet, in this office, also locked, whenever I'm not here." Her eyes are blue, and they twinkle when she smiles. "I'm always here."

Lydia nods. "We come from Acapulco."

The nun returns to her writing. "What is your intended destination?"

"We're going to Estados Unidos."

"What city?"

"Denver."

"A friendly city," the nun says. "Pretty there. Are you traveling for reasons of being reunited with a member of your immediate family?"

"No."

"Do you have family members currently living in the United States?"

"Yes, an uncle and two cousins." She hasn't seen that uncle, Abuela's younger brother, since she was a young girl. She's never met his children.

"They're in Denver?" Hermana Cecilia asks.

"Yes."

"They are expecting you?"

"No."

"Was your decision to migrate planned or spontaneous?"

"Spontaneous." Lydia squeezes her clasped hands together between her thighs.

"Was the primary reason for your journey financial?"

"No."

"Was the primary reason for your journey medical?"

"No."

"Was the primary reason for your journey domestic violence?"

"No."

"Was the primary reason for your journey related to gang violence or recruitment?"

"No." Lydia shakes her head.

"Was the primary reason for your journey related to violence by a cartel or drug traffickers in your place of origin?"

Lydia clears her throat. "Yes," she says quietly. She can hear Luca's crayon moving rapidly across the paper in silky strokes.

"Are you currently in fear for your life from a specific individual or individuals?"

"Yes."

"Have you received direct threats to your safety?"

Lydia nods. "Yes."

"Were the threats violent in nature?"

"Yes."

"Can you describe the threats?"

Lydia scoots her chair closer and places her elbows on the edge of the desk. She folds her fingers together and lowers her head and her voice.

"The cartel killed sixteen members of our family," she says, staring at the pen. The nun does not look up from her paper. "They came to a family party and they shot everyone. My husband, my mother, my sister, and her children. Everyone. We escaped."

Hermana Cecilia's pen is at a momentary loss. It hangs suspended over the page for a few seconds before the nun can make it move again. She scribbles everything down and then makes her voice go again, too.

"Has your spontaneous migration resolved the immediate threat to your safety and well-being?"

Lydia hesitates, because everything she's ever thought about protecting Luca has changed now. She doesn't want him to be afraid. But she needs him to be very afraid. And in any case, how can anything she does or does not say make any impact on him after what's already happened? She shakes her head. "No," she admits. "We are still in danger."

"You feel the threat has followed you?"

Lydia nods very slightly. "Yes. I mean, he doesn't know where we are right now. But it was a very powerful man who did this. His influence extends all the way to *el norte*. And he won't stop looking until he finds us."

"Do you know which *plazas* belong to him, or who his allies are in other organizations?" the nun asks. "Do you know which routes are safe for you to travel without his *halcones*?"

Lydia feels that this room has the sanctity of a confessional. "No," she whispers. "I don't know. I don't know."

"You are a long way from home," the nun says. "He cannot find you here. You are safe here."

Luca's crayon makes no sound behind her. The nun puts her pen in the cup beside her phone and tucks the paperwork into the folder. Then she stretches her hands across the desk toward Lydia, who takes them in hers, and bows her head. When Lydia closes her eyes, she realizes her hands are trembling. Hermana Cecilia's fingers are cool to the touch.

"*Padre nuestro*, bless these children with your love and grace. Protect them from any further harm, God, and provide them with comfort in their time of unspeakable grief. May Jesus walk the road with them and repair their broken hearts. May Mother Mary sweep all dangers from their road ahead and lead them safely where they're going. *Padre nuestro*, these two faithful servants have shouldered more than their share of life's burdens already. Please, God, may you see fit to relieve them of any further torment, yet not as we will it, but as thy will be done. In Jesus's name, Amen."

"Amen," Lydia says.

Behind her at the little desk, with closed eyes and clutched crayon, Luca is moving his lips.

Hermana Cecilia leans forward one last time. "Be careful who you talk to," she says.

That night Lydia wakes to the sound of raised voices in the corridor. She sits up in the half-light of the bunk room and notices several other women popping up from their beds as well. They move silently to check on their children, who sleep through the ruckus. Luca is above her in the top bunk, so Lydia has to disentangle her leg from the backpack strap she wrapped around it before she fell asleep. She stands, her bare feet cool against the tile floor, and reaches for his rumpled covers. Luca is not there. Panic rises in her throat.

"Luca!"

She checks her own bed again without meaning to, and then the surrounding beds as well. As if her child is an item she's unthinkingly misplaced. A cell phone, a book. A pair of glasses. There's a window on the door that leads to the corridor, and a rectangle of light shining through it. Lydia, without shoes or a bra, bolts toward that patch of light.

This is Luca's third trip to the bathroom since they got into bed a few hours ago. The murky lemonade returns. Being on the top bunk has made his frequent sprints to the toilet extra challenging, but Mami's so exhausted that she never wakes, not even when he nearly steps on her shoulder as he clambers down, not even when he lands with an indelicate thump just inches from her head, not even as he runs—the prickly, imbalanced gate of the diarrhetically infirm—from bunk to bathroom and back again.

He's just washed his hands and returned to the fluorescent light of the hallway when he sees Padre Rey and Néstor talking to a young man in the doorway of the men's bunk room. Luca recognizes the young man as a migrant who arrived late that afternoon, before dinner. He's wearing long, red shorts and a white T-shirt, socks but no shoes, and he's carrying his backpack in front of him, unzipped. There's a pair of clean, expensive, white sneakers on the floor beside him.

"At least let me get dressed first," he says. "Man, this is bullshit. You're supposed to help people."

Néstor steps behind him into the darkened interior of the dorm room, between the man and the sleeping migrants beyond.

"We can talk further, but not here. You are disturbing the whole facility," Padre Rey says calmly. "Please, just come with us to the main room, where we can talk without waking everyone."

"This is bullshit, Padre, that *puta* is lying," the man says, raising his voice to a shout. "Bullshit!"

Inside the dorm room, several men get out of their bunks and stand alongside Néstor, creating a kind of wall. They cross their arms, plant their legs wide. Luca stays frozen in his spot beside the bathroom door. He should turn and go the other way. He should scoot down the hall and back to the women and children's room, he should climb back up past Mami's head and settle himself into the covers, where he should allow his body, temporarily relieved of stomach cramps, to rest. But he's paralyzed, transfixed. He's unaware of his own racing pulse, his shallow breath, his fingers scrabbling into the smooth seams between the painted cinder blocks of the wall behind him.

"*¡Chinga tu madre!*" the young man yells.

"Let's go, *hermano.*" It's the first time Luca has heard Néstor use his voice. It's as solidly built as his body. "Don't make it harder than it has to be."

The young man stoops and grabs his sneakers with one hand as Néstor and the other men close the distance behind him, encouraging him into the hallway without touching him. When he straightens to follow Padre Rey down the corridor, Luca notes the shape of a sickle tattoo with three bloodred droplets on the blade jutting out from the man's sock. It's carved into the calf muscle of his right leg. Luca doesn't know what the tattoo means, exactly, but he doesn't need to understand it for it to amplify his sense of dread. That bloody sickle unsticks Luca from the wall and sends him dashing down the hallway back to the women's dorm. He runs bang into Mami as he barrels through the door.

"Luca," she says. "Oh my God, Luca, where were you?" She doesn't wait for an answer. Her hands are on his shoulders, and she places him farther inside the room before sticking her head out into the hallway to see what all the noise is about, but all she can see is Néstor and a few other men following Padre Rey toward the front of the building. She goes back inside and allows the door to click shut behind her. Luca is trembling.

"What happened?" she whispers.

He shakes his head.

"But what was all the shouting about?"

He shakes again, and his face looks all carved up with worry.

"It's okay," she says. "It's okay, it's okay."

She pulls him into her arms and crushes his head against her chest. His little arms reach around behind her and cling. They stay like that until she lifts him under the armpits. He's too big for it, and his weight is enough that she struggles beneath it. But he wraps his legs around her waist, and she carries him back to their bunk. He doesn't go up to the top bed this time. She makes her body into a shield behind and around him. She wraps one arm and leg over the top of his small figure, makes her breath deep and slow for him, so that his breath will line up with hers, so that he'll rest and sleep. But Lydia stays vigilant until morning.

CHAPTER THIRTEEN

The first time a head turned up by itself on the street in Aca- pulco, it was a big deal. It was a twenty-two-year-old head, with curly black hair shaved close on the sides and left long on top. It had a small gold hoop earring in its right ear. Its eyelids swelled and its tongue protruded from its mouth. It was left on top of a public phone booth outside Pizza Hut, right next to the Diana Cazadora fountain. Rolled up and stuck into the corner of its mouth like a cigarette was a note that read: "*Me gusta hablar.*" I like to talk.

The woman who found the head as she walked home from her shift as a night nurse at the Hospital del Pacífico was not a woman ordinarily horror-struck by the sight of blood. But that day, just as dawn tipped its westerly light across the pavements of Acapulco, causing the head to throw its queer, bodiless shadow from atop the phone booth and toward the feet of that weary nurse, she screamed, dropped her purse, and ran three blocks before retrieving her phone from her pocket and calling the police. The officers descended; the media swarmed. People passing through the area on their way to work or school were aghast. They took the time to get down on their knees and bless themselves, to offer up some thorough prayers on behalf of the anonymous soul who had once belonged to that head. It was famous.

Until the second one.

By the time the head count reached a dozen, a shameful, self-protective apathy began to spread in the gut of the city so that, in the mornings, when a call would come in that a head had been found, on the beach or at *el zócalo* or on the green of the ninth hole at *el club de golf,* the dispatcher answering the phone would sometimes make a joke.

"Go for the putter. That hole is an easy par three."

Back then, Sebastián had been the first one to recognize it for what it was: the city's steep, wholesale descent into the maw of the warring cartels. While other journalists were reluctant to acquiesce to the truth of their collapsing reality, Sebastián shouted it from his headlines:

CARTELS EXHIBIT BRUTAL SURGE IN VIOLENCE

TERROR AND IMPUNITY: CARTELS GET AWAY WITH MURDER

And most dramatically, after a particularly bad weekend, which saw the murders of two journalists, a city councilwoman, three shopkeepers, two bus drivers, a priest, an accountant, and a child holding a cob of buttered corn on the beach, his sandy feet still damp from the ocean, a simple pronouncement in two-inch letters:

ACAPULCO FALLS

That Monday morning Lydia sat behind her register in the bookshop reading her husband's unflinching account of the weekend's murders while her tea turned cold and bitter in its cup. She'd found it particularly difficult to leave Luca at the school gate that morning. She'd gripped his tiny hand with ferocity and rubbed the bumps of his knuckles with her thumb while they walked. Luca had pretended not to notice, but he'd swung his lunch box more vigorously than usual. When she kissed him goodbye at the gate, she spotted a powdering of dried toothpaste along his bottom lip. She licked her thumb and smeared it away, while he protested the gesture as *asqueroso.* Gross. Perhaps he had a point. But he'd kissed her back anyway, his lips all gloppy and wet, and for once, Lydia didn't discreetly wipe away the trail he left on her cheek. For once, she didn't turn and hurry off the moment he darted past the principal and into the courtyard. She waited there instead, one hand flat against the cinder block wall, and gazed after him. She didn't turn away until his little green-and-white uniform became invisible amid a sea of others.

To Lydia, the change had felt sudden, lurching. She'd gone to bed the night before in the same city where she'd been born and raised, where she'd lived her entire life except for the brief spin of years through college in Mexico City. Her dreams had been populated by the same whipped current of ocean air, the same bright, liquid colors, the same thrumming beats and aromas of her childhood, the same languorous swaying of hips that had always defined the pace of life here in this place she knew so well. Sure, there had been new violence, an unfamiliar hitch of anxiety. Sure, crime was on the rise. But until that morning, the truth had felt insulated beneath the illusory film of Acapulco's previous immunity. And then Sebastián's headline had ripped that protective skin away. All at once, the people had to look and to see. They could pretend no longer: *Acapulco Falls*. Briefly, Lydia hated her husband for that headline. She hated his editor.

"I mean, it's a little melodramatic, don't you think?" she'd challenged him when he stopped by the shop to pick her up for lunch. She flipped the sign to read CERRADO and then locked the door behind them.

Sebastián frowned at her. "Actually, I don't think it can be melodramatic enough. I don't think words exist that can sufficiently capture the atrocity of what's happening here." He slung his hands into his pockets and watched her face as they walked. He spoke carefully, endeavoring to suppress the accusatory note in his voice, but it was there. She could hear it. "You don't agree? That it's unspeakably horrific?" A kind of mild, repressed superiority.

"I mean, of course I do, Sebastián. It's insane." She dropped her keys into her bag and wouldn't meet his eye. "But *Acapulco Falls*? Like *Rome is burning*? I mean, look around. It's a regular day, the sun is shining. Look, there are tourists." She nodded toward a café on the corner where a group of rowdy *estadounidenses* sat at an outdoor table in the shade of an awning.

There were several nearly empty carafes of wine on their table. "We should get one of those," Sebastián said.

And though it was not yet noon, Lydia agreed, and they mostly drank their lunch that day instead of eating it. She cut her eyes at him across the table and did not say the things she wanted to say, that it was asinine of him to write this stuff, that he was turning himself into a target, that she wanted no part of his righteous campaign of truth, that she hoped he was satisfied with his byline and that it was worth the danger. She did not say: *You are a father. You are a husband.* But he felt all of it there, in the angle of her gaze across the table. And he didn't respond by condemning her lack of courage. He didn't bristle against her resentment or pick at the waiting scab. He knew her vigilance was not a shortcoming. He held her hand across the table and studied his menu in silence.

"I think I'll have the soup," he said.

That was more than a year and a half before she'd met Javier. But thinking back on it now, from the bottom bunk of the women's room at the Casa del Migrante in Huehuetoca with Luca sleeping heavily on her arm, she wonders if Javier had anything to do with those first heads, if he saw them or sanctioned them, if he swung the weapon responsible for severing one of them from its body. *Of course he did,* she thinks. *He must have.* What was once inconceivable now seems foolishly plain. *Por Dios,* how would her life be different at this very moment if she'd accepted that truth sooner?

There was a time once, perhaps a year ago, when a customer came into her shop on a windy day, his hair tossed up in a mess, and his cheeks reddened by the wind. A shiver of animation skated in on his shoulders. He was agitated and spoke quickly to Lydia. There'd been a shooting a few blocks away. Some men had pulled up on a motorcycle and shot a local journalist twelve times in the head. The man was still lying there dead in the street.

"Who was it, who was it?"

The customer shook his head. "I don't know. Some reporter."

Lydia bolted. She grabbed her cell phone and ran outside. She left the man standing at her counter unattended. She left without ringing up his purchases. She hit Sebastián's number while she ran down the street. Straight to voicemail. She panicked and cried out. When she got to the corner, she realized she didn't know which way she was running. Where was this shooting? Which street? She turned in circles. Hit redial. Straight to voicemail. The shopkeepers were standing in their doorways.

"Where was it?" she asked the shoe store owner and she hit Sebastián's number for a third time. Voicemail. The shoe salesman pointed, and Lydia ran. She turned another corner and another, hitting redial all the time. She called out for directions as she ran, and people pointed, and she kept going, and she kept hitting redial and she kept running, and then she stopped when she got to the street where *la policía* were just pulling up, where a crowd of onlookers had gathered in a clump around the body. She stopped because she didn't want to go any closer. She didn't want to see. Her husband lying there in the puddle of his spent life. Her thumb was cold as she redialed Sebastián's number three more times. Voicemail. She was crying before she approached, her hair stringing across her face in the wind, collecting her tears. She clasped the cell phone with both hands in front of her. She walked the double yellow line like it was the plank of a ship, her legs wilty beneath her.

And then it was not him. There was so much blood that it was at first difficult to ascertain, but within a few moments she could see clearly, no, those were not his shoes. No, Sebastián's hair was not that length, his legs were not that thick. Oh my God, the relief. It was not him. She cried harder and harder. It was not him. A stranger scooped Lydia into her big, doughy arms then and held her while she cried. The woman was enormous and smelled of powder, and Lydia did not resist her emphatic embrace, nor did she correct the woman's assumption that her breakdown was caused by some familiarity with the deceased reporter. After all, that notion did feel approximately true. So Lydia allowed the stranger to comfort her, to murmur over her tears, to offer her the kindness of a tissue from the pocket of her sweater, and in a few minutes it was all over. For Lydia. It was some other widow's turn that day. And when she finally extracted herself from the stranger's arms, Lydia's body felt jerky and clattery with adrenaline as she walked the several blocks back to her shop to find that her customer had left his money, plus a little extra, on the counter beside the register.

She's still afraid that, one day, it will be Sebastián. She's been afraid for so long that now she can't catch up to the facts: it was already him, and the rest of her family. It really did happen; all those years of worry did not prevent it. And not only Sebastián, but Mamá, too, and Yemi and her beautiful children, and none of them had chosen to marry Sebastián, or to take on the risks of his profession as their own. Only she had done that, and now her family had paid for her choice. The fears of her past and the horrors of her present are so mixed up they feel like the unmatching pieces of a *rompecabezas,* like she's trying to piece together things that were never meant to fit.

Perhaps she's just not ready. Lydia knows the stages of grief, and this is denial. Instead of acceptance she wants to recall Sebastián's face, lunch that day in the café, the boyish tilt of his posture at the small table after their first glass of wine. They'd laughed together, and Sebastián had made a show of looking discreetly down her top, of rubbing her thigh beneath the table, of asking if she wanted to head back to the shop early so he could help her "check inventory." But in the slick heat of the memory that follows, she cannot conjure Sebastián's face. The absolute absence of him feels like unmitigated terror.

Lydia is startled by the lateness of the daylight when she opens her eyes, and for a moment, she doesn't know where she is. Luca is already awake beside her, watching her, his black eyes clear through the curtain of his sleep-sticky lashes. She can smell something cooking, and there's the distant clinking of forks against dishes. "Come on, let's get some food." She sits up, but then leans back and presses her lips against the warm expanse of Luca's cheek. There's such comfort there that she stays for a minute, her hands against the softness of his skin.

Luca sits bolt upright in bed, his hands flying up to his head to confirm what he already knows, that Papi's hat is not there. He wears it even when he sleeps now, and when he has to remove it to shower, he makes Lydia hold it in her hands until he comes out. She's not allowed even to set it down. Neither is she allowed to put it on her own head, because it must maintain the precise smell of Papi mingled with Luca, a mix that Luca is very pleased to note has not diminished but only intensified in the time he's been wearing it. Perhaps Papi's smell is also his smell, and he can keep enhancing it by its continued use. They mustn't accidentally introduce any new ingredients, therefore, to corrupt the purity of the hat. It must've fallen off last night, when he was sleeping, or during one of his many trips up and down from the top bunk to the bathroom.

"Don't worry, *mijo,*" Lydia says, sitting up after him, because it's immediately evident what he's looking for, and he's already left the warm nest of the bottom bunk and clambered up to riffle through the top bunk.

The bed frame squeaks as he digs through the covers. There's an audible sigh of relief from above, and then the hat appears, perched triumphantly on the end of Luca's outstretched arm, over the edge of the bed.

There are plenty of *jóvenes,* teenagers, at the shelter, but only a few younger children, and at breakfast they all sit together at a round table in the center of the room. A little girl pops up from this table when Luca enters, and draws him by the elbow to an empty seat. Lydia makes him a plate, and one for herself, and then sits at a table nearby with two other women, Neli and Julia, both in their early twenties, both from Guatemala. Neli is pudgy with curly hair. Julia is slender, with dark skin and almond-shaped eyes. Lydia nods and smiles politely as they introduce themselves, but she keeps quiet, afraid of her own voice, afraid she'll betray herself in some way she hasn't considered. Her accent, a turn of phrase, some unconscious custom that might identify her. She does not reach for the loops at her neck. Neli and Julia recognize caution, and they understand. They don't press her. Lydia turns her face toward her plate, briefly closes her eyes, and blesses herself. Neli and Julia resume their conversation.

"She wasn't even going to tell anyone?" Neli asks. "God bless her."

"Said she didn't want to make a fuss. It's only because I happened to step into the hallway just at that moment," Julia says. "And I saw it with my own eyes! I saw what he did to her. I chased him away from her and then got the padre right away."

"And what did the padre do?" Neli wants a play-by-play. She's taking her time with her food, shredding a tortilla into host-size pieces, which she places on her tongue one at a time.

"The padre was great, he went in and fished that cholo right out of his cot. Sent him packing."

"And I slept through the whole thing!" Neli seems disappointed. "I heard he put up a bit of a fight, too."

Across the room, the girl at the center of last night's scandal, a sixteen-year-old from San Salvador, keeps her face tipped down toward her own plate. Her shoulders are rolled in so far toward each other that her body seems to be trying to swallow itself. Lydia chews even though the eggs are scrambled and the chewing is unnecessary. Her mouth needs something to do. Another woman approaches their table and points to the empty chair beside Lydia. Neli waves her hand to indicate that it's free. The woman sets her plate down and pulls out the chair. She's wearing a pink skirt and flip-flops, and has a multicolored ribbon woven into the two long braids down her back. If her clothing didn't mark her as an indigenous woman, then her heavily accented Spanish would. Neli and Julia steal glances at each other as the woman takes her seat. She smiles at them and offers her name as Ixchel, but Neli and Julia continue their conversation without pause, turning their bodies almost imperceptibly away from her. It's a rudeness that Lydia would've endeavored to counteract in her old life, with a smile and a kind word. Perhaps even a rebuke to the offending party. Because Lydia perceives that the Guatemalan women are snubbing the newcomer due to bigotry, because she's an *india*. And Lydia is suitably offended on Ixchel's behalf, but performing an act of decorum would mean putting herself at risk, so instead she keeps her eyes on her plate, scoops some eggs into a tortilla.

"I saw them together last night after dinner," Julia says. "I saw the way he looked at her, and I just presumed they were together. But what I saw then after, there was no question it was one-sided."

"She tried to fight him off?" Neli asks, placing a speckled white square in her mouth.

"Worse than that, she struggled but then seemed resigned to it." Julia shakes her head sadly but there's a spiky anger in her voice. "Like she knew there was nothing she could do if he'd made up his mind. *Qué chingadera.*"

"They should be castrated, every one of them," Neli says, shaking her headful of black curls.

Julia looks across at the young girl. "She's so pretty, too. She's going to have a rough journey."

"A lot of return trips to the *cuerpomático*," Neli agrees.

"The what?" Ixchel asks.

"The *cuerpomático*?" Neli repeats.

Ixchel shakes her head. She may have an accent, but her Spanish is excellent, and yet she hasn't heard this word before. Perhaps it's slang. Perhaps it's made-up. Lydia doesn't know it either.

"You don't know this word?" Julia asks.

Ixchel shakes her head a second time. Lydia watches Luca at the round table while she listens to the women talk.

"I thought all the *guatemaltecas* knew it." Neli allows the remainder of her tortilla to wilt back onto her plate.

"*Las guanacas también, y las catrachas.*" Julia leans forward on her elbows and pushes her plate aside. "It means your body is an ATM machine."

Lydia tries to swallow, but the eggs and tortilla have formed a paste in her mouth. Her fork is full of rice, a crispy disk of *plátano frito* speared onto its tines. The fork hovers.

"This is the price of getting to *el norte*," Neli says.

After some excruciating measure of seconds, Ixchel finds her voice, the Spanish words that are familiar. *La violación.* "Rape? Is the price?"

Both women look at her blankly. They cannot believe this is news to her. Has she been living under a rock before now?

"How did you end up here, *mamita*?" Neli asks, returning her attention to the food.

Ixchel does not answer.

Julia leans in and drops her voice low. "I have paid twice already."

This disclosure, shared with a woman she seemed to shun only moments ago, is such an unexpected intimacy that Lydia makes a noise in her throat without meaning to. A wound of a sound. All three women look at her as she takes a sip of fruit punch and sets her still-full fork on the edge of her plate.

"How about you?" Julia returns her attention to Neli. "Have you paid?"

"Not yet," Neli says grimly.

"You?" They all look expectantly at Lydia.

She shakes her head.

A smiling young woman approaches the table where Luca is sitting with the other children. "Who's ready for a puppet show?" she asks.

The little girl beside Luca shoots out of her chair, arms raised. "Me, me!" she says.

"Good, I need lots of helpers!"

"I heard he was a *sicario*."

This information snaps Lydia's focus back to her own table. "What?" she says, accidentally.

"That's the rumor." Julia shrugs. "Seems like they should know better than to let those narcos in."

"But he told the padre he was getting out," Neli intercedes. "Told him he got recruited by the cartel when he was just a kid and he never had any choice, you know the story. Had enough of that life and wanted to go to *el norte*."

"Which cartel?" Ixchel asks because like most people, because of her personal experience, she's more afraid of one particular cartel than others.

"What does it matter?" Neli says. "They're all the same. *Animales*."

"They're not," Julia insists. "Some of them are way worse than others."

Neli makes a face like she's skeptical, but doesn't argue.

"Like Los Jardineros," Julia says. "I heard they donated money to build a new cancer hospital in Acapulco."

Lydia takes a sharp breath, but Neli waves a hand dismissively. "That's just trying to buy people's loyalty," she says. "Propaganda."

"But maybe the reason is less important than the fact," Julia says. Then she drops her voice to a whisper and leans in again, closing the space across the table to a tight circle. She names the unnameable cartel. "Los Zetas feed people their own body parts. Los Zetas hang babies from bridges."

Lydia covers her mouth with her hand. Her fingers are cold and stiff, and beside her, Ixchel is crossing herself. Lydia will ask a question now, but she'll make her voice light. Neutral.

"So last night, the guy who got kicked out—which cartel was he?"

Julia shrugs. "I don't know," she says. "But if he really wants out, he better run. Far and fast, right? They don't let those guys go."

Lydia pushes her plate away. *Far and fast,* she thinks. Some things are so simple.

CHAPTER FOURTEEN

Six days and 282 miles from absolute calamity, Lydia and Luca take their leave from Huehuetoca and head north once again, following the trail of La Bestia. When Lydia considers how they've managed to survive the last week, to get this far from Acapulco and remain alive, her mind seizes. Because she knows she's made both good and bad decisions in those six days, and that ultimately, it's only by the grace of God that none of those choices have met with bad luck and resulted in catastrophe. That awareness incapacitates her. She can't conceive of a plan to board the train, which is what they must do. They must get on the train. Meanwhile, walking will give her time to think. They filled their canteens before they left the shelter, but they stop at a small shop down the road and Lydia jams her bag with snacks. Because it's a shop that's used to migrants, they stock the kinds of things that migrants can carry and eat: nuts, apples, candy, granola, chips, *carne seca*. Lydia buys as much as she can fit in her pack. She buys a floppy hat, too, pink with white flowers, to protect her neck from the sun. It reminds her of the ugly thing Mamá used to put on when she gardened, and any time Lydia and Yemi caught their mother wearing it, they would titter and tease.

"You laugh, but this hat is the reason I have the skin of a twenty-four-year-old!" their mother would chide them.

Back outside, the freight tracks stretch out across the Mexican landscape like a beanstalk migrants must climb, and Luca and Mami go step

by step, tie by tie, leaf by leaf. The sun is bright, but not too hot this early
in the day. They hold hands briefly, and then sweat and separate, and then
the cycle repeats. They take the westernmost route because Luca's mind-
map was convinced that, though that way was longer than the others,
the relative topography would be kinder if they end up making much
of the journey by foot, as it appears they might. He's glad Mami didn't
press him to explain his instinct; she simply yielded to the gentle pressure of his hand as they'd set off.

Lydia knows that her plan to go to Denver is inadequate, that it might
be difficult to track down her *tío* Gustavo. Abuela used to complain that
her baby brother had turned into a gringo when he left for *el norte* all
those years ago, when he was still a young man, and never looked back.
Lydia knows only that her *tío* married a white lady, changed his name to
Gus, and started his own company, something in construction. Was it
plumbing or electric? And what if he changed his last name, too? She's
never met his children, her *primos* yanquis. She doesn't even know their
names. When she dwells too long on these facts, she begins to panic,
so she strips it all back to manageable, step-by-step pieces: *Move north.
Reach the border. Find a coyote. Get across. Take a bus to Denver.* There
will be churches there. Libraries, internet access, immigrant communities. People willing to help. For now just move north, move north. Get
Luca out of danger.

A couple hours' walk northwest of the migrant shelter, Luca and
Mami encounter two teenage sisters wearing matching rainbow wristbands on their slender left arms, sitting on an overpass above the train
tracks, and dangling their feet below. Both girls are very beautiful, but
the slightly older one is dangerously so. She wears baggy clothing and an
intense scowl in a failing effort to suppress that calamitous beauty. The
younger one leans back on her stuffed backpack, but they both sit up
when they see Luca. The studied hardness of their expressions melts.
Together they make the "oh" of cuteness that teenage girls often emit for
smaller children.

"¡*Mira, qué guapo!*" the younger sister sings out in an unfamiliar
accent.

"So cute," the older one agrees.

They both have abundant black hair; stark, expressive eyebrows;

dark, penetrating eyes; perfectly aligned teeth; full lips; and apple-shaped cheeks. The older one has something extra, something undefinable that makes her entirely arresting. Luca fixes his eyes on her accidentally and cannot seem to remove his gaze once it's alighted upon her. Mami does, too. The girl is so beautiful she seems almost to glow, more colorful than the landscape in which she sits. The dingy gray of the concrete over-pass, the pebble brown of the tracks and the earth, the faded blue of her baggy jeans, the dirty white of her oversize T-shirt, the bleached arc of the sky, it all recedes behind her. Her presence is a vivid throb of color that deflates everything else around her. An accident of biology. A living miracle of splendor. It's a real problem.

"*Oye, ¿adónde van, amigos?*" the less beautiful one calls out to them when they're directly beneath her feet.

"Where everyone goes," Lydia says, shielding her eyes so she can look up at the girls above them. "To *el norte.*" She removes the ugly pink hat from her head and uses it to fan herself. Beneath it, her sweaty hair sticks to her forehead.

"Us, too!" she says, swinging her feet. "Your son is so cute!"

Lydia looks over at Luca, who's smiling up at the girls, the most gen-uine smile that's escaped his face since the morning of Yénifer's *quince-añera.*

"My name is Rebeca, and this is my sister, Soledad." The girl speaks to Luca directly. "*¿Cómo te llamas, chiquito?*"

Lydia, who's fallen into the habit of answering for her silent son, opens her mouth to reply but—

"Luca," he says. His voice clear like a bell, no hint of rust from all those days without use. Lydia snaps her mouth shut in surprise.

"How old are you, Luca?" Rebeca asks.

"I am eight years old."

The sisters look at each other with animation, and the younger one claps her hands together. "I knew it! Just exactly the same age as our little cousin at home. His name is Juanito. He looks like you! Doesn't he look like Juanito, Sole?"

Soledad the Beauty smiles reluctantly. "He does," she admits. "Like twins."

"You want to see his picture?" Rebeca asks. Luca looks at Mami, who's been very cautious about stopping to talk with people. But these girls have returned her boy's voice to him. She nods. "Come up!" Rebeca says.

She removes a fragile plastic bag of wrapped photographs from the front pocket of her sister's backpack and flips through them. Luca scrambles up to join the girls on the overpass while Mami watches from below. She tries to survey their location, but the seam of land cut by the tracks here makes a poor vantage point for visibility, so she follows Luca up the steep, sandy little hill. The girls aren't actually sitting on the overpass at all, but on a metal grate that sticks off the roadway on one side of the overpass like a hazardous catwalk. Lydia tests it with her foot before stepping over. Luca squats on the roadway side, leaning his elbows on the low guardrail. Rebeca leans back against this, and together they stare at the pictures.

"See?" she says. *"Guapo como tú."*

Luca grins again, and nods. "He does look like me, Mami, look," he says. "Except no teeth."

Rebeca holds the photograph so Lydia can see. "He lost those two both on the same day, and then he was like a vampire," the girl says to Luca. "Did you lose yours yet?"

A potent memory. It looms up unbidden: Papi pulling his first tooth—a bottom one, from the middle. The tooth had been loose for weeks and then one night during dinner, Luca took a bite of his *tampiqueña* and a point of pain shot through his gums. He dropped his fork, moved the food to the back of his mouth, swallowed it in an unchewed lump, and then examined the damage. The tooth, he found, had been pushed askew. It leaned like an ancient grave in soft ground. He touched it softly with one finger, and was horrified by its slackness. Mami and Papi both put down their forks to watch. But Luca was so afraid of the pain that he found himself unable to do anything. And then Mami had tried, for perhaps twenty minutes, to coax him to open his mouth just a little so she could have a look. But Luca was steadfast and mute, his lips clamped shut. When Mami finally lost her patience, Papi eased into place beside Luca. He made funny faces intended to illustrate what happened to children who didn't allow for the timely removal of ejected teeth. And

Luca laughed despite his fear, and in the gap of that laughter, he finally submitted to opening his little mouth while Mami watched from across the table. Papi reached in there so gently Luca didn't even feel the presence of his fingers against the tooth. But he does remember Papi's hands along his face, one securely cupping his chin, the other reaching inside. Luca remembers the salty tang of Papi's fingers and the triumphant smile when those fingers emerged with the prize of that tiny tooth. Luca's eyes popped so wide when he saw it, and he gasped. He couldn't believe there was no pain, no feeling at all. Papi had simply reached in there and lifted the little thing out. And then they all laughed and squealed at the table together, and Luca jumped out of his chair, disbelieving, and his parents both hugged and kissed him. He ate the rest of his *tampiqueña* while the new hole in his mouth gathered small pieces of food he had to sluice out with milk. That night they left the tooth beneath his pillow and El Ratoncito Pérez came to retrieve it, leaving Luca a poem and a new toothbrush in its place.

Luca lifts one hand to his mouth now and sucks on his knuckle, but it's not the same, and he has to bat at that memory like a pesky bug. A horsefly. The gone taste of his father's hands. Mami sees this, reaches out, and squeezes his toe through his sneaker, just a gentle pressure that brings him back to this dusty overpass. He breathes into his body.

"Couldn't get on the train, huh?" Among other things, Soledad has a gift for changing the subject at exactly the right moment. She's more tentative than her sister, but it's hard to remain standoffish with Luca there, all eyelashes and coy dimples.

Lydia wriggles out of her backpack and retrieves a canteen. "Not yet."

"They've made it a lot harder. *Safety first!*" Rebeca discharges a puff of air that, in another setting, might pass for laughter.

"Yeah." Mami shakes her head. "Safety."

"You've been on the trains?" Luca asks.

Soledad twists to look at him, resting her chin on her shoulder. "All the way from Tapachula, more or less."

Luca thinks of the men running alongside the train in the clearing outside Lechería, the way they ascended, one by one, and disappeared, while he and Mami watched, unable to move. He thinks of the deafening roar and clatter of La Bestia, shouting its warnings into their hearts and bones while they watched, and he feels awed by these two powerful sisters. "How?" he asks.

Soledad shrugs. "We've learned some tricks."

Mami hands Luca a canteen, and he drinks. "Like what?" Mami asks. "We need some tricks."

Soledad retracts her dangling legs and folds them beneath her, shifting her spine and shoulders into a stretched posture, and Lydia sees, even in this minor animation of the girl's body, how the danger rattles off her relentlessly. These sisters haven't befriended anyone since they left home; they, too, have kept to themselves as much as possible. But they haven't yet met anyone so young as Luca on their journey. Neither have they met anyone so watchfully maternal as Lydia. So it's a great pleasure to feel normal for a minute, to inhabit the softness of a friendly conversation. There can't be any harm in sharing some advice with their fellow travelers.

"Like this," Soledad says, gesturing at the tracks beneath them. "One thing we noticed is they spend all that money on fences around the train stations, but nobody has thought yet to fence the overpasses."

Luca watches Mami's face as she surveys their position now from the angle of this new information. Mami leans ever so slightly forward and gauges the distance to the ground beneath them. It's not that far. But then she tries to imagine how this space would change with the noise and weight and presence of La Bestia charging through it. "You board from here?" she asks incredulously.

"Not here," Soledad corrects her. "Because you'd hit your head as soon as you dropped. The overpass would knock you right off before you got your balance. We sit on this side to watch for it coming. But then you jump on over there." She points.

Luca follows the direction of her gesture across the roadway, and he sees there, affixed to the guardrail, a bleached white cross with a burst of faded orange flowers at its center. Likely a memorial, he realizes, for someone else who attempted to board the train at this place, and didn't manage it. He bites his lip. "You just jump on top?"

"Well, not always," Soledad says. "But, yes, if the conditions are right, you just jump on top."

"And what makes the conditions right?" Lydia asks. "Or wrong?"

"Well. The first thing is, you have to choose carefully where to do it. So this place is good because you see," she says, standing and pointing across the roadway to the tracks beyond, "you see the curve there, just ahead?"

Lydia stands, too, so she can see where the girl is pointing.

"The train always slows down for a curve. When it's a big curve, it slows way down. So we know it'll be going slow when it passes. And then the next thing is to make sure there are no other hazards ahead. That's why we chose this overpass instead of the first one."

Lydia looks south, back along the path they just walked. She hadn't even noticed that first overpass when they'd walked beneath it. She'd only been grateful for its momentary shade, a shallow respite from the sun.

"Because if you jumped on over there, on that one," Rebeca adds, taking up the explanation for her sister, "you'd only have a moment to get your balance before you'd have to hit the deck to pass beneath this one. Tricky."

Lydia blinks and shakes her head. She can't envision it.

"So we sit here," Soledad continues. "We watch. We wait for the train. And when we see one we like, we cross the road, we gauge the speed, we make the decision to board, and then we drop."

"Like going off a diving board?" Luca asks, thinking of the water park at El Rollo.

"Not exactly," Soledad says. "First you lower your backpack, because it makes you top-heavy, wobbly. So you toss that first. And then you squat down really low. You don't dangle, because if you do that your feet will get going with the train and then your top half won't catch up. You get stretched like a slingshot. So you roll your body up small and hop on like a frog. Low and tight. And just make sure your fingers grab something right away."

Luca's heart is hammering in his chest just thinking about it. He reminds himself to breathe. Then he looks at Mami, taking it in, considering their likelihood of survival. He feels a sudden surge of manic energy coursing through his body, so he has to stand and spring and kick and let it loose into the world.

"If you get really lucky, sometimes the train might even stop," Rebeca says. "And then you just climb down. Simple."

"But there's plenty of times we let a train go by, too," Soledad says.

"If it's moving fast, we don't even try. We've already seen two people who tried to board and didn't make it."

Lydia looks at Luca to see how this information will affect him, but he gives nothing away.

"Were those people boarding the same as you? From the top like this?"

"No!" Rebeca seems almost proud. "We're the only ones who board like this. I haven't seen anybody else do it."

Lydia screws up her mouth. So these girls are either brilliant or insane. "How many times have you done this?" she asks.

The sisters look at each other, and it's Soledad who answers. "Five, maybe? Six?"

Lydia lets out a deep, low breath. She nods. "Okay."

"You want to come with us?" Rebeca asks. It's not until after the words are out that she glances at her sister, remembering they're always supposed to check with each other first about everything. Soledad touches the top of Rebeca's head, and the gesture reassures her sister in the language of their lifelong intimacy that it's fine.

"Maybe," Lydia answers, ignoring the hitch in her lungs as she expels the word.

They talk a little while they wait, and Lydia learns that the girls are fifteen and fourteen years old, that they've traveled over a thousand miles so far, that they miss their family very much, and that they've never been on their own before. They don't say why they left home, and Lydia doesn't ask. They both remind her of Yénifer, though it's probably only their age. The sisters are taller and more slender, darker skinned than her niece, and both are luminous and funny. Yénifer had been studious and solemn. Even as a baby she'd had a certain gravity to her.

Lydia's older sister, Yemi, had selected Lydia, who was just seventeen the year their father died and Yénifer was born, to be the girl's godmother. Lydia remembers holding the baby over the baptismal font and crying. She made sure not to wear mascara that day so she wouldn't stain the baptismal dress. She'd known she would cry, not from joy or the honor of being the godmother or the emotion of the moment, but because her father wasn't there to see it. So Lydia's own tears had splattered across the child's forehead along with the holy water, and Lydia was surprised to see, through the blur of her vision, that the baby in her arms didn't join in her tears. Yénifer's eyes were wide and blinking. Her mouth, a perfect and puckered pink bow. Lydia loved that baby so much that she couldn't imagine she'd ever love her own child more. When Luca was born, years later, Lydia learned the incomparability of that kind of love, of course. But it was still Yénifer, that somber, shining girl, who had allayed her grief when she lost the second baby. Wise little Yénifer at nine years old, who'd cried with her and stroked her forehead and reassured her, "But you do have a daughter, Tía. You have me."

The enormity of Lydia's loss is incomprehensible. There are so many griefs at once that she can't separate them. She can't feel them. Beside her, the sisters talk lightly to Luca and he responds with his reanimated words. There's an effervescence among them that feels extraordinary. The sound of Luca's voice is an elixir.

The sun feels hotter when they're sitting still, and Lydia notices that her arms are as tan as childhood. Luca, too, is a shade browner than usual, and there are dots of perspiration all along his hairline beneath Sebastián's cap. But the wait beneath that sapping sun is almost too brief, Lydia thinks. She could've used more time to talk herself into this. It's not even two hours before the distant rumble of the train grows into their consciousness and all four of them rise without speaking and begin to ready themselves. In truth, Lydia's in no way convinced that they're actually going to go through with it. She hopes they do because they need to be on that train. And she hopes they don't, because she doesn't want to die. She doesn't want Luca to die. She feels as if she's outside her own body, listening to that train approach, moving her backpack to the other side of the roadway, prompting Luca along in front of her. She packs their canteen into the front pocket of her backpack and zips it up. Even if she felt confident that she could jump onto a moving train, how can she ask her son to do this crazy thing? Her shoulders feel loose, her legs erratic beneath her. Adrenaline sluices all through her jittery body.

Beside her, Luca follows a crack in the asphalt beneath his sneakers. He keeps his eyes and thoughts fixed on the minutiae. He leaves it to Mami to take in the broad sweep of the task at hand: the dun-colored grasses and scrubby trees crowding the embankment, the dome of blue overhead, the overpass and train tracks intersecting like a cross.

The wind fuzzes through Luca's hair as the noise of the train grows closer, the booming clatter and reverberation of those monster wheels hauling themselves along the metal of the track—the very loudness of that noise seems designed as a warning that enters through your ears but lodges in your sternum: *stay away, stay away, stay away, don't be crazy, don't be crazy, don't be crazy.* Luca holds his backpack by the top handle, low in front of him with both hands. There's one kid at school who's a daredevil. Her name is Pilar, and she's always doing crazy stunts. She leaps from the very top of the jungle gym. She flies from the highest arc of the swing. Once, she climbed a tree beside the school gate and shimmied out on an upper limb, from where she climbed onto the roof of the school building. She did cartwheels up there until the principal called her *abuela* to come talk her down. But not even Pilar would jump onto a moving train from an overpass, Luca thinks. Pilar would never, in a million years, believe steady, rule-following Luca capable of participating in such madness. He watches the nose of the train approach and disappear beneath the southern edge of the roadway. He turns then, and sees it emerge from beneath his feet. Mami peers over the edge of the low guardrail just as the train pulls itself into view.

"It's good." Rebeca smiles at them. "Nice and slow."

"Ready?" Soledad says.

Her little sister nods. Lydia's face is grim while she watches the girls. Luca studies the stretch of the train and sees a few migrants clustered near the tail end, on the last five or six cars. One is standing, silhouetting his body into an X, and he waves at them. Luca waves back.

"Let's go," Soledad says.

She and her sister line up beside each other, smack in the center of the track. They squat, holding their packs beneath them, and wait for the right car. They look for one that's flat on top. One that has the kind of grating you can walk on, sit on, grab onto. The first half of the train is all rounded tanker cars, so they wait. And then finally, quite slowly, Soledad tosses her pack and then follows it. With one graceful, chaotic, suicidal lurch, she moves her body from the fixed to the moving, she drops—Lydia can't tell how far it is—six feet? ten?—and then the girl is instantly receding, her form growing smaller as she moves away with the train.

"Come on!" she shouts back to her sister. "Now!"

And then Rebeca, too, is gone, and Lydia realizes how quickly this has to happen, that they have no time to weigh their options, no time to consider best practices. She rejects the awareness that all her life she's been afraid she would jump accidentally, like that girl from her favorite novel, from cliffs, from balconies, from bridges. But now she knows, with 100 percent certainty, she knows she would never have jumped, that the fear has always been an elaborate trick of her mind. Her heels are glued to the roadway. A week ago she'd have screamed at Luca to get back from there. She'd have told him not to stand so close to the edge. She'd have reached out and grabbed his arm to convince herself that he was safe, that he would stay put. Now she has to launch her child onto this moving train beneath them. The small cluster of migrants on the last few cars is approaching. They duck low to pass beneath the roadway and then, when they emerge on the other side, they're facing Lydia, their arms open wide, they gesture at her to toss the backpacks. She tosses the backpacks. And then she grabs Luca by his two shoulders, stands behind him.

"Step over," she instructs him.

Luca steps over without hesitation or objection. His heels are on the roadway. The toes of his little blue sneakers stick out into the air as the train passes beneath them. Luca hums to cover the dreadful noise of the train.

"Squat low," she tells him. "Just like the girls did."

He squats low. If he jumps from this place and dies, it will be because he did exactly what Lydia told him to do. She feels as though she's watching herself in a nightmare doing a monstrous thing that makes her panic. A thing, thank God, that she would never do in real life. And then just as she's about to reel him in, to crush his small head against her chest, to wrap him in her arms and weep with relief that she wakened in time, she hears it. With conviction, Sebastián's voice, cutting through all the external and internal noise.

The voice, then, when she opens her mouth and screams into Luca's ear, is almost not her own. "Go, Luca! Jump!"

Luca jumps. And every molecule in Lydia's body jumps with him. She sees him, the tight tuck of him, how small he is, how absurdly brave he is, his muscles and bones, his skin and hair, his thoughts and words and ideas, the very bigness of his soul, she sees all of him in the moment when his body leaves the safety of the overpass and flies, just momentarily, upward because of the effort of his exertion, until gravity catches him and he descends toward the top of La Bestia. Lydia watches him drop, her eyes so big with fear they've almost left her body. And then he lands like a cat on all fours, and the velocity of his leap clashes with the velocity of the train, and he topples and rolls, and one leg splays toward the edge of the train, pulling his weight with it, and Lydia tries to scream his name, but her voice has snagged and gone, and then one of the migrant men catches him. One big, rough hand on Luca's arm, the other on the seat of his pants. And Luca, caught, safe in the strong arms of this train-top stranger, lifts his moving face to seek her. His eyes catch her eyes.

"I did it, Mami!" he screams. "Mami! Jump!"

Without a thought in her head except Luca, she jumps.

CHAPTER FIFTEEN

The year before Sebastián's murder, Mexico was the deadliest country in the world to be a journalist, no safer than an active war zone. No safer even than Syria or Iraq. Journalists were being murdered in cities all across the country. Tijuana, Ciudad Juárez, Chihuahua. And yet, because Los Jardineros didn't specifically target reporters the way most cartels did, Sebastián hadn't received an official cartel death threat for almost two years. So it's not quite accurate to say that Sebastián and Lydia felt a false sense of security; no one in Acapulco felt secure. The free press was a critically endangered species in Mexico. But in the aftermath of their discovery that Lydia's friend was La Lechuza, the absence of an explicit warning from him, combined with the fact of her fraught but genuine attachment to Javier, functioned as a sort of short-term analgesic for the worst of their personal fears.

Sebastián continued to take the usual precautions: he avoided adhering too closely to a daily routine, he limited driving his recognizable orange Beetle to crime scenes, and whenever he wrote a particularly risky piece, he used the anonymous byline STAFF WRITER to conceal his identity. In those cases, the paper also sprang for a hotel room in the tourist district. He'd take Lydia and Luca and they'd hunker down for a few days out of sight. When it appeared that retaliation was not forthcoming, they'd reemerge and continue with their lives. But those safeguards were largely illusory. Sebastián knew that any research he conducted, any crime he investigated, any source he contacted, was a potential land mine. He was as careful as a truth-telling Mexican journalist can be.

For her part, Lydia became hypervigilant for any signs of danger. Javier continued to visit her in the bookstore almost weekly, and the torment she'd felt the first night she'd discovered the truth about him slowly gave way to something else. She still sat with him, served him coffee, spoke with him about a range of subjects. She listened twice more when he read her poems from his Moleskine notebook. She even smiled authentically at him, and despite a sickening feeling of culpability and a reluctance to admit it, she was still charmed by him. His intellect, his warmth, his vulnerability and sense of humor—none of it had changed. Yet, when there was news of a fresh murder, which happened more infrequently than before but not infrequently enough, Lydia experienced a sort of exaggerated emotional flinch, and she knew that her careful retreat from him was not only necessary but also inevitable. Her behavior need only follow what her heart had already accomplished.

"What if we tell him?" Lydia said to Sebastián the week before Yénifer's *quinceañera*.

They'd dropped Luca at her sister, Yemi's, house earlier for a sleepover with Adrián.

"Tell who what?"

"Tell Javier about the article. Before it comes out."

Sebastián closed his leather menu and set it down on his plate.

"*¿Estás loca, mujer?*"

She was buttering a warm roll from the covered basket, and didn't look up at him. "Yes. But I think I'm serious, too." She pressed the butter into the bread and waited for it to soften.

Sebastián looked away from her, out over the water. The restaurant was on a hilltop above the bay and it was dusk, and he could see lights winking through the valley below, their ghost-lights glimmering echoes in the water. He didn't want to consider the idea. He wanted to consider the view and the menu and his beautiful wife. After years of narco journalism he'd become good at compartmentalizing, at putting all the ugliness away. Sebastián was skilled at enjoying himself. But he respected Lydia and didn't want to be dismissive.

"If we talk about this for two minutes, do you promise then that we can not talk about it for the rest of the night?" he asked.

"Yes." She smiled and bit into her bread.

"Okay," he said. "Why would we tell him? What's the benefit of doing that?"

She took a sip of water. "To gauge his response ahead of time, to know what we're up against." Sebastián sat very still while he listened. "Maybe he'd even meet with you. You could get him to go on the record."

"Do you think he'd do that?"

"I don't know. Maybe? I mean, we know how smart he is. Maybe he'd see it as an opportunity to try and control the message. Get some good PR, get out ahead of the curve."

"Every narco has a Robin Hood complex."

"Right, so you appeal to that. Maybe he'd even like it."

"But that's exactly what I'm afraid of. I can't be beholden to him."

"No, I know."

"But *he* might not know. He might think this means I'm his new PR guy. I'm on his payroll after this."

"*Ay.*" Lydia grimaced.

"It's too risky," Sebastián said, opening his menu. "What are you going to eat?"

Lydia read the article on Monday evening, the night before it went to press. She and Sebastián had to calculate the level of risk, to determine their safest course of action for the coming days. The paper had offered to put them up in a hotel again, to get them out of sight. The piece would not be published under his name, but it would be easy enough to figure out who'd written it. Any one of his sources could reveal him to Javier. They already may have.

Sebastián paced behind her while she read at the kitchen table from his laptop: LA LECHUZA REVEALED: PORTRAIT OF A DRUG LORD. The story was accompanied by several photographs. Sebastián and his editor had selected a flattering picture of Javier, sitting elegantly with his legs crossed at the knee, one arm draped across the back of a velvet couch. He wore dark jeans and a tweed blazer, and looked every inch the bookish professor, his eyes warm behind the thick glasses, his face smiling but not smug. Lydia thought again of the first morning he'd come into the shop, how deeply his friendship, his vulnerability, had affected her in the months before she understood who he was. She still felt reluctant to learn more unpleasant things about him. She still felt a memory of fondness for him, which unnerved her. She pressed her eyes closed and took a deep breath before she began.

She was amazed by Sebastián's familiarity with his subject—he clearly knew a very different Javier than she did, and yet the account was both objective and compassionate. In her husband's words, she recognized her friend's intensity, but she also discovered for the first time the gruesome details of Javier's capacity for cruelty. The beheadings were only the beginning. Los Jardineros were also known to dismember their victims and rearrange their body parts into horror show tableaux. According to Sebastián's report, during Los Jardineros' war with the previous cartel, Javier was rumored to have shot the two-year-old son of a rival while the boy's father watched. He'd painted the man's face with the blood of his murdered child. Those details had been mythologized, of course; there was no proof of that brutality, but when she read that, Lydia closed her eyes for nearly three minutes before she could continue. The article also highlighted the grisly statistics of Javier's ascension: during the transition of power, Acapulco's murder rate was the highest in Mexico and one of the highest in the world. The city hemorrhaged tourism, investment, young people, and that kind of bleeding was difficult to stanch even after the violence tapered off. It was also true that, though the bloodshed had become less visible to the average citizen in recent months, there were still a dozen or more murders in the city each week. In addition to those numbers, countless more had silently disappeared. The very essence of Acapulco had changed; its people were permanently altered. Entire neighborhoods were abandoned as people fled the rubble of their lives and headed north. For those who left, *el norte* was the only destination. If a tourist mecca like Acapulco could fall, then nowhere in Mexico was safe.

The profile drew a bright line between Javier's ascent and the truth of the city's ruin. It was a brutal new cosmopolis, and its ugliness was underscored by the memory of Acapulco's glorious past. Sebastián's account was heartbreaking, unvarnished, and utterly convincing. It also credited Javier with the dawning peace, commended the control he exercised over his men, and appealed to him for continued restraint. It ended with a psychological profile of the man himself, and as Lydia read it, she knew it to be exactly true. Unlike his contemporaries and predecessors, La Lechuza was not flashy, gregarious, or even particularly charismatic. He seemed enlightened. But like every drug lord who's ever risen to such a rank, he was also shrewd, merciless, and ultimately delusional. He was a vicious mass murderer who mistook himself for a gentleman. A thug who fancied himself a poet. The article ended with the inclusion of a poem written by Javier himself, and Lydia's mouth dropped clean open when she saw it there in print. She knew this poem. The first one he'd ever shared with her.

"How in God's name did you get this?" she whispered.

Sebastián stopped pacing long enough to lean over her shoulder. Lydia read the poem again, even more terrible printed there on-screen than it had been when Javier had entrusted it to her.

"Oh, yeah," Sebastián said. "That was crazy. You know we run that annual poetry contest? His daughter, Javier's daughter, sent it in. She submitted it on his behalf. I guess she wanted to surprise him."

"Wow," Lydia said. "Marta."

The inclusion of the poem was mortifying. It served to coalesce all the facts into a vivid portrayal and to corroborate, somehow, the accuracy of Sebastián's description. As she closed the browser and leaned back in her chair, Lydia discovered that there were many different ways to feel horrified at once.

"Well?" Sebastián shoved his hands into the pockets of his jeans and leaned back against the kitchen counter. He was barefoot and his socks were twisted into a small heap on the counter behind him. Lydia stared at those socks. "What do you think?"

She folded her hands beneath her chin and shook her head. "I think it's fine."

"Fine? Not *good*?"

"No, I mean it's good. It's good, Sebastián, I'm not talking about that. I mean I think it'll be fine with Javier."

He nodded at her. "Okay."

They were quiet while she contemplated further. "In fact, I think it will be better than fine with Javier. I think he'll like it. It's fair. More than fair, almost flattering."

He nodded some more. "You feel confident?"

Again, she waited a moment to make sure her answer was true before she said it. "Yes."

Sebastián went to the fridge, retrieved two beers, twisted off both caps, and set one down in front of his wife.

"I'm not gonna lie, I'm a little nervous." He tipped the bottle into his mouth and drained half at once. "I'm relieved you feel good about it, though. You're sure it's okay." He watched Lydia twist her brown bottle in circles on the table. "You don't think we need to disappear for a few days, just to be on the safe side?"

She knew how important it was to be sure. She didn't fling the answer out recklessly; she measured it first. And then, "No, I think we're fine," she said.

"A hundred percent?"

"Yes. A hundred percent." She closed the laptop and pushed it away.

Sebastián was leaning against the counter. He hadn't shaved that morning, and there was a shadow of stubble across his chin. "Are you surprised? You think it's too sympathetic?" he asked.

"No. I mean, it's still horrifying." She sipped from the bottle. "But accurate. You show that he's human. So as far as the truth goes, I think he'll be pleased."

That was a Monday evening, less than two weeks ago. Lydia remembers it was Monday because she'd just brought Luca home from *fútbol* practice and he'd been hungry, so she'd given him a slice of toast and a banana, even though he was late getting to bed. He'd tracked dirt into the hallway because he forgot to take his cleats off at the door, and Lydia had been annoyed because she'd just swept. Less than two weeks ago, dirt on the floor in her hallway was a thing that could annoy her. It's unimaginable. The reality of what happened is so much worse than the very worst of her imaginary fears had ever been.

But it could be worse still.

Because there is still Luca.

On top of the train, Lydia takes two of the canvas belts from her pack and secures one through the back belt loop of Luca's jeans before threading it through a metal loop atop the grating where they sit. Then she belts herself to the top of the train in the same way. She doesn't know if that small strap of canvas would actually do much to save Luca, should he fall. All she can do is try. She imagines that most accidents happen when migrants are trying to get on and off the trains anyway.

Her feet smart in a way they haven't since she was a young girl leaping from the swings at a full arc, when she'd land with a thud, and feel that echo of tenderness reverberate up her legs. They're sore, but it's not a bad pain. It's only a reminder that she's alive, that her legs can be used like pistons and springs, that her feet can still make a racket beneath her. She flexes one leg and then the other, bangs her feet against the metal grating to loosen the ache. Rebeca and Soledad are a few cars ahead of them because they jumped earlier, but soon the girls make their way back to them, stepping along the tops of the freight cars, leaping across the gaps, ducking flat when the train passes beneath a roadway. Lydia performs a series of elaborate flinches while she watches them.

Soon they're all seated together, along with the four young men who were already here, including the one who caught Luca when he jumped. Lydia watches the men react to the girls' arrival. She studies their faces as, one by one, they absorb the circumstance of the girls' extreme beauty and one by one, they shift their bodies ever so slightly away from the teenage sisters. The men are deferential. They know what hardship lies along the road for these girls, and they're sympathetic to that danger. Soon they all move past it. The men smile at Luca. They tap him and point out interesting sights as they pass: a mother cow with her calf, a huddle of trees like a rugby scrum, a stark white cross atop a low hill. The men bless themselves when they go by a steeple or a roadside grave. They pray.

Those first few hours on La Bestia are exhilarating. The train ambles west and west and north, and Luca feels a giddy sense that they are really *going* now. It feels so good to be a passenger, to make fast progress with the power of machinery doing the work. They drink water from their canteens and eat granola bars. Lydia gives one to the sisters to share. Soledad and Rebeca sit back to back, their knees propped up like tent poles. Soledad eats her half in one gulp. Rebeca savors hers, picking crumbs from the corners and allowing them to dissolve in her mouth before swallowing.

The landscape rolls beneath them, shifting colors. Sometimes the trees draw close to the tracks, squat and scrubby. Sometimes they stand back and pierce the sky. Sometimes obstructions press in at the top of the train and threaten to knock the passengers off: overgrown foliage, the narrow structure of a bridge crossing over a ravine, and most alarmingly, the cramped tunnels, where the ceilings seem to skim just inches above their heads, and the echo of deafening noise amplifies the fear of falling. The migrants are alert to these dangers: they crouch, flatten, lean. They draw their arms and legs in and hold their breath.

Periodically, the train stops, and after a while, Luca begins to understand how to predict those interruptions. First, there will be an abrupt change of direction—that means there's a town nearby, large enough that whoever laid these tracks determined the train should go there. The train turns and lurches, slowing first for the change of direction, and then further as the town approaches. The migrants shift into postures of alertness, make themselves flat atop the cars, so Luca and Lydia do the same. They watch for the dark trucks and white stars of *la policía federal,* whose job it is to clear migrants from the trains.

"What happens if we see *la policía*?" Luca asks. He's lying flat on his stomach, stretched out between Mami and Soledad. Soledad faces him and rests her ear in the crook of her elbow.

"You run for your life, *chiquito,*" she says.

Sometimes the stops are brief, a few minutes; sometimes they last an hour or more, while the migrants hold their collective breath, their muscles taut, their senses strained. Their eyes comb the landscape for movement beyond the men loading and unloading freight from the hollow cars beneath them. Sometimes the working men throw snacks up to the migrants on top of the train before it leaves, or refill their water bottles from a nearby hose. Other times, it's as if the men have been warned not to aid the migrants, like they're invisible on top of the train, and those times are like careful choreography, all pretending not to see or be seen. And then at last, there's a whistle, a jerk, and the gradual acceleration of relief as the train resumes its journey to the next place. When the light descends to that golden, glowing hour, when it touches Soledad's skin like an uninvited spotlight, the sisters put their heads together and talk quietly for a few moments.

"We don't stay on the trains at night," Soledad explains to Lydia, after.

"We'll get off at the next place," Rebeca adds. "Whenever it stops again."

Lydia nods. She doesn't ask why.

"We'll get off then, too, right, Mami?" Luca asks.

It feels like the sisters have invited them, indirectly, to go with them. Rebeca looks to Lydia, the girl's face nearly as hopeful as Luca's. Soledad is harder to read, turning askance so Lydia can see only her profile. Lydia's loath to get off, after their difficulty boarding. Now that they're finally moving, she'd like to stay on the train all the way to *el norte*. But on the other hand, it's precisely because of these girls and their instructions that she and Luca managed to get on La Bestia at all. They've returned Luca's voice to him. They know things. "Okay," Lydia says.

When the train stops at San Miguel de Allende just before sunset, Luca and Lydia follow Soledad and Rebeca down the ladder. They wave goodbye to the men who remain behind, and wave hello to the men who are opening one of the freight cars to unload the waiting cargo. They set off quickly into the town.

San Miguel de Allende is immaculate, with low stone walls lining the streets, and manicured trees and flowers in the plazas. They follow a wide avenue as it swoops past a pink church, rosy in the setting sun, with pennant flags strung festively from the facade to the front gates of the churchyard. Luca can still feel the leftover vibration of the train in his bones as they walk. The concrete underfoot has a new sensation of active stillness. They pass a furniture store, a pharmacy, a bar, a fancy house with balconies, three men loitering beneath a palm tree, causing the sisters to quicken their steps. They pass new houses of stucco and old houses of stone, a supermarket, a *fútbol* field, a woman begging on the street, a nicer supermarket, and finally, a roundabout that seems to demarcate the downtown's edge.

The sisters walk by instinct, and they've become good at it, following the signs and the people, wending their way into the denser parts of town in search of *la plaza central*. They feel safest where it's clean and crowded. A hotel, a hardware store, a bus station, a statue of a winged angel attacking somebody with a sword, and the daylight descends from pink to purple. Beside a fruit vendor, a man sits astride a milk crate wearing a white cowboy hat. His accordion grows and shrinks in his hands like flamboyant lungs. He makes the music the whole street moves to. A lady is grilling meat nearby, and the aroma makes Luca's stomach twist in hunger, but they keep walking as the streets become narrow instead of broad, stone instead of tarmac. Paper lanterns stretch across the spaces overhead, affixed to the wrought iron balconies and bobbing in the urban breeze. It's different from Acapulco in every conceivable way except one: it's like a sensory postcard of a Mexican town. The sun sets west at their backs, making everything blush.

Luca squeezes his mother's hand. "Mami, I'm hungry."

"Good timing, *chiquito,*" Soledad says. "We're here."

Here is the Plaza Principal of San Miguel de Allende. They duck beneath the arched stone portico of a cinnamon-colored building and take a moment to rest. Luca lets go of Mami's hand and leans his pack against the wall behind him. In the plaza, people are eating *tortas* and drinking Cokes. They're chatting and laughing. Three mariachi bands in competing colors—orange, white, powder blue—keep just enough distance between them to be heard above their rivals. They stroll the corners of the plaza and romance the tourists with the brightness of their music. There's a band of odd trees that fills the square between them, their trunks tight and compact. The weird spread of their limbs above blends their foliage into one thick, spongy green ceiling. A riot of pink spires topped by a golden cross rises from the canopy like a fairy palace. It's the Parroquia de San Miguel Arcángel, and the church makes a stunning silhouette against the dusky sky.

"Crazy." Rebeca says the word they're all thinking.

It's one of the strangest places Luca has ever seen. And just as the

last ray of sunlight lifts diagonally from the Plaza Principal and slides
up the steeples on its way out of town, all at once the studded lampposts
blaze to light. The strings of lights around the tree trunks pop and glow.
It's overwhelming, to be in a beautiful, festive place like this. Lydia is
overcome by guilt. Because it feels incongruous and seductive and wrong
to witness the simple charm of a pretty place. She can see that same kind
of notion land across Luca's features, and she reaches for his hand. His
mind does this awful thing to remind him not to be enchanted: it floods
him with the helpful memory of all his dead family, the endless roll of
gunfire through Abuela's bathroom window, the screams outside, the futile press of Mami's hands against his ears, the single spot of his bright
red blood against the green shower tile. Everyone gone. Luca is gone with
them for a moment, so he doesn't hear Mami when she says his name.
He doesn't see the faces of Soledad and Rebeca swarm toward him in
sisterly concern. He's unaware of his own sobbing, the way he clamps his
hands over his head. He doesn't know how long he's gone, but when he
returns, he's tucked into the curl of Mami's body and she's rocking him.
Her hands through his hair, her voice a hum of tight comfort in his ear.

"Sh, *amorcito,* it's okay," Lydia says.

He nods. "I'm sorry. I'm sorry. I'm okay now."

But she doesn't let go.

Soledad catches Lydia's eye across the top of Luca's head, and some
byway of recognition darts between them. They perceive each other, the
unspoken trauma they've both endured, their reasons for being here. It's
as subtle and significant as a heartbeat.

And then Soledad says, "Rebeca, let's hurry now, and get him some
food. Figure out where to sleep."

Lydia funnels gratitude into the slow blink of her lashes.

The sisters return quickly with dinner. It's like a magic trick, so that
Lydia can see for the first time some benefit to their beauty. It's the best
food Luca and Lydia have eaten since the *quinceañera,* because the sisters
have learned important things. They don't bother with the street vendors, whose generosity might be contingent on feeding their own families first. Instead, Soledad and Rebeca have learned, it's best to find a
fancy restaurant, and befriend a young man there who may emerge for a
cigarette break or to make a delivery. That young man may find himself

beholden to the beauty and raw need of two young girls who are alone so far from home. Very often, the sisters have learned, that young man will disappear momentarily and return with two heaping containers of hot spaghetti, still steaming and tossed with garlic, oil, and salt. Perhaps there may also be a spoonful of Bolognese or some vegetables. A heel of warm bread. There is always a smile, a blessing, a flare of recognition from the hardworking young man who, because of the way beauty begets empathy (among other things), imagines his own little sister or cousin or daughter in the place of these girls. He bids them a safe journey, implores them to look after themselves. Sometimes he also provides forks. The girls are always effusive in their thanks. They call all of God's blessings down upon the young man's head.

On the broad pink steps of the elaborate church, Luca and Lydia, Soledad and Rebeca fall gratefully on the spaghetti. They eat in silence, sharing the two forks, until every morsel is gone. Lydia thanks the girls, and her spoken gratitude feels entirely insufficient, because what she really needs to say is that the food, yes, but also their kindness, their humanity, their very existence, has nourished some withered, essential part of herself. Rebeca and Luca have wandered over to rinse their hands in the fountain, but Soledad is looking directly at Lydia's face.

"Maybe we should stick together for a while," she says.

Lydia nods. "Yes."

Night collapses over the city. The bars and restaurants empty and shutter their doors for the night, and eventually, even the lingering mariachis disperse to their homes. As the lights of San Miguel de Allende falter and quench, the four travelers move their packs and their bodies toward the center of the plaza. They stretch themselves out on the municipal benches. *Like bums,* Luca thinks. It's their first night sleeping outdoors, and it doesn't feel like an adventure at all. He wants his bedroom with its stack of books on the floor and his *balón de fútbol* lamp. He wants Papi's warm shadow on the wall. But his belly is full and his head is resting on the squishy part of Mami's thigh, and Luca is exhausted. There's a tug-of-war in his heart already, between wanting to remember and needing to forget. In the months to come, Luca will sometimes wish he hadn't squandered these early days of his grief. He'll wish he'd let it pierce and demolish him more. Because, as the forgetting part takes anchor and stays, it will feel like a treachery. He'll mistakenly believe it's his own cowardice erasing Papi's details—the mole above his left eyebrow, the tight, rough little curls of his hair, the timbre of his voice when he laughs, the sandpaper feel of his jaw against Luca's forehead when they read together at night in Luca's bed. But Luca doesn't know any of that yet, nor does he know that, no matter what he does right now, that creeping amnesia is inevitable, it's not his fault. So, in fatigue, he pushes those memories away and shuts them out. He recites to himself the geographic particulars of Nairobi, Toronto, Hong Kong. Soon, he's snoring softly on his mother's lap.

Despite her bone-deep exhaustion, Lydia's the only one unable to sleep. She stiffens when a young couple approaches, tipsy and giggling. They steal beneath the trees for a kiss and then stop in their tracks when they see the darkened silhouette of Lydia sitting up on the bench, her backpack clutched in front of her like a shield, the sleeping figures of Luca and the sisters nearby. The children don't stir, and the couple quickly retreats. Behind the noise of crickets, their footsteps echo and diminish.

Lydia envies the chorus of shuffling breath around her, how easily young people can slip into their weariness like a warm bath. She used to do that, too, she remembers, before she was a mother. She could do anything back then, before she had maternal fear to spark any real caution in her soul. She'd been reckless in her youth. As a teenager, she'd dived from the cliffs at La Quebrada, just for the thrill, for the quaver that jolted through her when she leaped. She shudders now at the memory of that unnecessary danger and turns to look at the sleeping girls stretched head-to-head on the next bench over.

When at last a dim light begins to creep through the canopy, signaling the coming safety of daylight, Lydia's mind releases her to sleep.

CHAPTER SIXTEEN

The joke at home had always been that Luca and Sebastián shouldn't talk to Lydia until she was well into her second mug of morning coffee. She always had two at home and a third in the shop when she opened. She got into the habit of cleaning the filters and filling the carafe at night, so she wouldn't have to contend with all that in the morning when she was still half-asleep. It was the first thing she did each day when her alarm went off, on her way to the bathroom: she'd flip the power switch on the coffeemaker and feel a gurgle of happy impatience when the red light came on. On Sundays when she had extra time, she'd steam milk for froth, or brew the grounds with cane sugar and cinnamon for *café de olla*. Now there's no coffee at all most mornings, which triggers a daily headache, made worse when Lydia's exhausted from lack of sleep.

They return to the tracks early, and there are a dozen or so other migrants gathered there waiting for the train. Nearby, a man wearing nice jeans and a clean collared shirt stands at the back of a pickup truck with the tailgate folded down. Inside there's a huge pot of rice and a cooler stacked with steaming tortillas. He's the padre from the trackside church with the pennant flags, and before he feeds the migrants, he offers them Communion and gives a blessing. Then he fills the tortillas with the rice and hands them out. He also has a big orange barrel that says GATORADE even though it's fruit punch. One of the other migrants fills paper cups and hands them around to whoever's thirsty. Lydia and the girls sit on one of the benches and eat in silence. It's Luca who notices.

"Why are they waiting on that side of the track?" He points.

"Huh," Lydia says, chewing.

The migrants are gathered on the southbound side. Rebeca takes her tortilla with her as she walks over to the waiting men. She speaks with them, and then returns to explain.

"We've missed the Pacific Route," she says.

"What?" Soledad sounds alarmed.

"Not by much, don't worry." Rebeca sits down beside her sister. "Only an hour south of here is Celaya."

"Ah, the third-largest city in the state of Guanajuato," Luca interjects quietly.

Both girls turn to gawk at him, and he slurps his fruit punch, embarrassed.

Rebeca continues, "So we can ride the train south and change at Celaya for the Pacific Route."

"But why?" Lydia asks, sitting forward. "Isn't it shorter if we go this way?"

"It's not safe," Rebeca says. "Our cousin told us—"

"Everyone told us," Soledad corrects her.

"Everyone told us we have to take the Pacific Route. All the other routes are super dangerous because of the cartels."

The food is pasty in Lydia's mouth.

"Everyone says the same thing," Soledad agrees. "Only the Pacific Route is safe."

Lydia doesn't need to be convinced, but she does have a question. The girls seem to know a lot more than she does. "Do you know which cartels run which routes?"

"No, but God is watching out for us," Rebeca says. She makes the sign of the cross. "We will be okay."

Just to make sure, the sisters go into the church to light a candle while they wait.

When the southbound train comes through San Miguel de Allende, it doesn't stop, but it's traveling slowly, and the gathered men all board with ease. Luca watches the sisters jog along beside the train. Their fear makes them graceful and strong, their movements precise. Men wait at the top of the ladder to grab their hands and haul them onto the roof. Luca will not be left behind. He runs, and Mami with him, and he feels very brave until just at the moment when he grabs onto the advancing ladder, and the cursory vibration echoes into the palm of his hand and all down into the bones of his body, and that reverberation reminds him how small he is, and how colossal the train is, and how dead he would be if he let go at the wrong time. Mami's behind him, and she boosts him from the backside, and he grips the ladder so hard his knuckles turn colors, and he's almost afraid to let go with one hand so he can climb up to the next rung, but he knows he must because he has to make room for Mami. So he climbs, and the fear is like a balloon in his throat but now there are two men at the top, and one reaches down and grabs him by the backpack and the other by his upper arm, and now he's on top of the train and Rebeca is smiling at him and here comes Mami over the edge. They did it.

"*Qué macizo, chiquito.*" Rebeca is impressed.

He grins.

Luca has never liked a girl before. Okay, that's not exactly true, because he liked daredevil Pilar from school because she was really good at *fútbol,* and he liked his cousin Yénifer because she was nice to him like 85 percent of the time, even when she was mean to her brother, and he liked this one girl Miranda, who lived in their same apartment building, because she wore bright yellow sneakers and could make her tongue into the shape of a shamrock. So maybe it's more accurate to say that Luca's never been in love before. On top of the train, Luca watches Rebeca and tries to act like he's not watching Rebeca. Not that anyone would notice anyway, because everybody's too busy watching Soledad to notice anything else. In the half-light left over from Soledad's corona, Rebeca glimmers like a secret sun. She's stretched out on her back next to Luca on top of the train.

"So why'd you guys leave home?" she asks him.

Luca grinds his teeth and tries to formulate an answer quickly, before she can feel bad for having asked, but he can't think of anything to say.

"You running from your dad?" she guesses.

"No," Luca says. "Papi was great." He rolls onto his side so he can look at her even though that means his arm is no longer stretched alongside hers.

"Are you a spy?" she asks. "I won't tell anyone, I swear." She's holding a piece of cardboard over her face for shade, and her black hair is all looped through the holes in the metal grate beneath them.

"Yes," Luca says. "I'm a spy. My government received a tip about a nuclear warhead on this train. I'm here to save the universe."

"Thank God, it's about time." Rebeca laughs. "The universe needs saving."

The train rocks unevenly beneath them. Nearby, Mami chats quietly with Soledad.

"What about you?" he asks. "Why did you leave home?"

"Sigh." Rebeca frowns. She actually says the word *suspiro* instead of sighing, which is funny despite the unhappiness of her expression. "Everything was bad, in the end." She sits up. "Soledad is super pretty, you know?" She lifts the cardboard to the side of her face where the sun is.

"Is she? I didn't notice," Luca says.

"Payaso." Rebeca laughs and uses the cardboard to swat him on top of the head. "Anyway. We come from a really small place, only a little scrap of a village in the mountains, or not even a village, really, because of how stretched out it is, just a collection of different tucked-away places where people live. And it's a really out-of-the-way place—the city people call it a cloud forest, but we just call it home."

"Why cloud forest?" Luca asks.

Rebeca shrugs. "I guess because of all the clouds?"

Luca laughs. "But every place has clouds."

"Not like this," Rebeca says. "In my place, the clouds are not in the sky; they're on the ground. They live with us, in the yard, sometimes even in the house."

"Wow."

Rebeca half smiles. "It was always soft there. Enchanted. And there was no cell service or electricity in the house or things like that, and we lived there with our *mami* and *papi* and *abuela,* but it was pretty impossible to make a living in that place because there was no work, you know?"

Luca nods.

"So our *papi,* he was mostly away, living all the time in the city, in San Pedro Sula."

In his head, Luca thinks, *San Pedro Sula: second-largest city in Honduras, a million and a half people, murder capital of the world.* Out loud, he says, "Ah, you are Honduran."

"No," Rebeca corrects him. "Ch'orti'."

Luca makes his face into a question.

"Indian," she explains. "My people are Ch'orti'."

Luca nods, even though he doesn't really understand the difference.

"Anyway, Papi was a cook in this big hotel in San Pedro Sula, and it was almost a three-hour journey by bus from where we lived, so he only came home maybe once every couple of months to visit us. But that was still okay because this place, our little cloud forest, even though we missed our *papi,* it was the most beautiful place you've ever seen. We didn't really know that then, because it was the only place we'd ever seen, except in pictures in books and magazines, but now that I've seen other places, I know. I know how beautiful it was. And we loved it anyway even before we knew. Because the trees had these enormous dark green leaves, as big as a bed, and they would sway in the wind. And when it rained you could hear the big, fat raindrops splatting onto those giant leaves, and you could only see the sky in bright blue patches if you were walking a long way off to a friend's house or to church or something, when you passed through a clearing and all those leaves would back away and open up and the hot sunshine would beat down all yellow and gold and sticky. And there were waterfalls everywhere with big rock pools where you could take a bath and the water was always warm and it smelled like sunlight. And at night there was the sound of the tree frogs and the music of the rushing water from the falls and all the songs of the night birds, and Mami would make the most delicious *chilate,* and Abuela would sing to us in the old language, and Soledad and I would gather herbs and dry them and bundle them for Papi to sell in the market when he had a day off, and that's how we passed our days."

Luca can see it. He's there, far away in the misty cloud forest, in a hut with a packed dirt floor and a cool breeze, with Rebeca and Soledad and their *mami* and *abuela,* and he can even see their father, far away down the mountain and through the streets of that clogged, enormous city, wearing a long apron and a chef's hat, and his pockets full of dried herbs. Luca can smell the wood of the fire, the cocoa and cinnamon of the *chilate,* and that's how he knows that Rebeca is magical, because she can transport him a thousand miles away into her own mountain homestead just by the sound of her voice.

"The clouds were so thick you could wash your hair in them," she says. "But then one day something awful happened, because we were so isolated up there in our place, so when the narcos came through, and all the men from the village were gone away into the city for work, those bad men could do whatever they wanted. They could take whatever girls they wanted for themselves, and there was no one there to stop them."

Luca blinks hard at her. He doesn't want to experience this part. He suddenly dislikes Rebeca's easy magic, the way he can feel those men barging through the forest, their steaming bodies vaporizing the clouds around them as they swipe and stomp their way through the undergrowth. But he can't stop himself from asking the question. "Those bad men. They took you?"

"No." Rebeca makes a kind of face that reveals all her straight, white teeth, but it isn't a smile, not at all. "We were lucky because we heard the screams coming from our neighbors, because of the way those clouds could trap and funnel the sound, even from far away. So we stopped the fire from making its smoke, and we hid. They never found our place."

"Oh." Luca feels relieved. "But then?"

"But then after they were gone, and we discovered what had happened, that they'd taken four girls from our side of the mountain with them, our *mami* decided that very day that Soledad and I had to leave that place, even though it was the only place we knew in the world. We didn't want to leave it."

Luca can feel his face crumpling for her, and he tries to arrange it into an expression of comfort instead of pain.

"So the next day, Mami walked Soledad and me down the mountain and she put us on the bus to San Pedro Sula."

"Wait, what? She didn't go with you?"

Rebeca draws her knees up in front of her and fans herself with the cardboard. She shakes her head. "She said nobody would bother two old ladies. So she and Abuela stayed behind."

Luca swallows. He doesn't want to ask the next question, but he does: "What happened to them?"

"I don't know, I haven't seen them since that day. We got to the city, we found our *papi* at his hotel. And we stayed with him in an apartment that was just a room. It was awful there. So bright and hot and loud because there was always noise from cars and radios and televisions and people, but Papi said we were safer, anyway. He liked having us with him even though we barely ever saw him because he was working all the time and he wanted us to start going to school."

"Was school the same there as it was back home?"

Rebeca makes a sad smile. "No, Luca. Nothing was the same." She turns to look over her shoulder at Soledad. "But we tried to make the best of it anyway. We never had much schooling at home, or only when we were little, so it was hard for us to catch up. And there weren't many other *indios* there, so we felt out of place. We hoped to take the bus back up the mountain some weekends with Papi so we could visit with Mami and Abuela and our friends, so we could gulp the clouds and refill our spirits, but weeks and then months went by, and Papi was always working, and we never had extra time or money for the bus, and then Sole, she accidentally got a boyfriend."

Luca holds up one hand. "Wait. How do you accidentally get a boyfriend?"

"Sh," Rebeca says. "Don't let her hear you."

Luca drops his voice, leans closer. "But how?"

"Like, she was walking home one day by herself and this boy noticed her, and he called to her. That was always happening to her wherever she went in the city, so she just did what she always did, which was to ignore him, but he didn't like that, so he chased after her and grabbed her by the throat and a few other parts and he told her that he was her boyfriend now."

Luca feels his face wash into a shade of gray.

"*Ay,* I shouldn't be telling you all this stuff," Rebeca says. "I'm sorry."

"No, I can handle it," Luca says. "You don't have to be sorry."

Rebeca picks at a loose orange thread on the seam of her jeans. "I haven't been able to talk to anybody about this since it happened," she says. "Only Soledad, and she won't speak of it."

Luca nods. "I understand."

"But it's like you're my friend, you know?" Rebeca smiles.

"I am," Luca says, and he feels proud.

"You seem a lot older than you are. Like you're this old man in this tiny body."

Luca tries to take this as a compliment. His body isn't tiny; it's only moderately smaller than a typical eight-year-old's. "I've seen bad things, too," he assures her.

"Yeah?"

He nods.

"I guess you wouldn't be on top of this train if you hadn't."

"*Es un prerrequisito,*" Luca says. A prerequisite.

Rebeca nods.

"My *papi* died," he whispers. He hasn't wanted to say those words out loud, to admit it. This is the first time, and he can feel the words leaving his chest, like something rotten has broken off inside him and fallen away. There is a ragged wound now, where he'd been holding those words.

"Oh no," Rebeca says. She leans forward like she's suddenly off balance, but then she touches her forehead against his and they both close their eyes.

The rest of the sisters' story emerges in stolen moments over the next several days. How Soledad's unwanted "boyfriend" turned out to be the *palabrero* of the local *clica* of an international gang. How he was, therefore, just violent and powerful enough to do whatever he liked to her without fear of reprisal, but not quite violent or powerful enough to preserve her all for himself. How Soledad's life quickly deteriorated into a series of lurid traumas. How Soledad confided some of it to Rebeca but went to extravagant lengths to hide the situation from their *papi* because she understood that, were he to discover her circumstances, his resulting efforts to protect her would get him killed.

Rebeca knows that Iván, which was the name of the unwanted boyfriend, sometimes allowed Soledad to go to school, and sometimes did not. But there is much she doesn't know—how he always allowed Soledad to go home at nights because the idea of her having a curfew served, in the depravity of his mind, to sustain her virtue. How her decency, her moral resistance to him, her very obvious loathing, all turned him on. How, as Soledad began to perceive this, she sometimes pretended to enjoy his company in hopes he'd grow tired of her. And how now, when Soledad remembers that pretend enjoyment, she feels flooded with shame. It was futile anyway, because that effort at subterfuge was no match for her beauty.

One day Iván showed Soledad a picture of the hotel where her father worked. He said her father's name to her, and then gave her a cell phone and instructed her to answer it whenever it rang or beeped, no matter what she was doing. He showed her how to text. "It's good to be alive, right, Sole?" he said, and she cringed at the way he shortened her name, as if he were someone she loved.

During all those weeks of suffering, Soledad, who knew the only flimsy protection she could offer her baby sister was her unaccustomed distance, barely saw Rebeca at all. When Iván called, Soledad stopped whatever she was doing, as instructed, and she went to him. She left her shopping basket in the middle of the aisle, or got out of the line where she waited for the bus, or lifted herself out of the chair in the middle of her reading class, and she moved across the city to him like a zombie magnet.

Twice, Soledad saw Iván shoot people in the back of the head. Once, she watched him kick a nine-year-old boy in the stomach until he coughed up blood because that was one of the ways they initiated new *chequeos* into the gang. That day, she asked him what would happen if she didn't answer her cell phone sometime, and he backhanded her in the mouth, leaving a bruise along her lower jaw and a welt on her lip that was difficult to explain to Papi. "I only meant if I was in the shower or something," she explained to Iván afterward, "or if my *papi* was there and I couldn't answer." And when she said this, Iván cocked back and pretended he was going to hit her again, and Soledad winced and cowered, and Iván laughed and said, "Just answer your phone, *puta*." And after that, he let one of his homeboys pay him to be alone with her for an hour.

Soledad didn't actively want to die, not really. She'd always been a happy child. She remembered how it had felt to be happy, and she wasn't sure she could ever feel that feeling again, but the memory of it provided her with some measure of hope. Still, during that long stretch of weeks with Iván, there were plenty of times when it crossed her mind to drag a razor blade across the raised tangle of vessels in her wrist. Or to lift the homemade gun from where Iván placed it on his bedside table before he did what he did to her, to train it on him and pull the trigger. To shoot him and watch his brains splatter satisfyingly against the ceiling above him, and then to turn the gun on herself before his homies could swoop in and punish her. To be done with it all, to be free from this repetitive torture. But then she thought of her *papi,* the suffering her release would cause him. Her *mami* and *abuela* back home in the cloud forest, too, when Papi would have to go home to their mountain place and deliver the news. But more than any of that, even, Soledad thought of Rebeca. Her sister was afraid, but still intact. Rebeca was still undiscovered, and it was the improbable miracle of that truth that kept Soledad going. The possibility of her baby sister's salvation.

Then one afternoon, Iván lay in bed wearing boxer shorts and smoking a cigarette. He blew the smoke toward Soledad where she sat slightly curled over herself on the edge of the bed near his feet. "So I heard you got a sister," he said, nudging her backside with his toe. Soledad was very grateful not to be facing him when he said this, because she knew her face would've told the whole story of panic that these words provoked. "How come you never mentioned her?"

Soledad was wrapped in a sheet; it was tucked beneath her arms. She made her face into the approximation of a smile and turned it toward him. "We're not close," she said. "She's nothing like me."

Outside she could hear two of Iván's homeboys arguing, but there were also children playing somewhere beyond, squealing, chasing one another up the block. The sunlight rocketed through the open window.

"Nothing like you, huh?" he said, sitting up and yanking the sheet down to her waist. He tapped the bottom of her breast and watched it react. "That's not what I heard." Then he tossed his still-full cigarette into the ashtray beside the bed and sat up on his knees. "Damn, girl. Lemme get in there again."

Soledad endured him with something more immediate and terrifying than her regular revulsion, and when he was finished, and he instructed her to come back in the morning and bring her sister, she went home, packed her backpack, took all the little bit of money Papi had managed to save from the coffee can on top of the refrigerator, and then sat down at the table to wait for Rebeca to get home. She wrote Papi a note:

Querido Papi:
I love you so so much, Papi, and I'm sorry for these words I have to write that I know will break your heart. And I'm sorry for taking all your savings, but I know that you work hard and save this money only for us, and I know that you'd insist we take it and use it to get away from here if you knew the terrible things that were happening to me. And I didn't tell you sooner because I thought I could protect you and Rebeca if I stayed quiet and just did what they told me to do, but there are monsters in this city, Papi, and now I'm so scared, and I have to get Rebeca out of here before they hurt her, too. So we're leaving today, Papi. We are already gone. And you must be very careful and look after yourself, please. We are taking you with us in our hearts, and we will call you when we get to el norte, Papi. And we'll send for you when we have jobs, and you can come to us, and you can bring Mami and Abuela, too, and we will all be together again as it is meant to be.
    God bless you, Papi, until we meet again.
        All my love, from your devoted daughter, full of sorrow,
                                                            Soledad

Much of this Rebeca doesn't know. But she does know that Soledad texted their cousin César in Maryland that afternoon while she waited for Rebeca to get home. And she knows that César didn't ask any questions because he already knew all the worst possible answers and all he wanted to do was get them out of there. Rebeca knows that César asked if they could wait a few days so he could try to arrange for a coyote to bring them all the way from Honduras to *el norte,* but Soledad told him they couldn't wait. They were leaving today, right now. Rebeca knows that César has since prepaid for their crossing with a trustworthy coyote who will meet them at the border. Rebeca doesn't know that the sum of money their cousin paid for their crossing was $4,000 each. But even if she had known, that kind of money doesn't even make sense to her. It's so far into the realm of the incomprehensible that it might as well have been $4 million.

As Rebeca reveals what scraps of story she does have to Luca, he starts to understand that this is the one thing all migrants have in common, this is the solidarity that exists among them, though they all come from different places and different circumstances, some urban, some rural, some middle-class, some poor, some well educated, some illiterate, Salvadoran, Honduran, Guatemalan, Mexican, Indian, each of them carries some story of suffering on top of that train and into *el norte* beyond. Some, like Rebeca, share their stories carefully, selectively, finding a faithful ear and then chanting their words like prayers. Other migrants are like blown-open grenades, telling their anguish compulsively to everyone they meet, dispensing their pain like shrapnel so they might one day wake to find their burdens have grown lighter. Luca wonders what it would feel like to blow up like that. But for now he remains undetonated, his horrors sealed tightly inside, his pin fixed snugly in place.

CHAPTER SEVENTEEN

For both Lydia and the sisters, there's a constant tug-of-war between the gruesome feeling that something's chasing them, that they must move quickly away, and a physical hesitation, a reluctance to move blindly toward whatever unknown demons may loom in the road ahead. The Casa del Migrante they find in Celaya is a respite from that tug-of-war, and as such, after a sleepless night outdoors for Lydia, a holy blessing without compare.

It's only midday when they arrive. Luca and Rebeca play basketball in the yard and no one else can join, some complicated game with jumbled rules of their own devising. Lydia and Soledad sit quietly together, watching from a nearby bench. They help in the kitchen, listening to *las noticias* on television, and then Lydia naps. When she wakens, she watches her son playing dominoes with Rebeca. She notes how quickly those two have bridged the gap between their respective ages, eight and fourteen—Luca seems to have grown up and Rebeca to have simplified quite neatly—so they meet seamlessly in the middle. It feels as though they've known each other forever, as though these girls have always been here, waiting to become a part of their lives. That night Luca asks if he can snuggle in beneath Rebeca's arm in her bunk.

"It's not appropriate." Lydia draws the line.

Luca knew it was a long shot anyway, but hardly any of the rules from his old life seem to apply anymore, so he figured it was worth asking.

He climbs in bed without complaint. Lydia hauls her backpack beneath the sheets by her feet and wraps its strap twice around her ankle. They all sleep soundly. Glory, glory to have a door with a lock.

Soledad has told Lydia nothing of where she and her sister came from or what they endured. Lydia's said nothing of her family's circumstances either, but there's that silent bond of knowing between them regardless, a magic that's marginally maternal, but entirely female. So it's not surprising that in the morning, the girl, who seems much older than just the eighteen months that separate her from her sister, and who's not typically so forthcoming about private matters regarding her body, confides to Lydia that she's pregnant. Taking her cue from Soledad, Lydia endeavors to deliver her response to this news in a calm, unvarnished manner.

"Your baby will be a US citizen," she whispers across the top of her coffee cup.

Soledad shakes her head and stands up from the table to clear her plate. "The baby isn't mine," she says. When she stretches her arms above her and her baggy T-shirt grazes the waist of her jeans, her tummy is still flat.

That day and night at *la casa* are so significant in their restorative value that, in the weeks to come, when they think back to the halcyon memory of this place, their stay here will seem much longer than it was. Like all priests in Mexico, the padre who runs *la casa* wears regular street clothes, a yellow polo shirt and a softened pair of blue jeans with a tar stain on one leg. His only religious adornment is a simple wooden cross that hangs from a leather cord around his neck. He's slender, with gray hair and glasses. There are more than twenty migrants resuming their journey today, and the padre gathers them in the yard before they leave. He gives a speech that Lydia thinks of as a kind of pep talk with an identity crisis—because he means to encourage them, but there's no pep in his talk. He stands on an upturned milk crate in front of the gathered crowd, and mostly, he warns them.

"If it's possible for you to turn back, do so now. If you can go home again and make a life for yourself where you came from, if you can return there safely, I implore you: please do so now. If there is any other place for you to go, to stay away from these trains, to stay away from *el norte,* go there now." Luca has his arm around Rebeca's waist, his head leaning in, her arm around his shoulder. Lydia looks at their faces; they do not flinch from these hard words. Some of the other migrants shift their weight nervously beneath them. "If it's only a better life you seek, seek it elsewhere," the padre continues. "This path is only for people who have no choice, no other option, only violence and misery behind you. And your journey will grow even more treacherous from here. Everything is working against you, to thwart you. Some of you will fall from the trains. Many will be maimed or injured. Many will die. Many, many of you will be kidnapped, tortured, trafficked, or ransomed. Some will be lucky enough to survive all of that and make it as far as Estados Unidos only to experience the privilege of dying alone in the desert beneath the sun, abandoned by a corrupt coyote, or shot by a narco who doesn't like the look of you. Every single one of you will be robbed. Every one. If you make it to *el norte,* you will arrive penniless, that's a guarantee. Look around you. Go ahead—look at each other. Only one out of three will make it to your destination alive. Will it be you?" He points at a man in his fifties with a neatly trimmed beard and a fresh T-shirt.

"*¡Sí, señor!*" the man answers.

"Will it be you?" He points to a woman about Lydia's age with a silent toddler on her hip.

"*¡Sí, señor!*" she says.

"Will it be you?" he points at Luca.

Lydia feels a crush of wild despair steal over her, but Luca lifts his small fist in the air and shouts his response. "*¡Sí, seré yo!*"

The speech does the job of energizing the migrants and steeling their resolve, which in turn makes them restless and impatient during the long wait for the train. In the third hour, a few give up waiting and begin to walk. In the fourth and fifth hours, more follow. Luca, Lydia, and the girls head toward the western edge of the city in search of an overpass, but the only one they find is way too high. Jumping from there would be suicide. So they search instead for a curve where the train might slow down. It's midafternoon by the time La Bestia finally arrives, and it's more crowded than they've seen it before. Even from a distance, Lydia can see the silhouette of migrants atop the cars. It's moving much faster than when they boarded yesterday at San Miguel de Allende.

Lydia nearly says they should wait, they're not going to make it. She wants to articulate her hesitation, but she's not quick enough, and now the train is too loud. The noise thunders into her bones. They all run, and she holds Luca's hand tightly in her fist. The men atop the train shout down to them, instructions and encouragement. Rebeca goes up first, and then Soledad, who reaches back for Luca. He grabs at her with his free hand, and there's a terrifying moment where he's stretched between them, one arm taut with Soledad on the shrieking beast, and the other linked to Lydia racing beneath. He's like taffy, soft and exposed. And then Lydia hurls his little arm toward the train, and he's up. Soledad has him, and then the men from above, lifting. He is safe, he is safe. Lydia runs, not yet relieved, not until she joins him there, she runs and the train is picking up speed and she's falling behind the ladder, and she can't keep up, and then a burst of panic makes her legs go like pistons and she grabs at the metal bars, terrified, terrified that her legs won't be able to maintain this speed, that they'll drop, that she'll go under, but this is not her day, because all at once her feet have found the bottom rung, and her hands are only one rung above them, and the train is picking up speed so quickly now, she can't believe the velocity, but her body, all four of her limbs are attached to the train now, and she's curled there at the bottom of the ladder like a bug, and she allows herself one tiny sob of relief before she uncurls herself and, pushing up from the bottom rung, begins to climb. When she gets to the top she reaches for Luca, and she straps them down quickly with the belts, and then she holds him and cries quietly into his hair until her heart begins to calm.

Lydia wants to keep Luca and the sisters to herself, to set their little group apart from the others as a unit. But the men are so friendly, so eager to help. Too eager, she worries. There aren't many women on La Bestia, and very few children, so Lydia feels noticed by every single man they see. She's aware that she and her companions *represent* something to these men. They look like home. Or they look like salvation. Or they look like prey. To an *halcón* they might look like reward money. And even if none of that were true, the two sisters cause a stir wherever they go, just by the very presence of their faces. Lydia is distracted by these observations, which is why, despite her constant watchfulness, she doesn't immediately notice the boy near the other end of their train car watching her.

But Luca does. And he remembers. And in the act of remembering, he experiences a strange, incongruous moment of satisfaction, a brief wash of endorphins he's never noticed before, but that his brain has been performing all his life, a slight chemical self-congratulatory pleasure for achieving this task of almost perfect recall: Luca has seen that face before. He recognizes that boy, and so even before the tattoo is visible from where the boy is sitting cross-legged at the other end of the train car, Luca recollects it—the bloody sickle creeping out of the sock. The three drops of bloodred ink dripping from the blade. Luca shivers beneath the hot sun. The boy is staring at Mami. And then, as Luca watches him, he retrieves a phone from his pocket, scrolls around a little bit, and then looks back at Mami again. Then he puts it in his pocket. Luca is paralyzed by fear. A moment passes before he can give wind to his voice.

"Mami," he says simply, and he thinks he says it quite calmly, though his body, still strapped to the top of that train, feels like a wild flap of panic. Mami leans in but not close enough. He flutters his hand so she understands. *Come here. Get closer. Do it quickly.* Lydia scoots closer to him.

"Mami, I recognize someone."

These words alone are enough to send a slice of cold down Lydia's spine. "Okay," she says, willing her brain to slow down. Okay. "Who is it?" Her arms and legs feel like they've turned to liquid, but the fingers of one hand stay tightly curled around the grating. The other hand goes automatically to the chain at her neck. She slips her index finger inside Sebastián's wedding ring.

"Don't look," Luca says. "He's staring at you, at us."

Lydia's mantra comes heroically crashing through her consciousness, penetrating the violent static of this new information. *Don't think, don't think, don't think,* her brain tells her. "Okay," she repeats. "Who?"

Luca leans so his lips graze the top of her ear. "The boy from the first Casa del Migrante at Huehuetoca."

Lydia breathes deeply. *Okay.* Some boy they crossed paths with along the way. She feels relief in the jellylike roll of her shoulders. "Oh, Luca," she says. And she wants to reprimand him for scaring her to death, but how is he supposed to know what may or may not provoke a stampede of dread in the confusing wasteland of their new life? So she also wants to laugh, to kiss him, to tell him not to worry so much. She puts her arm around him. "It's fine," she says. "It's okay."

"Don't you remember, that really bad kid—that cholo who got kicked out of the *casa* for bothering that girl? He did something bad to her?"

Yes, she remembers. *Oh shit.* The women at breakfast claimed he was a *sicario.*

Only moments ago, Lydia had dared to feel comforted by their unlikely progress. She'd allowed herself to indulge in the new fear of anonymous, indiscriminate threats. Now here is some *sicario* from God-knows-what cartel, staring her down from a hundred yards away. She looks at the other migrants seated around them. Any one of them could be a narco. Any one of them could be a Jardinero. She folds herself over her legs so her face is nearly touching the grating in front of her, or rather, her body does this without her mind instructing it to. An instinct to hide herself, to melt into the scenery, to disappear. Luca leans down, too.

"There's something else," he says, because he knows, although he doesn't understand how he knows it or what it means, that there's something deeply unsettling about the tattoo.

"What is it?" Lydia is ready for this information, whatever it is. She opens the door to it.

"A tattoo. He has a tattoo."

Her machete is strapped to her shin beneath her pant leg. She can feel the cinch of the holster, the way it presses into her skin. She whispers to Luca. "What sort of tattoo?"

"Like a big, curved knife, Mami," he says. "With three drops of blood."

Lydia's mouth goes dry, her fingers cold. Her body trembles from the inside out, core to tip, beginning in her lungs. But to Luca, her face looks calm and impassive.

"Like a sickle?" She needs, but does not want, clarity. "Like this?" She traces the shape of it on the palm of his hand with her finger.

Luca nods.

"Thank you for telling me, *mijo*," she says. "You did the right thing. Good boy." She touches his ear.

Before Lydia can formulate a plan, before she can absorb this information, indeed, before she can even turn her face in the direction Luca has indicated to glimpse the boy with the Jardinero tattoo, there's a collective shriek and terrible commotion two cars up. They turn instinctively in the direction of the clamor. Everyone holds their breath and then almost immediately, with a long hoot of its whistle, the train enters a tunnel and all is in darkness.

"Mami!" Luca screams.

"I'm here." Lydia gropes for his hand. "I'm here, *mijo*."

"What happened?"

"I don't know, *mijo*."

"I'm scared."

"I know, *mijo*, it's okay."

She reaches through the blackness and touches the soft fuzz at the back of his head. The tunnel is a short one, and soon they blast out into daylight again, and the sisters, who'd been dozing in a small heap until the commotion, sit up and blink rapidly at each other. A weary Morse code.

"What happened?" Soledad asks.

There's still a lot of yelling coming from the car two ahead of theirs, and a couple of voices begin to emerge from the fray, louder than the others. One man is wailing, *¡Hermano, hermano, hermano!* And then he stands up on top of the train, and his companions grab him and pull him back down, and then a moment later the scene repeats itself. He seems determined to jump off, and now the story is traveling back along the train until it gets to the cluster of men seated in front of the sisters. One young man turns to share it.

"His brother fell off."

Soledad gasps and crosses herself. "*Dios mío*, how?" she asks.

The man points back at the tunnel they just passed through. "Didn't see the tunnel. Was sitting up too tall on his knees, and bang. He hit his head on the top of the tunnel and got knocked right off."

Soledad's face is a twist of horrified compassion. She leans past the young man because she can see now, beyond him, that the wailing brother is back on his feet a third time. The words fly out of her mouth by instinct, her hand darts toward him. "Stop him!" she screams. "Grab him!"

But it's too late. The man has jumped. He's a distorted silhouette of arched arms and legs against the bleary yellow of the late-morning sky. His shadow makes the shape of grief as he hurtles toward the earth.

"Too far, it's too far." Soledad's voice is still working independently of her body. "Oh my God, oh my God."

Their train car is already passing where the jumper has landed. His body rolls down the steep embankment and away. Luca counts his arms and legs: one, two, three, four. He counts them again to make sure. He still has all four, but they don't seem to be working. His body comes to a stop in a thicket of weeds, and the train storms on without him. Without his brother.

Soledad is almost catatonic after watching the man jump, as if the incident loosened the fragile scab of her own suffering. She lies down again, and Rebeca pulls her sister's head into her lap. She strokes Soledad's long, black hair back away from her forehead, and quietly sings a song in a language Lydia has never heard before. Soledad stays there unblinking, but soon her expression softens, her dark eyebrows turn slack, and her lids flutter closed. She drifts into some state akin to sleep.

Lydia doesn't stare at the boy at the other end of the freight car, but she's hyperaware now of his attention. He sits with his legs outstretched and his weight leaned back on his propped hands, and he's watching them. Lydia does recognize him now, but only because Luca mentioned it. He's wearing oversize red shorts and a huge white T-shirt. Over that, the giant red-and-black tank top jersey of some professional basketball team, and big diamond earrings in both ears. The jewelry is probably fake, but it does the trick of making him look like a hip-hop star, which is exactly the look he was hoping to achieve when he shaved those two tiny pinstripes into his right eyebrow.

Lydia doesn't turn her head. With the precision of a huntress, she can sense his movements with her peripheral vision—when he lifts his flat-brimmed black baseball cap to scratch beneath it, when he leans slightly over the edge of the train car to spit, when he unscrews the cap from his water bottle to take a drink. She wonders if he can feel her anxiety, if her studied nonchalance is biologically ineffective, if her body is shooting off alarm pheromones he can detect. A primal consciousness has sprung up between them. So she's aware, too, of the ways her own body responds when, on a long stretch of straight, open track, he lifts himself up from his position and moves toward them. Lydia's heartbeat increases, her pupils dilate, her grip on Luca tightens, indeed all her muscles either constrict or twitch, and her skin prickles with goose bumps. Her palms grow slick and clammy. She lets go of Luca and gropes at the machete strapped to her lower leg beneath her pants.

Everyone watches the young man pick his way gingerly past the groups of migrants on the train top. Everyone always watches when someone is on the move—they look for signs of drunkenness or erratic behavior. They look for the gleam of a concealed blade. They're especially alert to this young man because it's so obvious what he is. They lean away from him as he passes.

"You looking for the café car, *amigo*?" an older man in a straw hat asks him. The nearby migrants laugh but it's a suspicious laughter. Why is he alone? Where does he think he's going?

"Just stretching my legs," the young man answers.

They keep an eye on his tattoo after he passes, their friendliness a tinny facade. Most migrants understand the significance of those three drops of tattooed blood: one for each kill.

Lydia pulls the machete from its small holster and draws it out from beneath her pant leg as the boy approaches. She presses the button to engage the blade and feels gratified by its appearance. Luca watches her silently as she conceals it beneath her sleeve. Some small flash of instinct advises Lydia to ditch the blade and watch instead for a passing bush, for some soft landing point, and then to pitch her son from the train as soon as she spots a place where he might survive the fall. She reaches over and briefly grabs his leg to make sure her body doesn't wildly obey that foolish impulse. She presses gravity onto his folded legs and feels grateful for the insurance of the canvas belt. The boy's shadow is upon them. Lydia doesn't look up.

"Yo, I think I know you," he says.

He puts his body down in the very small space between Lydia and the sisters. He squeezes in there, and if her body could tense up any further, it would. She can feel Rebeca trying to catch her eye, but she doesn't look at the girl, because she doesn't want to draw her into whatever this is. Rebeca reshuffles her body, making room for the newcomer, and meanwhile, Lydia's brain has been so busy telling her to run that it failed to come up with a suitable plan for this moment, so she says the first words that show up in her mouth.

"I didn't think so, but my son recognized you from back the road a way—outside Mexico City." She does not say *Huehuetoca* in case the memory of his eviction from that place provokes his anger. She holds her body like a cocked gun.

"*¿Ah, sí?*" He leans over to smile at Luca, which confuses Lydia. She can't understand the chitchat. If he's a *sicario,* then why is he plopped down here shooting the breeze? And where is his weapon inside all that abundant clothing? "Wuddup, *güey*?" he says to Luca. "Cool hat." He stretches to touch the brim of Papi's red baseball cap, but Luca moves out of his reach. "Anyway, I'm Lorenzo," he says, putting his hand out to Lydia. She's never been more reluctant to shake someone's hand, but she shakes it lightly and retracts herself quickly, replacing her grip on the machete beneath her sleeve. "And you are?"

He can't be any older than eighteen, twenty, Lydia thinks. How is it that he speaks like this, as if she owes him her name? "Araceli." She expels the fake name on her breath like a surfer riding a dying tide.

Lorenzo shakes his head. "I don't think so."

Lydia bites the inside of her mouth. If she ever doubted herself capable of stabbing another human being, that uncertainty is no more. "Pardon me?"

"You're not Araceli."

The only response she can manage is a soft snorting noise. Luca leans against her. When Lorenzo reaches into his pocket, she coils her body so tightly she begins to shake. She will thrust the blade into his neck. But no. She's in a bad position; there's no leverage. Would she be able to kill him? Or would she only injure him, incite him to repay her failed violence? It would be better to jump. To curl around Luca like a shell so at least he would survive this moment. The leap from the speeding train.

But could Luca survive whatever follows that, once she's gone? Lydia will get only one opportunity to sacrifice herself—then Luca's on his own forever. Her body twitches with indecision. She turns the handle of the concealed machete, cold against her palm. But then Lorenzo's hand emerges from his pocket with only a cell phone. No pistol, no blade. He clicks the thing to life and scrolls through the pictures.

Lydia's breath shudders through her.

"That's you, right?" He turns the phone so she can see. It's a selfie Javier took of the two of them together at the bookstore. They're on opposite sides of the counter, both leaning across, their foreheads touching at the temple. Lydia looks directly at the camera, but Javier's face is turned slightly in, his eyes pulled toward her. Lydia remembers the day he took it, how he told her that Marta had instructed him thoroughly in the art of the selfie, how hard they had laughed together.

"Lydia Quixano Pérez, right?" the boy beside her says.

She tucks her lips inside her mouth and twists her neck once, but there's nothing even marginally convincing in the gesture. Lorenzo holds the phone up beside her face to check her features against the likeness.

"Yep yep. Good-looking folks," he says. And then, in a voice that sounds uncannily sincere, "I'm sorry about your family."

What passes for silence on the train is the slow-motion roar of the engine hauling countless tons of chugging, clacking steel along the track behind it. The wheels shriek in their tracks, metal whines against metal, the couplers between the cars knuckle and grind and squeal. Several beats of that kind of silence pass before Lydia finds her voice.

"What do you want?"

Lorenzo powers the phone off and puts it back in his pocket. "What do I want? Shoot." He whistles. "Same things as anybody, I guess. Nice house, a little bling, a good-lookin' girl." He turns and smiles at Rebeca, who's still sitting quite close to them, but doesn't seem to be listening. She doesn't meet his gaze, and Lydia doubts she can hear their conversation over the noise of the train. On her lap, Soledad's eyes are still closed. Lorenzo examines his nails, looking for one to bite, while Lydia watches.

"What do you want *from me*?" she clarifies.

He finds a tiny, unassaulted white corner of fingernail and rips it off

with his teeth. He spits it over the edge. "Nothin'." He shrugs. "Just being neighborly."

"Where did you get that picture?" Lydia scrunches up her nose and
uses her chin to point in the direction of the phone in his pocket.

"Mami, I hate to tell you," he says. "Everybody in Guerrero got that
picture."

Lydia sucks in a breath. It's not exactly news, but it does validate
her fear. "For what purpose?" She wants absolute clarity.

Lorenzo smirks at her sideways. "You for real?"

"I need to know what we're up against."

Lorenzo pauses. Then shrugs. "Word was to bring you in."

This is a surprise. Maybe only Hollywood gangsters say things like
dead or alive, but that was what she'd expected. She tries to push this information into her internal hard drive, but it doesn't compute. "Not to
kill me?" she asks. "To kill us?"

Lorenzo sighs. This isn't how this conversation was supposed to go.
She's not supposed to be the one asking the questions. "*Güey,* I said too
much already. I'm not trying to get myself killed, too."

Lydia shifts uncomfortably beside him, the handle of the machete
growing sweaty in her hand. "So that's why you're here? To bring us in?"

Maybe Javier wants only to kill them himself, to witness her suffering. She and Luca will not go with this boy. She will kill him if she has
to; she'll do it in front of Luca if she must.

"Nah," Lorenzo says. "I left all that behind me in Guerrero." He
waves his arm toward the south.

Lydia does not loosen her grip on the machete. "Okay."

"*De verdad,* new leaf." He grins. "I'm out."

She feels unqualified to assess this claim. She makes no response.

"How'd you get outta Acapulco, though?" Lorenzo asks after a moment. "Everybody was looking for you. You got magic powers or something? You some kind of *santera*? *¿Una bruja?*"

Lydia surprises herself with a laugh, but it's only a husk of a sound.
"I suppose fear has certain magical properties." She'll never know how
narrow their escape really was, that two of Javier's men opened the door
to their room at the Hotel Duquesa Imperial just as she and Luca were
entering the lobby of the hotel next door.

"So where you heading to now?" Lorenzo asks.

"I don't know," she lies. "We haven't really decided."

Lorenzo pulls his knees up so his baggy shorts sag beneath. He gathers his arms around his legs. "I'm going to L.A.," he says. "I got a cousin out there in Hollywood, doing his thing."

"As good a place as any," she says.

And then the train silence returns, and in that thundering quiet, she wonders: *Why?* If he was well connected in Los Jardineros, if he was making enough money to afford those expensive sneakers and that decent cell phone? If he was okay with earning that first drop of tattooed blood, and the second, and the third, then what made him leave Guerrero? There are infinite possible answers, she knows. Perhaps he disliked murdering. Perhaps he felt that the acts of violence he committed had some undesirable effect on him. Perhaps he had nightmares, the faces of the people he'd killed floating up before him whenever he closed his eyes. Maybe he was haunted, hunted, ragged in his soul. Or maybe the precise opposite was true. Perhaps he was so entirely without conscience that he'd been unable, even, to adhere to whatever deformed excuse for a moral code Los Jardineros exercised. Maybe he raped the wrong woman. Or stole money from one of his *jefes*. Or maybe he murdered so gleefully that his depravity turned him into a liability. Maybe he's running, too. Or maybe none of these things are true. Perhaps he hasn't left Los Jardineros at all, and he really is here only for her.

Whatever the case, Lydia feels shriveled by Lorenzo's presence. He's a menace, sitting beside her, and now the threat feels urgent again. It's all around her. She breathes it, and it's the same as ever: senseless, confusing, categorically terrifying. Javier feels as close as the day she first confronted him in the bookshop. The Russian nesting dolls. He'd reached for her hand. She can feel his fingers pressing into the veins at her wrist. She can hear that *sicario* urinating into the toilet on the other side of Abuela's green-tiled wall.

Lydia wishes this boy would move away from them. Nine days and 426 miles from their escape, they haven't made any headway at all.

CHAPTER EIGHTEEN

Luca likes the estates where all the homes are lined up like soldiers wearing identical uniforms: indestructible white stucco walls, helmets of red Spanish tile, all tilted at the same angle to the sun. He likes the anonymity of them, and thinks how nice it would be to live inside one of those houses with Mami, how nobody'd ever find them there. One thing he doesn't like is when the train tracks temporarily veer south, because even though he misses home, he misses only the life that existed in Acapulco before the *quinceañera,* and he understands that to be a place that no longer exists. It's nostalgia for a phantom limb. So he's relieved when the tracks bend toward the west again, and then, near a neat little town in Jalisco, sidle up beside *el río* Grande de Santiago and, at long last, curve northward.

The city appears gradually and with several false starts where Luca observes all the familiar symptoms of an urban metropolis: food vendors who pause at their grills to wave up at the passing migrants, the occasional clothesline strung with bright colors snapping in the sunny wind, a gathering of rowdy kids along the fence of a schoolyard. And then boom, it all recedes, and it's just cornfields, cornfields, cornfields. Two times this happens. Three. Four. And then finally, unmistakably: Guadalajara.

Second-largest city in Mexico. State capital of Jalisco. Population: one and a half million people.

All across the top of the train, migrants prepare to disembark. They wake their friends, stuff wadded-up jacket-pillows into their bags; they tighten the straps on one another's backpacks. Mami unstraps herself from the train but leaves Luca's belt attached to the grating. Lorenzo sits in the same spot, in the same position, and observes. Luca doesn't like the way he watches Rebeca and Soledad.

"Mami," Luca says as the train slows enough that some of the men on their car begin to climb down the ladders and jump to the gravel below.

Lydia is rolling up her canvas belt, and she looks at Luca with her *what?* face.

"I don't need the belt," he says.

"You need the belt."

"Mami."

This time she does the more aggressive version of her *what?* face.

"If I'm able to jump on and off a moving train, don't you think it's a little silly to buckle me in like a toddler?" Luca juts out his chin at her. She grabs that chin in her hand, pulls her face down to his. The unchanged nature of her temper when he's ill-mannered is a comfort like a hot bath.

"It is not silly," she says. "We ride these trains because we have no choice, but they are extremely dangerous, Luca. Did you learn nothing back there when that man fell—"

"Okay," he says, irritably. "Fine." He tries to wriggle his chin away from her, but she only squeezes harder. He still has control of his own eyeballs, though. She can't squeeze those. He moves his gaze away from her face, to her left ear.

"Don't interrupt me," she says. "And look at me when I'm speaking to you."

He looks at that earlobe.

"Luca. Look at me."

He returns his gaze to her face momentarily and then moves it away again.

"Listen. I know this is all crazy. It's reckless and wild, riding these trains, sleeping in strange places, eating strange things. And I know I haven't said it before now, but, Luca, I'm so proud of you."

He looks her briefly in the eye.

"I am," she says. "It's incredible, how strong you are, that you're able to do these inconceivable things."

Luca has an unexpected thought. "Can you imagine what Papi would say?"

Lydia lets go of his chin and smiles at him. "Papi would say we are both crazy."

Tears spring into Luca's eyes, but he doesn't want them there, so he makes them disappear. Lydia drops her voice to a whisper. "Papi would be so proud of you. You're capable of things I had no idea you could do, Luca." She squeezes his knee. "I never knew." She reaches across the landscape of their tangled legs to grab Luca's hand. "But you are still my boy, do you understand?"

He nods.

"*Y por Dios,* if anything happened to you, Luca. I couldn't bear it. I know how much you've grown in these last days. But your body is still only eight years old."

"Almost nine," he says.

"Almost nine," she agrees. "But please, please listen. Never be complacent. Never assume you're safe on this train. No one is safe, do you understand? No one." She squeezes his hands. "Machismo will get you killed."

Luca nods again.

The train has slowed to a placid roll beneath them, and Soledad and Rebeca both tie up their hair to disembark. They're wearing their backpacks, and they're turned, talking with the group of four men who've been in front of them since Celaya. One of the men has made this journey before—he's been deported twice from San Diego, so this is his third pass through Guadalajara. He's warning them. Lorenzo eavesdrops.

"You have to get off before El Verde," the man tells the sisters. "You have to walk the next part of the tracks."

"Why?" Soledad reaches up to tighten her black hair in its fixed coil.

"The people in this city are kind to migrants, God bless them. You will find a good welcome here. But first you have to get past *la policía.* They clear the trains at El Verde, and if they catch you—" The man finishes only with a shake of his head.

"Don't let them catch you." Soledad fills in the blank for him.

"That's right," he says. "And stay with a group. You can come with us if you want." His friends, one by one, begin moving toward the ladder, and he follows.

Rebeca relays all this information quickly to Lydia and suggests going with them. Lydia hesitates. She knows how dangerous it is to trust anyone on La Bestia. There are thugs and rapists and thieves and narcos hidden in the ranks of *la policía* in every town, but it's not only the police who deserve their suspicion. It's every single person they meet—shopkeepers, food vendors, humanitarians, children, priests, even their fellow migrants. Especially their fellow migrants. She glances at Lorenzo's clean, expensive sneakers. It's a common tactic for bad actors to ride the trains posing as migrants, working to gain the trust of unsuspecting travelers, so they can lure them into a secluded place where they can commit some violence against them. Lydia understands the increased probability of that violence being leveled against the sisters. Any gesture of kindness, any valuable nugget of shared information, any pitiful story of heartbreak may be only a well-designed trap. A prequel to robbery or rape or kidnapping. Lydia's brain makes her do the work of considering all this before she decides. But there's no time. The train rolls on and the men are getting off. In fact the whole train seems to be emptying.

These four men seem kind. They have the steep accents of Central Americans. *They're probably Central Americans, right?* Lydia has to decide. Lorenzo's waiting for her to decide, too. *Why is he waiting?* His lingering presence makes the decision. She unbuckles Luca and stuffs his belt into her pack.

"Let's go."

Lorenzo follows.

For the first while, it's all warehouses to one side of the tracks, and all dirt and grass and open sky on the other, so Luca has the impression of walking just outside of something, like the warehouses are a kind of border, fencing something better beyond. They stick to the tracks, where dozens of migrants walk ahead of and behind them, in a sort of miniature caravan. The boy Lorenzo hangs close, not walking with them exactly, but following only a few feet behind, matching his pace to theirs. Luca is worried about that boy, but he's distracted by the unmistakable smell of chocolate, which adds to the sense that, nearby, there's something much better.

"Do you smell that?" Luca asks Rebeca.

"*¿Chocolate?*"

He nods.

"Nope. Don't smell it," she says.

Luca laughs. "Well, I sure do."

They trudge ahead, passing behind the Hershey's factory without ever realizing it's there. Luca presses a fist against his stomach to discourage the groaning. They haven't eaten since breakfast at the *casa* in Celaya, and now it's late afternoon.

"Hungry?" Mami asks.

He nods.

"Me, too."

When the warehouses give way to brick and cinder block homes, the migrants are cheered by the appearance of two pigtailed girls in school uniforms, one slightly larger than the other, one with dimples, and one with a scab on her knee. Their mother sits at a wooden stall nearby, with a cooler of drinks and a small grill. She's selling lemonade and hot ears of grilled corn. A fat baby sleeps in a stroller by her side. There's a large basket there, to which the girls return in swoops, retrieving armloads of little white paper bags. These they pass out to the migrants with their blessings.

"*Bienvenidos a Guadalajara,*" the girls say, "and may God bless you on your journey."

The one with the scabby knee presses a bag into Luca's hand and one into Rebeca's.

"Thank you," Luca says.

The girl skips away, the hem of her blue plaid skirt brushing against her brown legs as she goes. Luca rips into the bag.

"Mami! It's chocolate!" There are three Hershey's Kisses inside.

As the city grows dense around them, people come and go across the tracks, carrying lunch boxes or bags of groceries. Kids with brightly colored backpacks hold their mothers' hands and clamber across the rails. Many of them look Luca and Mami right in the eye, and say, "God bless you," and they smile. Luca would like to smile back, but he feels peculiar, too. He is unaccustomed to pity.

At El Verde, there's a bench outside a neat, walled-in garden. The bench is painted orange, pink, and yellow, and a sign on the wall behind it reads MIGRANTES PUEDEN DESCANSAR AQUÍ. Migrants can rest here. A large, mustached man is sitting on the bench, and when he sees the migrants approaching, he stands, fixes a cowboy hat over his bald head, and retrieves a bat-sized machete from the ground beneath him. He walks toward the tracks with the machete still in its sheath, and keeps it tipped back over one shoulder.

"Amigos, hoy es su día de suerte," he says loudly so they can all hear. Today is your lucky day. "I will walk with you."

The migrants in front of Luca and Mami cheer, but Rebeca and Soledad exchange worried glances. The man falls in step beside them.

"You are right to be afraid," he tells them. "But not of me."

Rebeca sticks her thumbs under the straps of her backpack and says nothing.

"You have come a long way, yes? Honduras? Guatemala?"

"Honduras." Rebeca is first to relent.

"Your journey has been okay so far?" he asks.

Rebeca shrugs. They walk for a few moments in silence, only the sound of their jeans swishing beneath them as they go. Luca holds Mami's hand, but he strains against it, pulling her arm nearly taut as he tries to hear what the man is saying to the sisters.

"Well, I want you to have happy memories of Guadalajara." He smiles, and catches Luca looking at him. He's so large he could use that machete as a toothpick. Luca shies back to Mami's side. "My name is Danilo, and when you get to wherever you're going, when you find a job and a good house, and you meet a beautiful gringo boy and you get married and have your children, one day, when you're an old lady and you're tucking your *nietos* into bed, I want you to tell them that long, long ago, you met a nice man in Guadalajara named Danilo, and that he walked with you, and that he swung his machete around to make sure the knuckleheads didn't get any ideas."

Rebeca laughs now; she can't help herself.

"See? I'm not so bad."

Soledad is still apprehensive. "Where are all these knuckleheads hiding out?"

"Oh, *amiguita*." Danilo frowns. "I am afraid you will meet many of them in short order."

Soledad raises her eyebrows but doesn't respond.

"It's like the good, the bad, and the ugly in this city," Danilo says.

"And the beautiful!" Lorenzo adds, gesturing toward the sisters.

Lydia cringes. *Why is he still here?* Walking just behind them and listening in on every word. She shudders at his remark, noting how the girls draw their bodies closer in instinctive response. Danilo continues as if Lorenzo hasn't spoken at all.

"It's a long walk from here into the migrant places," he says. "And there are many dangers."

"What kind of dangers?" Lydia asks.

"The usual kind," Danilo says. "*La policía,* railroad employees, security guards. Especially dangerous for you two." He looks at the sisters briefly. "It's better to get off the tracks before you get to Las Juntas—go into the streets and make your way to one of the shelters. There are signs for them, or shopkeepers will point the way. If anyone says they will take you there, don't go with them. If anyone offers you a job or a place to stay, don't go with them. If anyone talks to you first, don't speak with them. If you need directions, ask only the shopkeepers. I will go with you as far as La Piedrera. A few miles."

"Why?" Soledad asks.

"Why what?"

"Why walk with us?"

"Why not?" Danilo says. "I do this at least three times a week, a walk with the migrants. It's my hobby. Good exercise."

"But if it's as dangerous as you say, why do you it? What's in it for you?"

Danilo has the kind of eyes that protrude slightly from beneath his lids, so there's no possibility of hiding their expression when he's in conversation. Luca can see that he's not annoyed by Soledad's inquiry. He appreciates her skepticism. "I will tell you the truth," he says. Then he pauses for a moment to smooth down his mustache with his thumb and index finger. "When I was a teenager, I stole a truck. My father died in a work accident, and I was angry with his employer, so I stole that man's truck. I destroyed all the windows and the headlights using my father's hammer. And then I slashed its tires and I drove it into a sewer ditch."

"Seems reasonable to me," Rebeca says.

"I drank for three months, and I did terrible things in my grief. But I never got caught, and God provided me with a good life anyway, despite my sins. So this is my penance. I am like the guardian devil for migrants who pass through my little neighborhood. I protect them."

Soledad looks up at him, narrowing one eye as she searches his expression for indications of deceit. She finds none. "Okay."

Danilo laughs. "Okay?"

"Yes, okay," Soledad says. They are quiet again for a few moments.

"You ever have any trouble?" Lorenzo asks from behind them. "Ever get beat up or anything?"

Danilo turns without removing the machete from his shoulder and looks back at him. "Not anymore," he says.

Lorenzo nods and jams his hands into his pockets. "Cool, cool."

Luca begins chatting with Danilo and the sisters, so Lydia drops back to walk beside Lorenzo. She's both repelled by him and drawn to the information he might be able to provide. Maybe he knows which cartels have alliances with Los Jardineros, which routes present the greatest dangers of her being recognized. She doesn't know how to begin the conversation, because in her mind, every question sounds like an accusation. Finally she speaks one out loud.

"How is it that you came to be traveling alone? Don't you have family in Guerrero?"

"Nah, not really." Lorenzo has plucked up a blade of dry grass from beside the tracks and tucked it into the corner of his mouth. He speaks past it. "My mom got married a few years ago and her husband didn't really want me around, so I split."

Lydia glances over at him. "How old are you?"

"Seventeen."

Younger than she thought. "And how old when you left home?"

Lorenzo looks up from his feet and snags the grass blade from his mouth. "Pssh, I dunno. Thirteen, fourteen. Old enough to look after myself." Lydia takes care not to contradict him, but he feels it anyway. "Not everybody has a *mami* like you, all right? Some mothers don't give a shit." He tosses the grass at his feet.

"I'm sorry," Lydia says.

"Whatever. *No importa.*" He slings his hands into the pockets of his baggy shorts. "I was traveling with my homeboy anyway. We left together because he wanted to get out, too, but then we got separated in Mexico City and I haven't heard from him since."

"But you have a cell phone," she says.

"Yeah, his stopped working."

"Oh."

They walk quietly for a few minutes, and then he says, "Yo, it was really sad what happened to *el jefe*'s daughter, but for real, what he did to your family? *Eso fue de locos.*"

Lydia frowns. "What?"

"La Lechuza. What he did to your family, it was too much. When I saw that girl on the news in her *quinceañera* dress—"

That girl. "My niece."

"Yeah—"

"My goddaughter. Yénifer."

"Yeah, when I saw her on the news, I mean for real I was already thinking about leaving, but that was it for me. Shit is out of control down there."

Lydia cannot discuss this with him. They are only bodies to him, strangers on the news, people like the ones he has killed himself. *That girl in her quinceañera dress.* But then Lydia's mind snags on a previous detail, an exit ramp.

"What happened to his daughter?" she asks. Lorenzo looks confused, so Lydia clarifies. "Javier's daughter, La Lechuza's daughter. You said it was sad, what happened to her."

"Yeah, you didn't hear?"

"Hear what? What happened?"

On the day Sebastián's article was published, Javier read it in the back-seat of his car while his driver shuffled him through the sluggish morning streets of Acapulco. All his life, Javier had enjoyed an almost preternatural ability to predict incidents and their outcomes. When he was eleven years old and his father was diagnosed with colon cancer, Javier knew that death would be swift; he knew that his mother, who'd previously been a good mother, devoted and affectionate, would handle it poorly, that she'd medicate her grief with alcohol and new men. He foretold and accepted her abandonment well before it came to pass. As a result of that aptitude, Javier was almost immutably composed. Nothing ever really surprised him.

So it was uncharacteristic that he failed to see the article coming. He wondered if his love for Lydia had blinded him to the inevitability of it, and that possibility caused him to feel a faint wrinkle of resentment toward her. Even before he read it and even with the anonymous byline, Javier, who read the article with his usual equanimity, presumed the article was the work of Lydia's husband, whose journalistic expertise in the drug trade was well-known. Initially, he didn't need to measure his response, because the article didn't provoke much feeling in him. On the contrary, Javier regarded it to be a mostly fair depiction of his life. There were, of course, some marginal inaccuracies, one or two instances of exaggeration. There was more righteous condemnation than Javier was prepared to accept, but that was to be expected. Beyond those details, Javier thought, Sebastián had managed to apprehend something true about the essence of Los Jardineros in Acapulco. And he was bewildered but unexpectedly pleased by the inclusion of his poem. Javier presumed that Lydia had somehow given it to her husband. Had she memorized it? (A flattering notion.) Secretly photographed it with her cell phone during a moment of lapsed judgment? Though the poem revealed something intimate about him, it also illuminated his humanity, he thought. He therefore portended that it might make him beloved by the people. He neither smiled nor scowled as he folded the newspaper and set it in the sunbeam on the leather seat beside him.

Instead, he tried to anticipate the impact the article might have on his future. He understood immediately that there would be ramifications, that his relative anonymity was a thing of the past, that his liberty had been permanently compromised. He'd always known this would happen one day. He hadn't expected it to be so soon, but he would adapt. It was, at worst, a nuisance. Perhaps it could even be fun. He couldn't recall another time the press had devoted so much attention to a cartel as young as Los Jardineros. It had taken years of established work before ordinary people began to recognize the names El Chapo Guzmán or Pablo Escobar, and there were plenty of people who still loved those men for their generosity and mythos, even after their spectacular downfalls.

The only thing that truly unsettled Javier was his speculation that Lydia, his dear Lydia, had betrayed his confidence with the poem. That betrayal he had not foreseen, and it caused a treacherous quickening in his chest. But then it occurred to him that perhaps she hadn't been disloyal at all. Maybe she'd provided the poem as a faithful contribution, a nod to his true self. Maybe the poem was a gift.

Lydia knew Javier as well as anyone knew him. His first response to the article was exactly as she'd predicted.

At that same moment, several miles away, just at the outskirts of the city, on a sprawling *finca* with glittering all-day views of the turquoise sea, Javier's wife was also reading the article. She was a woman who had never been beautiful, but who took care to appear as if she might once have been. Her hair was platinum, her mascara and lipstick tastefully applied, her bosoms maintained by the architecture of expensive lingerie, her nails, gleaming and square and only a shade pinker than natural. She hadn't had a cigarette in almost three years, yet here she was, smoke curling from the tip of her quivering menthol. She had a name, but she seldom heard it. Instead, she heard *Mamá* or *Mi Reina* or *Doña*. She'd reached an age where she expected each day to be the unveiling of some quiet new sorrow, and where she simultaneously believed there was nothing left in life that could truly surprise her. As she pursed her lips to draw on the menthol, the fine lines around her mouth became grooves. She stained the filter of her cigarette with a shimmer of gold-coral lipstick and blew the smoke out over one shoulder. A nervous maid soundlessly approached and tipped extra coffee into her waiting cup. There were gulls out wheeling over the dappled blue horizon. The bougainvillea sang. But she sat, wordlessly rereading Sebastián's article for the third time. It troubled her. It's unsettling to see, emboldened by the veracity of black and white, the most deeply suppressed grapplings of your own smothered conscience, printed right there in the newspaper for all the world to read. Javier's wife had failed to sufficiently calm herself when their daughter,

Marta, called from boarding school in Barcelona later that afternoon and destroyed her with the simplicity of a single question: *Mamá, is it true?* And because of her failure, in that moment, to adequately reassure her daughter, she would forever blame herself for what happened next.

Three days later, on the day before Yénifer's *quinceañera*, the boarding school dean called to relay the news that Marta had been found hanging from the air-conditioning vent in her dorm room by a pair of her roommate's knotted tights. The suicide note was addressed only to her father.

"One more death should not matter much."

CHAPTER NINETEEN

Just on the outskirts of Guadalajara, inhaling the fragrance of chocolate, Lydia stops dead in her tracks. Her hand flies up to her mouth. Lorenzo turns to face her.

"Yeah, so I guess the daughter read that article your husband wrote," he says.

"Oh my God," Lydia says.

"You didn't know this?"

Lydia's voice falters.

"Yeah, somebody sent her the article, and when she read it, she freaked out and killed herself. Left her *papi* a suicide note. Shit was ugly. That's why." Lydia's mind races to put the pieces together while the boy *sicario* talks. "That's why he went *loco*. Said you betrayed him, said your husband was responsible, said you were all gonna pay. He was really fucked-up."

"Wait." Because her brain has seized. It's too full. *Marta.* Isolated memories surge up in Lydia's consciousness one after another and then pop like bubbles. Javier in the bookstore, Skyping with his daughter in Barcelona before an exam. Her apprehension, his fatherly encouragement. Javier laughing when he told Lydia about the pogo stick Marta bought him for his fiftieth birthday. How he'd tried it out just to please her and ended up with his back in spasms. Javier's insistence that Marta was the only good thing he'd ever done in his life. *Es mi cielo, mi luna, y todas mis estrellas.* My sky, my moon, and all my stars. There's an unwelcome pang in Lydia's chest.

"She didn't know? She didn't know about her father, about the cartel?"

"I guess not."

"How could she not know?" It seems so unlikely, but Lydia immediately perceives her own hypocrisy. She hadn't known either. The first domino of her understanding teeters and falls.

Lorenzo shrugs. "I don't know. But he made your family like a straight-up vendetta. It was practically a press release for Los Jardineros. Usually when there's a job, you only hear what you need to hear, and it's only the people involved who know anything about it, but this time was different. Everybody in the city knew, everybody in Guerrero."

Lydia begins shuffling her feet beneath her again, but her mind is whirring like a disengaged motor. She is blindsided. All this time, all these miles, the same futile, idiotic refrain kept presenting itself through her thoughts. *This wasn't supposed to happen. It wasn't supposed to happen.* She'd misjudged him. She had missed something. A thousand times, she'd replayed the conversation she'd had with Sebastián the night before the article came out. He'd asked if they should go to a hotel for a few days, to be on the safe side.

"No, I think we're fine," she'd told him.

"A hundred percent?"

"Yes," she'd said. "A hundred percent."

How that answer has haunted her. It has followed her into sleep every night. It has twisted in her gut without reprieve. All the frivolous reasons she hadn't wanted to go to the hotel: She hated to uproot Luca, for him to miss school, for her business to suffer. She hated the interruption to their routine. And she'd believed, truly, that Javier wouldn't hurt them. What she wouldn't give to go back to that moment with Sebastián, to say anything else. To suck those words back in and obliterate them. *A hundred percent,* she'd said. How presumptuous she'd been, how foolhardy! Of course she couldn't account for every eventuality. Why hadn't she seen that sooner? She could never have predicted this, but she could've predicted that something unpredictable might happen. *Why, why, why.* Her body feels like cracked glass, already shattered, and held in place only by a trick of temporary gravity. One wrong move and she will come to pieces.

Marta's death changed everything, of course. It changed everything. Behind her shock, Lydia can sense waves of competing emotions, but she shuts them all down. *De ninguna manera.* She will feel nothing about Javier's dead daughter. No, Lydia will not even say her name. She will feel nothing about his anguish. The note he sent her at the Duquesa Imperial: *I'm sorry for your pain and mine. Now we are bound forever in this grief.*

No.

No.

His grief is not the same as hers. Lydia will not feel empathy for him. She will rage. She will inhabit the fury of her own senseless bereavement, the one that Javier invented for her. Instead, she will walk, she will leave him behind, she will repeat the sixteen names of her murdered family. Innocents, all of them. Sebastián especially. An honorable man doing his job.

She will list them and repeat them and remember. Sebastián, Yemi, Alex, Yénifer, Adrián, Paula, Arturo, Estéfani, Nico, Joaquín, Diana, Vicente, Rafael, Lucía, and Rafaelito. Mamá. Repeat. Her husband, her sister, her niece and nephew, her aunt, her two cousins, all their beautiful children. Her *mamá.* Lydia will not stop saying their names.

Lorenzo is saying something beside her, but his voice recedes behind her own recitation. She needs to be away from him. She will walk beside Luca instead, press his warm fingers into the palm of her hand.

Her repetition will become a prayer.

They pass into busier neighborhoods with curious dogs and kids riding bikes and women pushing strollers. Luca sees one man with a white cowboy hat riding an old pony and talking on his cell phone, which makes him laugh. There are also girls who look to be around the sisters' age who stand near the tracks in groups of two and three. They wear clothes that look like Mami's underwear, and white high heels or knee-high boots. They have neon pink lips, and they call out to their countrymen in their Central American accents as they walk past. The girls invite the men to come have a beer or a smoke or a rest, and Luca knows there's something off about their appearance, their dress, something improper about their posture—so languorous against the bustle of the day. But he doesn't understand how it all works. He doesn't understand the difference between the men who shake their heads sadly and avert their eyes, and the ones who leer and whistle, who trot off to disappear into darkened doorways with those young dress-up girls. When he tries to ask Mami about them, she only shakes her head and squeezes his hand.

Several times they pass clusters of uniformed men who rouse themselves when they notice the passing migrants, but each time this happens, Danilo removes the still-sheathed machete from his shoulder and swings it alongside his body as he walks. He does some elaborate shuffle that passes for a dance, and sings as they go, "*¡Guadalajara, Guadalajara! Tienes el alma de provinciana, hueles a limpio, a rosa temprana . . .*" When the men in their uniforms notice him, they return their interest elsewhere, so by the time they reach La Piedrera, Lydia feels as though Danilo has saved their lives perhaps seven times. She grips his hand and says thank you, but he shrugs it off and wishes them a safe continued journey. He turns and ambles back down the tracks the way they came. They hear him singing as he goes. "*¡Guadalajara, Guadalajara! Sabes a pura tierra mojada.*"

"I wish he could come with us all the way to *el norte*," Rebeca says to Soledad as they watch him go.

"I can take care of you," Lorenzo says in response.

The sisters turn to look at him.

"Nah, we're all set," Rebeca says. "Thanks."

Lorenzo shrugs, but Soledad has no patience for this cholo and has never been a champion of subtlety anyway. She wheels on him.

"Are you still here? Did we invite you to join us or something? Because I don't remember doing that."

"Damn, girl. *Cálmate.* We're all going to the same place, aren't we?"

"Are we?"

"I mean, what, you own Guadalajara now?"

She turns away. "Come on," she says to Rebeca.

The girls start to walk, and Luca with them. Lydia doesn't move. She knows Lorenzo could use that phone in his pocket to call Javier right now. He could snap her neck and then snap her picture, collect a big reward. Her death could make him a Jardineros hero. But isn't it possible that, beneath the shield of his baby narco swagger, he's also a scared boy, alone in the world and running for his life? And isn't it also probably true that if he persists in not murdering them, he might know more things about the cartels that could help them? He's already been a wellspring, and Lydia would like the chance to interview him further, to pump him for more information. Luca and the girls look back at her from the corner they're about to turn. Luca is holding Rebeca's hand. The pace of their life has become so fast and so slow; Lydia never has enough time to make decisions. She works from instinct alone, and her instinct is strong in this instance. It tells her to go, to get away from him.

"Can I ask you one thing?" she says.

He shrugs.

"Do you think he's still looking for us?"

"*Sin duda alguna,*" he says. Without a doubt.

It's not surprising, but still, there's no comfort in the validation. Her body feels leaden. "But we're safer here, yes?"

Lorenzo's wearing a string backpack. He squints and looks around. "I don't know," he says. "I mean, anywhere is safer than Acapulco."

"But he has alliances in other *plazas*?"

"*Claro que sí,* there's a lot more cooperation with the other cartels than there was before him. He's got reach. Deep into rival territories."

"Which ones?" she asks.

"I don't know. What do I look like, some kind of *maldito* expert?"

Well. Yes, she thinks. She moves her lips to one side. "I'm just trying to determine our safest route."

"There is no safest route, far as I can tell," he says. "You just gotta run like hell."

She looks into his face, broad and young. His eyes are heavily lidded, his upper lip softened by a feeble crop of hair. He has the remnants of a breakout high on one cheekbone. He's a veritable kid. Who has murdered at least three people.

"Lorenzo, you're not going to tell anyone, are you?" she asks. She tries to anchor his gaze, but he looks away.

"Nah, I told you already. I'm done with all that. I'm out." He jams his hands into the pockets of his shorts.

She nods skeptically. "Thank you."

"*Ni modo.*"

It's an effort to turn her back to him, because she is still afraid. The shock of a blade entering her flesh, severing her spine. The pile of her body in the road beside the tracks. "*Suerte,* Lorenzo," she says, and she turns to go. It's even harder not to look back after she rejoins Luca and the sisters, but she knows he might interpret any backward glance as a weakness or an invitation, so she only imagines him falling behind. She pictures him following from a hidden distance, but she doesn't turn to confront her suspicions. She keeps moving, *adelante,* keeps Luca and the girls moving. It's not until hours later, on the doorstep of a migrant shelter, that she accords herself a pause of reassurance. Just before she enters, she turns and allows her gaze to sweep up and down the vacant road, to linger and search in every shadow, and to thank God. He is gone.

They're exhausted by the time they arrive. There are good migrant services in the city, and between that and Danilo's modest heroics, the Hershey's Kisses, Luca has difficulty reconciling all the genuine kindness of strangers. It seems impossible that good people—so many good people—can exist in the same world where men shoot up whole families at birthday parties and then stand over their corpses and eat their chicken. There's a frazzling thrum of confusion that arcs out of Luca's brain when he tries to make those two facts sit side by side.

At the shelter, Rebeca and Soledad stand guard for each other outside the bathroom door. It's a luxury to slough the dust of the road off your skin, to soap up and stand beneath a spray of warm water, to watch it pool at your feet, grimy and brown, before it circles the drain and disappears forever. Soledad likes to think of the water molecules racing down the drainpipes, intermingling and dispersing, joining other pipes beneath the streets of the city, gathering volume and speed as they rush and tumble toward some unknown destination. She likes to think of the filth she washes from her skin, diluted and diluted until it no longer exists as filth at all.

Although Soledad has the cell phone Iván gave her, she can't use it to make phone calls or text because it has no credit. If it did have credit, Soledad still wouldn't use it, for two reasons: first, except for her *primo* César, no one she knows has a cell phone anyway, and second, like Lydia, she's afraid that if she uses the phone, Iván will then somehow be able to find her. So the phone functions mostly as a repository of photographs, but also as a propeller that reminds Soledad how far she has come, and how much better her life will be when she gets to *el norte*.

So when, after their showers, the director of the *casa* asks them if they'd like to use the communications room to email or call anyone, the girls' excitement is almost too much to articulate. Finally, they can call Papi. Rebeca has never used a phone before, never lifted a device to her ear and heard the familiar voice of a faraway loved one. Soledad has never initiated a call. It's an ordinary modern convenience that, for the sisters, still carries the full weight of the miraculous.

"How do we do it?" Rebeca asks her sister after the director has shown them into the quiet room and closed the door behind them.

Soledad frowns. "Get Luca."

The room is small, and it contains a desk with a glowing computer, one rolling office chair, and a small, floral-print couch. The phone sits on the desk beside the monitor. Rebeca returns quickly with Luca, who sits down at the computer, asks the sisters for the name of the hotel where her father works, and finds the phone number within seconds. He writes it down on the lone yellow notepad, but when he stands to go, Soledad asks him to dial it, too.

"What's your father's name?" he asks, covering the mouthpiece as the line rings in his ear.

"Elmer," Soledad says. "Ask for Elmer Abarca Lobo in the main kitchen."

So Luca does, but as he prepares to immediately hand the phone over to Soledad, the receptionist says, "I'm sorry, but Elmer isn't working today. Hold on."

Luca hears the sound of her voice, muffled for a moment before she returns to speaking clearly.

"Can I ask who's calling?" she says.

"I'm here with his daughters. I was just putting in the call for them."

"I see," she says.

"Hold on, I'll put Soledad on," Luca says.

He hands the phone to Soledad, who takes his seat, her face brightening in nervous anticipation. She hopes Papi won't be angry with them. She hopes he'll understand why they had to leave the way they did, without warning, without a proper goodbye. She's been haunted, these last weeks, by the thought of him coming home alone to the dark apartment, exhausted from a double shift, and finding her note. She's tried not to think about the anguish it might've caused him. She bites her lip.

"Hello?" she says.

"Hello," a woman's voice on the line—still the receptionist. "You're calling for Elmer? Is this Elmer's daughter?"

"Yes, it's Soledad. Is he there? May we speak with him?"

"I'm afraid Elmer's not working right now, Soledad."

Soledad's shoulders slump, and she leans back in the chair. "Okay," she says. "Can we leave a message for him? It's an important message and I don't know when we'll have an opportunity to use a telephone again. I'm here with my sister, Rebeca, and we want to tell him we're okay."

"Soledad," the woman says.

Just that, just her name. *Soledad.* But something about the hesitation in those three syllables makes Soledad's stomach drop. She straightens up in the chair.

"I'm sorry, but your father won't be back to work for quite some time."

Soledad grabs the edge of the desk, and turns her back to her sister. Luca reaches for the doorknob, but Soledad puts a hand on his shoulder. Her mouth is open, but she refuses to ask the questions that will lead to her enlightenment. She doesn't want to know.

"I'm sorry, Soledad, but your father had an accident. Not an accident. Your father, he—he's in the hospital."

Soledad clamps her knees together and stands up, sending the chair rolling away behind her. "Why? What happened?"

Rebeca stands up then, too, and Luca moves next to her.

"Is he okay?" Soledad asks.

The woman's voice is low. "I think he's stable, that was the last we heard."

Soledad takes one breath. *Stable.* "But what happened?"

"He was attacked coming into work last week."

She moves to collapse into the chair again, but the chair is no longer behind her, and she almost falls to the floor. Luca grabs the chair and rolls it over. She sits.

"He was stabbed," the woman is saying. "I'm so sorry."

"Which hospital?"

"*El* Nacional. I'm sorry, Soledad."

Soledad hangs up the phone, and it takes Luca less than one minute to find the number for the Hospital Nacional in San Pedro Sula. Again, he dials for them, but this time he hits the speakerphone button so they can all hear. And 1,360 miles away, in the ICU unit in a six-story green-and-blue building, a nurse wearing clean white scrubs and a blue stethoscope darts into the nurses' station and tosses a chart onto the cluttered desk. Luca, Rebeca, and Soledad all hear her pick up the phone. They lean forward.

"I think my father is there," Soledad says. Her voice sounds swollen and cobwebby in her ears. "My father, Elmer Abarca Lobo. The woman at his work told us he was there since last week?"

They can hear things clicking and beeping in the background. Voices. A child crying. The nurse does not immediately reply.

"Hello?" Rebeca says.

"I'm looking," the nurse replies. There are folders, charts. She's flipping through them.

Soledad's hand darts over and grabs her sister's across the desk. Together, their knuckles turn hard and shiny.

"A woman at his work told us he was stabbed."

"Oh," as if the nurse suddenly remembers. "Yes, Elmer," she says. "He's here. Not in great shape, I'm afraid, but he's stable now. He lost a lot of blood."

Rebeca clamps her free hand over her mouth. Soledad digs her fingers into the skin of her face, her lower jaw. "Can we speak with him?"

"No, he's not conscious," the nurse says. "Can you come in?"

Rebeca shakes her head, but Soledad answers out loud. "We're not in Honduras," she explains. "We're in Mexico."

Rebeca is stuck on a different detail. "What do you mean he's not conscious? What does that mean?"

"It means we have him sleeping right now because of the damage to his brain. He needs to sleep until the swelling and trauma are under control."

Soledad pitches forward, curling her body over her knees.

"Damage to his brain?" Rebeca says. "I don't understand."

"Yes," the nurse says. "He was stabbed in the face."

"Oh my God." Both girls begin to cry.

Luca is shifting his weight ever more rapidly from foot to foot. He backs away from the phone until he's leaning against the wall beside the door.

"He was stabbed once in the stomach and twice in the face." The nurse keeps talking. She's not oblivious to the sisters' pain, but she knows she has to impart this information, and it's better to do it quickly, like ripping off a Band-Aid, so they can move on to the next part, where they already know all the awful information and can begin to process it. "The stab wound that did the most damage was to the right-hand side of his infraorbital region—"

"Infraorbital? What is that?" asks Soledad. "Please speak simply."

Even the most hardened trauma nurse in the most violent city in the world would have difficulty conveying this detail to the family.

"His eye," she explains.

"They stabbed him in the eye?" Soledad asks.

"Yes," the nurse says.

"Oh my God," Rebeca says again.

"Yes," the nurse says.

She tells them he's resting comfortably, that he's stable, that they will keep him in the medically induced coma until the doctor feels it's safe to wake him up. She doesn't know how long that will be. She warns them that the stab wounds were significant, and that there may be lasting damage to his brain. She explains that there's no way to assess that damage until the initial period of rest and healing has concluded.

"Girls," the nurse says quietly, and they hear a door close on her end of the line, followed by a peripheral silence. "Do you know who did this to your father?"

Soledad lets out a sob and then answers, "Yes, I think yes. I do."

Rebeca's black eyes grow even larger and darker. A storm in her face.

"Listen to me," the nurse says then. "I need you to listen carefully."

Both girls breathe raggedly. They are shaking.

"Don't you dare come back here," the nurse says. "Don't even think about it. Do you hear me?"

Their faces are wet, their noses filled with snot and tears. Rebeca sniffs loudly and lets a small cry loose into the room.

"He's getting the best care possible, okay?" the nurse says. There's a catch in her voice, too. "We are doing everything we can to make him well again. And if you come back here just to sit in our waiting room and wring your hands and cry and get yourselves both stabbed in the eye, too, well, it's not going to do him one bit of good, you understand?"

They do not answer.

"How old are you girls?"

"Fifteen," Soledad says.

"Fourteen," says Rebeca.

"Good. Your *papi* wants you to live until you are one hundred years old, okay? You cannot do that if you come back here. Keep going."

In San Pedro Sula, at the Hospital Nacional, they can hear the nurse blowing her nose.

"My name's Ángela. Call me again next time you get to a phone, and I'll give you an update."

"Thank you," Rebeca says.

The nurse clears her throat. "I'll tell your father you called."

After they hang up, they stay in the room without speaking. Soledad stands up and sits down and stands up again at least ten times. Rebeca sits on the edge of the couch and shreds a Kleenex into pulp. Luca does not move. He hopes the sisters will forget he's there. He hopes they won't speak to him or ask anything of him. He needs to get out of this room but cannot move. His *papi* is dead. Luca lifts a hand to touch the red brim of his dead father's hat. He pictures Papi on the back patio of Abuela's house without nurses or blankets or beeping machines that might save him. He pictures the silence of pooling blood. Luca stands there and blends into the wall.

Soon, there's a knock on the door. Soledad is grateful for the knock, as it gives her something outside her body to attend to. She opens the door.

"About finished?" A staff counselor stands in the hallway with an-other migrant. "There's a fifteen-minute time limit when people are waiting."

"Yes, sorry," Soledad says. "We'll be right out."

Luca slips out just before the counselor closes the door.

Inside, Soledad whispers, "I'm sorry."

"What?" Rebeca looks up from her tormented Kleenex.

"I'm sorry. I'm sorry. It's my fault, Rebeca. Forgive me."

Rebeca moves swiftly across the small space and throws her arms around Soledad so her rainbow wristband presses against the still-wet blackness of her sister's hair.

"Sh," she says.

"It's all my fault," Soledad says over and over again, until finally Re-beca pushes back from her and shakes her roughly by her two shoulders.

"Don't be ridiculous. It's no one's fault. Only *ese hijo de puta*."

Soledad crumples even smaller into her sister's arms. "But I had to make a horrible choice," she cries. "It was you or Papi, I knew that. I knew we were putting him in danger if we left. Iván warned me. I just, I didn't really think he'd go through with it. I thought if we left, he . . ."

She doesn't bother finishing the sentence because it doesn't matter what she thought. She was wrong. The sisters take two shaky breaths to-gether, and Rebeca wipes Soledad's tears with her thumbs.

"Stop," Rebeca says. "Stop it, Sole. Papi would've made the same choice. When he's better he'll be so proud of you. You'll see."

Soledad dries her face with a fresh Kleenex. She blows her nose. "You're right."

"He'll be okay," Rebeca says.

"He has to."

Into the clicking, beeping silence of Papi's hospital room in San Pedro Sula, the nurse Ángela enters solemnly in her white sneakers. She had known his name, of course, because of the identification they found in his wallet. But there had been no visitors, no inquiries, until today. Sometimes it's easier that way—you can provide the care the patient needs, manage his pain, and administer to his broken body without the weight of additional sorrow. Ángela has been a nurse in this city long enough to know that the pain of the family often eclipses the pain of the patient.

It's relatively quiet in the ward this evening, so after she checks his vitals and changes his waste bag, Ángela has time to sit with him. It's still light out, but she turns on the table lamp anyway because she finds its soft glow comforting. She closes her eyes briefly before she speaks to him. Her colleagues don't do this anymore because it's too taxing. Too heavy. Ángela is the only one. The violence is overwhelming in this place now. It's become a gang pageant of blood and grisly one-upmanship. The ICU is always busy, but it's not as overcrowded as the morgue. The other nurses use irreverent humor to cope. They use a secret rating system of smiley faces to forecast their patients' chances of survival. Ángela doesn't judge them for it. They have to go home to their children at the end of their shifts. They want to stay married. They want to eat dinner and drink a beer in the yard with the neighbors. But after twenty years on the job, Ángela still can't shut it off. She doesn't even want to.

She pulls the chair closer to Elmer's bedside and lifts his hand, careful not to disturb his IV line. She rubs the back of his hand with her thumb. "Elmer, your daughters called today," she says quietly. "Soledad and Rebeca called from Mexico, and they're doing well, Elmer. Your daughters are okay. They're on their way to *el norte.*"

CHAPTER TWENTY

Later that night, when the initial wash of shock has lost its bite and the sisters are beginning to feel calm beneath the new distress of the terrible news, Lorenzo shows up at the shelter. Lydia is helping in the kitchen, stirring a huge pot of beans on the cooktop, when she sees him through the open door to the large dining room. From a distance, he's not as menacing as he'd appeared on the train. He's not as tall, not as bulky as his first impression would've suggested. Like every other migrant here, he looks bone-weary, and relieved to be indoors where the aroma of a hot meal greets him. Still, Lydia instinctively moves her body out of his line of vision and accidentally drops the long wooden spoon into the vat of beans.

"*¡Carajo!*" she says out loud.

She presses her eyes and mouth closed for just a moment, and when the woman who runs the kitchen notices, she tells Lydia not to worry, and hands her a pair of tongs so she can fish the wooden spoon out of the beans.

Lydia helps serve the dinner, too, on paper plates, and the migrants have to line up cafeteria-style for their food. When Lorenzo comes through, and Lydia ladles a spoonful of beans onto his plate, he nods at her without making eye contact, without further comment, and that strange behavior makes Lydia even more afraid. Has she offended him, provoked him to change his mind about letting them be?

"Would you like a little more?" she asks him, but he's already moved along to the rice station.

The sisters and Luca are behind him in line, and while they're waiting, Soledad feels a hand slip beneath her arm and grope her breast. It's so fast, like a sparrow. Her whole body recoils from that hand, but when she whips her head around to confront her offender, there are three migrant men all standing there facing one another. They're so deep in conversation, and so oblivious to her presence, that there's no way to determine who it was that grabbed her. Their disinterest is so convincing that Soledad finds herself wondering if she imagined the violation. *No,* she tells herself. *I am not crazy.* She grinds her teeth and clamps her arms in front of her. She keeps her body hunched into a warning.

After dinner, everyone gathers in *la sala* to watch television, but not Lorenzo. Lydia doesn't know if she's relieved or concerned about his absence. It's both. She wants to keep an eye on him and hopes to never see him, ever again.

On TV, no one wants to watch the news because it's all too familiar, so they put on *Los Simpson.* At home, Mami doesn't like Luca watching *Los Simpson* because she thinks Bart is rude, and she doesn't want Luca to start saying things like *cómete mis calzoncillos,* but what Mami doesn't know is that Luca and Papi used to watch it together all the time when she wasn't home, and Papi would stretch out on the couch with his shoes off and his toes wiggling in his socks, and Luca would drape himself across Papi's chest like a blanket, and Papi would rub Luca's back while they watched. It was their secret ceremony. They'd imitate the voices, and Papi would keep the remote control close by so, if Mami came in unexpectedly, he could change the channel to *Arte Ninja* real quick. Luca doesn't like watching *Los Simpson* here in this tiled room with its fluorescent lights and everyone sitting on folding chairs with their arms crossed and their shoes on. He endures it by unlacing and relacing his sneakers three times, and when it's over, Mami suggests to Soledad and Rebeca that they might all say a rosary together, for the full restoration of their father's health. Also, she knows the practice will serve to calm her nerves, to soothe her agitation before she attempts to sleep. They retreat to the corner of the room where the tables are, and several other women join them. The sisters are grateful, and it's the first time in Luca's life that the rosary doesn't feel like a chore. He listens to the chanting voices of the gathered women, first his mother's lone cadence.

Blessed are you among women.

And then the chorus of response.

Pray for us sinners now and at the hour of our death.

Amen.

Otra vez.

Luca holds his *abuela*'s blue stone rosary in both hands and he counts out the prayers. He squeezes the stones between his fingers so hard their shapes are temporarily etched into the press of his skin. He wonders if Abuela ever did that, wonders how many times she passed these stones through the grasp of her aged hands, and when that thought occurs to him, he can nearly hear Abuela's voice among the chorus, *Santa María, Madre de Dios*. There's a catch in his throat, so he can't speak, can't add his own voice to the prayer, but it's okay, because listening is its own kind of reverence, and in any case, he feels an energy flowing out of the beads and into his fingertips like a throb, like a heartbeat. The rosary is a kind of tether, and if he clings to it tightly enough, it will preserve his connection to Abuela and Adrián, to all of them. To Acapulco, his little bedroom with the *balón de fútbol* lamp and the blanket with the race cars on it. To home. Luca closes his eyes and listens to the chain of prayers that binds him to Papi.

All the while there's a new posture about the sisters that slouches them into a diminished curl. When Luca opens his eyes and emerges from his own thoughts, he recognizes that posture because it's familiar to him. It's relatively new to Mami, too, and Luca thinks of it as a grief-curl. He feels truly sorry for the sisters' anguish and for Mami's, so he asks God to alleviate their suffering.

That night, Luca sleeps the best kind of sleep; he sleeps without dreaming.

That Lydia and Luca will travel with Soledad and Rebeca for as long as possible has not been detailed aloud, yet it's an arrangement all four of them intuitively understand. So much has happened that each hour of this journey feels like a year, but there's something more than that. It's the bond of trauma, the bond of sharing an indescribable experience together.

Whatever happens, no one else in their lives will ever fully comprehend the ordeal of this pilgrimage, the characters they've met, the fear that travels with them, the grief and fatigue that eat at them. Their collective determination to keep pressing north. It solders them together so they feel like an almost-family now. It's also true that selfishly, strategically, Lydia hopes the addition of two extra people to their traveling party might serve as an extra layer of camouflage, might confuse anyone who, at first glance, suspects she might be the dead reporter's missing widow. Before sleep, Lydia closes the ugliest box in her mind, and instead allows herself to think forward, to Estados Unidos. Instead of Denver she thinks of a little white house in the desert with thick adobe walls. She's seen pictures of Arizona: cactuses and lizards, the ruddy red landscape and hot blue sky. She pictures Luca with a clean backpack and a haircut, getting on a big yellow school bus and waving at her from the window. And then she conjures a third bedroom in that house for the sisters. Soledad's new baby, perhaps a girl. The smell of diapers. A bath in the kitchen sink.

They're all eager to get clear of Lorenzo—Lydia, most of all. So even though the shelter is comfortable and they are weary and, were he not here, it would be tempting to stay another night or two, in the morning, Luca, Lydia, Soledad, and Rebeca rouse themselves while it's still dark out. They are careful to creep past the men's bunk room without making a sound. They leave before dawn.

Lydia feels a tremendous sense of urgency about getting out of Guadalajara, and it's not only because of Lorenzo. This city is a Venus flytrap, and she sees evidence all around as they rush through the indigo predawn streets. Migrants come here with momentum, on their way to *el norte,* and they may find a welcome, a slice of comfort, some relative safety away from the rails, so they stay an extra day to catch their breath. Then three more. Then a hundred. Look there, sleeping stretched out on a piece of cardboard in a disused corner of a parking lot, a shoeless mother and toddler in dirty clothing. There, with his eyes glazed and a brown paper bag of God-knows-what clutched tightly in his fist, a skinny teenage boy, track-marked and bruised. There, there, and there, so many young girls tottering on heels in shadowy places, the whites of their eyes glowing brightly against the gloom. Lydia hustles Luca and the sisters away from the shelter and toward the tracks while the light around them grows toward sunrise.

For Soledad and Rebeca, on the other hand, there's some increased measure of reluctance about this leg of their journey, because they learned from a woman at the shelter last night that they will soon cross into the state of Sinaloa, a place that's famous among migrants for two things: its expertise at disappearing girls and the vigor of its cartel. Still, there's no way to get to *el norte* without passing through someplace that's famous for those things, and they chose the Pacific Route specifically because it's the most secure. So this is perhaps the most dangerous leg of the safest route, and in any case, the sooner they set out, the sooner they'll be past it. Soledad also has a new, increased sense of determination: what happened to Papi will not have been in vain. She is desperate to get to *el norte* now, to make a life there that is good and golden, a life that will honor her family's sacrifices. So there's an urgent sense of disquiet among them as they move northwest along the tracks, listening all the time for the hopeful sound of a train at their backs. Lydia looks over her shoulder compulsively now, and when at length the train approaches, they board easily, without even much forethought or communication. That fact startles Lydia when she reflects on it.

"We didn't even think about it," she says to Soledad, once she has Luca safely belted onto the grating.

"We're becoming professionals," Soledad answers.

But Lydia shakes her head. "No, we're becoming apathetic."

Soledad frowns. "It's natural to get used to it, though, right? We adapt."

Lydia touches a thick strand of Luca's hair that sticks out from beneath his father's baseball cap. It's too long, this hair. She coils one of the thick black curls around her finger, and in the tenderness of that act, she's momentarily transported back to her mother's garden. Leaning over Sebastián's lifeless body, the handle of the bent spatula digging into her knee. She had touched her husband's forehead, and the coarseness of his hair, still growing from its follicles, had tickled her wrist. Sebastián used shampoo with a scent of mint. A solitary sob rises up from Lydia's bones and is lost in the rumble of the train beneath her. She turns her eyes from Luca and looks at Soledad.

"From now on, when we board, each time we board, I will remind you to be terrified," she says. "And you remind me, too: this is not normal."

"This is not normal." Soledad nods.

The sky begins to brighten above them, and a ribbon of pale orange expands on the horizon, but it's still twilight where the tracks meet the earth. There's a handful of other migrants on top of the train, but it's not nearly as crowded as yesterday, and although that fact might be explained by the earliness of the hour, it serves to underscore Lydia's sense that Guadalajara has siphoned off some of their numbers. She feels her chest opening with something like relief as the train moves away from the city. A half hour north, the landscape is commandeered by miles of squat, spiky plants. They stretch into the distance along both sides of the tracks, their gray-green fronds like a million waving hands, and the train slows slightly at the outskirts of a town where the buildings are quaint and well kept. Lydia notes the sweet, sticky aroma of fermenting agave plants. Tequila. On the car behind them, two migrants climb down a side ladder and wait for a safe place to jump off. Luca tries to watch them, but the train turns, and the men disappear, and Luca has to content himself without proof that they landed safely. He has to create that truth with only the determination of his mind.

The train thunders on toward Tepic, toward Acaponeta, toward El Rosario. For a long time then, they pass nothing at all. Just grass and dirt and trees and sky. The occasional building, a rare cow. It's pastoral, beautiful, and the morning air is fresh. Lydia feels a treacherous pang of smothered delight, a bewilderment of migrant as fleeting tourist, as if they're on vacation looking out across some exotic landscape. It's brief.

Despite the growing distance between herself and Lorenzo, the pique of his presence remains. It's alarming that he found them so easily, so accidentally. He hadn't even been looking. But Javier is looking, with all his considerable resources, with all his connections. Lydia turns her face to the south, ridiculously, as if she'll see him standing there atop the train. As if he'll push his glasses up the bridge of his nose and approach her. It won't happen like that, she knows. When he comes for them, it won't be him, wearing a smile and a cardigan, clutching a volume of poetry to his chest. It will be some faceless assassin, some boy in a hoodie, cold in the dispatch of her death. *El sicario* won't feel anything when he delivers the bullet that murders her son. Lydia might be a hamster on a wheel. She knows their executioner might already be on this train, but she wills it to move faster regardless, that they might outrun that selfie of Lydia with Javier, as it pings its way from phone to phone, all the way across Mexico. Lydia shrinks between the sisters. She slips her finger inside Sebastián's ring.

At a tiny village surrounded by mango orchards, La Bestia crosses without notice into Sinaloa. Soledad is stretched out, her pack tucked beneath her as a pillow and her fingers wrapped into the grating. Her face looks awash in a sickly gray.

"How are you feeling?" Lydia asks. The vocabulary of her former life is inadequate now, but it's all she has.

Soledad opens her mouth, but then closes it again without answering and shakes her head.

"When I was pregnant with Luca, olives helped with the nausea," she says quietly. Then her mind does a litany of counterarguments. *When I was pregnant with Luca, I was not fifteen years old. When I was pregnant with Luca, I did not have to travel thousands of miles on top of a freight train. When I was pregnant with Luca, he was not conceived by rape.*

"Olives?" Soledad grimaces, readjusts her chin on her backpack, and closes her eyes, but it's no use. After two deep breaths, she lunges for the side of the train and vomits over the edge.

Rebeca watches, her eyes wide with worry. Then she hands her pack to Luca and crawls across to her sister. She rubs the small of Soledad's back and waits for the retching to subside.

There's a briny cut to the air as the tracks draw near the ocean. Mango groves give way to palm trees in sandy soil, and outside a tiny village, a couple dozen migrant men have made a large camp. They cheer when they see the train approaching, but the beast doesn't slow, it's moving too fast for them to board, so the men stand despondent, watching it thunder past. Luca waves, and a few wave back. Most reclaim their positions in the scanty shade to rest while they wait for the next train, but one man decides to try. He runs alongside the tracks while the others watch. They shout and whoop at him, a lot of competing noise, conflicting advice. He manages to get one hand up on a passing ladder, but his legs can't keep up. His arm is snagged, but the legs hang down. The watching men yell louder and more frantically.

"Luca." Mami tries to draw his attention away, but he's leaning over to watch, transfixed by the dangling man. They all are.

It's clear he won't make it, that he can't haul himself up from that position. One arm binds him to the velocity of La Bestia. They all hold their breath. The man's face is tipped up so Luca can see his expression, the moment he shifts from determination to acceptance. For a moment beyond that, he delays letting go, so Luca has the impression the man is savoring it, these final seconds when his life is intact. When at last his grip fails and he falls, there's still a hope, briefly, that he'll land clear of the tracks. That happens sometimes. A fluke of lucky physics and biology. But no. This man is sucked instantly beneath the wheels of the beast.

His mangled screams can be heard above the sounds of the churning train. Luca looks back and sees the migrants gathering in a knot on the tracks behind them, assessing the pieces of the severed man. Lydia does not cry for that wounded man, but she does pray for him. She prays that he won't survive his mutilation, that merciful death comes quickly for him. More fervently, she prays that whatever impression the incident has on Luca, it won't cause him any further harm. Surely her son may soon reach a limit of what a resilient child might endure without triggering some permanent internal decay.

"Don't worry, *amorcito*," she tells him. "That man will be fine."

Luca protests. "He was in two pieces, Mami."

Her voice is light. "That's what doctors are for." She feigns confidence in the way all mothers know how to do in front of their children. She wears the fierce maternal armor of deceit. She allows only a moment to pass before she changes the subject, turning to Rebeca. "So what will you girls do when you get to the border? You have a plan, how to cross?"

"Yes, our *primo* went last year, into Arizona, and then he got a ride from there to Maryland. That's where he lives, and we're going to stay with him. We're using the same route, the same coyote."

"How'd he find the coyote?" Lydia is constantly reminded that her education has no purchase here, that she has no access to the kind of information that has real currency on this journey. Among migrants, everyone knows more than she does. How do you find a coyote, make sure he's reputable, pay for your crossing, all without getting ripped off?

Thankfully, Rebeca is flush with insight. "Loads of people from our village used him before. He was recommended. Because you can't just pick any coyote. A lot of them will steal your money and then sell you to the cartel, you know?"

Lydia has never met a coyote. It's possible she's never even met anyone who's met a coyote.

"You should use our guy," Rebeca says. "Unless you already have one lined up."

Lydia shakes her head. "We don't."

Rebeca smiles. "So we can go together. *Mi primo* César—he says this guy is the best. It took them only two days of walking and then somebody picked them up in a camper van on the other side and drove them to Phoenix. Gave 'em bus tickets from there to wherever they were going. It's a lot of money, but he's safe."

"How much money?" Lydia asks.

Rebeca looks to Soledad, who's still lying down, her head resting in her folded arms. Rebeca continues rubbing her sister's back. "How much, Sole?"

Soledad answers without lifting her head or opening her eyes. "Four thousand each."

Lydia is startled by the sum. "I thought it would be much more than that, like ten thousand pesos at least."

"Dollars," Soledad says, her voice muffled by the sleeve of her shirt. "Four thousand dollars."

Dios Santo. Lydia does a quick intake of breath. She accepts dollars in the bookstore, so she's familiar with the typical exchange rates, but not in these quantities. She strains to do the math in her head. It's a lot of money, but they have enough, they have plenty. They will even have a small sum left, to get them started on the other side. But then she remembers the padre's pep talk in Celaya. *Every single one of you will be robbed. Every one. If you make it to* el norte, *you will arrive penniless, that's a guarantee.*

But it's good, anyway, to have a plan, to look beyond what they might eat today or where they might sleep tonight. Lydia doesn't feel ready for it, but she's beginning to consider the future. She's definitely not ready to look back, though, and she hopes she may accomplish one without necessitating the other.

"So where do you meet this coyote? He's expecting you?" she asks Rebeca.

"Yes, his name is El Chacal—"

Of course it is, Lydia thinks. *Why would a coyote be named Roberto or Luis or José when he can be named The Jackal?*

"—and he works out of Nogales. When we get there, we call his cell phone. Look." Rebeca loosens the rainbow wristband she wears on her left arm and sticks her finger into a tiny hole on the inside. From there she unrolls a scrap of paper with the coyote's phone number on it.

"Good." Lydia nods. "Okay."

So now they have a solid plan.

It's amazing that riding on the top of a freight train can become boring, but it's true. The tedium is spectacular. The chugging of the engine and the squeal of the metal are so constant that the migrants no longer hear those things. At towns where the train slows or stops, migrants get off, migrants get on, and they continue. The sun hikes high into the sky and glares down on them until their skin is so hot they can smell it, a little charred, and the brightness of the light bleaches the colors out of the landscape.

They pass through Mazatlán without stopping, where the tracks run alongside the ocean for a while, and the existence of sand there and the blueness of the sea remind Luca of home, which makes him feel obliterated instead of cheered. He's glad when they turn inland and leave the beach behind. But then it's back to hours of tedium, blended brown and green and gray, so it's almost a welcome diversion when, a few miles outside Culiacán, the monotony is broken by screaming. A lone voice repeats the words over and over, like a siren: *¡la migra, la migra!*

All around them, migrants grab their things quickly; some don't even bother with that—they look once at the dust trails kicked up by the tires of the approaching trucks, they choose the opposite side of the train, and they bail.

"Come on, Soledad, wake up," Rebeca says, her voice tight with panic. "We have to go."

The train is slowing but hasn't stopped, and the men on top aren't waiting. They scatter. They bolt.

"*¡A la mierda con esto!*" Soledad curses, slinging her pack onto her shoulders.

"What's happening, Mami?" Luca asks.

In theory, *la migra* is no threat to Lydia and Luca. As Mexican nationals, they cannot be deported back to Guatemala or El Salvador, and unlike most of their fellow migrants, they aren't in the country illegally. They're committing only the minor infraction of riding the train. So perhaps it's only the pervasive panic all around them, perhaps it's contagious. But no, Lydia just *knows*. She can tell that *los agentes de la migra* in their uniforms are not here to enforce law and order. She knows by the bone-deep fear born only of instinct that she can't rely on their citizenship now to protect them. They are in mortal danger, she can feel it in her pores, in her hair.

The trucks converge like pack animals. The men inside are masked and armed. Lydia scrabbles frantically at the buckle on Luca's belt, but her hands are shaking and she has to try three times before she can free him.

"Mami?" Luca's voice is rising in pitch.

Hers is low. "We have to run."

CHAPTER TWENTY-ONE

There are three trucks, all black and white with enormous roll bars, and together they speed across the roadless dirt and sidle up beside the tracks, spewing gravel and dust behind them. There are at least four *agentes* standing in the back of each truck, plus more inside, and they're all kitted out like they're going to war. Luca stares at them with his mouth open. They wear boots and kneepads and helmets and giant, studded Kevlar vests and gloves and dark black visors so you can't see their eyes, and their faces are entirely covered by black balaclavas. Each one of them has weapons strapped all over his body and a really large gun slung diagonally across his chest, and Luca can't even begin to imagine what they'd need all that weaponry for, just to catch a few migrants, and then he also thinks it would be impossible to tell the difference, in all that gear, between an *agente federal de migración* and a *narcotraficante* in disguise, and Luca isn't sure there's much difference between them anyway because a gun is a gun is a gun. Luca pees in his pants.

No one cares. Migrants are spilling over the edges of the train. The ladders are full, and some men don't wait their turn; they jump from the top, and Luca cringes as he watches them land. One man doesn't get up again after he leaps. He writhes on the ground clutching his broken leg. Many stumble and puff when they hit the ground, but they have to make a swift recovery. They stagger and pick up speed. Luca has many questions, but he understands that now is not the time to ask them, so he listens to Mami and does exactly as she instructs. They are the last ones to reach the top of the ladder, and the only good part about that is that it's empty now—all the men have gone, and Luca can see them loping like jackrabbits through the fields, but it's no use. Luca can see that it's no use. Because *la migra* has planned the raid perfectly—the train, where they are now, is in the middle of just fields and fields and fields, all harvested, flat, brown, and bald. There is nowhere for those migrants to go, never mind how quick or clever or jackrabbity they might be. As soon as the migrants disembark from the train, they are done for. There is no town, no building, no tree, no bush, no ditch, no cover. And Luca nearly opens his mouth to share this observation with his mother, to suggest that maybe they'd be better off staying put, but then the train engages its brakes and they all lurch forward and Rebeca loses her grip on the ladder, and Soledad lunges for her, but misses her hand, but then catches her stringing hair only because it has come loose in the rush, and when she hauls her sister back in by the hair, they are both crying. They can all taste their hearts in their throats, and Luca says nothing at all as the train finally pulls to a jerky halt.

They run not because they have any feeling that they might actually escape, but rather against the certain futility of running, because their terror compels them to run. They run because every one of them understands that if they are caught, when they are caught, all the hard-fought progress they've managed up to this point will come to an abrupt end. Whatever they have suffered in order to get this far on their journey will have been for naught. They understand that the best-case scenario now is to be captured by a man who obeys the dictates of his uniform, a man who will detain them and process them, and then erase their entire journey, and send them back to wherever they started. That is the best-case scenario. On the other hand, they know, this capture might not be bureaucratic at all. Perhaps there's no one waiting to process them, fingerprint them, and send them home. Instead, this capture may turn out to be much more nefarious than that: kidnapping, torture, extortion, a finger chopped off and photographed for the threatening text they will send to your family in *el norte*. A slow, excruciating death if your family doesn't pay up. The stories are as common as the rocks in this field. Every migrant has heard them; they run.

Lydia's mind is clear of all thoughts except running as she propels herself and Luca along the furrowed earth as quickly as their bodies can go. Ahead of them, the sisters begin to pull away. Luca's moving as fast as he can, but his legs are so small. It doesn't matter. The train has chugged ahead to where it was instructed to stop, and the trucks have crossed the tracks behind it, and an *agente* in one of those trucks speaks into a bullhorn.

"Stop running. There is nowhere for you to go. *Hermanos migrantes,* sit down and rest where you are. We are here to collect you. We will collect you with or without your cooperation. Your choice now is to make us happy or to make us angry. *Hermanos migrantes,* we have food and water for you. Sit down and rest where you are."

The disembodied voice coming, as it does, from the barrel chest of a masked man and traveling across the bald fields with the attached squawk of the bullhorn, is the creepiest thing Luca's ever heard. The message is intended to enfeeble them, to make them understand the powerlessness of their position, and on some of the men, it works. Among the breakaway clusters, a few stop running. They put their hands on their hips, their knees, their chests heaving. They look up at the sky with some mixture of impotent rage and dread and acceptance. They sit down in the dirt, their legs extended, their heads collapsing into the cradles of their hands.

But the voice doesn't debilitate Luca; on the contrary, it makes him run faster. It reminds him of the times at Abuela's house when she'd ask him to go down to the basement and get another bottle of ginger ale to put in the refrigerator, and he knew he had to go down there and do it, but Abuela's basement was creepy. Even if you turned on all the lights and sang loudly to yourself the whole time, you'd still get only halfway back up the stairs before you'd feel that ice-cold certainty that something evil was chasing you, that it was right behind you grazing the slick of your neck, that it would, in another second, clutch at your ankle and yank you into the depths. The bullhorn engenders that same feeling, except a thousand times worse, because it's real.

Luca runs with his wet pants and his *mami*'s hand and all the horrific memories of Abuela's green shower stall. And then Mami cries out and it all goes into slow motion: Mami's cry, a shrill, corporeal thing, it bubbles out of her like a fully formed bird and it flies, but Mami doesn't.

She goes the other direction, down, down. She tumbles, slow, slow. And Luca, because he's familiar with people being shot, because he has just observed the many, many guns of *la migra,* because everyone else in his family was killed by a bullet, presumes quite naturally that Mami is dead. Why else would she cry out like that? Why else would she fall? It's so slow. First her hands. Then her head, her shoulder. Because of her significant velocity, she tumbles. Her back, her bottom. Her knees. She is on her knees in the dirt and Luca is no longer holding her hand. She is on her knees and her hands. Luca reaches for her arm. He's afraid to pull. Afraid that she's propped up like that only by some strange trick, and that if he unsettles the weight that's resting on her arms and legs, her body will collapse, and that it will never animate itself again. He pushes past that fear. He grabs for her arm.

"Mami, come on. Mami, run."

There is no blood, he notices. No blood. *Gracias a Dios.* He feels himself begin to breathe.

"I can't run," Mami says. "I can't run. I'm sorry, Luca. My ankle." She stands. It's her ankle! It's only her ankle. She tests her weight on it. A slice of pain. Not too bad. She hobbles in a small circle. She can walk, but she can't run.

"Okay," Luca says. His face is very wet.

He turns and sees Rebeca and Soledad still going, growing smaller into the distance as they run, and everything feels like euphoria now, in this terrible moment. Because Mami's voice still works and the sisters are still running. He clutches Mami around her belly, and she drapes an arm over him. *Nothing else matters,* Luca thinks. *As long as she's okay.*

Lydia keeps Luca's head there, pressed against her side so he won't see the tears sliding down her face. She doesn't know how caked with dirt she is, doesn't know that the tears are cleaning telltale trails down her face that will divulge her tears later, even after she dries them.

"It's okay, *mijo,*" she says. "We have every right to be here, to travel in our own country. We are Mexican. They can't do anything to us. We will be okay."

Luca believes her, but she doesn't manage to convince herself. The trucks have spread out to round everyone up. The farthest one has already passed the sisters, and is circling back, hemming them in.

"*Hermanos migrantes,* stop running. Sit down and rest where you are."

An *agente* hops out of the nearest truck and approaches Luca and Lydia, keeping one hand on his biggest gun. He uses it to gesture at them without using his voice so they know where to go.

When Lydia was a teenager and her *tío* died, her *tía* remarried a man who owned a cattle ranch in Jalisco. It was a two-day drive up the coast to the wedding with her parents and sister, and Lydia never forgot what it was like being there on that *hacienda,* how the wind was loud in their ears and the new *tío's* dogs herded the spooked cattle. They were tireless, those black-and-white working dogs, and they ran in big, swooping arcs to hem in the nervous cows. The cattle stamped and twisted fretfully. Lydia remembers how everyone else that day was amazed by those dogs, smiling, panting, running in happy arcs. How disciplined they were! How effortless it seemed for them! Lydia was the only one who felt sorry for the frightened cows. Everyone seemed to forget that they were animals, too. That memory returns now as the trucks swoop in arcs around the panicked migrants. Lydia has never before likened herself, on purpose or by any metaphorical accident of psychology, to an animal. So there's a crushing despair that accompanies this recollection. How animalistic they are in this field. She feels like prey.

Once *la migra* has rounded everyone up, Soledad and Rebeca included, the *agentes* march them to the nearest paved road. Everyone is sweaty, disheveled, and out of breath from running. Soledad and Rebeca made it farther than almost anyone before the truck looped around and forced them to turn back. Rebeca pauses and plants her hands on her knees to catch her breath. Soledad spits into the dirt. Everyone is angry and frustrated and reluctant to obey, but *los agentes* prod them roughly when they don't walk fast enough. Luca counts the gathered migrants, which doesn't provide any information about potential escapees because he didn't count them before they were scattered, so there's no baseline number. It doesn't matter, he thinks, because he can see all the way to the horizon from here, the slight brown arc of the earth. No one got away. Beside him, Lydia limps, the pain in her ankle subsiding to a dull throb. They wait at the side of the road, and no one tells them what they're waiting for, or how long the wait will be. There are twenty-three migrants here, and despair has settled into their features like a powdery dust. While they wait, Lydia keeps her face low beneath the floppy pink hat and watches *los agentes* for clues about what manner of captivity this might turn out to be. One of the other migrants is outraged. He has no intention of cooperating.

"*¿Quién está a cargo aquí?*" The man stands, even though they've been told to sit, and speaks past the shoulder of the officer who's been set to guard them, to the man they all suspect of being in charge, *el agente* who's sitting on the folded-down tailgate of his pickup truck with one foot planted in the dirt beneath him and the other dangling from the tailgate. His posture is casual, so it's surprising when he stands quickly and approaches the migrant who addressed him. Lydia watches, barely breathing, because this exchange might tell them everything they need to know about the hours ahead. She doesn't realize she's digging her fingernails into Luca's arm until he begins to squirm. She lets go, rubbing apologetically at the little gouge marks she accidentally made in his skin.

"What do you need?" *El agente* stands very close to the migrant, and Lydia understands that this is deliberate, that he hopes to frighten the other man, which strikes her as both juvenile and effective.

"I am a Mexican national. You have no right to detain me," the migrant says. "I want to know who's in command of this unit." *El agente* is tall enough that the migrant has to crane his neck to look up, his chin level with the top of the Kevlar vest.

"I am in charge," *el agente* says, and then he claps a hand onto the shoulder of his comrade beside him. "And he is in charge. And you see that guy over there? With the gun? He is also in charge. Everyone who looks like me? This uniform? We are in charge. And we have the right to detain whoever we like. Take a seat."

After a few minutes and some removed conversation, most of *los agentes* get into two of the three trucks and leave, so only five remain on the roadside with the migrants. With those two departing vehicles, so, too, disappear the migrants' hopes that this might be a clean, administrative experience. Fewer uniforms means fewer witnesses. The captives eye one another nervously, but no one moves. Even if the five remaining agents weren't so heavily armed, even if one of the migrants felt inclined to run, there's nowhere for them to go. Because of these circumstances, the hand-cuffs, when they appear, feel both gratuitous and alarming. They're not real handcuffs, but plastic zip ties. At first Lydia hopes they're only going to shackle the men. They begin at the end, standing the migrants up one at a time. They pat them down for weapons, cell phones, money. They take their backpacks and zip-tie their wrists behind them. One man complains when they take his money, and *el agente* backhands him across the face with his radio. Luca's eyes grow wide.

"*Mijo,* look," Mami says, pulling Luca close. "Look at that cloud." She points.

"It looks like an elephant," he says.

"Yes, and then see there? What's it picking up in its trunk?"

Luca squints. He knows what she's doing, trying to distract him. She doesn't want him to see. And he could tell her it doesn't matter anymore, that he's seen so much worse than this already, but he understands that it's as much for her as it is for him, this distraction. She needs to feel like she can still mother him, still provide him with some relief, no matter what horrible things are happening fifteen feet away. Luca can hear that man crying softly. Luca can imagine, without raising his eyes to confirm such things, that there's a glossy trickle of bright blood leaking from that man's nose or lip. Luca focuses on the cloud-elephant because it's something he can do for Mami.

"I think he's picking a flower."

Mami touches her cheek to his. "I think he's shaking hands with a little mouse."

When all the migrant men are handcuffed, nineteen of them, Luca counts, *los agentes* come to the sisters. They move to take Rebeca first, but Soledad steps in front of her.

"Everybody wants to be a hero," one of *los agentes* mutters. His partner laughs.

They turn Soledad around and take a long time patting her down. Much longer than they took on any of the men. Luca can feel Mami trembling beside him. The officers flap the bottom of Soledad's oversize white T-shirt, billowing air beneath it, and then they bend down to look up it. They stick their hands up there.

"Think she's packing?" the partner asks.

"Oh, she's packing all right."

When they cuff her, they pull her T-shirt at the back so it's stretched tight against the white outline of her bra, and they gather up all the loose material and bind it into the zip ties behind her, along with her wrists. The material rides up to show a few inches of her brown tummy, and all the migrant men show their solidarity for her by turning their eyes to the ground.

"That's better," says *el agente* who cuffed her. He tosses Soledad's confiscated backpack into the bed of the truck along with the others, but when Soledad moves to sit back down on the ground with the other migrants, he grabs her by the elbow. "You sit up here instead." He points to the folded-down tailgate.

Soledad's face betrays nothing. She sits where instructed, and makes sure not to watch while they do the same to Rebeca. Soon her sister is seated up beside her, and they lean against each other, consoling each other with the heat of their touching shoulders. Lydia endures her turn next. They face her away from Luca and remove her hat to study her face. She squints in the sunlight, but they replace the hat without comment before groping her breasts and her backside. They find the machete strapped to her leg, and they laugh while they unbuckle the holster. One of the men throws it into the bed of the pickup truck with a *thunk*.

"Don't worry, *mijo*, it will be okay," she says to Luca without turning to face him.

Luca is sitting cross-legged with his elbows on his knees. Soledad and Rebeca both stare silently at him, as if they can make a bubble of protection around him just by the resolve of their eyes.

The officer speaks to Lydia without inflection, without anger or hostility, in exactly the same tone of voice Lydia would use if she were talking to the automated teller when she does her banking by phone. "Shut up," he says, and he slides his hand between her legs. He brushes his pinky finger back and forth along the crotch of her jeans. Lydia clamps her mouth shut and begins to cry.

Luca leans forward to stand up, but Rebeca calls out to him. "What is the third-largest city in the United States?" she asks.

Luca is confused. "What?"

Rebeca repeats the question.

"Well, that's easy, it's Chicago," Luca says. "Once you get down to around the fifth- and sixth-largest it's a lot trickier because those populations are changing by a significant percentage year by year, but—wait, why?"

Seated on the tailgate with her hands tied behind her, Rebeca shrugs. "Just curious."

The officers have finished with Lydia, and they seat her back on the ground beside Luca.

"Come on, little man," they say to him.

Luca stands. He puts his arms and legs out and makes his body into the shape of an X. They remove his backpack and throw it into the back of the truck with the others. He does not complain. They turn his pockets inside out. He does not complain. They remove Papi's red baseball hat from his head.

"Nice hat. You a Yankees fan?" one of them says.

"You can't have it," Luca says. "It belonged to my *papi.*"

"Oh yeah? Where's your *papi* now?"

"He's dead." Luca wields that truth like a battle-ax.

The officer is impassive, but he nods and sticks the hat back onto Luca's head. Luca turns and puts his wrists together so they can cuff him. The officers laugh.

"Nah, *chiquito,* we're not going to cuff you," the first one says. "That your *mami* over there? Go sit with your *mami.*"

Luca doesn't understand why, but he feels ashamed not to be cuffed. Diminished. His face flushes hot, but he goes and sits down on Mami's lap, nonetheless, which is a thing he hasn't done for at least two years.

When the two vans arrive, the officers open the back doors and usher the migrants inside. There are no seats or windows. They are unmarked cargo vans, and Lydia knows that probably means they're all going to die. Her mind is racing and blank at once. She doesn't recall the details, the words, the exact numbers or dates, but she's remembering the disappearance of those forty-three college students from that bus in Guerrero in 2014. The massacre of 193 people in San Fernando in 2011. Just a few months ago, 168 human skulls found in a mass grave in Veracruz. Who will miss Luca and Lydia if they disappear? *We have already disappeared,* she thinks. *We already do not exist.* When she looks at Luca, she sees the shape of his cranium beneath his skin.

The migrant men are loaded into the dark vans first. They sit awkwardly inside with their legs extended and their hands cuffed behind them, trying not to tip over on one another. Some of them are already crying. The first van is full; the doors are closed. Lydia and Luca are last to be loaded into the second van. Rebeca and Soledad are still seated on the tailgate of *la migra* truck.

"My daughters," Lydia says to the officer who fondled her as he hoists her now into the back of the van.

"Your what?"

Lydia points with her chin to the sisters in the back of the truck.

"Those are your daughters?" he asks, even though they both know that the two Central American girls with their Honduran accents and their skin an entirely different shade than Luca's are not Lydia's daughters.

"Yes," she says. "We need to stay together."

"No room," he says, lifting Luca into the van beside her. "Van's full."

He slams the left-hand door, but Lydia sticks her leg out to block the second door with her foot.

"Please," she says, looking across at the silent sisters. Rebeca and Soledad stare back at her, their expressions ranging like a quarrel of sparrows across their faces. "Please, we have to stay together."

"Don't worry," the man says, pushing Lydia's leg back inside the van. "We'll give the girls a ride."

When he slams the door, Lydia's almost grateful for the blackness.

CHAPTER TWENTY-TWO

Behind Lydia's most immediate fear of being murdered in ob-scurity, or worse, watching Luca suffer some act of brutality, she's also afraid that, whomever these men are working for, they may find out who she is and submit her to a different kind of murder instead. Even if they're not actively looking for her, they might discover her accidentally, as Lorenzo did. If they are working for a cartel, which seems increasingly undeniable, and they do recognize her, they wouldn't necessarily have to be allies of Los Jardineros to identify her as a valuable commodity. There are any number of ways they could use her: as a bargaining chip, a peace offering, a humiliating prize, an expression of competitive violence. Lydia still has her voter ID card in her wallet. Why? Why hadn't she gotten rid of it? If she survives this captivity, she will destroy it before they go any farther. She will surrender her name; she has already relinquished everything else. Lydia thinks again of Marta, swinging from the vent of that distant dorm room. She thinks of Javier in grief. And though she can't conceive of forgiving him for what he's done, she also wonders, now that she knows about his daughter, if she might've been able to reason with him, given the chance, to appeal to that decimated, fatherly part of him. To plead for mercy, for her life and Luca's.

Beside her, Luca presses his head against her arm. "Mami, I'm scared."

"I know, *amorcito*."

"Where did they take Rebeca?"

"I don't know, *amorcito.*"

She curls her head over his because it's all the comfort she can give him. She tries not to think about what Soledad and Rebeca are enduring right now. Her body shudders in an effort to sling her imagination shut. Sweat trickles down her spine, and the hot air in the van feels damp and close. The reek of fear is thick. But when Luca slips his little hand up beneath her hair and clutches the nape of her neck, the sensation of his slick palm against her skin is like a shot of determination. They will survive this. They must. She curves her whole body toward him in the dark.

When finally the van doors open, the light is painful after all the blackness. The migrants feel sweaty and dizzy and thirsty. Luca's pants haven't dried because it was so humid inside the van. The stale urine has a piquant odor, but no one mentions it. Maybe not all of it is coming from Luca. The migrants scoot on their butts toward the open doors and try to hop down without falling. It's a cement floor beneath them. Dim fluorescent lights high overhead. They're inside a large warehouse, and the men in charge are no longer wearing uniforms. It takes a moment for these facts to land in Lydia's consciousness. It's not a precinct or a jail or an immigration detention center, but a dingy, anonymous warehouse. *Carajo.*

In one corner, there's a utility sink with water running, and the migrants are permitted one at a time to stick their heads under the murky tap and take a drink. The water tastes of rust and hard-boiled eggs. Luca can't reach.

"Please, can you untie me so I can help my son?" Lydia asks one of the guards.

He doesn't answer her but instead lifts Luca so he can stick his mouth beneath the faucet.

"What stinks?" the man asks and then, realizing it's Luca, tosses him down. "*¡Qué cochino!*"

Luca manages not to cry. He stands next to his *mami.* They are made to sit on the floor, and for a long time that's all they do, lined up along a wall, listening to whatever sounds they can hear: a steady trickle of water dripping into that filthy sink, the clacking of some metal rollers nearby, the occasional furtive whisper of one migrant to another, the unafraid voices of the guards echoing from a nearby room where they're talking and laughing. They're smoking in there, too. Luca can smell it. The migrants don't ask questions or complain. No one moves. Some of them pray quietly together. After what feels like hours, a door in one wall rolls up on its tracks, and all the migrants squint from the onslaught of unexpected daylight. A truck rolls in, the one with all their backpacks, the one with Rebeca and Soledad seated in the bed, facing the rear with their backs to the cab, their wrists still bound behind them. The door quickly rolls shut again.

"Mami! They're here," Luca says, and he starts to stand, but Mami tells him to sit back down again.

"Luca, don't look at them or talk to them yet," Lydia says. "Wait a minute. Let's see how they are."

Luca sits, even though he doesn't fully understand what Mami means by "how they are." *They're here!* He was worried he'd never see them again. Mami leans forward in the dirty light. She asserts her face into his so Luca has no choice but to look at her.

"Luca, these are very bad people. You understand?"

Luca hardens his lips against each other. He investigates a small tag of rubber tread that's come loose from the sole of his shoe.

"We have to be careful not to draw extra attention to ourselves now, okay? You have to be very quiet and still until we figure out what's going to happen."

Luca tugs at the rubber tag until it snaps.

"Okay, *mijo?*"

He doesn't answer.

Lydia is amazed by the girls' arrival. She, too, presumed they would never see one another again. When the men were finished with the sisters, they could've chosen to keep them or sell them or kill them, and that's frankly what Lydia expected, insofar as she permitted herself to expect anything at all. Lydia had buried that presumption in a shallow place, an unmarked place, for the last several hours. She'd pushed it away because she didn't have room for it. The girls do not look well.

Soledad has a black eye and a scraped cheek on the same side. Her hair is wild and full of grit. Rebeca is bleeding at the temple. Just a thin, bright red cord against her skin. Her mouth is swollen and raw. A guard pulls them by the ankles, one at a time, toward the liftgate of the truck and flings them to the floor like sacks of rice. Soledad and Rebeca don't complain with their voices or faces or bodies. They're both limp—all the flinch has gone out of them. The sisters land near the far end of the line of migrants, and they don't move from where they're placed. Rebeca closes her eyes at once. Soledad keeps hers open. She lifts her chin, leans forward, and looks down the line until she sees Luca sticking out a little from the rest of the migrants. She nods at him once.

"Soledad," he says, just loudly enough for her to hear. Because he knows without knowing that the act of saying her name in that moment is the flag she needs in order to return to herself.

"Rebeca," he says also. But Rebeca squeezes her eyes shut even tighter. She's not ready. She pulls her knees up in front of her and buries her face there.

Now the five men who were in that truck with the sisters are uncarefully unloading the backpacks. They wear untucked white T-shirts over their dark blue uniform pants, and Lydia wonders if they're real *agentes* who also work for the cartel, or if the uniforms and trucks are just elaborate costumes and props. *Qué importa.* They stand in the bed and toss everything down in a heap. Luca can feel the whole line of migrants clicking to attention, their spines snapping them upright. A fizz of nervousness in the air. A few more men from the office come to join them, and soon the one in charge stands before them. The others call him *comandante.*

"Is anyone here a Mexican citizen?" he asks.

"I am," Lydia says. Three or four other voices join hers.

El comandante steps up to the first man, seated directly beside Rebeca. *El comandante* nudges the migrant's worn shoe with the toe of his boot. "You're Mexican?"

"Yes, sir."

"You're not lying to me?"

"No, sir."

"You wouldn't lie to me?"

"No, sir."

"Where are you from?"

"From Oaxaca."

"City?"

The man nods.

"In what state is the city of Oaxaca?" *el comandante* asks.

The man hesitates. "Oaxaca state?" He is unsure.

"Yes, *amigo*. The city of Oaxaca is in the state of Oaxaca. Congratulations. You must have done very well in school, in Oaxaca."

The migrant squirms where he sits.

"And tell me," *el comandante* continues. "Who is the governor of Oaxaca now?"

"The governor?"

"Yes, the governor. Of the state of Oaxaca. Where you are from."

Another hesitation. "We, uh. We had elections recently. The governor, the last governor, he was um . . ." The man shakes his head.

"Surely you know the governor's name?" *el comandante* says.

"Esperanza?"

El comandante turns to a guard standing behind him, who's googling Oaxaca on his phone. He shakes his head. "Governor of Oaxaca is Hinojosa."

El comandante returns his attention to the migrant. "Now. Would you like to tell me again where it is you're from?"

The man swallows. He says quietly, "Oaxaca."

El comandante draws his pistol and shoots the man between the eyebrows.

Rebeca jumps, her skin and her bones. Lydia cries out. Every migrant in the line cries out. Luca begins sobbing and screaming. He clamps his hands over his ears and squeezes his eyes closed and rocks himself. "No, no, no." *El comandante* clears his throat irritably, a tiny sound which is louder than all the reverberating noise in the room. With huge eyes and a cracked mouth, Rebeca is staring at the slump of a man beside her. His eyes are still open as he falls over onto her lap. He bleeds onto her legs. Rebeca doesn't move.

"Should anyone else be interested in lying to me about where you are from, allow me to suggest that you reconsider," *el comandante* says. "Now I will ask again: Who here is a Mexican national?"

Luca is shaking his head frantically, but Lydia takes a deep breath, and "I am," she says. This time she's the only one.

El comandante turns and approaches her. "This is your son?"

She doesn't breathe. "We are from Acapulco, in the state of Guerrero," she says. "The governor is Héctor Astudillo Flores, and the state capital is Chilpancingo."

Before she can stop him, Luca moves swiftly to his feet. He's trembling, but he stands up straight, tips his head back, and closes his eyes. His voice is clear as he takes over for his *mami*. "Although the site of Acapulco has cultural influences ranging back to the eighth-century Olmecs, it wasn't established as a major port until the arrival of Cortés in the 1520s. The city has a current population of more than six hundred thousand inhabitants, and a tropical climate with distinct wet and dry seasons—"

"Is he for real?" *el comandante* interrupts. He's looking at Lydia.

"Yes," she says.

The man's face looks very different when he's smiling, as he now is at Luca. He looks grandfatherly. Portly. Wild, bushy eyebrows. A pebbly wash of gray around the temples. This man who just shot a shackled human being between the eyes.

"Tourism is the main eco—"

"*Mijo,* stop," Mami says.

Luca snaps his mouth closed and sits back down on her lap. He turns sideways there, so his body is mostly covering her. *El comandante* leans his hands on his knees.

"Where did you learn all that?" he asks.

Luca shrugs.

"Did you make it up?"

"No."

"You wouldn't lie to me?"

"No." Luca would pee again if he wasn't dehydrated. He buries his face in Mami's neck.

El comandante straightens himself up again. "So you are from Acapulco."

She hesitates even though it's too late. She already told the truth because there was no alternative; she can't change her answer now. "Yes," she says.

"And why did you leave such a glorious place?"

El comandante looks into her face, and Lydia doesn't see any recognition there. Sebastián's face, the slain reporter, has made the national news, but hers has not. Neither has Luca's nor Abuela's nor Yénifer's, nor any of their other sixteen slaughtered loved ones. It's only that traveling text message that might identify her. Lydia takes a deep breath. She will not lie; she will tell some of the truth.

"The city has become extremely violent, frightening. I could no longer afford the costs of running my business."

"So you left."

"Yes."

"In search of a better life for your remarkable son." He smiles a toothy smile at Luca.

"Yes."

"Smart."

Lydia does not answer.

"Stand up then," *el comandante* instructs.

Luca stands like a baby fawn and helps Lydia, who struggles with her wrists tied behind her. She leans on Luca and gets to her feet. The pain in her ankle is still there, but it's diminished. The twang of a slight sprain. If she were at home she might think to ice it, to use it as an excuse to get out of cooking dinner for the evening. She'd send Sebastián out to pick up *tortas*.

"Anyone else?" *el comandante* asks.

Rebeca stares open-mouthed at the dead man on her lap. Soledad looks as if she's considering speaking, but Lydia silences her with a panicky twist of her neck.

"Untie her," *el comandante* says to one of the guards, who approaches Lydia with a sharp blade. She winces when she feels the unpleasant pressure against her skin, but a moment later, there's a snap and her arms drop loose. The plastic zip tie is still attached to one arm, which she holds out now so the man can cut it and snag it from her wrist. Should she thank him? Lydia doesn't make a sound.

"Gather your belongings," *el comandante* instructs her.

Luca steps forward with her, and together they collect their packs from the pile. Lydia knows it's foolish to look for the machete and its holster, but she does anyway. It's gone, of course.

"Follow me." *El comandante* returns to the office, and Lydia and Luca follow.

Inside, he tells them to sit. There's a notebook at an old metal desk, behind which *el comandante* sits in an upholstered office chair. The pen atop the notebook is gold with something engraved on its edge, and the incongruity of that pen, of the impending paperwork, while the corpse of a recent man is still warm just beyond the door, is too much. Lydia feels her mind slipping. Surely this is the worst moment of their lives. Wait, no. All their family was murdered. Nothing can ever be worse than that. Once again, she and Luca seem about to escape the horrific fate of everyone around them. How does this keep happening? When will their luck run out? Will it happen right now? Will he recognize her, pull up her picture on his phone, give her a forehead bullet from Javier? Her breathing feels rapid and shallow.

"Now then," *el comandante* says. He opens a drawer in the desk and retrieves a cell phone, which makes her heartbeat hammer in her ears. "Stand just there against the blue poster." He indicates a patch of blue pinned to the wall. Lydia stares at it, reluctant to obey. Reluctant to disobey. She stands in front of the poster, and *el comandante* takes her photograph. "You next," he says to Luca. Luca does as he's bid, and then sits back in the chair beside his mother.

"You have identification?" *el comandante* asks.

"Yes."

"Let's see it, please."

The gunshot that killed that non-Oaxacan migrant is still a sensory echo in her ears. Lydia opens her pack with trembling fingers and finds her wallet. From this she withdraws her voter ID card, proof both that she's a Mexican citizen and that she's the woman Javier Crespo Fuentes is hunting. It feels like a rescue boat and a torpedo at once. She places it in his open hand, careful not to touch his skin. He waves his fingers at her to indicate that she should hand over the rest of the wallet as well. He photographs the ID, and then tucks it back in the clear pocket where it lives. Then he withdraws the money from the billfold and counts it: just shy of 75,000 pesos, or about $3,900. Lydia put a lot of thought into the way she divided and stored their money, anticipating robbery. At the first Casa del Migrante back in Huehuetoca, another migrant had advised her to make sure she stashed money in different places, so if they got robbed, when they got robbed, the thieves might not find all of it. So she'd put a third of everything they had into the billfold. It was a decent sum. Most people wouldn't expect her to have more than that. She'd divided the rest into ten equal portions of 15,000 pesos each and hidden them in various places: one wad is sewn into her bra strap beneath her left armpit, one's in her underwear against her right hip. One remains in the banker's envelope zipped into the hidden bottom compartment of Luca's backpack. Another is flattened and tucked beneath the insoles of her mother's gold lamé sneakers. Right now Lydia feels both grateful that she did that and terrified that there will be some punishment if *el comandante* finds some portion of the reserves. He opens another drawer in the desk and places most of their 75,000 pesos in an envelope. He returns the rest to the wallet.

Lydia can't believe her eyes. *What the fuck is this, some kind of moral code this monster has? He's leaving us with money?* A guard stands in the corner watching them. He's the same man who googled the governor of Oaxaca earlier. He's staring hard at Lydia while *el comandante* writes her name in the book, along with the sum of money he took from them. He frowns at the name written there in his own hand and taps the back of his pen against the page. The guard clears his throat.

"Something on your mind, Rafa?"

He's been leaning against the wall and now he stands erect, shakes his head slightly. "She looks familiar. Doesn't she look familiar to you?"

El comandante looks up from the notebook to regard Lydia more closely.

"I can't say she does. Do you look familiar to us?"

Lydia's throat has gone dry. "I have one of those faces," she says.

El comandante returns his attention to the paperwork, but Rafa pins his eyes to her face, and she can see it in his expression, the way he's riffling through the file cabinet of his memory, trying to place her. She can see it in the set of his mouth and eyes, the way he examines her, *Where has he seen her before?* And Lydia's whole body feels juddery with panic. Whatever this transaction is going to be, dear God, let it be fast, before this man remembers. She twists in her chair, an effort to subtly obscure her face. She leans toward Luca but she can still feel the guard's scrutiny like a malevolent clock. The time of their anonymity is expiring.

But *el comandante* has moved on. "What is your name, son?" he says to Luca.

Luca looks sideways at his *mami*. "Tell him the truth."

"Luca Mateo Pérez Quixano."

"How old are you?"

"I'm eight years old."

On the line beneath her name, using the fancy pen, *el comandante* writes +1, with Luca's name and age.

"In what city do you intend to live?"

"We're not sure yet," Lydia says. "Maybe Denver."

He writes that down, too.

"You understand what's going on here," *el comandante* says.

Lydia doesn't know how to answer. She doesn't want to say *Violence, kidnapping, extortion, rape*. She doesn't want to say *Evil and wickedness*. She doesn't want to say, *My death if we don't get out of here quickly*. There's no agreeable reply.

"Sometimes there's unfortunate fallout." *El comandante* waves his hand vaguely in the direction of the murdered man in the next room, and smiles at Luca, whose face is entirely blank. "But you will remember this fallout. And that memory will serve you well in maintaining your silence, and thereby your future well-being."

The words *future well-being* pierce Lydia's heart like a bell. She holds herself very still. *El comandante* replaces the cap on his pen, closes the cover of his notebook, and leans across it with his hands folded on top.

"Most of these people are bad guys anyway, young man. It's important for you to understand that. They're not innocents. They're gang members, they're running drugs. They're thieves or rapists or murderers, like the *norteño* president says. Bad *hambres*." He mispronounces the word *hombres* in the style of the US president who, attempting to call migrants *bad men,* inadvertently referred to them as *bad hunger* instead. It's a joke now, full of irony. Bad hunger. *El comandante* toes the line. "They had to leave where they came from because they got in trouble there, you understand. Good people do not run away."

Luca opens his mouth, and Lydia watches him consider speaking. With every molecule in her body, she wills him to be silent. Luca closes his mouth.

"Nevertheless, most of them will be okay," *el comandante* continues. "Some of them will be able to pay their own ransom. Like you. Those who can't are likely to have family in *el norte* who can help. They will be here only one or two days, they will pay their toll, and they'll be on their way. Understand? Nothing to worry about." He stands up from his chair but remains behind the desk. "I'm sure I don't have to tell you to keep this business to yourselves."

Lydia shakes her head. "No, señor."

"You needn't hear about the dreadful things that happen to people who tell tales in Sinaloa."

She shakes her head again. Who would she tell?

"Good, then," *el comandante* says. "Our business is concluded. Rafa?" He turns to the guard behind him. "See them out and send the next one in."

Rafa turns from Lydia, which movement underlines her overwhelming hope of deliverance. They are being dismissed. She can hardly believe it. She grips Luca's hand and stands shakily from her chair. In the corner behind the desk, Rafa opens a metal door Lydia hadn't noticed before. It's bolted at the top, but he reaches up and unlatches it. He presses on the bar that opens the door, and a slice of daylight pours in around its perimeter. Lydia moves her body toward that miraculous light.

But Luca doesn't move, and her arm snags with his fixed weight.

"Luca, come on," she says with a capricious note of hysteria in her voice. She lunges for him, but he dodges her grasp. "Luca, what are you doing?" She grabs his arm, so agitated she could kill him herself.

"We can't leave them," he says.

Luca's heart feels like a flapping bird in his chest, like that time a sparrow accidentally flew into their apartment from the balcony and couldn't find its way out again, and then it beat itself against the glass over and over until Papi caught it in a towel and smuggled it out the door to freedom. Luca's heart is in a similar terror, so it feels as if the glass of his rib cage might shatter and fall if the bloodied carcass of his heart doesn't smash itself into dead pulp first.

His mother stares at him in awe. *What is he doing?* "Luca—"

"No, Mami, they can't pay," he says. "They don't have any money."

El comandante slumps back into his chair with his elbows on the rests and makes a tent of his fingers. He seems amused by the exchange. Luca turns to face him.

"What happens to people who can't pay?"

"Young man, your loyalty is admirable—"

"What will happen?"

Something frightful flashes across *el comandante*'s face, and once again Lydia reaches for Luca. But the man relents. "It's okay, I won't harm him," he says to Lydia. "I respect his courage. Please, sit."

Lydia looks to the door. It had been opened. She had seen the fading daylight beyond, and she's loath to relinquish that promise of freedom. But there is Luca, back in the chair, more afraid of leaving the sisters than he is of staying longer in this nightmare. Despite everything he's been through, or maybe also because of it, her boy has weighed the call of his conscience above the call of his own salvation. *If we survive this,* Lydia thinks, *I shall feel very proud.* She shrinks two inches, her whole body collapsing from the lungs inward, and sits down beside her son, careful to keep her face turned away from the guard.

"Who is he talking about?" *el comandante* asks.

"The two girls," Lydia says, "with the rainbow wristbands."

"Your son is a very impressive young man," *el comandante* says.

It's deeply unsettling for Lydia to field a compliment from him. "The girls have no family to help them," she says.

"They only have us," Luca says.

El comandante breathes heavily, bounces the end of his pen lightly across the top of the notebook. "Those girls would fetch a price on the open market. Two beauties like that?" He whistles, then looks again to Luca. "But I wish to reward your bravery and fidelity. Very impressive." He sits up. Back to Lydia. "You have money?"

Lydia hesitates.

El comandante grins. "A woman who looks like you, who speaks like you? You have more money, yes?"

Lydia closes her eyes, and in that darkness she sees Soledad and Rebeca as she first encountered them on that overpass outside Huehuetoca, their singsong voices, their legs dangling down. She sees their vivacity and spirit. Her mind also reproduces, in that moment, the white lace, the dark red stain of Yénifer's *quinceañera* dress. A sob cuts into her gut but doesn't rise. Lydia opens her eyes. She nods.

El comandante raises his voice. "Rafa, bring the girls in." To Lydia, "Seventy-five thousand pesos."

She gapes.

"Each."

That sum is almost all the money they have left. He's demanding more for each sister than he took for Luca and Lydia combined, and she has a sickening moment of understanding that this amount is predetermined. It's the calculated value of their worth as human capital. If Lydia doesn't pay, someone else will buy the sisters. And then she also immediately perceives how her own price will skyrocket if that guard is able to recall why he recognizes her. The possibility of that recollection is like a ticking bomb in this box of a room.

Luca studies her face, and for him, she does not waver.

"We will pay."

CHAPTER TWENTY-THREE

All that's left of Lydia and Sebastián's life savings is the paltry sum *el comandante* returned to Lydia's wallet after he collected the price for her and Luca. It's a total of 4,941 pesos, or around $243. In regular life, that kind of money is substantial. It would buy many weeks' worth of groceries. It would go toward rent or doctors' bills or putting gas in the Beetle. But now the amount feels negligible. They have nothing. If they get to *el norte,* they will have to start from scratch. Already they need new shoes; Luca's are beginning to run thin in the soles, Abuela's gold lamé sneakers are peeling apart at the toe. The $243 minus some new shoes—it's not enough. Lydia feels destitute. But thank God they still have her mother's money in the bank, enough to pay a coyote to help them cross. That's all she can think about for now.

When at last the guard opens the door and they stagger out of captivity, Lydia's not thinking about the money anyway. The guard stays in her mind, his searching expression, his groping for the memory of her face. She knows he's back there still, that he could remember her at any moment: *yes,* Dios mío, *that's her, the one who belongs to Los Jardineros.*

They run. They don't know where they are, how far they are from the train or the city. They've emerged from a large warehouse in a rural landscape and they don't hear any distant rumble of locomotive or car engine. They run toward the leftover glow in the sky, pink fading to purple where the sun recently descended, due west over the uneven

ground, through ruts and ditches and holes burrowed by unseen animals, across rocks and roots and twisted clumps of plant life, hoping to
intercept a road that runs from south to north. The pain in Lydia's ankle
asserts itself only when she flexes her foot, so she tries to keep it straight.
Both girls limp, too, but Soledad is like a ball of fire, and she batters herself against the pain while she runs. Luca encourages all of them like a
breathless cheerleader as they go.

"Come on, Rebeca, you can do it. Keep up, Mami, let's go."

Soledad pushes ahead. She would run all the way to *el norte*. When
they come to a road, they pause. No cars in sight, the twilight still pink
around them. Soledad stands close to Lydia. She reaches for Lydia's hand.

"Thank you." She trembles.

Lydia is beset by guilt. She'd been ready to leave them there. "It was
Luca," she says.

Soledad grabs the top of Luca's hair. She bends down and looks into
his face. "You saved our lives. You know that? You and your *mami*." She
doesn't let go of Lydia's hand.

Luca smiles, and Rebeca begins to cry, a tight, high-pitched sound
that startles him. Her face is a twist of distress and her breath crashes
out of her between sharp hums. Her jeans are covered in the dead man's
blood mixed with some of her own, and the button has been ripped off
the fly, so they no longer stay up. Lydia retrieves one of the belts from her
backpack and laces it through the girl's belt loops for her. Rebeca winces
and shakes but endures Lydia's kindness. She fastens the buckle herself.
Soledad stands behind and twists her sister's black hair into a ponytail,
revealing a dark purple bruise on her neck. She touches the spot softly
with her finger. Rebeca turns to her, and the girls embrace. Rebeca shudders and cries and they all wait close together until she's able to walk
again. She folds her arms in front of her because her bra is gone.

They turn north to follow the road, and the light fades from purple
to indigo to blue, and by the time they pass the outskirts of a village,
they're walking in darkness. Lydia watches over her shoulder the whole
time, waiting for the approach of a distant light, a distant gunshot. Her
exhaustion is no match for her fear, and she keeps pushing ahead as
quickly as they can go. They're all very thirsty because they finished whatever water they had with them hours ago, and there's no shop here, no

river or stream. It seems too dangerous to venture into the tiny village. They're not yet far enough away from the warehouse, those men. They don't want to reveal themselves. But they haven't eaten today, and they are hungry. Despite their adrenaline, they weaken as they go. Occasionally the headlights of a car approach, and they dart away from the road to hold still against whatever cover they can find. They know without speaking that this new fear is a burden they're all carrying together, this sense that they haven't really escaped, that they're not safe. Any one of those cars could be carrying the men who abducted them earlier. Those men, with or without the knowledge of their *comandante*, may decide to come after them, to repeat and repeat and repeat the things they did to Rebeca and Soledad in the back of their truck earlier. They may decide to drag Lydia into the trunk of a car by her hair, to rip Luca from her arms, to shoot him on the side of the road and then drive her through the night back to Acapulco, to Javier. He's waiting for her there.

At length they begin to sense the ragged glow of a town to the north. They pass a juncture, and the traffic becomes steadier. They can no longer flee from the road each time a car passes because there are too many.

"We'll get water," Lydia says. "Soon there will be a place. Someone will give us water." There is no real indication of how true this might be, but she says it because she needs it, and it's encouragement enough for the others to quicken their pace. The land is flat, and the lights of the town soon come into view. A car passes them, slows down ahead, pulls onto the shoulder, and stops. Lydia puts a hand out to stop Luca from walking any farther. Rebeca and Soledad both freeze. They draw their bodies close together. The car reverses some way toward them, and the girls run from the road, but there's nowhere for them to go. Lydia stands her ground. She leans down automatically to retrieve her machete from its holster, forgetting that it's gone now. She curses mildly under her breath—$243 minus two pairs of shoes and a new machete. She puts Luca behind her. The door on the driver's side opens, and a man steps out. He's wearing cowboy boots, jeans, a button-up shirt. He stays beside his car, doesn't attempt to approach them.

"Are you okay?" he calls into the darkness.

"Fine," Lydia answers.

"Migrants?"

Lydia does not respond.

"We see many migrants on this road at night, some in very poor condition," the man explains. "And no one knows where they're coming from. You're well off the migrant trail here. How did you come to be in this neighborhood?"

Lydia tightens her lips, but he continues talking, undeterred by their reticence to speak to him.

"I'm a doctor," he says. "I have a clinic, not far. If you want, I can take you to safety."

Soledad snorts, but Rebeca squeezes her arm. "It's not funny."

Soledad dissolves into full-on hysterics.

"Is something wrong?" the man asks.

"Safety!" Soledad howls with laughter.

Luca presses in beside his *mami*. "Why is she laughing, Mami? What's wrong with her?"

"Sh," Mami says. "She has been through so much. Sometimes people break down for a minute. She will come back to herself, *mijo*."

They watch as the man walks to the trunk of his car and opens it. Lydia grips Luca's neck and takes two steps back, but when the man reaches into the trunk, he retrieves only a gallon jug of water. He sets it on the side of the road.

"Listen, I'll leave this here for you," he says. "I might have . . ." He interrupts himself and turns back into the trunk. "I thought I had some cookies here, too, but my son must have eaten them. I'll leave the water." He's holding his keys in his hand, and Luca can hear them clink against one another. "But if any of you need medical attention, I may be able to help. If you are hungry, I can get you some food."

Lydia peers through the darkness at the sisters off the side of the road. Her eyes have adjusted to the light so she can make out their faces but can't read their expressions.

"How far is it to town?" Soledad asks.

"Not far," the doctor says. "Another two or three miles. A half hour's walk will get you to the edge of the city."

"What city is it?" This is Luca. The word *city* has excited him, as it indicates a place larger than he expected.

"Navolato," the doctor says. "About twenty miles west of Culiacán."

Luca closes his eyes to look at the map in his mind. He can see Navolato there, a small dot next to Culiacán's large dot, but he hasn't stored any information about this place. *Twenty miles,* Lydia thinks. *How in God's name will we get back to the train?* The sisters are in no condition to walk much farther.

"Are there migrant services in Navolato?" Lydia asks.

"No," the man says. "I don't think so. But there's a church. They always help."

"What about in Culiacán? Are there migrant services there?"

"Maybe. I'm not sure."

Lydia allows a big gust of a breath to billow out of her. The surge of stunned gratitude she experienced when all four of them emerged from that warehouse, alive and together, is still with her, but it's beginning to fade behind exhaustion and lingering fear.

"Are you hungry?" the man asks.

"Yes," Luca says.

"Do you want a ride?"

Again, Lydia looks to the sisters.

"Nope," Soledad says.

Lydia's own disappointment, her eagerness to trust this man, surprises her, but she wants trace evidence of goodness in the world. She needs a glimmer. She can see only the outline of the man's body ahead, lit by the peripheral glow of his car, the headlights pointing the opposite direction behind him.

"Thank you anyway," Lydia says.

She ventures a few steps toward him, and Luca trots ahead. The jug of water sits near the back bumper, close to the man's feet. Luca pries the cap off the jug and lifts it, but it's too heavy for him and it sloshes awkwardly. The man helps. He holds the jug steady while Luca drinks and drinks. Luca turns his face away to breathe before going back for another long drink. Lydia stands behind him and waits for him to finish. She can hear the sisters approaching behind her, but they hang back in the shadows.

"Listen, I don't want to press you," the doctor says. "But it's not safe for you to be out on this road at night. There's a lot of activity in this area. There have been some terrible stories. Maybe you already know."

Soledad snorts again, but this time it's a solitary sound. She can no longer locate what was funny about it before. Concern creases the doctor's face. A miniflashlight dangles from his key chain, and this he clicks on. He turns the small beam toward the girls' legs to confirm what he thought he could see or smell there in the darkness: a significant amount of blood. And not only on Rebeca's jeans, Lydia can see now. Soledad's are covered as well, and the blood there isn't dry. Luca is still drinking. The doctor clicks off the flashlight.

"Please," he says. "Won't you let me help you?"

Soledad crosses her arms. Rebeca makes her jaw into the shape of a square. It's Luca who speaks up.

"How do we know you're really a doctor?"

"Ah." The man puts a finger in the air, then retrieves a wallet from his back pocket. There's an identification card there. The man's picture. It says "Doctor Ricardo Montañero-Alcán." Luca breathes on it before handing it back.

"That doesn't prove anything," Soledad observes. "You can be a doctor and still be a narco, too. You can be a doctor, a teacher, a priest. You can be a federal police officer and still murder people."

The doctor nods, slipping the wallet back into the pocket of his jeans. "It's true," he concedes.

"And why do you want to help us anyway?" Soledad asks.

The man touches the gold crucifix around his neck. *For I was hungry and you gave me food, I was thirsty and you gave me drink.*

Lydia automatically blesses herself. *A stranger and you welcomed me.* She completes the line of scripture, passing the water jug to Rebeca, who drinks only a little before passing it to Soledad.

"We should go with him," Luca declares.

The man lets Soledad scroll through his phone first. He shows her his Facebook page, photographs of his wife and children. She's so hungry, so depleted. She relents.

The doctor wants to take them to his clinic, but they refuse, so he drives them into the city, to a poorly whitewashed two-story building instead, with a shop on the bottom floor and bars on the windows above. Large red letters proclaim the building to be the Techorojo Motel. The shop beneath has a red awning and an open-air counter where two young women wear smock-aprons and eye the approaching patrons with considerable suspicion. Behind them are shiny tinfoil snacks and bottled soft drinks in neon colors. There's also a grill, the aroma of cooking meat, and the shallow sound of a cheap radio playing *música norteña,* heavy on the accordion. The doctor buys them food and pays for their room.

"If you want a ride to Culiacán tomorrow, I can come back in the morning," he says, and then he's gone before they even have time to thank him.

After they've eaten and locked themselves inside their tiny room, after they've managed to lug the wide, heavy nightstand across the carpet and wedge it beneath the doorknob for extra security, Lydia collects everyone's pants. The room does not have a bathroom, but there is, oddly, a toilet in one corner, and a yellow sink beside it. The water that emerges from the faucet of that sink is the color of sand, but Lydia doesn't mind because the discoloration serves to camouflage the colors she has to wash out of those jeans. Luca's, Rebeca's, and Soledad's. She uses the cracked bar of soap in the dish, and she scrubs and scrubs until finally the water she wrings from the denim returns to its original murky dun color.

By the time she's finished, Luca is snoring softly on one of the room's two single beds, and the sisters, too, are already asleep, curled up together. Soledad cradles her sister's head in her arms, and their hair is fanned out in one twisted, black wave across their shared pillow. Lydia rummages through her pack for her toothbrush, and rations a smear of paste onto the bristles. She considers the brown water from the tap before sticking the toothbrush under there and wetting it. At home, there was a whole routine before she got into bed. It could take twenty minutes some nights. Cold cream, toner, moisturizer, floss, toothpaste, mouthwash, lip balm. Some nights tweezers, too, or clippers or nail files. Of course, the occasional exfoliant or mask. Hand cream. Fluffy socks if her feet were chilly. Sebastián would whisper-call from the bedroom, trying not to wake Luca in his impatience, *"Madre de Dios,* wife, the Eiffel Tower was built faster!" But when she was finished, he'd always fold back the covers to invite her in. He'd drape them over her when she was settled, along with the top half of himself. His breath was clean when he kissed her.

Lydia avoids her reflection in the harsh yellow light of the rusty mirror. She spits into the sink and rinses her mouth. She splashes murky water over her face and neck and dries herself off with the shirt she wore for the last two days. When she finally slips into bed beside Luca, before she can even invoke her *don't think* mantra, exhaustion descends like anesthesia and blots out everything else. They sleep.

Some hours later and well before dawn, Rebeca wakens Lydia from a black sleep.

"It's Soledad," Rebeca whispers to Lydia. "Something's wrong with her."

Lydia disentangles herself from Luca, who smacks his lips in his sleep, and then rolls tighter into a ball facing the wall. A good deal of light comes in through the room's only window, which has an insufficient curtain and is positioned beneath an overzealous streetlamp. Lydia moves to the other twin bed, where Soledad sits rocking over her legs and clutching her stomach.

"Soledad? Are you okay?"

She clenches her jaw and rocks her body forward. "Just bad cramps."

Lydia looks up at Rebeca, whose face is a cloud of worry. "Just sit with Luca," Lydia says. "Make sure he stays asleep."

Rebeca sits at the foot of Luca's bed.

"Can you stand?" Lydia asks.

Soledad gathers her strength and then rocks herself onto her feet. There's a dark stain on the mattress beneath her and the mineral scent of blood. Lydia grips her under the elbow and steers her around the bed toward the corner of the room where the plumbing is. She positions the flimsy curtain to give Soledad as much privacy as possible while she miscarries her baby.

Good to his word, the doctor returns in the morning and drives them to Culiacán. The girls' jeans are still damp and stiff from Lydia's scrubbing, but they wear them anyway, and the sun isn't long drying them. It eats the moisture from their clothes and their hair and skin. Rebeca moves a little easier and Soledad with a little more difficulty than yesterday. Lydia wants to buy a packet of sanitary napkins for Soledad, but they're expensive, so she puts her embarrassment away and asks the doctor, who, being a doctor, thinks nothing of the request and complies without hesitation. He also buys them breakfast and a tube of sunscreen, which he urges them to use, and for Luca, a comic book. When he takes his leave, he does so abruptly, to release them from the effort of gratitude.

Lydia cannot wait to get back on the train, to get away from the nightmarish memories of this place, to be traveling north at high speed. She's terrified as they walk the tracks through the city that they will be spotted, that the guard from yesterday will be out driving to work—*Do these men commute to work? Is that what they call it? Do they kiss their wives and children goodbye each morning and then climb into the family sedan and set out for a day of raping and extortion, and then return home exhausted in the evenings and hungry for their pot roast?*—and he'll see her, he'll see the four of them walking north along the tracks, and the information will snap into place, and he'll remember: her face smiling beside Javier's in that picture. She pushes Luca gently in the back, ushers him into a faster pace. They cross over a muddy river on a skeletal railway bridge, and discover a train yard where the tracks are lined on one side with giant boulders. A few clusters of migrants wait there, surrounded by the dirty colors of litter and debris, mud and weeds. There's a boy among them, slightly older than Luca, but certainly younger than Rebeca. He stands while the other migrants sit hunching their shoulders against him. His eyes are unfocused and his posture is the shape of a question mark. His hands float unsteadily in front of him, and he sways strangely on his curved legs.

"Mami, what's wrong with him?" Luca asks.

He's the most disturbing child Luca has ever seen. He seems unaware of them, unaware of anything. Mami shakes her head, but Soledad provides a one-word answer: *drogas*. They move quickly past the boy, away from the cluster of migrants he seems to be orbiting. In fact they are nearly ready to quit the railway yard altogether when three well-dressed young women appear at a crossing ahead on the tracks. They wave their arms overhead and call out, *"Hermanos, ¡tenemos comida!"* The men stand up from their clusters, pat the dust from their jeans, and gather for the offer of food. One of the three women reads loudly from the Bible while the other two hand out tamales and *atole*. Luca's not hungry because, thanks to the doctor, they already had breakfast, but he's learned never to turn down a gift of calories. They eat gratefully, and when the women begin packing up their pots and gathering the spent rubbish, Lydia wonders if they should leave this place, too. It feels squalid and dangerous, but there's a rumor that one of the trains parked here is being loaded, that soon it will journey north. Men are already climbing the ladders and spreading their packs out on top of the train. The railway workers watch and make no move to stop them. It seems so senseless and arbitrary, the way the government clears migrants from the trains in some places, spending millions of pesos and dollars to build those track-fences in Oaxaca and Chiapas and Mexico state, all while turning a blind eye in other locations. There's even a *policía municipal* parked just there on the corner, watching the migrants board. He sips coffee from a paper cup. It feels almost like a trap, but Lydia's too grateful to flex her suspicion.

The sisters' bodies are battered and weakened, especially Soledad's, from the miscarriage. Being able to board while the train is stopped feels like luck, so they climb up gingerly, and Lydia can still get a whiff of blood from Soledad on the ladder above her. They move back along the top of the train until they come to a car where there's room for all four of them to be comfortable. Just as they're setting down, just as Lydia is pulling the canvas belts from her pack, a little girl peeks her head up over the edge of the train car. She clambers up quickly and approaches Soledad without hesitation. The girl is younger than Luca, perhaps six years old, and she's alone. Her black hair is cut short and shiny, and she wears jeans and brown leather boots. She hunkers down very close to Soledad, who's startled by the girl's boldness, the intimacy of her posture. She speaks rapidly, her upturned face very close to Soledad's. Soledad leans away from her.

"Do you need work?" the girl asks quickly. "My *tía* has a restaurant here and she needs a waitress. Do you want a job?" The girl puts her hand on Soledad's arm, and tugs at her. "Come on, quick. Come with me, I'll show you the place." She pulls at Soledad's elbow, and Soledad is so taken aback that she nearly rises to follow the child. She knows she shouldn't, that the girl is presumptuous, almost bullying. But there's a conflict between Soledad's mind and her body, because her mind knows to mistrust this pushy little girl, but her body is biologically susceptible to the child's cuteness, to the beautiful innocence of her young face. Soledad feels momentarily distended between those two truths, but the spell is quickly broken because *el policía municipal* has gotten out of his car now, and is standing in a patch of mud beneath the train, still carrying his paper cup of coffee. He yells up to the little girl.

"Ximenita, leave those people alone! Get down from there."

The little girl snaps her head in his direction and bolts. She drops Soledad's arm and flings herself over the edge of the freight car and back down the ladder. She reappears a moment later in the distance, dashing away among the boulders and debris.

El policía calls after her. "Tell your *papi* I said no *víctimas* for you today!"

Soledad is eager for the hiss of the disengaged brakes and the rumble of the locomotive. When at last they begin to move, instead of happiness or relief, they all feel a tentative, miniature suspension of dread.

As they travel, Luca pays attention to the signs so he can check off familiar place-names on his mind-map, or add new dots for unfamiliar ones: Guamúchil, Bamoa, Los Mochis, check, check, check. Roughly three hours after pulling out of Culiacán, in the middle of nowhere, they come to a place where other tracks meet the ones they're traveling on, and then there are more and more tracks, until the rails are at least a dozen wide, and when the train slows down, Luca can see there are many migrants gathered here waiting, and again, no fence, no *policías*. Nothing at all to prevent the whole crowd of them from boarding La Bestia. The train stops, and easily a hundred men get on while the train sits idling, but then the locomotive cuts its engine, and the workers disembark and scatter to cars parked in a nearby lot, and everyone atop the train groans and curses. La Bestia doesn't move again for three nights.

CHAPTER TWENTY-FOUR

There are cultivated fields on both sides of the tracks, and Luca watches the farmer, sometimes on a tractor, sometimes on foot, as he tends to the rows of whatever crop he's hoping to grow there in the rich seams of dirt. The farmer lets the stranded migrants fill their bottles from a long hose, and the water it dispenses is warm but clean. Sometimes a family comes and sells food and *refrescos* out of the back of their truck, but sometimes they don't come, and Luca is very hungry. They rely on the kindness of their fellow migrants, who share their limited provisions. At night it gets cold, and some of the men build cheerful little campfires. Some folks sleep huddled up inside one of the empty freight cars, but it's crowded and smelly, and even though the box car cuts the wind, the metal seems to conduct the cold into the migrants' bones while they sleep. So Luca and Mami stay tucked in near one of the fires, wearing all of their clothes, and wrapped up together in their blanket like a colorful burrito. Everyone is exhausted and edgy, and by the middle of the second day in that arid, desolate place, some migrants give up waiting and start to walk. Luca can't imagine where they'll walk to, because there was no town for miles before they stopped here, and what if there's no town for miles ahead either? He worries about that, and he prays when he watches the migrants strike out along the tracks. When a crew of *ferrocarril* workers arrives on the morning of the fourth day and prepares the train to depart, a cheer gathers in the camp and all the migrants begin to board, but Luca presses on his *mami*'s hand and insists they should wait.

"Because this one is all the way on the right-hand track," he explains. "That one must go east, when the tracks split."

He points north up the rails to where the dozen different tracks begin to merge, and then to merge again. Beyond a highway overpass, the number of tracks decreases to three, and then beyond that again, they merge to two. He and Rebeca walked there yesterday to explore, and they found the place where eventually the two tracks veered in different directions, one east, one west. But Lydia is anxious. They've waited so long already, and she can't imagine not getting on this train. She shakes her head in exasperation.

"He's right." Two men at least a generation older than Mami are still seated on the far side of an empty track. "There are two tracks," one of the men says. "They run parallel from here to the village, and then they split. That train is going all the way to Chihuahua."

"We're waiting for the Pacific Route train," his companion says. They might be identical twins. They have the same weather-beaten faces, the same neatly trimmed mustaches, the same warm timbre to their quiet voices. "If you want to cross at Nogales or Baja, you have to take the left-hand track from here."

"Thank you," Lydia says.

"How do you know?" Soledad asks them. She wants to understand how to learn these things.

"We make this journey every other year. We've done it eight times."

Lydia's mouth drops open.

"Why?" Soledad asks.

The men shrug in unison. "We go where the work is," the first one says.

"Come back to visit our wives and children," the second one adds.

"Then we do it again." They both laugh, as if it's a comedy routine they've been performing for years.

Soledad removes the backpack she'd put on in preparation for their departure, and slams it to the ground. "We've been waiting three days," she says. "Where is this train? What if it never comes?" It's difficult not to feel hysterical with the passing of the hours, the setting and rising of the sun. Honduras is no farther away today than it was yesterday.

"It will come, *mija.*" One of the men nods at her. "And your patience shall be rewarded." He reaches into the front pocket of his backpack and opens a wrapped parcel of *carne seca.* He hands two strips to Soledad, and then shares with the others. "The train will be along soon," he reassures them.

Luca bites gratefully into the salty, leathery strip. He rips it with his teeth. The second man leans forward and speaks softly to Soledad, who's sitting on her pack now with her elbows resting on her knees. "And do not worry, *morrita.* Soon, Sinaloa will be well behind you. You will survive this. You have the look of a survivor."

She drops her head low for a moment, so Luca worries about her. He expects that she's crying, that everything she's suffered is finally weighing her down, pressing her into the ground. But when she lifts her head, it's the opposite of that. The man's words have landed on her face and she does—she looks like an Aztec warrior.

The twin brothers tell stories while they wait, about their homes in Yucatán, about their wives and children, about the farms where they do seasonal labor in *el norte,* and about their third brother, a triplet, who they both agreed was the handsomest brother, before he was killed, six years ago, when the combine harvester he was driving on a farm in Iowa struck an overhead powerline. They bless themselves when they say his name. *Eugenio.* Luca recognizes the alchemy of recounting their brother's name, and he blesses himself because it's an eighth holy sacrament for migrants, repeating the names of your beloved dead. He tries it quietly on his own tongue: "Sebastián Pérez Delgado." But the shapes of it are too raw, still, too sharp. They flood his mouth with grief and for a moment, he has to bury his face. He has to breathe into the dark angles of his elbows. He has to fill his mind with other things. *The capital of Norway is Olso. There are 6,852 islands in the Japanese archipelago.*

The brothers are a deeply calming presence. They are warm bread. They are shelter. And soon, just as the brothers assured them it would, the train arrives. It stops briefly, so they're able to board easily, and after they help them up the ladder, the brothers move along to another car, where they can spread out, and give Lydia and the children some space of their own.

"See you in *el norte, manito*," one of them says to Luca. "Look me up when you get to Iowa. We can have an *hamburguesa* together." He gives Luca a high-five, and then turns to follow his brother across the top of the train.

Rebeca sits down right where they are.

"First class," Soledad jokes as Mami straps Luca onto the grating. She waves her arm around them. "I got us a private cabin."

The train goes, and when they cross *el río* Fuerte, the landscape changes almost immediately from green to brown. They chug through the difficult farmland for an hour and a half, finally passing a sign that indicates they've crossed into the next state. Luca reads it out loud.

"Bienvenido a Sonora."

"Y vete con viento fresco a Sinaloa." Rebeca bids good riddance to Sinaloa, but that invisible border does little to ease their newly intensified sense of constant fear.

Bacabachi, Navojoa, Ciudad Obregón, check, check, check. The desert asserts itself. Soon Luca can smell the ocean, but this time it reminds him of nothing about Acapulco because there's no green here, no trees, no mountains, no dense mineral soil. No nightclubs or cruise ships or *estadounidenses*. Everything is sandy and dusty and dry, and the rock formations that lurch up from the ground have a brutal beauty. Even the trees look thirsty here, and Mami doesn't have to pester Luca to drink. He sips frequently from his canteen, and his hair grows damp with sweat beneath Papi's cap. By sunset they have, almost unbelievably, reached the city of Hermosillo, which is a place as parched and brown and alien as any Luca has ever seen, but its strangeness makes no impression on him, such is his mounting excitement.

"Rebeca, we're almost there," he says.

He's been trying to pump oxygen back into her flagging person for days. He's like a small, human bellows, and she a fire that's dimmed to embers.

"Almost where?" she says.

The light is drawing out of the sky, the train is slowing, and on the car ahead of them, the twin brothers are making to disembark.

"Almost to *el norte*," Luca says.

She gives him a skeptical look, which wasn't the response he was hoping for. He snuffles his chin inside the zipper of his hoodie, but Mami leans forward and asks him to repeat himself.

"We're almost to *el norte*," he says. "We're due south of Nogales now, only about three hundred miles."

"Three hundred miles," Soledad repeats. "What does that mean? How far have we come already?"

"From Honduras?"

"Yes."

He tips his head up and squints with thought. "I'd say that is more than two thousand miles."

Soledad's eyes get big. A hesitant smile seeps into her features. She makes minimal effort to defeat it. She nods her head. "More than two thousand miles. We've come more than two thousand miles?"

"Yes."

"And now we have only three hundred left to go?"

"Yes, that's what I'm telling you. We're getting close."

"How long will that take, three hundred miles?" Soledad asks.

Luca shakes his head. "I don't know, a few hours?"

"Why, you want to stay on the train?" Rebeca sounds worried. "It's getting dark soon."

"Look, we're stopping," Mami says.

The brothers have disembarked and walked a decent stretch already, so it would be easy to miss the sound they emit at that moment, were it not for the fact that Luca, Lydia, Soledad, and Rebeca are all acquainted with that sound now. It's a sound recognizable from both their recent experiences and their nightmares. The brothers are yelling.

"*¡Migra! ¡La migra! ¡Huyan, apúrense! ¡Viene la migra!*"

This time the terror doesn't gather or grow; it crashes in on them all at once. Lydia yanks the belt off Luca in a movement so swift and violent he nearly cries. The sisters are already halfway down the ladder and they don't wait for a reasonable place to get off. The memory of Sinaloa makes them fast, not despite their damaged bodies, but because of them. They leap wildly down to the uneven ground with their unfastened backpacks thudding against them. Luca is next, and then Lydia, and thank God they're in the city already because they scramble down the shallow embankment and immediately there are alleys and roads and walls and gardens and houses and open garages and a barefoot little girl gaping at them while she licks at an ice pop and a woman who has a food cart attached to her bicycle and a dog with a spot over one eye and tall grass around their ankles and then concrete underfoot and the brothers have gone in a different direction and there are still three or four other migrants behind them. It's been four days since Lydia twisted her ankle, and she's relieved to feel that the twinge has disappeared. It's strong beneath her weight. She looks at the sisters ahead of her and considers what would happen if they got separated now; how or if they'd ever find each other again. She chases after them as quickly as she can, dragging Luca frantically behind her. They run past a shaded garden where a little boy is juggling a *balón de fútbol* on his knees, and a woman wearing faded jeans and flip-flops is watering her boxed herbs. She stops when she sees them, and without moving her head or raising her voice, she says, "*¡Oye!*" in a manner that's so subtle Lydia almost misses it. But the woman's face has snagged her attention, and again almost without moving any part of her body, she juts her chin toward the darkened doorway of a covered shed in the back corner of her garden. "*Rápido,*" she says, again without raising her voice.

Lydia doesn't hesitate to consider the pros and cons. She restrains Luca with one hand on his shoulder, and then calls out as quietly as she can, "Rebeca. Here."

And the sisters skid, turning to look at them. Lydia has already pushed Luca through the gate, and he's running beneath a shade tree with riotous pink blossoms, and he's ducking inside the darkened doorway of that shed, and Lydia is right behind him and now here come the sisters until they are all there together, squeezed into the cooled and musty little space, and the exertion of their breath sounds terribly loud, and Lydia can hear the pumping of blood in her ears, a dreadful, vulgar pulse, and she curls her head over her knees and laces her fingers together behind her head and Luca throws an arm around her lower back and they all sit as still and silent as possible until, after a few minutes, they hear the mother calling to the little boy, and she says, "Come on, I've picked some oregano for dinner. Inside, let's go." And in the silent moment that follows, the fears that Lydia hadn't paused to entertain before come flocking in and lodge in her throat. *This woman has trapped us here; she has gone to get la policía; she has gone to get someone much worse than la policía, this will be the end for us, why did I trust her, why didn't we keep running.* It's too late for these fears, of course, because the decision has been made, and they can't venture out now because they've given up their lead, and now they're stuck here while *la migra* combs the neighborhood. Lydia gets hold of herself in the only way she can. *Don't think, don't think, don't think.* And then they hear the bang of a door and the woman calls out again to her child. "Close that gate before you come in!" And there's a creak and a clang as he slams the gate, the echoing bounce of the *balón* when the little boy lets it drop, and then the rumble of a car or truck, a vehicle door opening, slamming, footsteps, and a new voice.

"You seen any visitors?" the voice says. *"Migrantes?"*

Lydia's heart feels like machinery in her chest. Rebeca and Soledad are standing, facing each other, their fingers tangled together in the darkness, their heads tipped down in prayer. They cannot hear the little boy's answer, but then the bang of the door and the mother's voice is there again.

"Víctor, I told you to come inside," she says.

A man's voice, beyond the gate. "We were just asking him if he'd seen any migrants. We had a few get off the train just at the end of the street."

"We haven't seen anyone," she says. "I was out here with him until only a moment ago. Go inside."

The door bangs once again.

"Little girl down the street saw them heading this way."

"They must have turned before they got here. We were outside all afternoon. You have a cell phone, or I just call the station house if we see them?"

The voices drop lower, become momentarily indiscernible. Lydia opens her eyes wide, as if she can increase her range of hearing that way. At this very moment, Lydia knows, the woman may be pointing to the doorway of this shed. She may be mouthing the words *There are four of them, inside the shed. Los agentes de la migra* may be unholstering their weapons. Lydia trembles with the thought and closes her eyes again. Her finger slips inside Sebastián's wedding ring. *Don't think, don't think, don't think.* And then there's a kind of miracle, a tiny distraction: her finger moves absently through the void of Sebastián's ring and provokes a funny idea, that it's like the magic ring from *The Hobbit,* that if she slips her finger fully inside and holds on to Luca, it will make them both invisible. *Seguro.* She can make out the woman's words again. A shift of the wind.

"I picked too much oregano for supper," she's saying. "Please, here, take some with you."

After the footsteps retreat to the vehicle, and the engine rumbles away, and the woman opens and closes the door to her house again, Soledad and Rebeca join Lydia and Luca in sitting on the floor. Slowly, their collective heartbeats return to a normal pace. Slowly, they begin whispering to one another in the darkness.

"Should we leave?" Soledad asks.

"Not yet," Lydia says. "They're still searching the neighborhood. Let's wait until it's really dark out."

Rebeca is crying, hunched over her legs. Luca touches her hand, and she flinches, which hurts his feelings. But instead of withdrawing, he persists, and then Rebeca softens, melts into him like a pat of butter on a pan. Luca pulls her head onto his shoulder and strokes her hair.

"It's okay, nothing bad happened," he tells her. "It's okay."

"I can't do this anymore," she says. "It's too frightening."

"Stop it," Soledad says.

"I just want to die. I want it to be over," Rebeca says without any inflection to her voice at all.

"Well, you don't get to decide that, Rebeca," her sister says.

"I want to go home."

"There is no home. We're going to make a new home. This is the only way forward, so we go forward. *Adelante.* No more crying now."

Soledad wipes at her sister's face with her thumbs, and the tough love works. Rebeca sits up and makes a loud sniff, and is finished with her despair.

"We're almost there," Soledad says. "You heard Luca earlier. Three hundred miles, right, *chiquito?*"

"That's right," Luca says.

"Three hundred miles," Soledad says. "And then it's all over. All this nightmare, the whole thing, all of it. We will be in *el norte,* where no one can hurt us anymore. We'll make a good, safe life. And Papi will get better and we'll send for him, and then we'll bring Mami and Abuela, too. Everything will be better, you'll see."

Rebeca doesn't believe a single word of it. She doesn't even understand how Soledad can preserve that kind of naïveté after everything she's been through. Rebeca has been cured of innocence. She knows there's no safe place for them in the world, that *el norte* will be the same as anywhere else. Hope cannot survive the poison of her recent proof: the world is a terrible place. San Pedro Sula was terrible, Mexico is terrible, *el norte* will be terrible. Even her gold-dappled memories of the cloud forest are beginning to rot and decay. When she reaches back in her mind now, it's not her mother's voice she remembers, or the scent of drying herbs, or the chorus of the tree frogs at night, or the cool wash of the clouds on her arms and hair. It's the poverty that drove her father and all the men away to the cities. It's the advancing threat of the cartels, the want of resources, the ever-present hunger. So it's only for the sake of her sister that Rebeca nods her head.

"Everything we've been through?" Soledad says. "It'll all be worth it. We'll leave it behind and have a new beginning."

Rebeca looks at the floor but her eyes are unfocused. "Like it never happened," she says.

They stay in the shed while Víctor and his mother eat supper in the house, while the neighbors come home from work and greet their families, while the clouds skid across the lid of Hermosillo, and the sun sinks orange into the horizon. Beyond the perimeter of the city, the Sonoran Desert trades heat with the sky. As twilight cools the land and the human city prepares for sleep, the desert pops and teems with life. Lydia and the sisters plan to rest until the neighborhood is entirely quiet, to slip out during the darkest hours of the night. Luca is too hungry to sleep, so he's very grateful when the woman appears with a pot of cold beans and a stack of dry tortillas. She places these items on the floor among them and then steps back toward the doorway. Luca doesn't wait for her to leave; he uses a tortilla to scoop up the beans, and almost bites his finger in his hurry. There's no light, but their eyes have adjusted to the dark.

The woman whispers, "You can rest here for a while. But please be gone before daylight."

CHAPTER TWENTY-FIVE

Before dawn, Lydia, Luca, and the sisters walk deeper into the city, where they discover that the railway fence in Hermosillo is serious business, expensive infrastructure. Tax pesos at work. In fact, it's not a fence at all, but a concrete wall topped with razor wire in threatening coils. Inside that wall, a train rumbles past with migrants asleep on top, their arms folded across their chests, their hats over their faces. On this side of the wall, six migrant men sleep wrapped around their packs while one keeps watch. He has no shoes. He greets them as they approach.

"What happened to your shoes?" Lydia asks.

"Stolen," he says.

Soledad recognizes his Honduran accent. *"Ay, catracho, ¡qué barbaridad!"*

He nods, scratches his chin. "At least they didn't get my beard," he says.

Lydia cannot stop thinking about the man, even after they've passed well beyond him, farther into the city, where they have to find breakfast and stock up their water supply. How could he make a joke like that, a man so destitute that even his shoes have been taken from him? Lydia is rationing toothpaste. Her hair feels greasy and her skin dry. She's aware of these discomforts daily. If someone took her shoes, she would give up, she thinks. That would be the ultimate indignity. Sixteen dead family members she can survive, as long as her toes are not naked before the world.

They find a large park with broad, paved walkways and a string of orange Porta Potties left over from a concert the night before. Luca leans over the edge of a fountain and submerges his arms up to the elbow. Lydia has a growing sense that her very humanity is under siege, so as a flimsy defense against that attack, she permits herself to spend 10 pesos on a cup of coffee from a vendor. The caffeine hits her bloodstream like a dream of another life. She sips it slowly and allows the steam to curl around her face while she thinks about that man and his shoes. The encounter has provoked in her an urgent feeling about the importance of shoes. So she will convert some portion of their remaining money to new shoes now, she decides. Here in Hermosillo, today. She looks to the girls' feet as well, and notices that both of their sneakers could use replacing. They wear low-top Converses; Soledad's are black and Rebeca's gray. The shoes are sun-faded and worn, but at least they're comfortable, well broken-in, Lydia tells herself. She wishes she had extra money. They wait in the park until the shops open, and Lydia spends almost half their remaining cash on two decent pairs of hiking boots for herself and Luca. They're just ordinary leather with heavy stitching and thick rubber soles. But no. These boots are miraculous, extraordinary; they are mythological winged sandals. These are the boots that will cross the desert passage to *el norte*. It feels like a crater in her chest when Lydia hands over her money.

There are many migrants gathered beside the tracks in Hermosillo, and some of the campsites appear permanent. An older couple sits on a plaid couch beneath a tarp while the woman tends to a fire where you might expect a coffee table to be. Just outside the expensive gate, no one seems to care that migrants are waiting for La Bestia. The fence ends at the gated opening across the tracks, and just inside that gate, two guards sit in the shade of a small hut, waiting to open and close the gate when the train is ready. The gate, like the fence, is topped with razor wire, but there's nothing to stop migrants from slipping underneath the gate, where there's a two-foot gap Luca could easily roll through. Anyone could go under the fence here, and the guards don't seem interested in preventing them, but no one tries. They're content to wait just outside the gate instead, where, the other migrants inform Lydia, the train will emerge from its cage eventually, slowly, and everyone will clamber on.

The wait there with the other migrants feels like the longest stretch of hours in Soledad's life. Ever since Luca told her how close they are to *el norte*, she fancies she can smell it there on the horizon, all McNuggets and fresh Nikes. She can almost see it shimmering in the distance, and her whole body twitches with the yearning for it. She leans north with her spine, her eyes, her lungs. While the others sleep that night on the cold, packed earth against the cinder block wall of the bordering gardens, she paces the tracks in the moonlight, tense with fear that something more will happen now that they're this close, some fresh horror will swoop down on them and steal the dream they've almost accomplished. She tries to doze, and when her head begins to pound, she realizes she's been holding her breath.

In the morning, a local resident drapes a hose over the garden wall so the migrants can brush their teeth, wet their faces, and fill their canteens. A contingent of older ladies walks the tracks, passing out blessings with homemade bagged sandwiches and pickles. A guard from the hut calls Luca over and passes him a grape lollipop through the chain-link fence. Lydia is on alert at all times now, for Lorenzo, or for anyone like Lorenzo, for anyone who might recognize her. Whenever there's a delay of this sort, her worry grows that he'll catch up to them, that he'll appear walking toward them at any moment. Or that someone else will have too much time to think it over and there will be a *snap*! An *ah-ha*! She keeps the ugly pink hat flopped over her face all the time.

"Mami, can I wear my sneakers?" Luca asks.

He's been wearing the new boots since yesterday, and they're stiff. She wants him to break them in, but he has to do it in small doses. There's no point in him getting blisters before they even get to the desert. His blue sneakers are tied together by the laces and strung through one strap of his backpack.

"Go ahead and change," she says.

When he takes the boots off, she gathers them up and ties them together in the same fashion. She changes hers, too.

It's late morning when there's a squawk from the radio in the guards' hut, and the migrants sit up and take notice. Minutes later, the guards swing their expensive gates wide open for the train that appears in the distance. The cage is open, and now all they have to do is wait while the train chugs slowly toward them. The migrants clamber aboard in groups, women and children first. The men help, and the guards watch. One guard even tosses a migrant's backpack up to him after it rolls off the edge.

Lydia catches Soledad's eye. "Don't forget to be afraid," she says.

"This is not normal," Soledad responds.

But they're up quickly. Easily. And the train doesn't pick up substantial speed until everyone is aboard, almost as if the engineer was taking care to safely accommodate the migrants. To give them a boost. Lydia blesses herself anyway. She traces the sign of the cross on Luca's forehead every time.

And then a strange thing happens as they travel north out of Hermosillo and deeper into the Sonoran Desert: they begin to notice other migrants moving in the opposite direction. Just a trickle at first, two on foot, and then another two, and Lydia cannot imagine where they've come from, walking south as they are, and emerging from what seem to be endless tracts of vast and barren desert. They are unmistakably migrants. She's not sure how she knows this, but she does. Still, there's something different about them, and it's not only that they're traveling in the wrong direction. Lydia can't put her finger on it. Then, only a few miles north of Hermosillo, a second line of track sidles up alongside theirs. Because the vast majority of the Mexican railways are single-track lines, these lay-bys, these miniature exit ramps, exist at intervals so one train can pull off and idle, to await the approach of another coming from the opposite direction. In this way the trains can pass one another, north and south, and carry on, using the same line of track to their destinations. It's in just such a lay-by that they see a southbound train now idling, and Soledad sits up taller as they approach it. She shields her eyes from the sun in case they're playing tricks on her. But no, it's true—the southbound train is packed with migrants. They wave and salute and call out greetings to them as their train slows to a clacking crawl to pass.

"Where are they going?" Rebeca asks no one.

The second line of track is separated from theirs by a space of only five or six feet, and one young boy, not much older than Luca, is standing atop the southbound train. He seems to be gauging whether or not he could jump the gap. A group of men yell and gesture wildly at him, so he clambers down the nearby ladder instead, and jumps down to the ground. Then he runs north alongside the northbound train. The train is traveling quite slowly now, and Luca leans over the edge in astonishment to watch the running boy beneath. He looks up at Luca and grins. He grips the moving ladder of Luca's freight car and hauls himself up. Luca leans back up and waits for the boy's head to emerge over the lip, which is black and shiny in the desert sunlight. On the idling southbound train, a loud cheer goes up for the boy's victorious transfer, and the boy shouts back to the men, who all wave and smile.

"*¡Vaya con Dios!*" the boy yells at the men he's leaving behind. "*¡Ya me voy pa'l otro la'o!*"

Another cheer. "Be careful and God bless you!" another man yells.

And then the train begins to gain speed again, and the clacking returns to its shriek and rumble, and the boy walks over to them without even crouching, and he plops himself down carelessly. Unlike most migrants, the boy does not carry anything, nor does he wear a hat to shield his berry-brown face from the sun. Because of that fact, his exposed features are dry and burnished. His lips are cracked with peels of white, but the chapping doesn't interfere with the brightness of his smile. He puts his hand out to bump fists with Luca, who responds reflexively, the way any eight-year-old boy would, without even thinking.

"*¿Qué onda, güey?*" the boy says, using the borderland slang that marks him immediately as a northerner.

Luca doesn't know exactly what *qué onda, güey* means because he doesn't know anyone who talks like this, but he understands enough to know it's a friendly greeting, so he replies by saying hello. Lydia, who believed her capacity for surprise had been exhausted, is genuinely taken aback by the boy's arrival. She doesn't know what to make of him. On the one hand, he gives the instant impression of being gregarious, friendly, charismatic. On the other hand, she's wary of everyone she meets now, and although this child seems very young, she knows that boys this age are prime candidates for gang recruitment. And why is he alone? Why so friendly with Luca? She puts one arm defensively around her son. This child's face is round, his eyes, nose, and cheeks, all round. His eyelids look puffy, but the black eyes beneath them are clear and intense. He's wheezing slightly, and as they all watch, he removes an inhaler from the pocket of his jeans, shakes it vigorously, places it to his lips, and takes a puff. Then he breathes deeply and coughs a little.

"It's empty." He shrugs, replacing the inhaler in his pocket. "But the memory of the medicine helps."

Luca smiles, but Lydia furrows her brow.

"Will you be okay?" she asks. Despite her instinctive suspicion, she's still a mother, and you can't fake a wheeze like that.

The boy coughs again, once, twice, and then spits something solid over the edge of the train car. "It will pass in a minute," he wheezes.

They watch him for signs of a medical emergency, though it's unclear how they could help if the episode does not, in fact, pass. He sits up straight, looks out across the landscape, folds his legs into the shape of a pretzel, and concentrates on breathing slowly. As he does this, Lydia's relieved to see the existence of a hole in the sole of his sneaker. No boy with an empty inhaler and a hole in his sneaker could belong to a gang or cartel.

After he manages to regain a steady breath, the boy turns to Luca and says, "I'm Beto. What's your name?"

"Hello, Beto. I'm Luca."

Beto nods. Their train is passing a village that seems to have grown right out of the tracks—just a cluster of houses the same rusty color as the land, and two competing taquerías that face off across the lone street.

"Is your breathing better now?" Luca asks.

"Yeah, it's fine," Beto says. "Happens whenever I run too fast, but you learn how to be calm until it passes, because if you freak out, that makes it worse."

Luca nods.

"It's cool to meet another kid," Beto announces then. "I don't see that many kids out here. How old are you?"

"Eight."

"I'm ten. Almost eleven, though." He says this like a very wise old man.

Luca has about a thousand questions for Beto, but the effect of having them all packed so tightly together in his brain is that none of them shakes loose and gets through the gate. Lydia leans into the opening left by Luca's silence.

"Beto, are you traveling alone?" Luca can tell that his *mami* is trying not to sound judgmental, but the effort isn't entirely successful. Beto doesn't seem to care, or even to notice.

"Yep, just me." He grins, displaying the absence of two teeth on the bottom, a canine and a molar side by side, so the hole is a double-wide. Beto sticks his tongue through it.

Now it's Soledad's turn. "Were you traveling south?" she asks.

"I was. Temporarily. But now I'm traveling north," he says without irony.

Soledad doesn't know quite how to respond, but Beto saves her the trouble by changing the subject.

"*Guau,* you're really pretty," he says.

Soledad blinks but doesn't respond.

"Must be a pain in the ass, huh?"

She laughs.

He returns his attention to Luca. "So where you guys from?"

Luca glances at Mami, who responds with only the tiniest shake of her head. "Mami and I are from . . . Puebla," he decides. "And the sisters are Ecuadorian."

Beto nods. The lie doesn't matter at all; those places may as well be Antarctica or Mars as far as he's concerned.

"How about you?" Luca asks. "Where are you from?"

"I'm from Tijuana," Beto says. "But we call it TJ. I was born there, in the *dompe.*"

An utterly bizarre piece of information. So odd, in fact, that Luca's not sure he understands. Again, this is an unfamiliar word, *dompe.* Luca looks at Mami to translate, but she seems confused as well.

"What's a *dompe*?" Luca asks.

Beto smirks. "You know, a *dompe,* where people dump their garbage. The trucks come. You know, a *dompe.*"

"You mean like a *vertedero*?" Luca asks, using the Spanish word for "dump."

"Yeah, yeah, a *vertedero,*" Beto says.

Lydia, because her English is slightly more sophisticated than Luca's, begins to understand that this boy's native language is not exactly the Spanish of Mexico, nor is it the English of the United States, but rather some kind of semantic borderland crossbreed. Still, this insight does nothing to clarify what the boy means when he says he was born in a *dompe*. Luca literally scratches his head—a gesture Lydia hasn't seen him make, she now realizes, since the decimation of their family. It's a gesture that in fact she never noticed before, and therefore she didn't miss when it vanished, but now that she sees it again, she's floored by an accompanying revelation that the gesture, one thumb on top of his ear, three fingers raking through his hair above, is specific to Luca's intellectual curiosity. It's a tic that happens only when he's intrigued by something, when he finds something interesting. The reappearance of it, therefore, feels to Lydia like evidence that her son might survive, that he might be capable, after fifteen days and fourteen hundred miles, of temporarily losing himself in a moment of uncorrupted curiosity. The feeling that thuds through her sternum is *hope*.

"So you were born in a garbage dump?" Luca asks carefully, trying not to be rude, and not understanding that there's nothing at all discourteous about the question, because Beto is neither ashamed of the facts of his origin nor, for that matter, even aware that the facts of his origin might, in other people, incite feelings of discomfort. His origin is simply his origin, and he tells the story without any kind of appreciation of the effect it might provoke.

He laughs. "Yeah, well, I wasn't born *in* the garbage, though. Just near it. In Colonia Fausto González. You heard of it?"

Luca shakes his head.

"It's kinda famous," Beto says proudly.

Lydia knows a little about *las colonias* of Tijuana because she's read the books, because Luis Alberto Urrea is one of her favorite writers, and he's written about the dumps, about kids like Beto who live there. That flare of recognition makes her feel like she knows him already, at least slightly, but that feeling is half-hollow, a shadow puppet. Because though she may understand something of this boy's circumstances, she doesn't know *him*. Still, the familiarity has the effect of thawing the part of her that would otherwise remain hardened to him.

And then Beto tells them his whole life story, all of it without stopping, without even really taking a breath, how he doesn't remember his father, who went to *el norte* when Beto was still a baby. But he remembers his *mami,* who was a garbage picker in *el dompe* before they closed it. And he remembers his big brother, Ignacio, who's still there in *el dompe,* buried beneath a sky-blue, hand-painted cross with his name, IGNACIO, and the words MIJO, 10 AÑOS.

Beto reminds Luca that he's ten years old, and explains that that's the same age his brother, Ignacio, was when he was squashed by the back tire of a garbage truck while reaching for the miraculous, round, unblemished sphere of a *balón de fútbol* he'd spotted amid the refuse. An unprecedented treasure. Beto, who was eight years old and standing nearby at the time, was so stunned by Ignacio's screams that he failed to secure the *balón* for his dying brother. (Instead, a pimple-faced kid named Omar got it.) Because of the softness of the ground beneath the truck's tires, Beto explains, Ignacio was not entirely flattened, but rather compressed into the garbage beneath him—crushed just enough that he survived for three dreadful days. It wasn't long after that, and the sky-blue cross, that Beto's *mami* disappeared, too, first into a drunken stupor, next into a new, more rancid haze, and finally, into the ether.

Beto is afraid of turning eleven, because it feels like a treachery to his brother. "But I guess it would be worse to not turn eleven, right?" He laughs, and Lydia and the sisters attempt to join him in that sound.

Luca does not laugh but feels compelled to give the boy something in return for his story. He unzips the side pocket of his backpack, which is sitting in his lap, and fishes out his tube of Orange Mango Blast Blistex. He hands it to Beto, who takes it without saying anything, removes the cap, smears it across his lips, and then makes a loud *ah* sound. He hands it back to Luca, and doesn't say thank you, but Luca knows the *ah* was an expression of gratitude.

"So wait," Soledad says, finally turning her whole body toward him instead of just her head. "Isn't Tijuana right at the border?"

"Yeah, it is," Luca says, looking at Soledad with approval.

She intercepts the look. "You're not the only one who can read a map around here," she says, and then back to the newcomer, "So then what are you doing here if you were already right at the border? Why were you traveling south? And all those other migrants, too, traveling south?"

"Oh, those guys are all *deportados*."

Soledad cringes. "All of them?"

"Sure." Beto shrugs. "TJ is full of *deportados*. There's more people going south than north in Tijuana. You can tell them apart from the regular migrants because of their uniforms."

"Uniforms?" Luca asks.

"Yeah, all the migrants wear the same uniforms, right? Dirty jeans, busted shoes, baseball hats."

"You don't have a hat," Luca observes.

Beto shrugs. "I'm not a real migrant. I'm just a poser."

"So what's different about the *deportados* then?" Soledad prompts him back to the subject.

"They are haunted by the cries of their absent children in *el norte*." They all stare at him.

"I'm just messing," he says. "It's that they don't have backpacks."

Lydia snaps her fingers. "The backpacks," she says. "Yes, that's what they were missing. The backpacks."

"Why don't they have backpacks?" Luca asks.

"Because they're *deportados*. They live in the United States, *güey*. Like forever. Like, for ten years maybe. Since they were babies, maybe. And then they're on their way to work one morning, or coming home from school one day, or playing *fútbol* in the park, or shopping at the mall for some fresh new kicks, and then *bam*! They get deported with whatever they happen to be carrying when they're picked up. So unless they happen to be carrying a backpack when *la migra* gets them, they usually come empty-handed. Sometimes the women have their purse with them or whatever. They don't get to go home and pack a bag. But they usually have nice clothes, at least. Clean shoes."

Lydia clutches her pack in front of her. She doesn't want to think about this. The dream of getting to Estados Unidos is the only thing sustaining them right now. She's not prepared to begin considering all the horrible things that might happen after, if they're lucky enough to achieve that first, most fundamental goal.

Soledad sits back and bites her lip. "So when they get deported they just give up and go home?" she asks. "Why don't they try to cross back over?"

"I mean, some of them try," Beto explains. "But it's impossible to cross at Tijuana now. Unless you have, like, tons of money or you're working with one of the cartels. They got tunnels. A few years ago it was easy. I even knew some guys from *el dompe* who would make extra money taking migrants across. The fence was full of holes, plus ladders, boats—there were a thousand ways to get across."

"And now?"

"Now it's like a war zone, all drones and cameras and *la migra* just waiting over there like a gang of overpaid goalkeepers. Plus, *los deportados* got money. They're are all rich from working in *el norte*. So they can afford a vacation before they go back. They go home to visit."

Soledad bites nervously at the inside of her lip.

"But don't worry," Beto says. "Nogales is supposed to be better. I mean, it's supposed to be easier to get across, because nobody wants to cross in the desert and stuff, so there's not as much Border Patrol. That's why I didn't try to cross at TJ. I'm going to Nogales to get across."

Beto presses his lips together, and Luca can smell the orange and mango of the Blistex. It gives him a feeling of gladness.

"That's where this train is going, right? Nogales?" Beto asks, leaning back on his elbows and stretching his legs in front of him.

"We hope so," Luca says.

"There's one more major junction," Beto says. "At Benjamín Hill, the tracks split. Straight north to Nogales, or west to Baja. When I was coming down, I was supposed to get off there and change trains, but we didn't stop, so I just kept rolling south until we hit that lay-by." He sighs. "I hope we don't end up back in Tijuana. Imagine if I just did a Bestia sightseeing tour of the countryside and wound up back in *el dompe*?"

Soledad groans. "So you mean we might have to change again?" she says. "When we're this close?"

"I guess we'll see," Beto says, reaching into his pocket and drawing out a fistful of sunflower seeds. He munches them and spits the shells over the edge of the train without sitting up. He offers to share them with the others, but his hands are sweaty, and no one takes him up on his generosity.

"How long you been traveling?" Soledad asks him.

"Only a few days," he says. "I guess this is my third or fourth day. That your sister?"

He points at Rebeca with his chin. She's only half facing them, watching the passage of the impossible landscape: scrubby welters of green growing from the powdery earth, the arc of hot blue above them, the serrated brown of the distant mountains, the increasingly rare sight of a vehicle on the parallel highway.

"Yes, that's Rebeca," she says. "And I'm Soledad."

"How come she's so quiet?" Beto asks. "She doesn't talk?"

Rebeca turns her face but not her eyes toward him. "I used to talk," she says. "Now I don't talk anymore."

Beto sits up and brushes the salt and the sunflower-seed dust from his fingertips. "Fair enough," he says.

Two hours later they slow but do not stop as they pass through the small town of Benjamín Hill, and Luca feels encouraged by the fact that, after the tangle of tracks recedes back to a single line, they've emerged on the easternmost route, which continues due north toward Nogales.

Santa Ana, Los Janos, Bambuto, check, check, check. By early afternoon, Luca spots an airplane low in the sky. It becomes larger and flies lower until it seems like it will collide with their train. They all duck, pinning themselves flat to the top of the train as they pass the runway of Nogales International Airport.

CHAPTER TWENTY-SIX

Nogales makes them feel almost as if they've arrived in the United States already. The train slows way down and chugs right through the middle of the city. The streets are wider than Luca has seen elsewhere. The cars are bigger. There's a giant Coca-Cola can perched atop a building and countless radio towers stretching up into the sky. And then. They all see it at the same time. A huge green highway sign with white writing and an arrow. There are only three letters on the sign: USA.

Soledad begins to cry. She doesn't even try to keep from crying— she lets the tears stream down and the snot fill her nose and overflow, and this she wipes with the back of her wrist, but Rebeca puts an arm around her, which makes Soledad cry even harder.

"We made it," she whispers to her little sister.

Beto stands up on top of the train (an action that makes Lydia feel almost instantly hysterical) and says without deliberate cruelty, "Not yet, you didn't."

Luca pinches him on the back of the leg.

"Ow," Beto says. "I mean, you will. You will, you're going to make it."

"You have no idea how far we've come," Soledad says. "Even just to see it."

The train is slowing, and there's the lurching they've all become accustomed to, so that Beto has to stagger a bit, one or two steps forward, half a step back, and then Lydia can't take it any longer and she yells at him, "For God's sake, would you sit down before you get yourself killed—you're not made of rubber!" And she feels self-conscious about the unintentional sharpness of her outburst, but Beto sits down without argument and grins at her. She clutches at her chest. "Thank you," she says.

They wait until the train stops before they all climb down to the pavement. There's no station here, but it's stopped for a red signal, and they're close enough to the border that they won't have to walk for miles, and yet far enough to avoid a run-in with *la migra.*

As soon as she sets foot on the asphalt, Lydia feels a tremor of excitement travel through her whole body. She feels the exhaustion of this journey drop away from her shoulders, all the trauma and grief and guilt and horror submerge beneath a skin of new possibility. She turns back to the ladder and lifts Luca down by the armpits.

"Mami, stop, I can do it," he says, and Lydia realizes that the presence of Beto has returned yet another of her son's temporarily suspended features: parental embarrassment. She's happy to see it.

"Sorry," she says.

"You guys hungry?" Beto asks. "I'm starving, I'm going to go find some *lonche.* You wanna come?"

"*¿Lonche?*" Luca asks.

"*Almuerzo,*" Mami translates. Lunch.

"Yeah, I want some *lonche,*" Luca says.

"I could go for some *lonche,*" Soledad agrees.

Lydia thinks about the cash they have left: just over a hundred dollars. They need to eat, but that money won't last.

Beto sees her hesitation. "I'm buying," he says.

They walk north along the main avenue, and when Beto spots a *birrie-ría,* they stop and order five portions of the spicy stew. When he opens his pocket wide enough to take some money out, Lydia sees the big wad of cash he has in there, and all at once, her fear returns. They'd been foolish to trust this kid so easily, regardless of the hole in his shoe, regardless of the empty inhaler. No ten-year-old should be walking around with that kind of money in Nogales. There's only one source of potential income for a kid like this, Lydia knows. She stiffens, but the vendor is passing her a Styrofoam bowl with fragrant steam curling up the handle of the spoon. She can't help but fall onto it with vigor. The last time they ate well was in Culiacán. Her suspicions can wait until after *lonche.*

"*Ay, Dios mío,* thank you," Soledad says with her mouth full of food. Beto nods.

"Let's go see it, I want to go see it," Soledad says.

"Then just look," Beto says, gesturing with his spoon.

Soledad follows the direction of the spoon, and she sees, not half a block from where they're standing with their toes pointing north, flapping against the stark sunshine, the red and white stripes, the blue starfield of the American flag.

"It's right there?" she says, forgetting her food for a moment. "That's not it, is it?"

"That's it." Beto nods, shoveling in a mouthful.

"But it looks so . . ." Soledad doesn't know how to finish the sentence.

This street dead-ends in a fishbowl of concrete: a line of shops to the right, some formidable, blockish government buildings to the left, and a wall directly in front, which is topped with a second wall, which is topped with a third wall, which is topped with razor wire and mounted cameras. It's behind this wall, stretching high up into the sky, that the American flag moves stiffly in the mild wind. Only a few feet away from it, on this side of the fence, a Mexican flag also flies.

"See," Beto says, pointing to the Mexican flag. "This is the whole problem, right? Look at that American flag over there—you see it? All bright and shiny; it looks brand-new. And then look at ours. It's all busted up and raggedy. The red doesn't even look red anymore. It's pink."

Luca and the sisters walk toward the Mexican flag and then past it. They approach the wall at a section of open screen where they can see through to the other side. Lydia hangs back with Beto, who's seen it all before. It's good to have a minute alone with him anyway. She wants to interrogate him about the money.

"It's like we don't have any pride, like we don't even care," Beto is saying. "I mean, why does their flag have to be so much higher? How hard would it be to get a taller flagpole?"

Lydia looks up and sees that he's right. The Mexican flag here does look tattered and sun bleached, and the red, white, and blue one appears pristine behind it, like it was replaced just this morning.

"I don't know," she says. "Imagine replacing that flag every week, how expensive that would be. What's the point?"

Beto tosses his spoon into a planter and tips the Styrofoam into his mouth. He slurps it.

"Seems like a lot of jingoism if you ask me," Lydia says.

"A lot of what?"

"Wasted money."

"I guess." Beto shrugs. "I mean, those *estadounidenses* are obsessed with their flag." He tosses the remainder of the stew into his mouth and then pitches the Styrofoam into the planter after the spoon.

"Can I ask you something?" Lydia asks. "Speaking of money?"

"Sure." But the mention of money makes him shift his weight.

She clears her throat. "I couldn't help but notice you're carrying quite a lot of it there."

Beto slings his hand instinctively into his pocket. Lydia keeps one eye on Luca and the sisters while she bends to retrieve Beto's discarded spoon and bowl. She sets her own bowl of half-eaten stew on the edge of the planter and takes Beto's garbage to a nearby trash can. When she returns, he's seated on the edge of the planter beside her *birria*. She lifts it and sits beside him, taking another bite.

"It's my money," he says. "I didn't steal it."

"No," Lydia says. "I'm not accusing you."

"I didn't do anything bad for it either."

Lydia continues to eat. "It's none of my business, I know," she says between bites. "But of course it makes me curious. Sometimes money is cause for concern. Especially here. Especially when it's a young person who has a lot of money without having a job or a rich family."

Beto stares at a wad of gum beside his feet. "I could have a rich uncle."

Lydia frowns. "Listen, you seem like a nice kid, but we've had enough trouble already," she says. "We really can't afford any more."

Beto sits up out of his slouch and answers defensively. "I got it by selling some stuff."

Lydia sets her spoon into her empty Styrofoam bowl and waits a beat to see if he'll continue. When he doesn't, she prompts him. "What kind of stuff?"

Beto leans down to rest his elbows on his knees, which isn't easy for him, since his feet don't quite reach the ground. "I found a gun," he says, and then he looks at her to gauge her response before continuing. She doesn't seem alarmed, so he goes on. "And I found some drugs."

She nods. "Okay."

"And I didn't even really sell the stuff, I just returned it to the guy in *el dompe* who I knew it probably belonged to."

"So the money was more like a reward?"

"Yeah, I guess. He asked me if I wanted to work for him, and I said what I really wanted was to get out of *el dompe* and go north, so he gave me the money."

"But that much?"

Beto shrugs. "I think he felt bad for me because of Ignacio and stuff. Everybody in *el dompe* was always feeling bad for me after that, and after my *mami* disappeared."

Lydia bites her lip.

"He didn't even count it. He just went to his lockbox and grabbed me a fat stack of cash. Told me to go to Nogales if I really wanted to cross."

"He didn't even count it?"

"Nah."

Lydia doesn't think he'd bother lying. He seems completely guileless, and he doesn't owe her an explanation anyway. But it's so far-fetched. Why would anyone give a kid that much money? It seems almost impossible to offend Beto, so she pushes it.

"Are you sure you didn't take it when he was sleeping or something?"

He laughs. "*Güey*, I'd have to have some *huevazos* to do a thing like that!" He shakes his head. "Or a death wish."

"Okay," she says.

"I don't have a death wish," he clarifies. "I like being alive."

"Good," she says.

"Despite everything."

Lydia crushes the Styrofoam bowl in her fist without meaning to, and a dribble of sauce runs into her palm. She wipes it on her jeans and then looks at Beto's round face. He's a philosopher, she thinks. He's rough, but he means what he says, and his openness is a provocation. *Despite everything, he likes being alive.* Lydia doesn't know whether that's true for herself. For mothers, the question is immaterial anyway. Her survival is a matter of instinct rather than desire.

"If you want to know the truth, I think it's more than he meant to give me," Beto confesses suddenly. "He was pretty stoned."

"Ah." Now it makes sense.

"I told him I'd pay him back when I got a job *en el otro lado,* but he said, 'After you get across, just keep walking. Don't ever look back here.'"

Lydia nods. "So that was it?"

"That was it, here I am!"

"Here you are."

Luca looks over at them, a little boomerang of reassurance—just verifying they're still there. Then he returns his gaze northward.

"And nobody's coming after you, right?"

"I hope not," he says. "I've paid my taxes, stayed out of prison, always kept up with my child support." He clears his throat and spits into the sidewalk. He squints north toward the wall. "I'm a free man."

Lydia laughs. "You're a character."

"That's the word they always use," he says. "Character."

She tosses her bowl into the trash can as well. "Well, it sounds like you were overdue for some good luck anyway."

"That's right, it's my turn," he says. *"Darle la vuelta a la tortilla."*

"So how are you going to cross?" she asks. "You have plans?"

Beto sits up taller and studies *la línea* from where they sit. It looks as impenetrable as it does in TJ. "Sometimes kids just walk right up to the booth and hand themselves in," he says. "Some of the Central American ones can get asylum. You know about that?"

"Sure, I heard about the caravans."

Lydia had been aware of the migrant caravans coming from Guatemala and Honduras in the way comfortable people living stable lives are peripherally aware of destitution. She heard their stories on the news radio while she cooked dinner in her kitchen. Mothers pushing strollers thousands of miles, small children walking holes into the bottoms of their pink Crocs, hundreds of families banding together for safety, gathering numbers as they walked north for weeks, hitching rides in the backs of trucks whenever they could, riding La Bestia whenever they could, sleeping in *fútbol* stadiums and churches, coming all that way to *el norte* to plead for asylum. Lydia chopped onions and cilantro in her kitchen while she listened to their histories. They fled violence and poverty, gangs more powerful than their governments. She listened to their fear and determination, how resolved they were to reach Estados Unidos or die on the road in that effort, because staying at home meant their odds of survival were even worse. On the radio, Lydia heard those walking mothers singing to their children, and she felt a pang of emotion for them. She tossed chopped vegetables into hot oil, and the pan sizzled in response. That pang Lydia felt had many parts: it was anger at the injustice, it was worry, compassion, helplessness. But in truth, it was a small feeling, and when she realized she was out of garlic, the pang was subsumed by domestic irritation. Dinner would be bland. Sebastián wouldn't complain, but she'd register the mild disapproval on his features, and she'd feel provoked. She'd try not to start an argument.

Beto is talking beside her. "I heard if your life is in danger wherever you come from, they're not allowed to send you back there."

To Lydia it sounds like mythology, but she can't help asking anyway, "You have to be Central American? To apply for asylum?"

Beto shrugs. "Why? Your life in danger?"

Lydia sighs. "Isn't everyone's?"

CHAPTER TWENTY-SEVEN

The sisters call the coyote from a pay phone. They feel like professional telephone users now, and they make the call without Luca's assistance. Soledad tells the coyote they've arrived in Nogales, and they have three more people now who want to join their crossing.

"Can they walk?" he asks. "This is the no-frills package. They have to be in good shape."

"Yeah," Soledad assures him. "They're good."

"Where are you now?"

Soledad presses the receiver to her ear and looks around. "I don't know, we're right by the border," she says. "By the train tracks."

"You can see the American flag there, on that big white building?"

"Yes."

"Yeah, I know where you are."

The coyote tells her to meet him at a plaza a couple blocks away. He'll be there within the hour. She's excited when she hangs up the phone. She tells Lydia and the boys the news.

"He says it's good if you come. We have to go meet him now."

They want to call Papi first, and they try three times, but it's an international call and they don't understand all the codes, so they finally have to enlist Luca's help. It turns out they don't have enough money anyway, so they settle on a prayer instead.

"He'll be okay," Rebeca insists. If she says it enough times, she can maybe make it true.

At the Plaza Niños Héroes, there are ornate benches painted a vivid gold, but all the ones set in the shade are already taken, so Luca and Beto sit on the edge of another planter, and Lydia sits on a low step nearby. The sisters walk quiet laps together through the square, their arms folded tightly in front of themselves, and their heads tipped toward each other. Lydia watches people notice them, their remarkable beauty, their visible exhaustion.

Lydia's worried about so many things she can't pin one down to examine it. She's worried about being out in the open like this, about being recognized. Whenever someone looks at her and then looks at their cell phone, there's a little racehorse of adrenaline that clobbers through her body. She feels it mostly in her stomach and her joints. She sits close to the wall with her pack at her feet, where she imagines she's inconspicuous. This is the one benefit of being a migrant, of having effected this disguise so completely: they are nearly invisible. No one looks at them, and in fact, people take pains *not* to look at them. She hopes that general indifference extends to the *halcones,* if Javier has them here in Nogales. She also worries about money. How expensive the coyote might be, how she'll gain access to her mother's bank account, and even if it works, how little money they'll have left after they cross. She worries about the coyote, too. Her mother's money is their last hope, and the idea of withdrawing that money and handing it over to a stranger is maddening. What questions will she ask him to ascertain the worth of his character? After he has their money, what incentive does he have to get them safely to their destination? What's to keep him from leading them all deep into the desert and abandoning them there to die? And ultimately: What choice does she have?

Luca and Beto talk quietly nearby, swinging their feet from the planter, banging their heels against the wall beneath them. Beto scratches a twig along the top of the planter like a pencil. Luca plucks two leaves off a shrub and intertwines their stems, twisting them around in his fingers. So Lydia is worried about all these things, and yet, she has a new understanding about the futility of worry. The worst will either happen or not happen, and there's no worry that will make a difference in either direction. *Don't think.* She leans her elbows on her knees.

When he arrives, El Chacal finds the sisters without trying.

"*Dios mío,*" he says, by way of introduction, shaking his head.

Soledad can feel him assessing them, the angles of their faces, the problem of their beauty. She feels the hesitation this causes him, and she likes that hesitation is the thing it causes rather than something else. She's relieved as she watches him push past his reluctance. He nods at them.

"Soledad?" he says.

"Me," she responds. "And this is my sister, Rebeca." She pinches her sister's elbow, and Rebeca nods.

He's a small man, only slightly taller than the sisters. His face is handsome, with angular cheekbones and a clean shave. His cheeks are a shade rosier than the rest of his skin, which makes him look more cheerful than he otherwise might. He's wiry and lean in his clean Levi's and red Gap T-shirt. He looks like a migrant himself, except his Adidas sneakers appear brand-new. "Where are the others?" he asks.

"They're sitting," Soledad says. "Over there." She walks toward them and the coyote follows.

"*Ay,*" he says, when he sees them. "A lady and two kids?" He shakes his head.

The boys are already in earshot, and they both hop down from the planter.

"You don't have to worry about me," Beto says. "I'm twenty-three. I just have a growth disorder."

Beto knows the words *growth disorder* because one of the kids he knew in *el dompe* had a growth disorder, and even though that kid was the same age as Beto, he stopped growing when they were both six, and Beto kept going until he was twice that boy's height. It was one of the visiting priests from San Diego who told them about growth disorders. It didn't matter anyway, because knowing the words didn't make the kid start growing again. Beto grins at the coyote.

"Twenty-three, *de verdad*?" El Chacal says.

"Plus, I have the voice of an angel," Beto says, and then he places one hand on his heart and breaks into song. A very loud, not entirely off-key rendition of some pop song Luca's heard before but doesn't know the name of. When he gets to the rap part, El Chacal holds up one hand to shush him. "Impressive, though, right?" Beto says. "They called me the J Balvin of *el dompe.*"

The coyote looks unblinkingly at Beto, who does an impromptu tap dance right there in the middle of the square.

"Okay, okay, *siéntate.*" El Chacal doesn't like to draw attention.

Beto hoists himself back onto the edge of the planter.

Lydia stands. "My son and I have come all the way from Guerrero. We rode La Bestia. We are capable; we won't slow you down."

Rebeca speaks up. "You wouldn't believe the things that little dude can do. He could walk a week in the desert if he had to."

The coyote frowns, turns to Soledad. "Your cousin told you I have a good track record, yes?"

"Yes."

"You know why I have a good track record?"

She shakes her head.

"Because I don't take kids. I don't like leaving people behind. I don't like people dying in the desert. So I choose people who won't die."

Luca holds on to his mother's hand. "I have no intention of dying," he says.

El Chacal turns his attention to the boy. "No one *intends* to die," he says to Luca.

"Yes," Luca concedes. "But I intend *not* to die." Lydia holds her breath. She can see that Luca's making an impression. "There's a difference," Luca says.

"Oh?" The coyote leans back to get a better look at Luca's face beneath Papi's cap.

"Yes," Luca says. "I have considered it."

"You've considered it!" El Chacal laughs. "You have considered dying?"

"Of course," Luca says.

"And?"

"And I'm not interested in dying yet."

The coyote nods. "I see."

"So I will stay alive."

"Okay."

"With or without your help," Luca says. Lydia pinches the back of his neck lightly. "But of course, your help would be a significant advantage."

Now the coyote laughs harder. "*¡Órale!*" he says, holding his hands up in front of him. "Okay, okay."

Beto hops down to the ground. The kid knows when to keep quiet; he doesn't say a word.

"Okay," the coyote says again. Then he looks at Lydia. "You can pay?"

She tries to make her face blank, her voice loose. "What is the price?"

"Five thousand for you. Six each for the kids."

"Dollars?" Lydia's mouth drops open.

"*Claro.*"

The sisters paid only four each. "But I thought—"

The coyote intercepts her argument. "It's not a negotiation. I have enough *pollitos* to cross without you. I don't need the money. If you want to come, that is the price."

Lydia closes her mouth. She's short. She doesn't know exactly how short, but they don't have enough. Her stomach drops, and for the first time in days, she feels like she's going to cry. The flare of her nostrils, the swamp of fluid into her sinuses, it's almost a relief. She wasn't sure she was still capable of crying.

"How much is that in pesos?" Beto removes the wad of cash from his pocket, and is flicking through it, counting.

The coyote pushes Beto's hands down out of sight. "Put it away," he says. "You trying to get killed or just robbed?" Beto stuffs the money back into his pocket while the coyote looks around to see if anyone's watching them. "Listen, if we're going to do this, the first thing is, you have to not be an idiot, okay?"

Beto looks sheepish and doesn't clown. "Okay," he says with genuine remorse. "Sorry."

The coyote nods. "Don't do anything until I tell you to do it, right?"

Beto nods again.

"You don't even piss or sneeze without my permission. And for God's sake, you don't ball out with a wad of money and start counting it in the middle of the street."

"Okay."

El Chacal returns his attention to Soledad. "It's going to be tight quarters in the apartment with the extra people, but it's only a couple days."

"Apartment?" she asks. She's taken her backpack off to drink from her water bottle. Luca and Beto collect their things.

"Yeah, a place I use for staging. You'll be there a day or two until the others arrive." He begins to walk, and Lydia grabs her backpack to fall in step behind him.

"I need to go to a bank first," she says.

He turns and looks at her, eyebrows up. "A bank?" he says, as if she's requested they stop by the moon for a moment.

"Yes. To get your money," she says.

"A bank!" El Chacal says again. "Maybe I should've charged you more!" He laughs when he says this, and although Lydia is cheered by his unexpected congeniality, by his quickness to laugh, she can't manage to join him.

Lydia is relieved to find a branch of her mother's bank nearby, and she leaves Luca outside with the sisters. The building looks freshly white-washed, and it makes her aware of how worn-looking and dirty she is. She pauses to check her reflection in the window. She's been wearing the same powder-blue, button-up blouse for three days. Her armpits feel damp, and her hair is a mess. She hopes she smells okay; she can't tell anymore. Lydia never wore makeup when she was younger, but since she turned thirty, she's taken extra care with a bit of powder most mornings, a light dusting to cover the lines across her forehead. At work, she wore a light coat of mascara and a slick of nude lip gloss. She washed her hair every second day, and usually wore it in a ponytail when she was stocking the shelves. The woman in the window looks nothing like that recent Lydia. This woman is thinner and darker, with ropes of muscles in her neck and arms. This unshowered woman has dark circles beneath her eyes and a grim visage. She wishes for the armor of her small makeup pouch at home, hanging by its drawstring from a wooden hook in the family bathroom, but the bewilderment is almost comforting; perhaps no one would recognize her from Javier's photograph after all. She'd like to take off the floppy hat, too, and stuff it into her backpack, because she feels ridiculous, like she's going to church in her bathing suit. But even with the changes to her appearance, she'd feel too conspicuous without it. *Enough wishing.* There's a security camera mounted on a bracket above her, and Lydia doesn't want to be on it. She lowers her face beneath the hat as she opens the door of the bank, and steps inside.

In the fluorescent-lit, air-conditioned vestibule, Lydia's arms immediately come up in goose bumps. Her body has become unused to electric comforts. She rubs both arms to warm herself, removes her mother's bank card from the purse, and checks the account balance again at the ATM. It's still all there, still untouched, 212,871 pesos. Lydia blows air through her parted lips. There's a withdrawal limit of 6,000 pesos per day, and Lydia has delayed this moment for many reasons, not least of which is that she's not sure how she'll get her hands on the money without the required documentation. She knew it was safer to leave the money in the bank while they traveled anyway. But it's also true that delaying the withdrawal was easier for Lydia, who isn't ready to ratify the awful truth that her mother is really gone. She knows it will feel like stealing her mother's money. She wants it to feel that way. Because Lydia has not been able to grieve, there's still some significant way in which it feels like only she and Luca have gone, that the rest of their family is still intact and happy, living their lives as usual in Acapulco. She imagines Sebastián brushing past her hanging makeup pouch in the bathroom each morning, damp from the shower, his bare body wrapped in the blue towel. Lydia wishes she could further delay pulling the plug on that artifice.

But the existence of this electronic money is a miracle. A one-shot parachute. She writes her mother's name in a binder on the counter, and then waits in a chair until the branch manager calls her into a private cubicle. Lydia sits, setting her backpack on the empty chair beside her. It's a woman who sits in the chair facing her, so that feels like a bit of luck. The woman wears a navy blazer and has a single streak of gray in her hair. Her face is kind. Lydia studies the woman's features for a moment and makes a snap decision. She will tell her everything. All of it. She will throw herself on the mercy of this stranger's kind face.

It's only the third time Lydia has told her story. The first was to Carlos in the office above the church in Chilpancingo and the second was to the nun, Hermana Cecilia, at the first Casa del Migrante in Huehuetoca. Both times, the telling had taken a toll on Lydia, but both times, she'd received in return something that felt like salvation.

"What can I do for you today?" the branch manager asks, folding her hands in front of her on the desk. She doesn't lean away, or eye the backpack suspiciously. She is gracious, and her name is Paola, according to her square, brown name tag.

"I—" Lydia begins, but then her nostrils flare and all the words catch in her throat. Lydia presses her eyes closed once, slowly, and begins again. "I need to close my mother's account."

"Okay," Paola says. "I can help you with that. Is your mother . . . can she come with you to do that, or . . ."

"She's deceased," Lydia says.

"Oh, I'm so sorry for your loss." Paola says this not unkindly, but mechanically, and only because it's the thing people say.

This isn't at all how Lydia wanted to begin, so formal, so cold. She shakes her head, inches her chair closer to the desk. Paola does not back away.

"I need your help," Lydia says.

Paola nods. "Of course," she says, reaching out to pat Lydia's hand before clasping her own hands together on the desk again. "All we need, then, is her death certificate and a copy of her will, if you have it—"

Lydia stops the woman from talking by clearing her throat. She looks not at Paola's face but at the knot of her hands on the desk between them, at the simple gold wedding band. She speaks without looking up.

"My mother was murdered. My whole family was murdered by the cartel in Acapulco. My husband, my sister. Sixteen of my family members." She is speaking very quietly now, leaning toward Paola across the desk, and she can hear that Paola's breathing has changed—no—has stopped, actually. She glances up at the woman's face and sees the same stillness there. It's a paralysis born of empathy, so Lydia chases the rest of the words out of her mouth quickly, before she loses her nerve or her track, before she begins to cry. "My son and I escaped. He's there, just outside. We had money, but we were kidnapped in Sinaloa and now it's gone. And we need my mother's money to pay the coyote now. To get across. I'm my mother's only remaining child."

There's only one hand left on the desk now, the one with the wedding ring. The other has gone up to Paola's face, to Paola's mouth, where its presence might prevent the escape of some of Paola's informal reaction. "Oh my God," Paola says. Because what else could she possibly say? She opens a lower drawer and withdraws a box of tissues, which she places on the desk between them. "That birthday party massacre in Acapulco, I read about you. Your family, oh my God. I'm so sorry."

"Thank you," Lydia says. "It was my niece's *quinceañera*. Yénifer."

Paola crumples a tissue from the box and holds it beneath her nose. Lydia takes one, too. Then they look each other in the eye. Lydia whispers.

"Do you have children?"

Paola nods. "Three."

"I'm afraid we're going to die. This money is the only way to save my son."

Paola pushes her rolling chair back from the desk. "Wait here," she says.

She's gone for what feels like a very long time, and when she returns, she's carrying a folder stacked with documents. She sits back into the chair, and Lydia straightens her posture. Paola opens the folder and, using the mouse, clicks the computer monitor to life. "Do you have any identification?"

"Yes." Lydia digs into her backpack and finds her voter ID card. She hands it to Paola, who studies it for a moment, looks more closely at Lydia's face, and then sets it on the folder.

"Bank card?"

"Yes." She produces this as well.

"Are you a custodian on your mother's account?"

"No."

"And you don't have a death certificate for her, I'm sure," Paola says.

"No."

"Or a copy of her will?"

"No." Lydia tries not to panic. Surely this woman is going to try to help her. She understands. She knows that Lydia has none of these documents, has no way of obtaining any of these documents without returning to Guerrero and getting herself killed. But what if it's simply impossible? What if Paola is trying to help Lydia find a loophole, but all she's really doing is confirming the inevitable bad news that Lydia has no legal right to this money? Lydia tries to breathe deeply, but everything shakes.

"What is your line of work?" Paola asks.

"I own a bookstore in Acapulco. Or I did. I guess I still do."

Paola types into the computer. "Name of the business?"

"Palabras y Páginas."

She types some more, and then twists the monitor so Lydia can see. She's not filling in forms, Lydia realizes. She's googling her. Verifying her story. Making sure this is not a con job. "This is you?"

She's opened the website Lydia's been meaning to update. There is her picture on the "contact" page. She's wearing black leggings and an oversize sweater. It's an outfit she'll never wear again. It's in her dirty clothes hamper in Acapulco. Lydia's unremarkable happiness in the photograph takes her breath away, and a sob cuts loose into the cubicle. Lydia wishes the walls stretched all the way to the ceiling. Her eyes are two lines, her mouth, a line. She nods her head at Paola, who reaches across the desk and squeezes Lydia's hand. Then she stands and steps around the desk. She removes Lydia's backpack from the chair and sits down beside her.

"My nephew disappeared last August," Paola whispers. "He was missing for three days. When they found him, his head . . ." She pauses for a long moment, so Lydia thinks she might not continue. But she's only gathering strength. "His head was separated from his body." Her hand trembles in Lydia's. They squeeze each other tightly. "He was a beautiful boy," she says.

And now it's Lydia's turn to experience that empathy-paralysis. The depth of her feeling surprises her, because how can she have any leftover grief available for other people, for Paola's murdered nephew? But there it is—an anguish that makes her feel hollow in the bones, despair for a beautiful boy Lydia never met. For the innumerable griefs of all those stolen boys, stretching from family to family like one of Luca's connect-the-dots. It's so big, the pain. It's exponential. Each violent death amplifies itself a hundred times, a thousand times. Everyone in this bank knows some small or large portion of that grief. Everyone in Nogales. Everyone who lives in a place that's been carved up into *plazas* and parceled out for governance by men like Javier. *For what?*

Lydia lets go. All the torrent of emotion she's been corralling for weeks, it all tries to squeeze through at once. She curls into a tight ball in the wooden chair and she sobs quietly, and her body is a knot of grief, and Paola is a stranger, but her hands on Lydia's back are the hands of God. They are Sebastián's and Yemi's and Yénifer's. They are her mother's hands. Lydia weeps into Paola's lap, and Paola weeps with her. They weep for themselves and for each other. And when they're finished, they clean themselves up using only the Kleenex on Paola's desk.

Paola rubs Lydia's knee roughly and then honks her nose into a tissue. She tosses it like a three-pointer into the wastebasket on the far side of the little cubicle. And then, "I might lose my job," she says quietly. "But I will get you that money."

Lydia's head pounds. She closes her eyes in grateful disbelief. The aftermath is like a jackhammer in her sinuses.

It takes a few minutes, but soon there's an envelope fat with cash, and then Paola produces her own purse from a locked drawer in the bottom of her filing cabinet, and hands Lydia an extra 500-peso note. "For your son," she says.

Lydia hugs her, and there's no way to thank her. It's impossible.

CHAPTER TWENTY-EIGHT

The apartment is weirdly nice, if impersonal and sparsely fur-nished. It's the lower level of a house that's built into a hill, so it's half a flight down from the street. It has four large rooms: a living room (with two black leather couches, a flat-screen television, and some grim art-work), a kitchen (whose refrigerator contains only a jar of mayonnaise and two eggs), and the two bedrooms (which are entirely empty, save a lone wire hanger on the tile floor in one, and an aerosol can of Raid on the high windowsill in the other). At the sleek kitchen counter, Lydia hands over their money. The price El Chacal demanded was $11,000. She gives it to him half in pesos and half in dollars because the bank didn't have enough cash to give her all one currency. The two stacks of bills she hands him include all the money from her mother's account, the 500-peso note Paola gave her, and every penny she had left in her wal-let. The exchange rate has been dismal, so the total sum of her money is roughly $10,628. A few weeks ago, when the peso was stronger, it would've been enough. Today, she's $372 short. The coyote counts the money, works out the exchange on his cell phone, and when he realizes she's short, pushes the cash back at her, shaking his head.

"*No es suficiente.*"

"But we're only a little short. Maybe I can pay you when we get to the other side. When I get a job, I can make up the difference."

"That's not how it works."

It's inconceivable that it might come down to this. $372.

"We had more, but we got robbed on the way." She hears the desperation in her voice.

"Everyone gets robbed on the way," he says, unmoved.

"No," Soledad says. "She paid to ransom us."

"She saved our lives with that money." Rebeca turns to her sister. "We can ask César. We have to."

Soledad looks worried about asking their cousin for even more money, but she nods. There's a note of hysteria in the room, hopping from face to face. Only the coyote is immune to it.

"We won't be leaving for at least a day or two," he says. "You can stay here with your son. You come up with the cash before then, you can come."

Two days, Lydia thinks. They'd lived frugally in Acapulco, never touching their savings, taking a packed lunch to work most days, buying new clothes only when the old ones could no longer be repaired. The rare dinner out, an occasional movie. This is how they splurged. For their anniversary last year, Sebastián bought her a vial of lavender oil, so she could put a drop on her pillow each night before bed. What a luxury that had been! But when she thinks now of their small, sunny two-bedroom apartment, filled with shoes and books gathering dust, its kitchen pantry stocked with uneaten maize, dry beans, and cereal, the linens folded in the hall closet, two bubble-shaped wineglasses drying in the rack beside the sink, it all feels like extravagance. She has nothing now. What can she sell? How can she possibly get $400 in two days? Her mind searches for people she can ask for money. *Dead. All dead.* If she had her uncle's number in Denver she might call. She thinks wildly, shamefully, of her body. How much could she get for sex? It's sickening and obscene, and she's grateful when she manages to discard the thought without real analysis. She will find a way.

Beto and Luca are sitting on one of the black leather couches behind them, playing some game about cars, but they can feel the strange tremor of agitation in the room, and they are drawn to it. They appear magnetically, one on each side of Lydia.

"What's wrong, Mami?" Luca asks.

"Nothing, *amorcito, no te preocupes.*"

But Beto, who's accustomed to having to work things out without people explaining them to him, looks at the stacks of money on the counter, and then at Lydia's face, and then at El Chacal, and says, "How much is she short?"

El Chacal lifts his phone from the counter and reads from the screen—"Three hundred and seventy-two dollars"—and then sets the phone back down.

"How much is that in pesos?" Beto asks.

The coyote does the math. "About seven thousand five hundred."

Beto goes into his pocket and flicks out his wad of cash while Lydia watches. He already paid for his crossing and still has money to burn. *We just met this kid this morning,* she thinks. *He doesn't even understand how much money this is.* She rejects her misgivings instantly. He covers it.

She draws him in and hugs him. "Thank you."

El Chacal tells them they'll cross when the other *pollitos* arrive, and they should make themselves comfortable while they wait. He leaves them with almost no instruction, and after he's gone, Lydia wonders if he'll ever come back. They've given him everything, their very last chance of escaping to *el norte.* He doesn't seem like a thief, but what if he is? Or what if he gets hit by a bus? She balls her hands into fists and tells herself to shut up. *Don't think.*

They all take their shoes off as soon as the coyote is gone, and it's incredible what a pleasure it is to be barefoot. To wiggle your toes freely without constraint. *Con un olor a queso.* Luca and Beto run up and down the hallway between the kitchen and the bedrooms, feeling the cool tiles beneath their sticky feet, and making tiny footprints of phantom condensation along the floor. Soledad tucks in her T-shirt and shows them a trick she can do: a handstand against the wall, her arms strong beneath her. The boys applaud. When they try to watch TV, they discover that the flat screen doesn't work. Lydia finds a dog-eared paperback in one of the kitchen drawers and reads while the boys and sisters nap. It's an older novel, a Stephen King book Lydia read many years ago, and slipping back into it is briefly transporting, like she can reach back through time and commune with the person she was when she first read it. That act of communion feels both lucky and holy. When the others awaken, she abandons the book with some reluctance, leaves it facedown on the couch, cracked open at the spine to page 73. They all look forward to taking showers, and are disappointed to find there's no hot water. There's also no food or pots, and only one frying pan in the kitchen, but Lydia heats up what little water she can in that, so they can sponge the dust and the sweat from their skin. They eat nothing, contenting themselves with the relatively recent memory of the *birria,* and fall asleep as the sun sets.

Early the next morning, just as they're discussing how and what to eat, the door opens, and Lydia buckles with relief when El Chacal descends the four steps, followed by two men and an older woman. He's still here. He hasn't abandoned them. This relief is soon followed by fear: Who are these people? Lydia watches them for clues, for recognition. The men seem to know each other. They are young and wear their baseball caps low over their eyes, talking quietly together while ignoring the others. Long sleeves and jeans hide any possible tattoos. Lydia experiences a trigger-wash of nausea, but it's chased off by her hunger.

"Don't go far," the coyote says. "If you're not here when it's time to go, we won't wait."

It's tense in the apartment after El Chacal leaves. The sisters and Luca retreat to the bedroom where they slept last night, and the new woman locks herself in the bathroom. Lydia wants to find out all she can about the newcomers, but she also wants to keep her distance, to remain imperceptible and vague. And anyway, she's hungry. Luca is hungry.

"Are you hungry?" she asks the new men, who are seated on the couch.

They are.

"I will cook, if you have money for food."

She will make omelets. A warm morsel of familiarity for Luca. The men give her some pesos, and she and Luca set out to find a grocery store.

"Wear your new boots," she tells him. "Let's break them in."

They're only a half a block from the apartment when they hear someone calling out behind them.

"*¡Hola! Perdón, señora, ¡disculpe!*"

Lydia turns with trepidation and finds the new woman from the apartment hurrying toward them. "I thought I might come with you if

you don't mind," the woman says. "I need to get a few things myself."
She carries a purple handbag and is dressed as if going out for a nice
meal: black trousers, an oversize blouse, and wedge sandals. She's slim and
dark-skinned with short-cropped hair, black with sparks of silver. A gold
bracelet on one wrist is too understated to be fake. She looks nothing like
a migrant, Lydia thinks, and then remembers that neither does she. Or
at least she didn't when first they embarked on this journey.

"I'm Marisol." The bracelet dangles when the woman extends her
hand for Lydia to shake.

"Lydia."

"Mucho gusto."

"And this is my son, Luca."

"Hello, Luca!"

At the corner, an elderly gentleman sits in his doorway, and Lydia
asks him to point the way to the nearest shop. He does.

"I need to buy fruit," Marisol says as they walk. "I'm used to eating
salad every day, and my stomach has been all messed up since I got back."

"Back?" Lydia asks.

"From California."

"Oh! You were in California already?"

"Yes, sixteen years," she says. "I'm practically a *gabacha* now."

They both laugh.

"But then why did you come back?" Lydia asks.

"Not by choice."

Lydia winces.

"My daughters are still there, in San Diego." She reaches into a side
pocket of her purse and draws out an iPhone with a shiny case. She un-
locks it with her thumb and scrolls to a photograph of two beautiful
young girls, perhaps close in age to Soledad and Rebeca. She shows them
to Lydia proudly. The younger one is wearing a *quinceañera* dress.

"That's my Daisy," she says. "She wanted to wear a Chiapas dress
for her birthday, even though she was born in San Diego. She doesn't even
speak Spanish!" She closes the phone and returns it to her purse. "And
my older one, América, she's in college now, trying to take care of her
younger sister, trying to take care of the house." Marisol's voice sounds
thick and tired.

"How long have you been gone?"

"Almost three weeks," Marisol says. "But I was in a detention center for more than two months before that." She shakes her head and presses her lips together in a gesture Lydia recognizes. It's the one when you're resolute about keeping your shit together despite the fact that your voice is quivering, and your chest feels cleaved with sorrow. Luca doesn't seem to be listening, but Lydia knows better. He's always listening now, walking a few steps ahead of them and watching the cars come and go.

"What happened?" Lydia asks.

Marisol takes a big breath before answering. "We went legally, when América was only four years old. My husband was an engineer—he had work there, so we got visas. And then Daisy was born, and years and years went by, you don't even notice the time going by."

Lydia finds herself instinctively drawing close to Marisol as they walk, up and down the sunny hillside streets, around corners, and through quiet intersections. Luca strides heavily in his new boots.

"Then five years ago, Rogelio was killed, my husband was killed." Marisol blesses herself and Lydia gasps involuntarily.

"I'm so sorry," Lydia says.

Marisol nods. "It was very sudden. A car accident as he was returning home from work."

Something treacherous and unkind lurches up in Lydia—a jealousy almost, of that kind of widowing. A normal, ungruesome death. But then she follows it: Rogelio is no less dead than Sebastián. By the time she squeezes Marisol's arm, her compassion is genuine again.

"Our visas lapsed when he died. We were supposed to return home to Oaxaca. Only Daisy was permitted to stay because she's a citizen."

"But that's absurd," Lydia says. "She's how old?"

"Fifteen."

"Ay." She's heard the stories, of course. But it's different talking to a mother who's actually living it. Lydia can't imagine being separated from Luca, on top of all the other griefs. He's there, walking just ahead of them, but Lydia has to fight the urge to lunge for him, to crush him to her chest.

Lydia's always been a devoted mother, but she's never been the co-dependent kind who misses her child when he goes to school or to sleep. She's always treasured that time to herself, to inhabit her own thoughts, to have a break from the nonstop emotional clamoring of motherhood. There were even times in Acapulco when she'd experienced a sliver of resentment at the way he barged into her heart and mind whenever he was around, how Luca's energy usurped everything else in the room. She loved that boy with her whole heart, but my God, there were days when she couldn't fully breathe until she'd left him at the schoolyard gate. That's all over now; she would staple him to her, sew him into her skin, affix her body permanently to his now, if she could. She'd grow her hair into his scalp, would become his conjoined twin-mother. She would forgo a private thought in her head for the rest of her life, if she could keep him safe. Luca waits at the corner, and Lydia looks beyond him, across the street, where the side of a building is painted with graffiti. A giant question mark. No. No, it's not a question mark. Lydia stops cold. She puts her hand out for Luca.

"*Mijo.*"

"Are you okay?" Marisol asks.

It's not a question mark. It's a sickle. And beneath the sickle, in fresh black paint, the slanted letters warn: VIENEN LOS JARDINEROS. Perched on the curved blade is an owl. La Lechuza. And then something new, something Lydia has not seen before: a perfect, faceless rendering of Javier's distinctive glasses. The exact shape as to provoke in her memory the man himself. Where the lenses would be, someone has scrawled, AÚN TE ESTÁ BUSCANDO. He is still looking for you.

For me. He is looking for me, Madre de Dios. Lydia turns on her heel. "Luca, come."

"But, Mami—"

"Come!" she snaps, her voice like a whip.

Marisol jogs to catch up with her. "Are you okay?" she asks again.

After seventeen days, sixteen hundred miles. Here, on the doorstep to *el norte, los pinche* Jardineros. How flawlessly the artist has rendered Javier's glasses! As if he's familiar with them. As if he's seen them in person, here, in Nogales. Lydia will fall down on the street. Her knees will give way. The wind passes through her body as if she's mostly holes, a ghost already. Marisol reaches out to steady her.

"We cannot go that way," Lydia says, and she's walking quickly now, but not too quickly, not quickly enough to draw the attention of those three boys leaning against the wall of the bodega. Her arms feel clattery in their sockets, her knees liquid with panic.

"Okay, it's okay." Marisol puts an arm around Lydia's shoulder, and they fall in step together, Lydia's stride matching the older woman's accidentally. And here's Luca, tucking beneath her other arm. And they're already half a block away, the other direction, and now they turn a corner onto a shadier street, and Lydia doesn't know if the direction they're going is any safer than the one they'd been traveling before, and does Marisol know where they're going? Is she leading them somewhere? Lydia shakes herself out from beneath the woman's arm.

"Thank you, I'm fine now," she says. "I'm fine, we're fine." She grabs Luca by the hand. "I just remembered something we have to do," she says. "We'll see you back at the apartment later."

Marisol stops, confused. "Oh."

"We'll be back soon," she says, and she drags Luca across another street, and they leave Marisol standing alone in the middle of the road.

They have to get off the street, out of sight. Away from anyone who might recognize them. Los Jardineros are here, in Nogales. Perhaps as an alliance. Perhaps as a test market, a turf war. Perhaps only to hunt her, to find her, to take her back to Javier so he can finish the job of eradicating Sebastián's entire family in return for Marta's death. Lydia can see it as if she's there, in that dorm room in Barcelona: a creaking sound from above. Marta's feet swinging slightly in their navy-blue tights, one chunky black shoe still clinging to her left foot, the right one fallen to the floor beneath. Lydia squeezes her mind closed against the image, and against the certainty that Javier would follow her here, will follow her indefinitely, across anyone's territory, until he finds her. Only in *el norte* will his power be diminished. In *el norte,* where there's no impunity for violent men. *At least not for violent men like him,* she thinks.

There are no sidewalks here; the garden gates and shopfronts sit directly at the edges of the streets. Cars have to swerve around the pedestrians. There's no place to hide. They turn at the next corner and head back the way they came. Lydia's not wearing her hat. Why didn't she wear her hat? She hates that floppy, pink thing. She'd liked the idea of liberating herself from it long enough to buy groceries and pretend normalcy for an hour. Until the graffiti it had felt like a jaunt. Things had gone well yesterday at the bank. The apartment was comfortable. They were so close! She had let her guard down. *Estúpida.*

An old woman leans against her door jamb and calls out to them as they pass, "*¿Fruta, pan, leche, huevos?*"

It's not the supermarket Lydia'd been in search of, but maybe it's better: a woman selling the basics out of a makeshift shop in the dark front room of her house. They duck inside and Lydia keeps an eye on the street through the open door. They buy eggs, tortillas, onions, an avocado, and some fruit.

"Do you have a hat?" Lydia asks her.

"A hat?" The woman shakes her head.

"Or a scarf? Anything for my hair?"

"No. *Lo siento.*"

"It's okay. Thanks anyway."

"Wait." The woman snaps her fingers and totters into the kitchen. She returns with a thin blue dish towel adorned by a pattern of flowers and hummingbirds. She presents it to Lydia like a bottle of fine wine, and gestures that she could use it to cover her hair.

"How much?" Lydia asks.

"*Cien pesos.*"

Lydia nods, and ties the cloth over her hair like a handkerchief.

"What about for him?" The old woman points at Luca with her chin, and Lydia turns to look at him, confused. "Are you crossing?" she asks, this time using her chin to point north, toward *la frontera.*

Lydia hesitates for only a moment and then confesses. "Yes, we're crossing."

"He needs a coat," the lady says. "It gets very cold."

"He has a sweatshirt and a warm jacket."

"Wait." The woman disappears into the kitchen again, and Lydia and Luca can hear her banging through cupboards or closets, shifting things around, dragging a box across the floor. Luca giggles in the left-over quiet, but Lydia's too nervous to join him. She eyes both doorways, interior and exterior. When the lady returns, she's carrying two lumps of knitted blue yarn, which she spreads out across the counter so Lydia can assess their shapes: a hat and scarf. Perhaps a little too big for Luca, but the yarn is thick and warm. Lydia touches the soft wool with her fingertips, and nods.

"How much?"

The old woman waves at Luca. "*Un regalito,*" she says. "*Para la suerte.*"

They move through the streets as quickly and carefully as they can. Each window and door they pass feels like a possible booby trap. She counts their steps to try and keep herself calm. Luca carries the eggs and tortillas. She carries the bag with the produce. She considers Marisol as they go, her apparent kindness and sorrow. Behind Lydia's fear, she might find room to feel bad about the abrupt way she left Marisol standing in the street. The fact that she hadn't followed them, hadn't insisted or attempted to redirect them, that feels to Lydia like probable evidence that she's no nefarious actor. She probably is who she claims to be: a deported mother, desperate to return to her daughters in California. When Lydia sees the house where their apartment is, she holds her breath. She looks behind her. Only one car on the street. It approaches slowly, and Lydia doesn't exhale until it rolls past them, the elderly couple inside giving Luca a friendly wave as they go.

"Thank you, God," she says out loud when they step through the door and close it behind them. She leans against it for a moment and allows herself to breathe before, together, she and Luca descend the steps back into the apartment. There are voices and laughter below, and it's warmer inside than on the street—humid with people. Lydia walks in, and when she gets to the bottom step, she drops her grocery bag to the floor.

"Surprise!"

Lorenzo is seated on the black leather couch.

Lydia cannot immediately respond. An avocado rolls out from the toppled bag. Her terror causes a speech delay. She pushes through it. "What are you doing here?" She picks up the wobbling avocado.

"Same as you, going to *el norte.*"

The avocado resting in her hand is like a still life. "But how did you find us?"

"*Puta,* don't flatter yourself," he says. "I didn't find you. I found El

Chacal. It just happened to be a nice surprise when I walked in and saw the hottie twins were here."

Marisol is in the kitchen with a glass of water, and the two men with the low hats are seated at the counter with a deck of cards. Lydia stands behind the couch across from Lorenzo, who's sprawled back on the facing sofa.

"Anyway, this guy is the best coyote in Nogales," Lorenzo says. "What'd you think, nobody else would know that?"

"You're not . . ." She doesn't know how to finish the question, so she doesn't. It hangs, half-formed.

He has black shorts on now, and his skin has been darkened a shade or two by the sun, but everything else about him is the same: the diamond stud earrings, the flat-brimmed baseball cap, slightly sun-faded, but still clean. His socks are remarkably white for a migrant, but his expensive shoes are beginning to look worn. He sits up and swings his feet to the floor in front of him. "Look, I know I make you uncomfortable, and I don't really give a shit. It's not my problem," he says. "But I swear I didn't follow you, I wasn't looking for you. Just like I told you, I'm done with all that Jardinero shit. I'm out."

Lydia studies him for a moment. Because there's nothing she can do about any of it, about the graffiti announcing Javier's presence, about the sickening proximity of Lorenzo, about feeling acutely distrustful of everyone she meets: Marisol, who emerges from the kitchen to retrieve and unpack the groceries, the men sitting at the counter playing cards, Lorenzo smirking on the couch. Any one of them could mean her harm. Any one of them could murder Luca in his sleep. They haven't done it yet. So perhaps they won't. Lydia rubs her thighs through her jeans. Maybe it's just a coincidence, his being here. The graffiti.

"Okay," she says.

"Así que tranquila."

She regards him for another moment. "But if it's true," she says. "If you're really out?" She lets a beat pass so she can focus, measure her words. "Then there's something you should know."

"Yeah? What's that?"

"Los Jardineros are here."

A calculated disclosure. Sharing this information may benefit her in a number of ways.

"In Nogales?" he asks.

She nods. Perhaps he'll feel indebted to her. In any case, there is this: the opportunity to observe his reaction. And he does react. He blanches. Gone is the smile, the arrogant posture. He sits up and clears his throat. His shoulders hunch automatically, so Lydia can see it's authentic. Lorenzo is afraid.

"How do you know?" he asks.

"I saw their graffiti." She sits down on the arm of the opposite couch. She's aware of the two men at the counter, listening. Their cards remain in their hands.

"Close by?"

"A few blocks from here." She turns to Luca. "Why don't you go check on the girls. See what Beto is up to." He scoots down the hall into the bedroom where they all slept last night. To Lorenzo she says, "You want an omelet?"

While the two women are cooking, Soledad escapes the apartment. What felt spacious for the five of them is cramped with nine, especially with the reappearance of that revolting *naco* Lorenzo.

They're in the far west of the city, only steps from the border, and Soledad paces the street outside, up and down the hill, watching the emptiness on the other side. The border is unnatural here, a sharp and arbitrary line that slashes through the desert, restraining the surging city behind it to the south. There is almost nothing Soledad can see on the northern side of that line—perhaps there really isn't anything over there, or perhaps whatever's there is hidden by the buckles and folds of the landscape. On her third trip down the hill, she goes a little farther and finds a remarkable place where the landscape funnels into itself. There's a bald patch of dirt beside the road, and a little berm built up there that looks like a ramp. Indeed, the berm is higher than the fence because of a significant dip where the border is lower than the road. Soledad stands on this ramp, and her heart soars across like a bird. She could almost run and launch herself across. She might manage to jump it from here. She scrambles the few feet down the gravelly embankment to where the rusty red fence digs into the earth, and she wraps her fingers around two of the thick red posts, and leans her forehead against the bars, and she can see very clearly then that the fence is only a psychological barrier, and that the real impediment to crossing here is the technology on the other side. There's a dirt road over there that follows the jagged landscape wherever it leads. The road is worn smooth by the regular accommodation of the heavy tires of the United States Border Patrol. Soledad cannot see them, but she can sense them there, just out of sight. She sees the evidence of their proximity in the whirring electronics mounted on tall poles that dot the hillsides. She doesn't know what those contraptions are—cameras or sensors or lights or speakers—but whatever they are, she can sense that they're aware of her presence. She sticks her hand through the fence and wiggles her fingers on the other side. Her fingers are in *el norte*. She spits through the fence. Only to leave a piece of herself there on American dirt.

CHAPTER TWENTY-NINE

Lydia borrows a machete from one of the men to cut the onions and avocado, because there isn't even a knife in the kitchen. There are paper plates in one of the drawers, but no forks, so they scoop the eggs into tortillas and eat them wrapped up. Lorenzo seems preoccupied.

"You have to eat more than that," Lydia tells him when he returns his plate to the counter still half-full. "You need lots of calories if you expect to walk through the desert."

He stands with one hand hanging loose by his side, and regards her. He seems at a loss. She takes the plate and adds another spoonful of eggs, a wedge of avocado.

"Here." She pushes it back to him. "Want a banana?"

He leans his elbows on the counter, picks at one corner of the tortilla, and eventually takes a bite. He talks with his mouth full. "Why you being so nice?"

She gathers up the empty paper plates the other men left behind, and selects a banana from the bunch for herself. She snaps the top and starts to peel it. "I know what it's like to run from them," she says simply. "I know what it's like to be afraid."

After the food, the day passes in excruciating eagerness. Lydia tries to engage the men in conversation, but they're sullen, and they stick to their card games for most of the day. When they do speak, infrequently, Lydia strains to discern their accents, but eventually she releases herself from the effort. Because again: Why? If they are violent men, if they know her or recognize her, and decide to trade her life for a small fortune, she will find out soon enough.

They all go to sleep early, stocking up on rest while they can. Lydia, the sisters, and the two boys share the same bedroom where they slept last night. Marisol joins them, and they all stack their packs against the closed door. They curl up in corners or stretch out with their jeans rolled into makeshift pillows. Rebeca throws one arm over Luca like a teddy bear, and the two of them snore softly together. Beto sleeps sprawled out on his back in the shape of an X with his mouth wide open. The two quiet men share the other bedroom, and Lorenzo takes the couch.

Luca dreams of a deep stone well. At the bottom of the well are the sixteen bullet-riddled bodies of his family. He knows this not because he looks into the well—in fact, he takes care to give the well a wide berth anytime he has to pass it during his day—but because he hears them talking down there. He hears the echoey sounds of their laughter and lively conversation. He hears Papi telling jokes to Yénifer and Tía Yemi. He hears Tío Alex playing monster-tag-wrestling with Adrián, hears his cousin squealing and laughing while his father tickles him. Luca even hears Abuela lightly scolding them all, not because she actually disapproves, Luca realizes, but because a casual reprimand is Abuela's way of participating, and that is the thing, really, that makes Luca understand that the dream is real. Because this insight about Abuela is new, a thing Luca didn't perceive about her when she was alive. So they are still there, Luca knows. They are at the bottom of the well. And he wants to go to them. He wants to be with them. He knows that the holy water down there is life, that it's essential, that it will satisfy his every need, that it has revived them all. So he goes, he goes to the well at last, without fear, without hesitation. But as he approaches, their voices and laughter cease. It's only the *plink* and trickle of some unseen droplets that echo into the shadowy depths. So Luca pulls on the rope instead. He thinks to draw up the bucket, that maybe he can ride it to the bottom. They can all be reunited. But he knows by the smell that something's wrong. Before the bucket is fully visible, he can tell. There's a rottenness. He draws the bucket into the light, and it's only a flash of gore. Fingers, eyeballs, teeth.

Papi's earlobe, a lock of Yénifer's hair. All floating in the putrid bucket of blood.

Luca awakens from the nightmare with his heart pounding, but he's not afraid. Or maybe it's more accurate to say that he's no more afraid than he always is now. His prevailing emotion is irritation, because Beto is sleeping beside him, farting. He lets another one rip while Luca lies there, blinking in the stench. It was such a nice dream until the odor turned it. "Papi," Luca says out loud in the dark. He rolls over and covers his nose with his sleeve.

They're all awakened at dawn to the sound of a key in the lock and a crush of heavy bootsteps on the wooden stairs. El Chacal has arrived with five more migrants—two brothers from Veracruz named Choncho and Slim, plus their two teenage sons, David and Ricardín. The brothers are big, strong men, and even their teenage sons are big, strong men, and it's impossible to tell which son belongs to which father because they all look so much alike. They have big voices and thick forearms and solid necks. They all wear jeans and plaid button-up shirts and enormous work boots. They have to duck their heads when they reach the bottom step. The four of them fill the apartment beyond its capacity. But there is a fifth man as well, named Nicolás, who's tiny in comparison with the others, average-size. Like Marisol, he's a *deportado,* and he has amazing blunt eyebrows, which look like they're drawn onto his face with a marker, Luca thinks. He wears an Arizona Wildcats T-shirt and thick-framed glasses. He's a lapsed PhD student at the University of Arizona.

El Chacal tells everyone to sleep today, to rest as much as they can, and to hydrate themselves. "Make sure you have the supplies you need. A warm jacket for the nights, and decent shoes for walking. No bright colors. Only things that will blend in with the desert, camouflage. If you don't have the right gear, you don't make the journey," he says. Lydia hadn't thought of the colors. She does a quick inventory of their clothing in her mind. She thinks they'll be okay. The coyote continues. "I'll provide water. We leave before sundown."

The apartment is stifling now, crowded with bodies and anticipation. In the bedroom, Lydia and Marisol are both on their knees, unpacking and repacking their belongings for the trip ahead.

"I don't know why I told my daughters to send all these clothes," Marisol says, rummaging through a small black suitcase. "I'm going to end up leaving all this behind. Now I'll have to go shopping in San Diego."

The woman seems to have forgotten Lydia's odd behavior on the street, or at least she's pretending to be untroubled by it.

"I'm sorry for yesterday." Lydia wants to explain, but there's so little she can say without revealing herself. "I got spooked. I've seen, we've seen so much atrocity, sometimes I can't tell what's real. Who to trust—"

"Please," Marisol interrupts her. "Don't apologize. You're right to be wary, I'm sure."

Lydia takes a deep breath. "If you want to stay alive, you have to be."

Marisol stops rolling the T-shirt she'd been packing and looks up at Lydia. She nods.

Marisol makes the trip to the grocery store alone this time, and when she returns, she stores half in the fridge for later, and then she and Lydia prepare the food together, a huge amount of food, they think. There are eggs again, and rice and beans and tortillas, and this time also some plantains and more avocado, and even a small bit of cheese and some nuts and some yogurt, all of which are expensive but dense with the protein their bodies will require for the journey. The large brothers and their sons are happy with the food, and chivalrous about making sure everyone has enough to eat, but when it's clear that the others are finished and there's food left, they devour every morsel. Soledad and Beto do the cleaning up, while the others sit talking on the couches and stools.

Luca sits on the floor between his mother's legs and listens to the grown-ups telling stories. Even though it's a bunch of strangers in the house, it has the atmosphere of a party. As such, it makes Luca feel very still and alert. The large brothers from Veracruz are gregarious. They tell stories and sing songs, and their voices boom out through the room regardless of their intended volume. They are demonstrating for their sons how to be in the world, how to fill up even more space than the bulk of your body demands, to leave no room for misconceptions, to put people around you at ease with your unusual size. They tell stories of their years working in *el norte,* picking corn and cauliflower in Indiana, working as line packers at a dairy plant in Vermont, sending every paycheck home to Veracruz. Slim's son Ricardín carries an *armónica* in his breast pocket, and when he takes it out to play it, his father slaps his leg in time with the song, which draws Beto out of the kitchen and into the center of the room, where he pushes aside the small coffee table to make room for break dancing. Rebeca flits away to the bedroom to rest, and the two quiet men who arrived first disappear as well, but the rest remain there, talking and sipping instant coffee from paper cups. Luca is drawn mostly to Ricardín, because of his quick smile and the *armónica*. Ricardín notices Luca watching him, and holds the *armónica* up.

"Want to try?" he asks.

Luca nods and stands up. He looks at Mami to make sure it's okay first, and then, with her encouragement, takes a step toward Ricardín to study how he plays the thing, how he uses it to draw music out of thin air. Even seated on the couch, Ricardín is taller than Luca, so Luca has to look up into his face. When he holds the *armónica* up to his mouth, his hand is so large, the instrument disappears behind it, like he's concealing it beneath a baseball mitt. His fingers move up and down, up and down, showing glimpses of the flat metal beneath. Luca watches carefully, and then Ricardín hands the *armónica* to him.

"Go ahead," he says. "Give it a try."

Luca takes it and holds it up to his mouth. He blows. And he's surprised that, right away, he can make such a lovely sound.

"Hey!" Ricardín grins at him. Luca smiles and tries to hand it back, but Ricardín pushes it toward him again. "Keep going. Again!"

He claps his giant hands while Luca runs the metal instrument up and down his lips, trying the different sounds it makes. It's easy.

"*Chido, güey*," Beto says. "Can I try?"

Luca hands him the *armónica*. While the boys pass the instrument around, Choncho asks Marisol about her family in California. She tells them she was arrested at a routine immigration check-in almost three months ago.

"Wait, you actually go to those things?" Nicolás, the PhD student, asks.

"Of course!" Marisol says. "I play by the rules!"

"What is it?" This is Lydia.

"A routine immigration check-in?" Marisol asks.

"Yes."

"It's an appointment, usually once a year, where I have to go and check in with an ICE officer," Marisol explains. "So they can review my case."

"But what for? So you can get your papers?"

"No, just so they can keep tabs on me," Marisol says.

Lydia is confused. "And ICE is . . . ?"

"Immigration and Customs Enforcement." Nicolás fills in the acronym. "I never went to a single one of my check-ins."

"I guess it doesn't matter now," Marisol says. "We both ended up in the same boat. To think of all that wasted bus fare."

"But I don't understand," Lydia says. "They always knew you were there?"

"Sure, for years," Marisol says. "After my husband died, and I didn't leave before the deadline they gave me, I received a notice to come for a check-in. I went every year. Never missed one."

"And they didn't deport you? Even though you were undocumented?"

"Not until now."

"But why not?"

Marisol shrugs. "I never committed any offenses. I have a daughter who's a citizen."

"They have discretion," Nicolás says. "They're supposed to be able to use their discretion, so they can divert their resources to deporting bad guys. Gang members, criminals."

"But now suddenly they're deporting people just for showing up at their check-ins," Marisol says.

"And that's what happened to you?" Lydia asks.

Marisol nods. She'd been dressed in her dark red scrubs, planning to head straight to her job as a dialysis technician after her appointment. It was a Tuesday morning, and both her daughters were at school. They'd been worried about the upcoming check-in for months, of course. Everyone worried now. The appointments used to be just procedural, an easy way for the government to exert some control over an overburdened system, and an opportunity for the migrant to improve her legal status by demonstrating her cooperation. But now everyone was alarmed by the spike in arrests, and some people stopped going to the check-ins altogether.

Not Marisol. She hadn't been willing to demote her daughters to a life in the shadows. San Diego was the only home they'd ever known, so she never really believed they'd deport someone like her, a middle-class woman with perfect English who came here legally, a homeowner, a medical professional. Three months later, she's still in a state of disbelief. Ricardín provides a bluesy riff on the *armónica* to conclude her story, which makes it funny instead of heartbreaking. They all laugh.

"So you were in detention for two months?" Nicolás asks.

Marisol nods.

"What was that like?"

She pauses to consider the question, and as she remembers, she winces. "I mean . . ." She gropes for a word to encompass her memories of that place, but she can't find one substantial enough. "Horrible?" she says. "Like you'd expect, I guess. I slept on a mat in a cold cell. It was freezing all the time, *como una hielera*. No blankets, no pillows, only those tinfoil things. I woke up stiff and sore every morning, with a kink in my neck. They wouldn't replace my contact lens solution, so when that ran out, at least I didn't have to look at the walls closing in."

Nicolás cringes while she talks. "I couldn't hack it. I'm claustrophobic."

"Yeah, it was utterly dehumanizing." Marisol sighs. "But my lawyer thought I had a good chance, so I told myself to be strong, that it would all be worth it."

"Good for you, sticking it out," Nicolás says. "I left after two days. They were going to transfer me to El Paso, so I did voluntary departure. I knew I'd rather walk through the desert than spend another day in that place."

"But it was such a waste of time!" Marisol says. "Two months I sat in that cell without my daughters." She presses her eyes closed and then opens them again. "So many mothers in there without their daughters, without their children." Her eyes fall to the floor and her voice drops to a whisper, but they can all hear it in the hushed room. "Most of those women were separated from their children at the border," she says. "When they were caught coming in. Some had babies taken right out of their arms. I thought those women would lose their minds. They didn't even know where their children were—some of them were too young to talk, too young to remember their names."

Lydia leans forward over Luca, who's sitting between her legs. She pinches his T-shirt between her finger and thumb. It's too much. They all glance at her without meaning to. They don't want her to think the same thoughts they're thinking, so they quickly look away. Marisol tries to change the subject. Back to Nicolás. "Weren't you eligible for a student visa? As a PhD candidate?"

"I took a sabbatical for one semester." He shrugs. "Didn't realize I had to file extra paperwork for that."

"So that was it?" Marisol asks. "You got deported because of paperwork?"

"Yep." He nods, straightens his spine, and spreads his hands wide, palms up, as if he's the product of a magic trick. His deportation is a ludicrous feat of wonder.

Lydia will not think about any of it. Most especially, she won't think about those families separated at the border. The children lifted straight out of their mothers' arms. She absolutely cannot. It's not possible, to have made it this far, and then to lose him. *No.* She runs her hands through Luca's hair. She makes her fingers into the shapes of scissors and thinks about the haircut she'll give him when they get to Arizona. This is what her brain can hold.

At midday, they take a siesta. They will sleep for the afternoon and get up in time to have one last meal in Mexico before tonight's journey. They stretch their bodies out in the spaces they've claimed for sleep, Choncho and Slim joining the two quiet men in the back bedroom, their sons David and Ricardín finding space in the hallway and on the kitchen floor. Lorenzo and Nicolás take the leather couches. Only Soledad cannot rest. She returns to pacing the street outside. Lorenzo goes to the window while everyone else is asleep and watches her.

When she returns to the hot, quiet apartment, she's startled to find Lorenzo sitting up on the couch looking at her. His shoes are off, but it doesn't appear he's been sleeping. She moves quickly past him and into the kitchen, where she fills her water bottle from the tap and takes a long drink. She can feel him looking at her back, but she doesn't turn to intercept his gaze. She refills the bottle again, and then turns toward the bedroom where her sister and the others are sleeping.

"Yo, what's your hurry?" His voice is quiet, careful not to wake Nicolás, who's breathing heavily on the facing couch. Lorenzo's attempt at a flirtatious tone comes out menacing instead.

But Soledad's not afraid of him. There are a dozen other people in this apartment; there's nothing he can do to her here. Besides, what Soledad has been through in these last months? She's hard as nails. Almost nothing scares her anymore. She turns and narrows her eyes at him. She makes her voice unambiguous. "I'm in a hurry to get some rest. You should be, too."

Lorenzo adjusts his position on the couch, stretches his torso out in front of him, and leans his head back against the cushions. "Yeah. Whatever," he says.

Soledad realizes then that he's holding a cell phone in his hand. He leans forward and tosses it toward the arm of the couch by his feet. She freezes, turns her back on him again, and takes one step toward the bedroom before changing her mind. She turns back to face him. "That phone work?"

He picks his head up off the couch. "Pssh, yeah, what you think, it's for decoration?"

She takes two steps back toward the living room, sets her water bottle on the counter, and hovers there for a moment. She doesn't want to be indebted to a person like this, but it could be days before she has another opportunity. "Can I make a call?"

Lorenzo smirks at her. "What's it worth to you?"

Soledad feels something sour swarm up in her mouth. She doesn't answer but pretends with her face that the joke's funny. Her smile is hollow, but she sees how it works on him—just that—a fake smile, and he goes all gooey and hopeful. In his mind, she's already naked. *What a scumbag,* she thinks.

He holds the phone out to her. "Go ahead."

She stretches so she can take the phone from a distance. "Thanks," she says. The door to the bedroom is already open for air circulation, and the lights are off inside. Rebeca and Luca sleep nearest the door, wrapped up together and dreaming, because Lydia's initial objection to that kind of closeness is so far gone they hardly remember it now. Sole takes two steps into the room and squats down beside her sleeping sister. She hesitates to wake her.

"Rebeca," she whispers, touching her sister's shoulder lightly. Luca's eyes pop open, but Rebeca is still asleep. "I'm sorry," she says to Luca, but he's already fallen back asleep. "Rebeca," she says again, shaking her sister more roughly. Her sister breathes deeply and doesn't move. Soledad stands and moves quietly through the apartment, up the stairs, and back out to the street.

She removes the tiny scrap of paper with the hospital's phone number from where it's folded into a tiny square in her pocket. She presses the numbers. It takes her two tries, but then the phone at the Hospital Nacional in San Pedro Sula is ringing.

"Hello?"

There are several transfers before Soledad hears the familiar voice of the nurse Ángela on the line. She can feel adrenaline coursing through her shoulders, her neck. When Soledad looks back on this moment for the rest of her life, when she relives it, really, she will come to believe that she already knew what the nurse was going to say, she knew it well before the words emerged from her mouth and traveled into that far-away phone, before they bounced out across cell towers and satellites and reverberated back into this borrowed cell phone here on the border of the United States, and fell into her waiting ear. She will come to believe that she knew it from the moment Lorenzo handed her that phone, from before that even, from when she first stood on the pavement in Nogales and wrapped her fingers around the bars that demarcated the border of Estados Unidos, from when she sat on that cold, dirty toilet in Navolato while that unwanted but still loved baby fell out of her, from the first day she felt the thudding and thrumming of La Bestia beneath her bones, from the first time Iván raped her, from way before that even, before she ever set eyes on the city of San Pedro Sula, from the days when her father used to hoist her onto his shoulders and she'd wrap her tiny baby-arms around his sweaty forehead while he swiped a path for them through the cloud forest with his machete. She will come to believe that she knew this truth from the day she was born, when her father first held her in his arms and gazed upon her beautiful face with love and love and love.

"I'm so sorry," Ángela says.

Alone in the street, Soledad bends in half, planting the palms of her hands hard against her knees. She doesn't cry, but instead shakes and shakes. She paces but cannot find anywhere to escape her panic. She says the word *no* out loud more than a hundred times, tight through the garble of her seizing throat. She flaps her hands to try to shake the adrenaline out of her, but the grief has descended like a demon beast, and she realizes immediately that the burden of that grief must be hers alone to bear. Rebeca must survive the desert, and she might not survive the desert if she has to do it while carrying this monster on her back. She will not tell her sister. *My fault.* So she gets down on her two knees right there in the street and feels the sharp pebbles pressing up through her jeans. She prays and prays that God has taken Papi quickly into heaven, that somehow her father will forgive her for the death she has caused him.

"I'm so sorry, Papi. Forgive me, Papi, please," she says over and over again.

Her legs feel shaky so she moves to sit on the curb, wondering vaguely how the news will travel up the mountain to the village. She wonders if Mami and Abuela already know. She wonders if she will ever see them or hear their voices again. Because Papi was the only hub connecting them, and now he's gone. One of the other men from the mountain who works in the city will hear, she thinks, and in sorrow he will carry that unholy news on the bus, three hours up the narrow, disappearing roads into the clouds. He'll deliver it to Mami and Abuela. She closes her eyes to that thought. She puts it away from her because Soledad has been through enough to know that she's at her limit, that she can go no further into that anguish without vanishing forever. The only thing that matters now is Rebeca. She can still save Rebeca.

When she stands up from that curb, Soledad is already a ghost of herself. Perhaps very deep within her, there's still some smoldering wick that was once the flame of her person, but she cannot feel it there. She opens the door of the apartment, and descends.

CHAPTER THIRTY

They've all packed their scant belongings, prepared and eaten the remaining food, and are drinking instant coffee by the time the sun begins to slant toward the horizon and El Chacal returns. Beto has nothing to pack. Marisol has ditched her black wedges in favor of some Adidas trail hikers. No one talks as they ascend the staircase out of the apartment one last time. There are two open-bed pickup trucks parked outside, and the back of one is half-filled with several dozen plastic gallon jugs of water, painted black. Lorenzo approaches the white truck, so Lydia herds Luca toward the blue one. Beto, the sisters, and Marisol all climb in after them, among the water jugs. Nicolás, too. He sits beside Marisol.

"So, do you have a girlfriend back at college?" she asks.

Nicolás shakes his head.

"You know, my daughter is a college student in San Diego. A sociology major. What's your field of study?"

Nicolás's eyebrows animate themselves across his forehead. "I study evolutionary biology and biodiversity in the desert," he says.

"Oh." Marisol is unable to muster any appropriate follow-up questions.

"What the hell is that?" Beto asks.

Nicolás laughs. "It means I study how organisms evolve, and what environmental factors influence that evolution, and vice versa."

Beto looks at him blankly.

"Specifically, I study the migration patterns of certain desert butterflies, and the effect of those changing migration patterns on certain
flowering shrubs."

"Desert butterflies, huh?" Beto says suspiciously.

"Yes."

"You study, like, where they go?"

"Yes."

"And that's, like, a whole job? That's all you do?"

Nicolás grins at Beto.

"Man, I want to go to college," the boy says.

El Chacal is securing the liftgate at the back of the other truck, and
now he walks over to theirs. He looks at them individually, checking
their gear. His own shoes are solid, lightweight hikers, dusty enough to
appear as if they could belong to any migrant, albeit one with the means
to buy himself boots for the trek. He's dressed like he was the day he met
them in the plaza—close-fitting jeans and a gray Under Armour T-shirt
this time. His backpack, sitting on the seat in the cab, is tiny. His jacket,
made of waterproof Gore-Tex, is light enough to tie around his slim waist.
His cheeks, as usual, are a cheerful shade of pink in the light brown
expanse of his face. Everything about his body seems designed for the
wilderness. He is lean, muscular, compact, and he moves with efficiency
as he steps from migrant to migrant, examining their footwear, their
moods, the weight of their packs. Nobody with a sniffle or a sneeze will
be allowed to make the journey. He stops when he gets to Beto.

"Where's your bag?" he asks.

Everyone else is clutching their pack in front of them. Beto has
nothing.

"I don't need no bag, *güey*," Beto says. "Everything I need is right
here." He taps on the side of his head with one finger.

"That crazy brain of yours going to keep you warm tonight?"

"What are you talking about, warm?" Beto says. "*No manches, güey.*
We're in the middle of a heat wave. It's like a million degrees outside."

It is April in the Sonoran Desert, and uncommonly warm this week.
Today's high was ninety-seven degrees Fahrenheit.

"So you don't have a jacket? A coat, sweater, nothing?" El Chacal
asks.

"I'll be fine!" Beto says.

"Out of the truck." El Chacal unlatches and folds down the tailgate.

"*Órale, güey*," Beto says. "For real, I'm fine, I don't need a jacket."

"Out," El Chacal repeats. "I was very specific. I told you what you needed, I told you what would happen if you didn't adequately prepare."

"But—"

"And you find yourself a coyote who says he will take you across without the right gear? Don't fucking pay him. Because he doesn't give a shit about you, and you will die, understand? Come on, now. Out."

"But I'll get one! I'll get a jacket!" Beto's voice is rising to a frantic pitch.

"It's too late," the coyote says, slapping a hand impatiently on the bed of the truck. "Get a jacket and I'll take you next time."

Beto stands up and begins to move slowly toward the tailgate, reluctance in every cell of his body. Luca tugs on Mami's arm, but she doesn't respond. She should have checked with him. He seems a thousand years old, but he's only ten, and he saved them; he bought their passage. So how hard would it have been for her to ask: *Now, Beto, you have a good jacket, right?* But she didn't. And now it's too late. There's nothing she can do. She squeezes Luca's hand, a meager apology for her failure of foresight, her scarcity of heroism. The rest of the migrants look helplessly at Beto, but Nicolás is unzipping his pack. Beto sits with a thump on the back of the liftgate, his feet dangling over, procrastinating. He riffles through his brain for an argument or plea he might make.

"Here." Nicolás tosses a heavy, fleece-lined, zippered hoodie onto the boy's lap.

Beto's face brightens at once, and Lydia heaves a relieved smile. Luca grins. Beto snatches up the thick, brown fabric and scrambles back to his feet. He ties the arms of the hoodie around his waist while Nicolás zips his backpack again.

El Chacal watches the young PhD student. "You have another one for yourself?"

"And a thermal, plus a rain poncho."

The coyote nods and slams the liftgate back into position. Beto has already returned to settle himself back into his spot beside Luca, but El Chacal walks around the side of the pickup truck and speaks quietly into the boy's ear. He leans his hands on the edge of the truck, and Beto twists to face him, one knee flopped over, the other propped up.

"You were lucky Nicolás helped you out," the coyote says to the boy. "I never take kids across, and this is why. I'm not trying to babysit, and I don't want anybody dying of stupidity. Don't make me regret bringing you."

Beto's face endures a rare slash of stillness, and the sincerity of it threatens to rob Lydia of her careful restraint.

"When I tell you that something's important, you heed me, understand?" El Chacal says. Beto nods earnestly. "Because when I say *importante* it means you will die if you don't listen. This journey is no joke. If I say jump, you jump. If I say *cállate,* you shut your mouth. If I say you need a jacket, you need a *pinche* jacket." He takes one step back and turns so he can see the migrants in both truck beds. He raises his voice so they can all hear. "Same goes for all of you. You hear? This is a grueling journey. Two and a half nights of arduous hiking, and I am your only lifeline. If there's any problem with that, or if you don't think you can make it, this is your last chance to say so."

The coyote carries a pistol on these crossings to aid in convincing reluctant migrants about the absolute nature of his authority. He makes sure the migrants know he has the gun by carrying it quite openly in a holster slung low around his jeans. It serves mostly as a useful psychological prop, and he very seldom has to use it. Beto isn't impressed by the gun, which he glimpsed when the coyote was standing beside the other truck, but he is affected by the subtle intensity of the man's words. Beto knows the truth when he hears it.

"*Oye,*" the boy says. "I'm sorry." Beto is like a wide-open moon shining up at the coyote, and something in his yearning sends the memory of Sebastián falling across Lydia's mind like a ruler across an outstretched knuckle. How long will the memory of his father sustain her own child? How long before he's looking up at strangers this way? Grief-adrenaline swamps through her body, but Lydia closes her eyes and waits for it to pass.

El Chacal nods, opens the passenger door, and climbs in.

They drive southwest into the desert sunset. There's nothing unusual about a couple of trucks full of migrants heading out into the wilderness from Nogales. No one will try to stop them; anyone who looks can see what they're up to, but no one here cares. Lydia is the only one concerned about hiding herself. She slumps low in the bed of the truck, and shields her face with her faded hat when other vehicles approach and pass.

"Why south?" Luca asks as they turn left out of the town, but she doesn't know.

She's relieved when the drive turns to barely paved roads that eventually become unpaved roads that eventually become trails that can hardly be called roads at all. They are pocked with holes and ruts, and the gravel feels loose beneath the tires. They're alone in the desert now, no other cars for miles around, and the migrants hang on to the edges and bounce uncomfortably in the beds of the pickup trucks, their bones juddering when they cross a dip they aren't expecting. Lydia holds Luca down to keep him from flying out, but their progress is careful and slow.

When the trucks eventually point west, and then northwest, Luca wonders if they're moving perpendicular to that boundary now, that place where the fence disappears and the only thing to delineate one country from the next is a line that some random guy drew on a map years and years ago. They haven't seen another vehicle for almost an hour, so to pass the time, Nicolás names some of the species of animals that live here, some they might encounter on their travels: ocelots, bobcats, coatimundi, javelina, whiptail lizards, mountain lions, coyotes, rattlesnakes.

"Rattlesnakes?" Marisol says.

Rabbits, quail, deer, hummingbirds, jaguars.

"Jaguars!" Beto says.

"Rare, but not yet extinct in Sonora, sure. Foxes, skunks," Nicolás says. "And don't even get me started on the butterflies."

Luca thinks of all of those animals running willy-nilly, back and forth across the border without their passports. It's a comforting notion. Rebeca is only half listening. She doesn't really want to consider what kind of wildlife they may encounter on their journey. She's unconcerned about it in any case. She thinks of her own remote, wild place, full of noisy, big-eyed creatures of its own. It feels almost impossible that the cloud forest still exists. She wants to close her eyes and travel back there. Wants to feel the cool softness of the clouds against her cheeks and eyelashes. She wants to hear the echoing drips of rainfall spattering among the big, fat leaves. The memory of that bright, liquid, ethereal place is fading from her grasp. When she closes her eyes now, she cannot recall the sound of her *abuela*'s singing or the smell of the *chilate*. It's all been obliterated from her, and the grief of that eradication feels like a weight she must carry in her limbs. When she breathes now, in this desert place, the air feels waterless in her nose, her scalp scorched by the sun where her hair parts.

Rebeca leans her head against her sister's shoulder and watches the changing colors of the landscape. The sun sinks in front of them and turns the sandy earth orange and pink. The sky, too, is filled with crazy, vivid pinks and purples and blues and yellows, and the colors are slow to deepen, slow to slip into blackness, but when at last they are gone, the darkness is deeper and more vast than anything Luca has ever seen. He cannot see his knees drawn up in front of him. He cannot see his own fingers wiggling in front of his eyes. He gropes for Mami's hand in the blackness, and when she feels him there, she pulls him closer and folds her wing around him. No one talks much after the sun is gone. Their eyes yawn open and seize on any suggestion of light. They stay each in their own mind, considering the hours ahead.

Lydia remembers a show from her childhood, not like these slick, indistinguishable cartoons Luca watches, shows that are beamed into televisions worldwide with their big-eyed, squeaky-voiced monsters of backtalk. It was a memorable show, an incredible low-budget job with handmade puppets and real junkyard magic. Lydia remembers the theme song, where all the characters would zoom around the earth in this rackety dumpster, except the dumpster was like a chariot, but only when all the friends were onboard, because if even one of them was missing, it was just a regular old dumpster, with hovering flies and sticky puddles. But when all the friends were together, the dumpster would glimmer and shoot off into the sky, and then stars would burst from its exhaust pipes, and don't ask Lydia why a dumpster had exhaust pipes, she was only six when she watched that show, but *Dios mío,* it was something.

She doesn't know why she's remembering that show right now—she hasn't thought of it in years, and this blue pickup truck is no magic dumpster. But Lydia has that same swooping, rocketing feeling she used to get when she watched that eruption of scrap-heap stars, when she saw how tightly the friends would curl their fingers around the lip of their vessel to keep themselves safely inside, never mind gravity or physics or the fiery reality of planetary atmosphere. Anything was possible.

"Do you remember that show, from when we were kids?" she asks Marisol in the blackness. "The one with the flying dumpster?"

Marisol remembers.

During the second hour of driving, there's a light on the path ahead, and the trucks roll to a stop at a checkpoint. There is light enough, just, for Soledad to recognize the uniform of *los agentes federales de migración*. Immediately, Rebeca begins to cry. She scrapes her heels along the bed of the pickup and writhes back into her sister's arms. Soledad shushes her and wraps an arm around her forehead. She presses Rebeca's face into the hollow of her neck and tells her to close her eyes. She hums softly to her sister in the comfort of their ancient language.

"Soon this will all be past. Soon we will be safe. Close your eyes, sister."

Rebeca breathes deeply into Soledad's neck, and her tears wet the soft brown curve of her sister's skin without sound. El Chacal gets out of the truck and steps toward the two guards, who are armed with flashlights and AR-15s. They greet him in a familiar manner, and he hands them an envelope. They talk for perhaps two minutes, and when the coyote returns to the truck, *los agentes* approach, shining their flashlights onto the faces of each migrant in turn. Rebeca does not lift her face from Soledad's shoulder when the beam touches her skin. Soledad sets her jaw and grits her teeth and stares directly into the light. Her eyes water, but she does not blink.

"*Oye, jefe,* maybe we'll keep this one," one of the guards says to El Chacal, whose window in the cab of the truck is rolled all the way down.

The coyote is leaning out, but before he has a chance to answer, Luca stands bolt upright, startling Lydia, who lunges for him.

"You cannot keep her!" he shouts. "You cannot have her, no one is allowed to have her. She is her own person, and she is coming with us!"

The beam of the flashlight swings toward Luca and the circle of light finds his face in the dark. His black eyes glimmer and his hands are balled into tight little fists.

"*¡Mira, el jefecito!*"

"Luca, sit down!" Lydia grabs him and wrestles him into her lap.

But the guard is laughing. He leans into the bed of the truck, and Soledad tightens her grip on Rebeca.

"Don't worry, little man," the guard says to Luca. "I was only joking." He swings the light back to Soledad. "You are lucky to have such a brave and fearsome bodyguard, señorita."

"Yes," Soledad says mechanically.

He returns his attention to Luca. "You keep fighting, little man. That's the kind of mettle you're going to need in *el norte*."

Lydia begins to breathe again but doesn't loosen her hold on Luca. When it's her turn to endure the beam of light on her features, she doesn't breathe. She keeps her eyes open and low, and prays these men don't work for Javier. She prays that her face isn't lodged in a text message on one of their cell phones. The flashlight lingers, and then swings across to Marisol. Lydia breathes.

"Godspeed!" the agent calls out, as he steps backward away from the truck.

"*¡Nos vemos pronto!*" El Chacal salutes the men with a parting wave as they continue their trek.

More than three hours after leaving the apartment in Nogales, the two pickup trucks, now with their headlights off, and covered in a thick layer of desert dust, pull to a stop. Without the ambient light of the trucks' dashboards and taillights, the migrants find themselves in absolute darkness. They are half a mile's walk from Estados Unidos. El Chacal lines them up outside the trucks and tells them they need only be aware of the person in front and the person behind them. It's too dark to see him, but his voice takes on such a warm animation it's almost visible itself, a shot of color against the black of night. He's all safety and faithful authority. He is perfectly contagious energy. With his guidance, they all believe this is possible. They don't even know his real name, but they entrust him with their lives. He tells them they're going to move quickly and it's vital to keep up. It's paramount that no one gets separated from the group.

"If you hear this noise, freeze." He makes a short, low-pitched whistle. "If I make that noise, it means you have to be absolutely still and silent until I say it's time to move again. This is the signal that it's time to move again." He makes a double-clicking noise with his tongue that's impressively audible. "If we get caught—is everybody listening? This is important. If we get caught, do not tell them which one of us is the coyote. Understood?"

"Why?" This is Lorenzo.

"You don't need to know why, but I'm going to tell you why, just so you don't get any stupid ideas," El Chacal says. "If we get picked up, and they find out I'm the coyote, you'll all be deported without me, right? I'll get arrested, and you'll get sent home. If *los carteles* find out who squealed on the coyote and interrupted their income stream, you'll have hell to pay. You have enough troubles from *los carteles,* yes?"

Lorenzo makes some noise that passes for an affirmative.

"So you keep your mouth shut. If we get caught, we all get deported together, we come back and try again. You get three tries for the price of one. Agreed?"

Everyone agrees, and then El Chacal lights a low lamp and spends a few minutes preparing. He unscrews the lid from a jar of minced garlic and instructs everyone to smear some on their shoes as a rattlesnake deterrent. The smell reminds Lydia of cooking, of home, but she's even more afraid of snakes than she is of nostalgia, so she's generous with her new boots and with Luca's. Then the coyote outfits everyone with the water they must carry. The jugs are heavy and awkward, but nothing's more critical. Lydia uses one of her canvas belts, looping it through the jug handles and then through the bottom straps of her backpack. The bottles slosh and bang against her hips as she walks, so she tightens the straps to fix them in place. Luca carries only one bottle; he can barely manage the weight of that. The men carry four gallons each, and Nicolás also has a fancy hiking backpack that's filled with water he can drink from a long tube over his shoulder. They all try not to think about the heat of the desert, the distance they must walk to reach safety after they cross, and the quantity of water they carry.

The migrants stay in the positions El Chacal assigns for them, so the coyote is first, followed by Choncho and Slim, followed by Beto and Luca, Lydia, the sisters, and then Marisol. The rest of the men are at the rear.

They move north at a pace that's rapid enough to be almost startling, and Lydia tries to watch Luca's nearly invisible outline ahead. The fresh air is cold moving through their lungs, and after those fidgety days in the apartment, it's exhilarating to be moving their bodies northward across the starlit earth. There's no talking, but their footfalls against the uneven terrain and their bodies' small sounds of exertion take on the qualities of conversation. Everyone concentrates on not falling, not stepping wrong, not bumping into the person in front of them. They stay alert to the real danger of twisting an ankle. They try, but mostly fail, to suppress their fear of the unseen, omnipresent Border Patrol.

There's no fence in this stretch of desert because there's no need of one. They are roughly twenty miles east of Sasabe and twenty miles west of Nogales, where the Pajarito Mountains serve as the border fence. It's cold. Luca is wearing every item of clothing they bought at that Walmart in Diamante before they left Acapulco: jeans, T-shirt, hoodie, warm jacket, and thick socks. His new boots are tied and double-knotted. Papi's baseball cap is stowed carefully in the side pocket of Luca's pack, and he's wearing the warm stocking hat and scarf he got from the old lady in Nogales, but even with all that, even though he feels damp with sweat along his spine, his nose and fingers are freezing. He wishes they'd thought to buy gloves, too. Sometimes El Chacal makes the quick whistle, and they all stand absolutely still and silent until he gives the double-click command for them to continue. There's one place where Luca can hear the electronic hum of some unseen machinery. Choncho falls into step beside Luca and points up to a blinking red light mounted high on a post nearby. They're almost directly beneath it. It swivels. And when the blinking red eye looks away, El Chacal makes the double-click, and they move very quickly, almost at a run through the darkness, until they are up and over a small ridge, beyond the sweep of that swiveling, mechanical eye.

"Congratulations," Choncho whispers loudly to Luca. "You've just outsmarted your first United States Border Patrol camera."

Luca grins in the dark, but Lydia feels a lurch in her stomach, a passing grief at what that must mean.

"We are in the United States already?" she whispers.

"Yes," Choncho says.

Lydia expected the crossing would be momentous. That it would happen in an instant, that she would, in the space of one footstep, leave Mexico and enter the United States. She expected to be able to pause, however briefly, so she might look back and reflect, both physically and metaphorically, at what she's leaving behind: the omnipresent fear of Javier and his henchmen. After eighteen days and sixteen hundred miles of endurance, she wants to feel that she's slipping his noose. But she wants to look further back than that, too, to her life before the massacre, to her happy childhood in Acapulco. The orange bathing suit she wore every day during the summer of her sixth birthday. Diving from the cliffs at La Quebrada when she was a teenager. Walking on Barra Vieja with her father when she was still small enough to hold his hand without embarrassment. The million endearing grievances of her mother. College, Sebastián, the bookstore. Holding Luca outside her body for the first time. Lydia expected there would be a moment when these notions would flood through her, all at once, like a small death. A portal. She'd hoped, like one of those desert rattlesnakes, to shed the skin of her anguish and leave it behind her in the Mexican dirt. But the moment of the crossing has already passed, and she didn't even realize it had happened. She never looked back, never committed any small act of ceremony to help launch her into the new life on the other side. Nothing can be undone. *Adelante.*

The sky is clear and there are stars overhead, but the moon is new, so even when it rises, it offers no light to their path. Ideal conditions for crossing, the coyote assures them as they stumble through the dark. For an hour they trudge through the desert without speaking. At eleven o'clock, they take shelter beneath a rocky outcrop because, the coyote explains, these are prime border patrolling hours, and *la migra* is thick in this sector. He tells them to rest, but none of them do. They sit in fear, their eyes blinking like inadequate lamps. They pass three hours that way, listening to the foreign sounds of the desert all around them. It's terrifying to hear grunting and snuffling and clicking and shrieking, sometimes at a distance, sometimes rather close, and to not be able to see what kinds of creatures are creating all that racket. It's a queer, vulnerable feeling to sit without armor among nocturnal animals, knowing they can see you and smell you and feel you there. Knowing that you're blind to their presence should they decide to approach. Every one of those migrants prays while they wait. Even Lorenzo remembers that he once believed in God.

CHAPTER THIRTY-ONE

Shortly before two o'clock in the morning, El Chacal gets them moving again. He wants to make camp before the morning twilight begins to ascend. He's walked this exact route dozens of times before. He knows just where they're going and how long it takes to get there. He knows they can make do with a lot less water if they avoid walking during the heat of the day. But now that it's late spring and the nights are growing shorter, he also knows there's little time to spare before the light comes. He pushes the group to the top of their pace. They're probably three miles north of the border but still hours from safety, from the nearest town, by the next time El Chacal makes the whistle. This time Beto, half-asleep on his feet, stumbles into Slim in front of him, and they tumble into a small heap together on the desert floor. Beto giggles and apologizes, but El Chacal snaps at him and puts one finger against his lips. Slim claps a meaty hand over Beto's mouth to ensure silence.

Ahead, at the foot of a hill they're nearly halfway down, Luca can see the faint white trace of a road, winding its way snakelike through the landscape. They're standing beneath a huddle of scrappy trees, but below them, there's little to no cover until the far side of the road. Several hundred yards to the right, four pickup trucks are parked together.

"*Carajo*," El Chacal says out loud.

Up to now, Luca has rather enjoyed this one perk of having his whole life annihilated: he's suddenly privy to a world where grown-ups sometimes curse out loud. He's even tried some of those words out on his own tongue, but in this instance, hearing El Chacal say *carajo* when he sees those pickup trucks makes Luca feel deeply unsettled.

"What are they doing here at this time of night?" Choncho asks the coyote quietly.

El Chacal shakes his head. "I don't know. There's a trailhead there." He points to the far side of the road. "Sometimes we hike that way if there's no one here. It's a little-used trail. But this . . ." The coyote spits into the dirt at his feet. "These are not day hikers." El Chacal wears a pair of binoculars from a length of cord around his neck, which he lifts and squints into now. It's too dark to see anything except the outline of the trucks, and an interior cab light that's been left on inside one of them. It's still very dark here, but the blackness is beginning to diffuse into a range of discernible grays. Soon the light will follow. El Chacal gathers the migrants out of their line and into a clump so he can speak to them all at once.

"There are four trucks parked at the trailhead below," he says. "It's a remote trailhead. I've never seen anyone parked out here before. So my guess, it's either a cartel waiting for a delivery, in which case, watch your backs because somebody might be coming along behind you."

Lydia's body goes rigid, and she reaches for Luca in the dark. She pulls him close.

"Or, more likely, it's one of those crazy fucking vigilante groups," the coyote says. "Out playing nighttime Power Rangers, in which case, watch your fronts, because those *hijos de puta* would like nothing better than to mount a stuffed migrant head over their mantel at home."

Luca grimaces, even though it strikes him as slightly funny, the notion of his head stuffed and mounted on a shiny slab of wood in a yanqui cabin somewhere.

None of it's funny to Lydia. She hadn't been naïve enough to think they were in the clear yet, but she did think the nature of the most pressing threat would've changed by now. She thought that here in *el norte,* she'd have to worry more about Border Patrol, about the possibility of Luca being taken from her, and less about random men with guns enforcing their own decrees. She avoids ranking the possibilities in terms of their potential for violence. Whatever their uniforms, their accents, their faces, *no importa*. She knows that anyone they encounter here, in this wild, desolate place, would mean the end.

"What are we going to do?" Marisol asks.

El Chacal is already removing his pack. "We'll wait here," he says. "This is the only cover. Anyway, the trucks look more like vigilantes than *carteleros*."

"How can you tell?" Choncho asks.

The coyote hands Choncho the binoculars without removing them from his neck. The big man peers into them. "They're not fancy enough to be narcos," El Chacal says. "And if they're vigilantes, as I suspect, they've probably gone migrant hunting up the trail on the far side. We wait here. They'll eventually go back to the trucks and we can pass after they leave."

"But what if they are narcos?" Marisol asks. Lydia shudders involuntarily, rubs her hands over her face, and shrugs her hood up. "Won't we be sitting ducks, right between them and whatever shipment they're waiting for?"

"*Mira,* I've already paid the toll to pass through here," El Chacal says. "I play by their rules."

"But whose rules?" Lydia can no longer keep the question to herself. She has to know which cartel is the self-appointed owner of this scrap of desert.

"Los Jardineros?" Lorenzo asks.

The coyote doesn't answer, and in the silence that follows, Lorenzo catches Lydia's eye. Lorenzo paces like a caged animal. This terrible hypothetical finally presses itself into Lydia's consciousness: Would it be worse to get caught by *estadounidenses,* who would take Luca from her? Or to get caught by *mexicanos,* who would return them to Javier? With effort, she represses the speculation. Neither thing can happen. They must succeed. She claps her fists against her thighs and stretches her cramping legs.

Choncho hands the binoculars back to El Chacal and begins removing his pack. Slim and their sons do the same, setting their water jugs wordlessly on the ground, and reclining against their backpacks.

El Chacal takes a measured sip of water from his own jug. "Find a place to tuck yourself in, in case the sun comes up before we're able to move."

The coverage isn't great here in this stand of scrappy trees, but there is a thicket nearby, and Rebeca, Soledad, and Lydia all set themselves up facing the rear, watching the path they've already taken halfway down the hill, waiting for the shapes of their nightmares to emerge from the dark. Luca sits back-to-back with Mami, and has time to consider how strange it is that being a *migrante* means you spend more time stopping than in motion. Their lives have become an erratic wheel of kinesis and paralysis. Beto falls asleep. Nicolás falls asleep. Marisol would like to fall asleep. They've all grown fatigued. Light grows in the eastern sky, and by the time the dozen men approach the four trucks on the road below, picking their way down the trail on the opposite hill, it's bright enough for El Chacal to see them clearly with the assistance of his binoculars. "Vigilantes," he confirms.

The men, dressed entirely in camouflage and bearing enough visible weaponry that anyone not knowing better would presume them to be authorized military, take their time at the trucks. They open coolers, remove drinks and food. They gather at the back of one of the trucks and pass a thermos of coffee. They're close enough now that, when the wind shifts in certain directions, the migrants can hear a whip of laughter here, a scrap of a sentence there. Those shifting acoustics are terrifying, because those sounds must also travel in reverse. The migrants all become aware of their anatomy. No one wants to sneeze or fart. They pray for the men to go away. Breakfast takes forever and then, just when it seems they are packed up and ready to go, they discover the interior cab light that was left on in one of the trucks. The battery is dead.

By the time the men locate some jumper cables, maneuver the trucks into position, hook everything up, get the truck running, spend five to ten minutes congratulating one another on getting the truck running, and finally, at long last, parade themselves down the road and out of sight, it is full daylight in the desert.

The migrants are still almost a mile from the hidden place where El Chacal intends to make camp for the day, and now they must contend with the danger of the glaring daylight. He shakes Nicolás and Beto to wake them.

"Let's go," he says. "Double time."

Luca's limbs feel stiff after the time spent shivering on the cold ground. He's happy to get them going again, and happy when the warmth begins to seep back into his legs. The road below is nothing like the roads Luca imagined he'd encounter in the USA. He thought every road here would be broad as a boulevard, paved to perfection, and lined with fluorescent shopfronts. This road is like the crappiest Mexican road he's ever seen. Dirt, dirt, and more dirt.

To the northwest there's a huddle of hills taller than the ones they've encountered so far, and after they cross the road, El Chacal begins to ascend the slope of the closest one. It's steep, and everyone focuses their energy on moving their bodies efficiently uphill.

"Why don't we go around?" Lorenzo complains.

"Because we take my route," El Chacal tells him.

"But that way looks way easier." Lorenzo points north.

"Vete entonces."

El Chacal dislikes Lorenzo. There's a tension between these two men, Luca understands, because there's a tension between Lorenzo and every person he encounters. Most people, because of decorum, attempt to disguise that conflict, but the coyote doesn't bother, and Luca likes that. Instead, when Lorenzo speaks, El Chacal makes a face that's like the opposite of rolling his eyes, where his features get really still, and he looks away from Lorenzo with his eyelids half-closed, and he just waits for the words to go away. After a moment, he reanimates himself and presses on.

When they reach the apex of the hill and behold the vista on the other side, an uncomfortable feeling of both thrill and dread shivers right through Luca's whole body. It's so severe that Mami actually sees the quake of his limbs from her peripheral vision, and turns her head to look at him. He makes sure not to catch her eye. He's enraptured, anyway, by the panorama that caused the feeling in him; they all are.

On the far side of this hill are a hundred more just like it, and probably a hundred more beyond those that they can't see, because the hills get taller and sharper and more formidable as they go. The sunlight cracks across them in crazy stabs of brightness. The hills are covered in golden, wind-beaten grasses, spiky plants, and scrubby trees. There are huge boulders everywhere, studded into the creases of the hills, perched on rickety ledges, gathered in hollows like intransigent families. A few of the rocks are so gargantuan they dwarf the hills beneath them. The sky is merciless above, wheeling clouds to shift the light, playing tricks, making it impossible to gauge distances, but never covering the hot, ruthless globe of the sun. Luca pauses there to snatch the hat from his head and stuff it into his coat pocket. He's suddenly covered with sweat. He peels the scarf and jacket off, and unzips his backpack to stuff them in. He retrieves Papi's red hat and takes a whiff of the hatband before fixing it back onto his head and reslinging the backpack onto his shoulders, but the coyote looks over and shakes his head.

"You can't wear the hat," he says. "You can spot that red from a mile away."

Luca frowns at Mami, but she nods, and Luca unhappily removes Papi's hat. He hands it to Mami, and she tries to zip it back into his pack.

"You can wear mine." Lydia removes her hat and holds it out to him.

"But it's pink," he protests.

"Hardly."

"I'll take it!" Beto says.

Lydia laughs. "I wish I had an extra one for you," she says. She plops it on Luca's head and returns to the zipper on Luca's pack, trying to get Papi's hat back in. The backpack is stuffed. She pauses to pull a white T-shirt out from inside. "Here," she says, handing the shirt to Beto. "Use this."

He fixes the neck of the T-shirt over his head and lets the fabric drape down his neck to shield his skin from the sun. He grins at Lydia. "Thanks."

Everyone has paused here, suddenly aware of the mounting heat. They're all peeling off layers and regrouping. Slim and Choncho are sharing water from one of their jugs. There's a reason this landscape is devoid of people, why it's still feasible to cross here without getting caught. It seems impossible that any creature could survive in such a place.

"It doesn't even look real," Mami says.

Beside Luca, Lorenzo removes his own cap and wipes his brow. That hat was pristine the first time Luca saw it, at the migrant shelter in Huehuetoca. Now the brim is still flat, but the sun has sapped its color from black to gray. That change is startling to Luca. He's unaccustomed to the potency of the Sonoran sun, how quickly it corrodes whatever's beneath its gaze. He pulls Mami's hat off his head to examine it more closely, and he realizes that the pink really isn't pink anymore. It's only the bleached memory of pink, a dirty sand color. That's what Mami meant when she said *hardly*. Lorenzo leans his hands on his knees and looks out across the hopeless vista.

"*Ay, no manches, cabrón,*" he says. "You've got to be kidding me."

"I guess this is what he meant by *grueling*." Beto wheezes, pulling the empty inhaler from his pocket to suck on it.

"You okay?" Luca asks, gesturing at the inhaler.

Beto shrugs and tries to regulate his breath, his eyes squinting against the brightness of the sun. "Why, you got some albuterol in there?" He pokes at Luca's backpack. "Because I'll take it if you do!"

Both boys laugh, and Beto's sounds like a dying balloon.

"*Venga, mijo,*" Mami says, prompting Luca to walk in front of her. "You, too, Beto. You okay to walk?"

He doesn't waste any more breath on words but nods and gets moving.

Each hill looks like it would take a half a day to walk up, and a half a day to walk back down. The migrants file downhill in El Chacal's wake. They're silent now, descending into the first seam of the valley, struggling to keep their minds strong as they face the enormity of their undertaking. The wind rockets across the landscape and whips Rebeca's hair into a black tornado. Their feet crunch through the witchy yellow grass, and Luca's body is flooded with awful excitement. They're in the United States now, and already it looks like a movie set, but with real desert animals that can kill you, like scorpions and rattlesnakes and mountain lions. Luca experiences a swamp of tingly, nauseating confusion.

"Luca." Mami's right behind him. Sometimes it's like she can hear what he's thinking. "You doing okay?"

He nods.

"I'm proud of you, *mijo*," she whispers so no one else can hear. She makes a muscle. "*Eres bien fuerte*. Papi would be proud."

El Chacal knows where there's a water station, a place where aid workers leave water for passing migrants. He's made them conserve their supplies anyway, because sometimes the water's not there—sometimes the Border Patrol or vigilantes find it first and destroy it. But today it's there,

marked by a whipping blue flag atop a pole, three huge jugs sitting on a
pallet beneath a tarp. It's not cold, but it's the best water Lydia has ever
tasted. Her head was beginning to pound because she was conserving
their supply, but now she drinks her fill from her canteen, and feels the
pain diminish at once. It feels like a miracle, to drink. She refills her canteen again and drinks some more. Luca drinks very little.

"As much as you can, *amorcito*," she insists.

"But I'll get a cramp. We have to walk so fast."

"Cramps you can live with," she says. "Drink."

They rest beside the water station for ten minutes, filling their jugs
and drinking and drinking, and filling them again before they strike out
deeper across the valley floor. El Chacal has warned them to stay quiet,
to listen all the time for the sound of engines, but the wind is too loud
for that. Beto starts chatting to Choncho.

"Where you guys from?" Beto asks.

Choncho is slow to respond, not from reluctance, but just because
that's his way. "Veracruz," he says eventually.

"That in Mexico?"

Another pause. "Yes."

"I didn't know they made Mexicans as big as you."

Choncho laughs, and it sends a ripple through the whole group.

Beto looks from Choncho to his brother Slim to their two sons.
"Everybody in Veracruz as tall as you?"

"No," Choncho says slowly. "Much taller."

Beto is listing all the tallest people he can think of from *el dompe,*
when El Chacal makes the low-pitched warning whistle. Marisol spots
the problem at the same time, and inadvertently cries out. She points
across the valley to a ridge on the far side where a trail of fawn, powdery
dust rises up through the foliage. El Chacal does his whistle once more,
commanding everyone to drop, and it's instant, the way they obey. They
drop like they were shot, all fifteen of them right where they stand. "Get
into the shade if you can," he says.

The light is vigorous here. To be in it is to be discovered, to be out
of it is to be concealed. When the desert sunlight shines on any scrap of
moving color, that color radiates like a beacon. Mami and Luca huddle
together beneath the shade of a rock, pressed up beside a silk tassel tree.

Catkins hang down from its branches in pale green curtains that drop their clinging flowers into Mami's hair. Tucked into this dark alcove and curled behind their backpacks, they're invisible from the ridge where that plume of dust is growing steadily across the hillside in a sputtering line. Around them, the other migrants squirm to find cover, flattening themselves into the parched grasses, twisting themselves into the spiky shadows of yuca fronds, folding themselves into the silhouette of a cypress tree. They all become perfectly motionless and silent. Even Beto is quiet, lying flat among the blond stalks, his toes pointing up to the sky. When three minutes have passed, they finally hear the vague rumble of an engine slurring itself into the wind. After another full minute, the vehicle appears on a slope not far above them, on the next hill over. It's the distinct white-and-green Chevy Tahoe of the US Border Patrol.

El Chacal's face betrays nothing. "Nobody move," he says quietly. He's well hidden between Marisol and Nicolás in the shade of a standing rock. Because he knows it might be some time before they can move again, he always makes sure to land in a comfortable position. He sits on his bottom with his knees up, and trains his binoculars on the passenger seat of the Chevy Tahoe, where a Border Patrol agent trains his own military-grade binoculars back toward them.

We are invisible, Luca says to himself, and he closes his eyes. *We are desert plants. We are rocks.* He breathes deeply and slowly, taking care that his chest doesn't rise and fall with the cycle of his breath. The stillness is a kind of meditation all migrants must master. *We are rocks, we are rocks. Somos piedras.* Luca's skin hardens into a stony shell, his arms become immovable, his legs permanently fixed in position, the cells of his backside and the bottoms of his feet amalgamate with the ground beneath him. He grows into the earth. No part of his body itches or twitches, because his body is not a body anymore, but a slab of native stone. He's been stationary in this place for millennia. This silk tassel tree has grown up from his spine, the indigenous plants have flourished and died here around his ankles, the fox sparrows and meadowlarks have nested in his hair, the rains and winds and sun have beaten down across the rigid expanse of his shoulders, and Luca has never moved. *We are rocks.* At length, the Tahoe finishes its noisy, indiscreet voyage across the ridge and disappears over a low rim into the next seam of the valley beyond.

El Chacal doesn't waste time on chitchat. The sun is lodging itself ever higher into the hot, bright shelf of the sky, and they should've made camp an hour ago. It's not safe for them to be exerting themselves beneath the burning lamp of the sun. It will sap them. "*Vámonos,*" he says. "*¡Apúrense!*" Just as quickly as they dropped, everyone rises, collects their belongings, and once again they're on the move.

By late morning, just as that sun is sucking all the moisture from their depleted bodies, just as Rebeca feels ready to give up, behind the skirting of a deep hill, they come to a shaded fold of land where a cluster of trees hides a good camp. Sumac and mountain mahogany band together beneath the jagged ridges, so their camp is entirely concealed from view. They are deeply in shade, and it's a blessed relief to be out from under the sun. There are signs all around the clearing of previous campers: discarded plastic water bottles, a ripped black T-shirt covered with salt stains, a worn pink sneaker, much smaller than Luca's. El Chacal goes directly to a soft clump of sand beneath a tree where all the rocks have been cleared. He pitches his pack down beside the trunk and immediately settles himself in to sleep. The others follow suit. It's easy for the men, who seem to sleep wherever they drop. Marisol lies flat on her stomach and rests her head on her outstretched arms. She, too, is asleep instantly. The sisters are restless, and they move several times before they find comfort.

Despite her exhaustion, Lydia expects to have trouble sleeping. She flings out their blanket anyway, and she and Luca collapse onto it. The desert sun is so bright that even here in the deep shade, Lydia finds herself squinting to block out the light. When she opens her eyes to look around, the landscape beyond this seam of shade is one wide expanse of sepia, everything bleached into varying fractures of brown by the adamant sun. Choncho notices her wakefulness and gives her a somber nod, which Lydia interprets as a promise to watch over her and her sleeping child. *You rest. I will make sure nothing happens to you,* is the meaning she chooses to attach to that ambiguous nod. And with that imagined vow of protection, at once, she drops into sleep.

CHAPTER THIRTY-TWO

They don't wait until dark to set out. As soon as the sun dips near the ridge at the western end of the valley, and their shadows lengthen to undulating streaks of black along the desert floor, El Chacal tells them to make themselves ready.

"Tonight is *difícil*," the coyote tells them. "Eight miles, rough terrain. You have to keep up. If you fall behind, we cannot wait for you. I won't risk the whole group for one individual. So listen up, *esto es importante*. It's life or death." El Chacal clears his throat to make sure everyone's listening. "Just west of here, the road we crossed early this morning cuts north and runs sort of parallel to the route we're taking, okay?"

They all nod.

"If you get separated from the group. If you fall, if you twist an ankle, if you decide you need a rest or a piss or a scratch or a sleep, if for any reason you cannot keep up, you go to that road. That is the Ruby Road. Border Patrol and locals pass there regularly. You won't die out here if you get to that road. In a few hours, someone will find you there."

It's a grim business, the Ruby Road, and none of them can picture it yet, not while things are going well. Right now that road is to be avoided at all costs, it's the very nexus of their fear. It's impossible for the migrants to imagine the desperation that might, only a few hours hence, convince them to seek deliverance there.

"We travel this way." El Chacal gestures with a slice of his hand.

"North. So which way is the road? I want you all to know it. Lorenzo! Which way is the road?"

Lorenzo doesn't answer.

"It's west," El Chacal repeats with exasperation. "Which way is west?"

Lorenzo reaches for his phone but there's no signal in the desert.

"It's that way." Luca points west.

"*Claro que sí.*" The coyote ruffles Luca's hair. "This kid's not gonna die in the desert."

They eat nuts and strips of beef jerky while they walk. The PhD student Nicolás has some kind of protein paste in single-serving tinfoil tubes. They look and smell disgusting, but they're packed with nutrients, and indeed, his energy is impressive. He's directly behind Lydia this evening, and he makes quiet conversation as they walk. She wonders if the protein tubes are caffeinated.

"Whatever you do, don't go to Arivaca," he's saying. "If you're dying of thirst, those people will pull up a lawn chair and sip lemonade while they watch."

"Ah, they're not so bad," El Chacal interrupts from ahead. "There are good people in Arivaca, too. Life is complicated for them, living so close to the line."

Nicolás raises his remarkable eyebrows. Although Arivaca is a tiny, remote town of fewer than seven hundred people, a forty-five-minute drive down empty roads from its nearest neighbor, Nicolás, like most people who live in southern Arizona, knows its reputation as a merciless, hardscrabble outpost, a place where vigilante militiamen murdered a nine-year-old girl and her father years ago, hoping to pin the blame on illegal migrants. The vigilantes wanted to stoke community fear and incite outrage by inventing a group of murderous migrant bogeymen, so they broke into the Flores family home, and shot little Brisenia in the head. She was wearing turquoise pajama bottoms and red-painted fingernails when she died, curled up on the love seat in her living room. But because Nicolás is a young, politicized liberal who's never been to Arivaca, he hasn't observed how the shame of that murder still weighs on the tiny town. He's never been close to a tragedy that barbaric, never experienced a shock so primitive that it shakes him to the very core of his beliefs. In short, Nicolás has never had a fundamental change of heart.

So he's unaware of the way Newton's third law can resonate in a place like this: for every wickedness, there is an equal and opposite possibility of redemption. In any case, the point is moot. Lydia has no intention of going to Arivaca, a place where the only way out is to turn yourself in, to ask for help. She and Luca are going to make it to Tucson, to safety.

They hike almost three miles without incident, and it's amazing to watch the colors leach back into the desert after the day's blanching. There's a moment, Lydia realizes, or no, more than a moment—a span of perhaps fifteen minutes just at twilight—when the desert is the most perfect place that exists. The temperature, the light, the colors, all hang and linger at some unflawed precipice, like the cars of a roller coaster ticking ever so slowly over the apex before the crash. The light droops ever farther from the sky, and Lydia can smell the heat of the day wicking away from her skin. Luca's backpack bobs in front of her. For the first time since she stood up from the chair on her mother's back patio in Acapulco and left her iced *paloma* sweating on the table, Lydia feels like they might survive. A weird lurch of something like exhilaration. And then, quite suddenly, it's very dark and very cold. Colder than the night before, if she's not imagining it, and that chill has the effect of prompting all fifteen of them to move faster. The ground is jagged, studded with rocks, pitching and rising unpredictably, pockmarked by the hidey-holes of unseen animals. Lydia prays that no one falls. The sisters have been uncommonly quiet, she notices, and she worries about their stamina, so soon after their bodies have endured those other traumas. Lydia prays, too, for Luca's feet in his new boots, and for Soledad's and Rebeca's feet, for her own feet. *Dear God, keep them strong and unblistered, let them step only in places where human feet are supposed to go.*

El Chacal moves at a brutal pace. The rendezvous point is just over a dozen miles north of the border as the crow flies, but those miles cover some of the roughest terrain in North America, with elevation changes of up to seven thousand feet. Their two-and-a-half-day path winds around the worst of the impassible sections, and funnels them toward cattle tanks in case they get desperate for water, all while keeping them as far away from popular hiking trails and known *migra* patrolling routes as possible. At the end of tonight's walk, near dawn, when they make camp in a cavelike formation a few miles west of Tumacacori-Carmen, Arizona, they'll be almost home free. The migrants don't know this yet. They don't know any of the details, really, because El Chacal likes to keep things relatively covert. If anything goes wrong, if a migrant wanders off, or lags behind and gets picked up, the coyote doesn't want that migrant confessing the whole thing to Border Patrol. All they need to know is to follow El Chacal. To do what he tells them to do. If they listen, if they obey, if they persevere, he'll see to it that they survive this journey. Tomorrow night, they'll be pleasantly surprised by the shortness of their walk. There will be the delighted sounds of wonder among them as they approach the campsite where two RVs are waiting to drive them up the crude, unpaved road that eventually ushers them onto the kind of smooth northern highway they've all envisioned; the flat, wide pavement of Route 19 awaits. The Border Patrol checkpoint there is closed for a specific number of hours each week. The coyote, with the exchange of regular money for reliable information, knows which hours those are.

It's a forty-five-minute drive from there to Tucson, to the optimistic anonymity of urban Arizona. It's so close. The migrants don't even realize how close. But now, in the fifth hour of their vigorous hike, as the loose gravel of the black slope they're descending in some unnamed canyon slips treacherously underfoot, just as their spirits are beginning to mirror the fatigue of their bodies, there's an almighty crack in the sky, followed by a downpour. They're shocked, all of them, and even Nicolás and El Chacal, who are both well prepared with rain gear, are soaked before they manage to get their ponchos on. Their bodies want them to seek shelter, and it takes some measure of minutes for them to quell those instincts and return to their pace, trudging through those curtains of rain.

Luca's jeans are heavy with rainwater and he has to walk with his legs spread apart because the wet denim chafes between his thighs and against one spot at the back of his left hip. He's glad for the new hiking boots, and glad that Mami insisted he wear them all around the apartment for the two days in Nogales, to break them in. He's glad he hadn't complained or argued, even though he'd wanted to. But even with that extra practice, with each step he's increasingly aware of a pinpoint, a tiny dot only the width of a thread, on the back of his left heel, that's beginning to trouble him. At first he ignores it. Then he addresses it. He tells it that no puny, insignificant speck of pain will prevent him from reaching his destination. He tells it that he would endure a hundred such pains, a thousand, without blinking an eye. He is Luca! His whole family has been murdered! He is unstoppable!

"Mami." His voice is soft with pain, curdled.

"What is it, *mijo*?"

"I have a blister," he confesses. It's excruciating. He cannot go on.

Mami presses her lips together and draws him to the side of the trail, out of the line. The other migrants don't stop or even slow. They continue at speed, and by the time Lydia's down on one knee with Luca's pant leg rolled up at the cuff and his sock pulled down, they've all passed. It's difficult to see in the dark and the rain, but El Chacal has forbidden the use of flashlights, so Lydia draws her face down close to Luca's heel to investigate. His socks are sopping, and she runs her hand across the back of his foot, where she can feel the forming bubble of a blister. There's nothing she can do for him because of the dampness of his skin, the dampness of his jeans, the dampness of everything. Band-Aids are impossible. But she has to try. She unslings her pack, finds the zippered compartment on one side where she stashed a handful of Band-Aids before they set out. They are wet, of course, but Lydia selects the driest one, from the middle of the stack. She opens her coat and leans over his ankle, trying to make an umbrella of her body.

"Take the boot off," she says.

"But, Mami, they're going," he says. "We don't have time."

"Do it quickly," she snaps.

Luca obeys, tugging on the laces, ripping off the boot, which somersaults to the ground beneath.

"Sit here." She points to her pack, and Luca sits. "Sock, too," she says, and then she glances up through the streamers of rain, to where she thinks she can still see the last of the group disappearing into the darkness. She stashes the wrapped Band-Aid between her lips. Luca whips off the wet sock, and she crams it into her pocket, untucks her shirt from beneath her hoodie, and uses her shirttail to dry his foot as best she can. His little toes are pruned. She tucks his foot into the warm fold of her armpit, and then reaches over Luca's shoulder to unzip the backpack he's still wearing. She knows there are two pairs of socks inside, right-hand side, near the bottom. She worries that her panic will make her clumsy, that she won't be able to find the socks, groping blindly into the pack this way, that she'll find them, and drop them, and they'll be drenched and useless, and they will have lost the group for nothing, that they will die here, not shot through with cartel bullets at a family party, but alone in the desert. They will both die because of a blister. Because of rain. No. There, her fingers brush against a soft ball of rolled socks, still dry. *Gracias a Dios.* She tugs them out and sticks them into her armpit with the foot, zips the pack. The other migrants are gone now. She can no longer see them or hear them, but all her senses strain after them, she sends her mind to follow the direction they were taking. *God, please let us find them,* she prays. She peels the wrapper off the Band-Aid, spits the papers onto the ground, gives Luca's foot another wipe with her shirttail, blows on the damp foot with her meager breath, and then presses the adhesive bandage against the curve of his skin. *Please, God, let it stick.* She unfolds the dry socks and tugs one onto his foot. It seems to take hours, the wriggling of the foot into the tube of material, the correct placement of the seam across the toe, the adjustment of the dry cotton into position around the afflicted heel. She thinks about putting the second one on him, too. An extra layer of protection between the boot and the skin. Would that be better or worse for the blister? Extra padding, but a tighter fit. The time constraint is the deciding factor. She tucks the other dry sock beneath her bra strap and retrieves the toppled boot. She loosens the laces and pulls at the tongue. She wipes the inside of the boot with her shirttail, and Luca jams his foot in. She yanks on the laces.

"I'll do it, Mami," he says.

She holds her coat over him while he ties the boot quickly, impressively, and then, "I'm good," he says. "I'm okay, Mami. Thank you." And he stands up from her backpack. He takes a few steps to test the repair. "Much better," he says.

Lydia has refastened the side zipper on her pack, and is already walking after him, jogging, really, while she slings the backpack around to her shoulders. The gallon jugs of water bang and slosh beneath. "Go, *mijo,* quickly, we have to catch up," she says.

Altogether, the delay cost them perhaps two and a half minutes. Maybe three. Enough time to become completely lost from the group. They're well out of earshot because all they can hear is the thundering wash of the rain hammering down all around them. Lydia feels panicky, all her fears compressed into a tight ball that lodges in her chest. *This is how it happens,* she thinks. And her voice becomes frantic as she urges Luca to move faster, but he's remembering, too, that day outside Culiacán when *la migra* were chasing them and Mami twisted her ankle and fell. They can't afford a twisted ankle on top of everything else, Luca thinks, and that worry slows him into a pace that's too cautious. So perhaps this will be it instead, they will die from caution.

"*Apúrate, mijo,* please." Lydia fights against a mounting scream in her throat, and now there's a new doubt: What if they're hurrying in the wrong direction, diverging only slightly from the path, a fork, so that with each step, they stray a little farther from the group? *This is the way they went, isn't it?* There's no possibility of tracking them in this rain, in this dark. They have to just go. Move. Keep moving. In desperation Lydia breaks the crucial rule about silence, and she calls out for them, but there's no response. They walk and stumble and hurry through the dark for some time, and every few minutes, she breaks that rule again, louder and more desperately each time Lydia tries a name.

Soledad.

Rebeca.

Beto.

Help.

Nicolás.

Choncho.

Where are you?

Luca is no longer in front of her or behind her, but beside her, holding her hand, and she glances infrequently at the darkness of his eyes, and she sees that he's calm. He doesn't share her panic.

"It's okay, Mami," he says at length. "This is the right way."

She believes him because she must. And he knows these things. Doesn't he?

Chacal.

Marisol.

Slim.

Hello?

The only answer is the whip of falling rain in thick cords upon their shoulders, fat drops spattering against their hoods. She pushes through the darkness, and in some detached corner of her mind where operations are still functioning normally, she makes jokes for herself, about being lost in the desert for forty days, for forty millennia. Her Catholic vision of hell is all wrong: there's no fire, no wretched burning. Hell is wet and cold and black and lost. Her brain tap-dances and contracts, and then. Then. She sees a shape moving through the darkness. A shadow. A barely discernible movement, a distant blotch of black that's a slightly dimmer shade of black than all the fixed blacks around it. Lydia yelps, and feels a shot of hope club through her sternum, and she squeezes Luca's hand, and drags him into a quicker pace, and she charges after that blotch of black as it moves through the invisible landscape, and she's not imagining it. It's no mirage. It continues its trajectory, bump, bump. It moves forward, and Lydia fixes her eyes on it and she follows, she pulls Luca, she runs, heedless of the treacherous ground beneath their feet, until the shape grows larger, closer, and it is a backpack. It is Ricardín's backpack. She calls out once more.

Ricardín.

David.

And the shape pauses. Turns toward her. They are found. They are saved.

Salvación. Salvación. Lydia cries.

Ricardín ushers her into the line ahead of him, ahead of his *primo* David. And here are the sisters, Rebeca. Soledad. It's easy for Lydia to believe the girls might not have noticed their absence. It's so dark and the rain is falling so hard, it's difficult to observe anything beyond the border of your own hood, your outstretched hands, your churning feet. Lydia doesn't want to know if the sisters noticed they were gone, if they mentioned it to El Chacal, or asked him to stop and wait. If she doesn't know, then she doesn't have to ask herself what she might have done in their position. It's okay now anyway, it doesn't matter. *It's okay.* Lydia crosses herself in the darkness. She breathes into her shoulders. She inhales the endless rain.

CHAPTER THIRTY-THREE

The downpour stops. Just as abruptly as it started. And in its wake, Luca hears a new chorus of uncomfortable music in their midst. Their shoes squelch beneath them. The drenched denim of their jeans murmurs stiffly when their legs move against each other. Luca's teeth chatter, and he becomes so cold he can almost hear his brain shivering in his skull. He begins to wonder if being freezing and wet in the aftermath of rain might be worse than the rain itself, the same way your body, once adapted to the cold Pacific water of Acapulco Bay, can yearn for the mantle of that water after you emerge onto the hot, dry sand of Playa Condesa. Your body can get mixed up about what's hot and what's cold, Luca thinks, but then it begins to rain again, and Luca knows that his hypothesis was *una mierda*. The night passes in misery, in bouts of torrential rain and intermittent periods of respite. Lydia tries to maintain her sense of relief, her feeling that they are saved. But their backpacks and jeans chafe their skin raw, and then it rains again. Every one of them, once or twice at least, every one of them despairs. The only thought that sustains them is the notion that each moment they endure this misery is one less moment they have yet to endure.

"There's a blessing of the rain," El Chacal says as they lace their way through the seam of a canyon. "Everybody hates it."

Luca and Lydia have returned to their place near the front of the line, behind Choncho and Slim and Beto. Rebeca and Soledad are directly behind them now, followed by Marisol, Nicolás, Lorenzo, David and Ricardín, and then the two quiet men who carry their names in secret. The boulders in this seam of land are broad and smooth underfoot, slick with water, and Luca notices that he can begin to make out their shapes in the dark. They come to a place where the boulders form a kind of natural staircase the migrants descend, and then the walls of the canyon rise up on either side of them, and they walk along the bottom of a gulch, where a stream of rainwater sloshes around their ankles. They follow El Chacal tight along the left-hand side of the gulley, where the path is driest, and irregular ledges jut from the canyon walls. It's just the kind of landscape the daredevil Pilar from school would like to climb if she were here, Luca thinks. He could climb it, too, he knows now. He can do things Pilar never dreamed of. The first traces of dark gray daylight brush the walls of the gorge by degrees while the coyote talks. "When it rains, the narcos stay in their SUVs. *La migra* agents stay in their dens. We sneak past while they take shelter."

"Only migrants venture out in the rain," Choncho says.

"Only lunatics," Slim corrects him.

But the rain is fickle in the desert, and as the lid of night slowly lifts, Luca watches the oppressive clouds rolling like the wheels of La Bestia across the still-dark sky. Those clouds gather and crush and demolish, and after they pass, they leave a blank void of gray nothing behind them. Soon the sun will come and fill that void with hot color. Soon *la migra* will return.

They walk in haste.

"How much farther?" Beto asks, because no one has spoken in a long time, and even more than he wants an answer, he wants to hear the reassuring sound of another human voice.

"An hour, maybe less," the coyote answers.

Most people who meet El Chacal at this stage of his life presume he got his moniker because of his work as a coyote, but in fact his family has called him that since he was twelve years old. When he was a boy in Tamaulipas, Juan Pedro, as he was known back then, found a pup one day on the side of the road. The pup's mother had been struck by a car and killed. The other littermates had scattered or been picked off by the time Juan Pedro arrived and found the lone pup sitting bereft beside the cold body of its mother. Juan Pedro took the pup home, and as it grew, despite the meticulous care and affection Juan Pedro gave it, it became a wild, rangy-looking thing. People in the village took to calling the pup "The Jackal," which was fine by Juan Pedro, who liked the wildness of it. But then they began calling Juan Pedro "Mother of Jackal," which he didn't like quite so much. He endured that name for some time and was glad when eventually folks stopped mentioning the dog entirely and shortened his nickname to "El Chacal."

Despite the name, El Chacal had no intention of becoming a coyote. Few people do. He crossed once many years ago, when he was still a young man looking for work, and he intended to make just the one crossing. It was much easier back then, but still no picnic—not in Arizona. The other migrants he was with during that first crossing found it strenuous and difficult. But El Chacal discovered that he liked these high-desert places. He found that they suited him, they opened his lungs and the good heat of his body. He spent a few months working as a dishwasher at a diner in Phoenix, and whenever he had time off, he liked to go hiking through the canyons. It wasn't long before he went home to Tamaulipas. The next time he crossed, he did it alone, without a guide. It was crazy, but he did it without difficulty. He did it with a map and a compass, and what's more, he enjoyed it the way some people enjoy boot camp or a marathon. He liked the strain it put on his muscles and his mind. He liked the undercurrent of survivalist danger. So then he did it again. Several more times without company, and each time he crossed, he grew stronger and smarter, he adjusted his route, perfected his bearings. Then he brought a group of friends from Tamaulipas with him. They were so impressed by his knowledge of the land, by the apparent ease with which he navigated the difficult terrain, that they hired him to bring their girlfriends, their children, their cousins, their parents. Quite accidentally, El Chacal found himself with a thriving business in human smuggling.

It was exciting for him to be good at something after a lifetime of mediocrity in Tamaulipas. His reputation grew, and as the border tightened and his previous routes became impassable, as he had to strike farther and farther into the desert, into more arduous, perilous tracks all the time, El Chacal realized he could charge a lot of money for this service. Then the cartels moved in.

So he doesn't make as much money now, and what's more, he doesn't enjoy the work as he once did. He used to feel like a minor hero, a guide with the power to lead people to the promised land. Now he pays *la migra* and the cartels both for the privilege of crossing this binational scrap of dirt. They eat his profits and his freedom. When they demand favors of him, he cannot say no. Sometimes they ask him to carry something he doesn't want to carry. Once in a while they tell him to take someone he doesn't want to take. Soon El Chacal will retire. He has enough money saved, and now that he's almost thirty-nine years old, the travails of this repetitive journey are beginning to outweigh his boyish sense of adventure. He'll go home to Tamaulipas. Maybe he'll marry Pamela, whom he's loved since he was a boy. Maybe she'll finally say yes. Why not? Meanwhile, he tries to be stern with the migrants. He tries to be detached because attachments can be fatal. He needs to be at liberty to make decisions for the good of the group, and if he grows too fond of one of his *pollitos,* that makes it harder to make a tough decision in a pinch, to leave someone behind if he sees they're not going to make it. But recently, it's difficult for him to discern how much of his callousness is still an act. He wears a rosary around his neck to countermand his worries about the flagging condition of his soul. The tattoo on his right forearm reads JESÚS ANDA CONMIGO, and mostly, he still believes it. He wants it to be true.

When they hear the cry behind them, the migrants instinctively duck, but El Chacal, still on his feet, turns toward the sound. Across the tops of the migrants' heads he sees, approaching from behind and moving as swiftly as a nightmare through the charcoal colors of the canyon, a fast-flowing black mass of water. It's descending the staircase behind them.

"Get up!" he shouts. "*¡Arriba!*" His voice bangs and echoes against the walls of the canyon, all his furtive inclinations suspended. He shouts at them, "Get up, up!"

He leaps from rock to rock ahead, and then reaches for a broad ledge just higher than his waist, and hoists himself aloft. The migrants follow, and El Chacal reaches back to help them up, first Luca and Beto, then the sisters and Lydia, and now Lorenzo is already up. "Help them!" El Chacal shouts at him, so Lorenzo leans down, gives Marisol his hand, and pulls her up, and in this way, one by one the migrants scramble up and away from the advancing wall of water, and those at the front try to move up again, to make room for the others to follow, and here's another ledge, just higher, so they climb up and up, ascending the wall, and they're almost all up out of the bottom of the gorge now, and it looks so obvious from here, with the water coming so quickly, with the discovery of the alternate path, this higher path, made up entirely of these jutting ledges, that it's an ancient riverbed beneath them. *Jesucristo*.

Even though they'd been near the front of the line, Choncho and Slim and their sons are still below in the gulch because they stayed to help the others. The migrants on the ledge step back to make room for the stragglers to scramble up. They spread out, hasten to scale the ascendant ledges, to reach higher ground. And now Slim is up on the first ledge below, and he reaches back for his nephew David, and their thick forearms slap against each other as they grab wrists and Slim hoists the boy up. And now Choncho is up, too, but Ricardín is last, Slim's son. And the water is so fast and so high that it doesn't reach Ricardín's ankles first and then engulf his legs, but rather it hits the entire back of his body at once and knocks him forward, and he's dragged along in its maw like a ragdoll, and they all shout and yelp, and El Chacal and the two brothers run and leap from ledge to ledge after him, or after his backpack really, because that's all they can see now, his large and floating backpack, the same one that was Lydia's redemption in the darkness, and then Ricardín's arms come flailing out of the water and he manages to flip himself somehow, and then the backpack is immediately dragged from his body, his arms slip right out and it's gone, and Ricardín makes one perfunctory effort to reach for the pack, and then realizes immediately that the pack is not the priority, so he returns his attention to his own flagging body, his unusually large frame, whose strength has never failed him before. His *papi* and *tío* are on the embankment above him, and the coyote is there, and no one can believe how fast this happened, how the water came out of nowhere, and how fast and strong and deep it is. They're reaching for him, and yelling for him, and he can hear his father's voice but he can't do anything because the water has his arms pinned, and his legs are churning and he keeps spitting out mouthfuls of water, but as soon as he spits out one, his mouth is already full again, and it's not only water, but water and soil and sticks and debris, and he's going to drown in it. Ricardín knows he's going to drown, and he has the thought that it would be almost funny to drown in a flash flood in the desert, and then he realizes that he doesn't want his death to be funny, or even almost funny, so he focuses all his energy on his abdominal muscles, on bending himself in half, so the top part of his body comes up out of the water and once, twice, he reaches for his father's hands and misses, and then—wham!—just like that, he bangs into a rock with his head, and then another right after that, and now he can taste blood, his tooth—his front tooth is sharper than it's always been, and his lip is bleeding. But he is not going to die here, he refuses to die here, in such a stupid, undignified way, when he has a big, strong body to save him, so he looks up at his father on the ledge above, and manages to turn himself just enough so the next rock he hits feet-first, and then another and again, until he's almost bouncing himself along in the water, from boulder to boulder, and when the next one comes, he uses it, and the momentum of the water, to catapult himself up toward the ledge above, and again he misses his *tío*'s outstretched hand, but the men are yelling encouragement at him, and keeping pace with his swift progress by leapfrogging each other, and he knows his plan is a good plan, and if he can do it again it will work, so again he twists in the water, except this time, when the next boulder comes and he reaches out his leg, it gets caught there, in an underwater crevasse, and the water pushes his body past, but keeps his leg wrenched under, and he can feel the bone snap, and he screams out in pain, but now his father and his *tío* are there just above him, and the pain is wicked, but their hands are on him, his *papi* has his arm, and his *tío* has the hood of his sweatshirt, and they are hauling him back against the current and toward his wrong-way leg. He feels no relief when the coyote is there, too, when they fix their six strong hands on him and together haul the top half of his weight up from the floodwaters and drape it over the lip of the earth above. His body is twisted awkwardly, but he has purchase now, they've got him. He will not drown. The water from his drenched body stains the dirt beneath him a darker color, and his fingers scrabble at the earth, but the lower half of his body is still in the water, stuck.

He feels no relief because he knows.

"My leg is broken." Ricardín does not cry. "It's definitely broken. I broke my leg."

And it's just as well the other migrants have not followed this far downstream, because no one wants to see or to hear the horrific business of removing the boy's leg from where it's caught in the crevasse below.

The only question is who will stay with him. Slim and Choncho have both done this journey enough times to know how it works, and to accept the terrible fate without complaint. They don't plead with El Chacal or the other migrants. They don't beg for help or ask them to stay. Although it would be a reasonable response in these circumstances, they don't drift toward hysteria at the thought of being left alone and immobilized here in the desert. It's Choncho who makes the final decision.

"Because I'm the older brother, that's why."

Slim nods.

"I'll stay with my godson," Choncho says. "We'll give you a head start, and when he's feeling up to it, I'll get him to the Ruby Road. You take David and go find work for both our families."

The brothers embrace, the hard, back-smacking embrace of working men. Then Slim pulls his son's wet head into his arms.

"I'm sorry, Papi," Ricardín says.

Slim shakes his head. "*Gracias a Dios,* you escaped with your life. That's all that matters."

Ricardín and David pray with their fathers before the four of them part ways.

"Call Teresa when you get to a phone, when you get picked up," Slim tells his brother. "And I'll call her when we get to Tucson, and make sure you're safe."

Choncho nods.

"And take this." Slim sets one of his water jugs down beside his son.

"Papi—"

"Take it, Ricky," Slim says. He squats down on his haunches and looks his son in the eye, and then squeezes his shoulder, and stands up with his hat pulled low. He turns his face quickly away.

Behind him, Choncho hugs his son, his hand like a mitt on the back of David's neck. They're both well over six feet tall. Choncho kisses his boy on top of the head, and then gives him a light shove toward his uncle. "Stay out of trouble," he says.

"Keep the rising sun to your backs," El Chacal tells them. "The Ruby Road is barely a mile from here."

A mile, Luca thinks. *With a broken leg.*

When the coyote herds the migrants back to their route, when they ascend from the canyon into the hot pink dawn, only Luca looks back from the gap at Ricardín and his *tío* still sitting on the ledge below. The others keep moving, and Luca can feel their unified will, pushing themselves forward like cogs in machinery, like an escalator. They can't stop the engine or even slow it down. It moves on despite the new rot in their collective spirit. Even the coyote's energy seems to be flagging. But they move on. They move on.

The migrants are shuffling past Luca, who hovers now, in the gap. Behind them, Choncho pulls his brown baseball cap low over his eyes, and Ricardín's face is a wet twist of pain. *How will they climb out of there when he can't walk?* Luca wonders. *How will they make it to the road?* Then he banishes that thought and prays instead. *Please let them make it to the road.*

"Luca, *ven,*" Mami says.

He scrambles to catch up.

CHAPTER THIRTY-FOUR

The cave, when they finally reach it, is warm and dry, and the
rising sun paints the back wall orange and pink and yellow. It's not a
sunken cave with a dark hole of a mouth like Luca expected when he
heard the word *cueva*, but rather, it's as if a huge divot has been hollowed
out of the earth with an ice-cream scoop, and then softened and cleaned
by the elements. There are several copper nails hammered into the top
of the cave's opening, and El Chacal takes a sheet from his pack that's
painted in earthy stripes the exact colors of the landscape. He tacks this
sheet onto the nails above, dropping the migrants into a light shade.

The migrants look different in this morning's light than they did in
yesterday's. Some of them had already known they were capable of walking away from a wounded man, of abandoning a person in the desert
to save themselves. Marisol, for example, believes there's almost no de-
spicable thing she wouldn't do in order to get back to her daughters.
Lorenzo would trample a baby to get to *el norte*. For others among them,
the discovery of their own compliance is an unpleasant surprise. They
all know how lucky they are that it was Ricardín who broke his leg, and
not them, and the recognition of that good fortune makes them each feel
damned, doomed. Unconscionable.

"Men outside first," the coyote orders them, when the sheet is fixed
in place.

Lorenzo groans, but the others duck through without complaint.

Rebeca is soaked and there's a dank smell rising off the back of her neck where the hood of her sweatshirt has gathered the oils running from her sopping hair. Her toes are frozen, and her feet feel raw in her shoes, but she's terrified of taking off her clothes.

"It's the only way to get dry." Soledad plops down on her backside and peels off her soggy sneakers. Her toes are tingly. "I feel better already," she says.

They all undress. They don't look at one another. Beto stays in only his underwear because he has nothing else to put on, so Lydia fishes out the same spare T-shirt he wore as a makeshift hat yesterday and hands it to him. The rain has had an unhealthy effect on his lungs, and he rattles and wheezes when he lifts his arms to pull the gifted T-shirt over his head. Lydia finds her own spare clothes, rolled inside a plastic bag in her pack, to be reasonably dry. Luca's, too. Soledad stands up and removes her sweater, which she holds up in front of Rebeca like a curtain so her sister can change. They all peel the clothes from their wet bodies. They slip into large T-shirts and change their underwear. They'll have to stretch their jeans to dry on the rocks outside.

Even though there's a new solemnity among them in the absence of Choncho and Ricardín, the solace of this place, this moment, is extraordinary. The ordeal of the rain makes Lydia appreciate the comfort of dryness in a way she never even considered before now. While the men strip and change in the cave, she and Luca sit just outside the sheet with their bare legs stretched out in the sunshine. It's still early morning in the desert, but the temperature is rising quickly. The rock is soft and dry beneath them, and the sun warms the patches where their skin is chafed and tender. Luca wants to ask Mami what they're going to do when they get to *el norte,* but he's afraid she won't have an answer, and besides, he doesn't want to jinx the nearness of their arrival. There's one question that won't leave him alone, though.

"What about Rebeca and Soledad?" he says. "Do you really think they'll go to Maryland?"

Lydia squints her eyes against the brightness of the growing day and pulls his feet onto her lap to examine his blister. The Band-Aid from last night is still surprisingly well fastened to his heel, so she doesn't mess with it. She can feel the warm weight of Sebastián's ring sitting in the hollow at the base of her throat. A mild breeze crosses her bare brown knees, and Luca wiggles his toes.

"It's always been their plan," Lydia says carefully.

"But couldn't they change their plan?" he says. "If we ask them?"

The sky is scrubbed fresh and stark blue by the gone rain, but every trace of that water has evaporated from the earth around them. It feels like a dream, all that rainfall. *This is a cycle,* she thinks. Every day a fresh horror, and when it's over, this feeling of surreal detachment. A disbelief, almost, in what they just endured. The mind is magical. Human beings are magical.

"Anything's possible, Luca," she says, looking past her toes and out across the ruddy landscape. And maybe they really could change their plans. Lydia thinks about how adaptable migrants must be. They must change their minds every day, every hour. They must be stubborn about one thing only: survival.

The moon has risen like a frail white eggshell against the blueness of the daytime sky.

"Can they stay with us?" Luca asks. "Can they live with us?"

"Yes," she answers him easily. "If they want to."

Lydia can't imagine saying goodbye to Soledad and Rebeca now. Another parting.

"And maybe Beto?" Luca asks.

"Oh my goodness!" She laughs. "We'll see."

Luca doesn't ask Mami if she thinks Choncho managed to get Ricardín to the Ruby Road. He doesn't ask if she thinks someone found them by now, if they're okay. He's already made up the answers to those questions in his own mind; they are the answers he needs them to be.

Their drinking supplies are beginning to run low, which feels ludicrous after all that water. The coyote instructs them to drink what they need, but conserve as much as they can. In the large cave, they sleep all morning, and by mid-afternoon they are thirsty and sweaty and hungry, and the relative comfort of this place has melted with the oppressive heat of the day. They endeavor to sleep through their discomfort. They know that tonight is the last night, and they're all eager to get out of here, to get where they're going, to descend from this airless, waterless, colorless nowhere and get to that road down there, to follow it to where there's life.

It becomes stifling in the cave because the camouflage of the hanging sheet, now weighted with rocks along its bottom to prevent the wind from billowing it in and out of the cave, also prevents that breeze from cooling them. Rest becomes difficult, and Rebeca is hot and frustrated when she sits up in the cave and finds everyone else asleep. All around her, the other migrants make the breathy noises of unquiet sleep. Beto is the loudest, wheezing impressively with every breath, but he doesn't stir. He uses one arm as a pillow, and sleeps with his mouth wide open, trying to draw the oxygen out of the air. Rebeca jams her bare feet into her sneakers and steps over him. The sneakers are scratchy and misshapen from being so wet and then drying out again, but she doesn't bother tying them. She only has to find somewhere to pee. Lorenzo opens his eyes as the girl picks her way across and around the sleeping migrants. He looks right up the smooth brown skin of her leg as she passes, and is rewarded by the sight of her yellow cotton underwear beneath her baggy white T-shirt. She ducks beneath the hanging sheet and steps outside. Without a sound, Lorenzo sits up from his place, leaves his shoes off, and follows her.

Rebeca rounds the side of the cave, leaves the softness of rock behind her, and steps into the scraggy tangle of undergrowth in search of a place to empty her bladder. There are scrubby trees here, and she ducks beneath one, pulling her cotton panties to her knees and squatting in the shade. She hears Lorenzo before she sees him, because he grunts at the prickly sharpness of plants and stones underfoot. She stands immediately, leaving a trickle of urine down the inside of one leg. She snatches her panties up around her hips and pulls the T-shirt down.

He gives her a crooked smile, an attempt at charm. "Should've worn my shoes," he says, stepping painfully toward her across the rocks. "Guess I'm not as smart as you."

Rebeca takes two steps back. Away from him. She puts one hand out and feels the rough bark of the rosewood she just watered. Its boughs are low overhead. A small branch tangles in her hair.

"I'm just taking a piss," he says. "Just like you." He's not wearing a shirt, only boxer shorts with a stretchy elastic waistband. He tugs them down right in front of her and pulls out his engorged penis. Rebeca does not want to see it. She looks at the path behind him, the path she took around the side of the cave, and knows she cannot return that way, not without walking toward him, without passing directly by him with his disgusting erect penis. She's already crying as she turns and ducks beneath the branch of the tree behind her, ripping out a strand of her hair as she goes. Lorenzo is quick, much quicker than she thought he'd be without shoes on, and before she's managed to get very far at all, he's already on her, first with a violent yank of her wrist in his grip, and then the hot wetness of his mouth all over her, her cheek, her neck, her ear. Rebeca fights, swinging with her free arm, but then he grabs that one, too, so now he has her pinned, her two wrists encircled by the fetters of his strong hands, and he presses all his weight on top of her. He pins her back against the rugged rock face and she can feel the hard club of his anatomy pushing against her stomach. She knows there are tears coming down her face, but she feels entirely powerless to change anything. She tries anyway, swinging her knee up to find that her legs, too, are now pinned beneath his weight. So then she strikes with the only thing she has left—her head. And she manages to connect, once, twice, she headbutts him, but he only laughs and tells her he likes it rough. She fights and cries, and tries to get her hands loose, tries to use her teeth, her elbows, tries to get her arms between their bodies, to push him off, but she doesn't scream, she holds in her scream, because they're in the United States now, and if she screams and she's lucky, it will be Slim or David who answers that cry, but if she's unlucky it will be *la migra*. When has she ever been lucky? Her head goes limp. Her neck, limp. Rebeca stares up past the contorted menace of Lorenzo's strained face. She stares up at the blank blue sky above him and waits for the worst part to happen. She wants it to be over with.

But then it doesn't. It doesn't happen. Because just as she feels the brutality of his hands traveling down the length of her rigid body, just as he pulls at the fabric of her underwear, there's another voice.

"*Oye naco,* get the fuck up off her this instant or I will blow your *pinche* brains out."

All at once, the violence recedes. The pressure recedes. The cruel weight of his body is lifted off her, and Rebeca slides down the rock face, trembling.

Lorenzo stands, stuffing himself back into his shorts. "*Chingada, güey,* we were just having some fun, right? *Relájate, hermano.*"

Rebeca is trembling and shaking, and she uncurls herself from his shadow and moves away from him as quickly as she can. The quaking of her limbs is a tremendous, rackety throb. She feels skeletal, juddery. She jerks and shudders and feels as though her legs might not hold her, but soon she's away from him and standing next to El Chacal, who has his pistol stretched out toward Lorenzo. Soledad is here, too, now, and Rebeca is crying as she reaches for her sister, but Sole moves past her. Soledad's eyes are hard and black in the ruthless light of the desert. They glitter as she stares at Lorenzo in his droopy boxer shorts. She looks at his tall, muscular frame, the slight smirk that twists across his mouth, his bare feet. She sees the sickle tattoo with its three drops of blood, just visible as he stands in profile, with one hand still leaning against the rock. She can see the shape of his erection beneath the fabric of his shorts, and she reaches out very deliberately to the coyote beside her.

El Chacal has never read academic theories of trauma psychology, but he has seen a thousand different varieties of it here in the desert. He is, in every practical sense, an expert in the field. He knows better than to give Soledad the gun. But on the other hand, the coyote feels nothing but disgust for Lorenzo. After seventeen years of ferrying people through the desert, he's learned to tell the good from the bad, even in difficult circumstances. He understands that once in a while, a person is not worth saving. So perhaps it's not entirely accidental, what happens; maybe El Chacal willfully mistakes Soledad's gesture for something else. When she reaches out and puts her hand on the pistol, he allows it, he lowers the weapon. He tells himself it's a tactical feminine intervention, a de-escalation. The coyote barely reacts when she disarms him.

And then it happens so quickly. She steps forward abruptly, swings the pistol up, and points it at her sister's would-be rapist. *Carajo.* This is not what El Chacal expected, not really. He steps after her, reaches toward her outstretched hands. "Soledad."

She swings it toward him for only a split second, but it's enough to convince him to freeze. She settles it swiftly back on Lorenzo, who's no longer smirking. He raises his hands in front of him.

"Yo," he says, and perhaps it was going to be *I'm sorry.*

CHAPTER THIRTY-FIVE

Soledad pulls the trigger, and Rebeca watches without any re-action at all. She doesn't wince or jump or gasp. She doesn't look away. Soledad would like to shoot him again and again. She imagines bullet holes in *todos los agentes* in Sinaloa, imagines Iván's brains splattered on the ceiling above her, and she'd like to keep shooting Lorenzo forever. She doesn't even need to leave the desert now because the satisfaction of standing here shooting is all she needs for the rest of her life. It feels like a buckle in time, like hours or years pass while she stands there holding that gun. So then it also feels like a slow-dawning realization she has, that she might yet use one of those bullets for herself, and in so doing, join Papi, but then she wonders if she can still make it to Papi, to the good place where he is. She looks at the gun in her hand, and sees it there at the end of her arm as if from a great distance, and as she watches, it turns slowly toward her, so the hole where the bullets come out is nearly facing her. But there are other hands covering hers now, strong and gentle, and together, all four hands point the gun toward the ground. El Chacal loosens the grip of Soledad's fingers and untangles the warm chunk of metal from her grasp.

When Soledad finally looks up from her hands and settles her eyes on her sister, what she sees in Rebeca's face is a mirror of what she feels inside herself. It's a nothingness. It's the blankness of that painted sheet blowing free in the hot desert wind. There is no joy, no relief, no regret, no disbelief. The sisters clasp hands and walk carefully back toward the cave, picking their way among the stones and the spiky plants with their eyes wide open.

El Chacal stands over the body. Guilty. It's not the first time one of his *pollitos* has died in the desert. Hell, it might not even be the first time today. But this one he could have prevented. He knows he's responsible. He makes the sign of the cross over the corpse, but it's God he addresses. *"Perdóname, Señor."*

They have to break camp quickly in case anyone nearby heard the shot. When the coyote returns to the cave, the migrants are already dressing in their dry, stiffened clothing. They're distressed, especially the two boys. Beto shakes his empty inhaler and takes a hollow puff, but they can all see the skin sucking into the depressions above his collarbones with each breath. He leans over and plants his hands on his knees. He closes his eyes to concentrate on deep, slow breathing. Marisol rubs his back.

"Is he okay to move?" El Chacal says. "We have to move."

Marisol leans down to Beto, the sleeve of her blouse making a small curtain for him, like the one a nurse might draw around his bed, were he in an emergency clinic in Tucson. Beto doesn't answer, but with his eyes still closed, he nods. Marisol gives El Chacal a thumbs-up. "He's okay." Beto's breath knocks like a rattlesnake.

The sisters move mechanically to dress themselves and pack their belongings. Their expressions are impassive. Marisol and Nicolás fall into helping them, zipping their backpacks, readying their shoes. The two silent men stand outside, apart. Slim and David look grim-faced and waxy. The confirmed death of one among them has forced them to contemplate what they'd heretofore managed not to consider too closely: That their brother and son, their uncle and father, may have by now met a similar end. Or no, not a similar end, in fact. A much worse one.

They probably made it out of the canyon, by Ricardín slinging his arm around his *tío*'s strong neck. Perhaps they fashioned a splint so they could stagger up from ledge to ledge, and climb out of the gorge. Maybe Ricardín was able to tolerate the pain of walking, somehow, another mile on that smashed and gnarled leg. Surely they drank their reserves of water on that journey, however long it took them, hot and exposed beneath the bald desert sun. Maybe they were able to save a few mouthfuls for the end. If they made it as far as the Ruby Road, while the sun sucked all the moisture from their bodies, how long were they able to last there, on that unshaded dirt, while they waited for someone to find them? How long does it take for a person to dehydrate and die in the Sonoran Desert? What happens when your body becomes so thirsty it no longer follows basic commands like *keep going, wave your arms, call for help. Don't close your eyes. Wake up. Wake up!* Are you aware, when your companion falls into the dirt beside you, when his body can't take another step? Can you feel your own kidneys shutting down, your liver failing, your skin shriveling onto your bones? Can you feel your brain cooking inside your skull? Or do you lose consciousness before all that?

Mercy.

The coyote tells everyone to move quickly. He pulls the sheet from its nails and wraps it into a ball. He knows he will never return to this place again.

Lydia is not sorry Lorenzo is dead. Neither does she feel bad that Soledad was the one to kill him, beyond whatever emotional fallout that truth might one day have for the girl she's grown so fond of. But she does worry that something vital may be broken inside herself, because Luca is suitably upset, but for her, it seems like death—even sudden, violent death— may no longer have the capacity to shock her. It's a fear she needs to press like a bruise, to test its tenderness. Both of Luca's heels are wrapped with Band-Aids and fresh socks, his boots tied snugly to his feet, and he's holding Rebeca's hand. The magic that exists between those two billows up and covers them like a force field. His presence reanimates Rebeca, erasing her blankness and filling her in with a trace of color. That energy, in turn, calms Luca, and returns him to himself.

"I'll only be a second," Lydia says to El Chacal as he stuffs the colored sheet into his pack. "I need to see him."

"Wait," the coyote says, and then he bends into the space where Lorenzo had been sleeping. His discarded T-shirt is there, his shorts and shoes. El Chacal reaches into the pocket of the shorts and pulls out a black canvas wallet with Minecraft characters on it. There's a *scritch* of Velcro as the coyote opens the wallet, but there's no ID inside. He'd been hoping for something he could leave with the body, because that act of identification is the smallest kindness, and one El Chacal can afford to give. Still, maybe someone will recognize the wallet, which will remain intact long after the skin is gone, long after the flesh is entirely scavenged or decomposed. Bodies disappear with astonishing speed in the desert. It's helpful to find some personal item near the bleached bones. He hands the wallet to Lydia. "Just leave this with him," he says.

When El Chacal returns to his packing, Lydia notices the cell phone, too, tucked inside one of Lorenzo's expensive sneakers. She picks it up. Luca watches her, but he's calm now, with Rebeca. She nods at him, and then climbs up the outside of the cave to where Lorenzo's body is still fresh in the dirt. It feels wrong to see him like this. Not only dead, but also without clothes. It's embarrassing to see the vulnerability of his bare chest. His eyes are open, and Lydia thinks about closing them, but she doesn't owe him that. She doesn't want to touch him, but she nudges his bare foot with her toe and watches his leg react. It wobbles and settles. He's really dead. And still she feels nothing. She stands so her shadow falls across his face and says a Hail Mary. She says the Fatima prayer, she tries.

O my Jesus, forgive us our sins, save us from the fires of hell, and lead all souls to heaven, especially those most in need of thy mercy. Amen.

It's not enough.

She's not praying for Lorenzo. She presses her lips together so hard her teeth bite into the flesh. She's praying for herself, for grace. For everything she lost. For all the mistakes she made. For the apology she can never give to Sebastián. For being wrong about Javier. For being wrong about everything. For surviving when everyone else died. For being so numb. She is praying for her boy and their decimated lives.

A sudden wind creaks through the nearby rosewood tree and flips through Lydia's hair. She squats down next to Lorenzo, and there's the violent flashback of this posture on Abuela's back patio. It floods in at her shoulders and at once she can feel it in her whole body. The sharp ache of tenderness, the half-moons of Sebastián's pink fingernails. There was love. There was love. She had a family, and then they were gone. All at once, their bodies splayed out in grotesque shapes across the patio. Yénifer's white dress, red. Her beautiful hair. Adrián's *balón de fútbol* abandoned in the grass near his feet.

Mamá.

So there it is. The welling reservoir of grief, keen and profound beneath the bruise, the proof of her humanity, still intact. She needs to bury it back where it was. She can't indulge it yet. She imagines a hole in the desert floor, all her pain inside. She imagines covering it with dirt, pressing down on the earth with her soiled hands. Lydia tucks the canvas Minecraft wallet beneath one slender, outstretched arm. She can see now, from the bareness of Lorenzo's chest, the mold of his shoulders, what he'd been concealing beneath that troublesome shell. He's only a boy. She stands and looks down again at the wreckage of the young body beneath her. And this is the moment.

This is the moment of Lydia's crossing. Here at the back of this cave somewhere in the Tumacacori Mountains, Lydia sheds the violent skin of everything that's happened to her. It rolls down from her tingling scalp off the mantle of her shoulders and down the length of her body. She breathes it out. She spits it into the dirt. Javier. Marta. Everything. Her entire life before this moment. Every person she loved who is gone. Her monumental regret. She will leave it here.

She stands at Lorenzo's feet.

She turns away from him.

"I forgive you," she says.

Lydia has already turned to go when she remembers his phone. She stoops again, to leave it where someone might find it. She stretches out her hand and sees it there, the innocuous, shiny thing, black plastic and gleaming metal in her hand. She closes her fingers around it and stands up again. She presses the button that makes it turn on, and she knows how, because it's a nicer, newer version of her own phone, the phone that's powered off, SIM card removed, stuffed inside her spare socks in the bottom of her pack right now. She is untraceable. But what about Lorenzo? Did he ever consider how his signal might be pinging between cell towers, triangulating his location? The thing glows to life in her hand, and there's no passcode or lock, it just opens right up, and Lydia has to cover the screen to see it beneath the glare of the sun. She walks to the rosewood tree and ducks into its shade. There are text messages, seven of them. Unread. Her thumb hovers over the screen. But then she jerks her head up and looks around, over her shoulder. They are miles from nowhere. Alone. What is she afraid of? She touches her thumb to the screen and the messages swarm up, they tumble open. They are from someone named *El Él*. The Him. Lydia curls over the phone, and it's instant, the way she consumes the information. It takes her no time at all to read them, and to know.

El Él.

L L.

La Lechuza.

The bottom drops out of her stomach. He's been tracking her.

Nineteen days. 1,626 miles.

Only seconds ago, she felt liberated. She was free of him, the fear of him. He cannot follow her where she is going. *No.*

"No!" she says out loud.

She almost throws the phone. She almost kicks Lorenzo in his dead ribs for his easy betrayal, for his treachery, for his nature. She'd like to bash his head against that rock, to kill him again, my God. It won't help. There's no act she can perform that would appease the violent rush she now feels in her limbs. There are no swear words magical enough to carry some piece of this violence away from her. She is a tornado. She's an eruption. She's an *huracán*.

She reads the texts again. She scrolls back, and back. To Guadalajara. Eleven days ago. Lorenzo had sold them out, proclaimed himself finished with Los Jardineros forever, and insisted that this piece of intel was a parting gift for the *jefe*, a gesture of good faith. He'd sent Javier a surreptitious photograph of Lydia in profile. She was wrapped around Luca, the two of them squinting out from atop La Bestia. Tus amigos están en Guadalajara, Patrón, the text read.

Javier had been in the coroner's office in Barcelona when the text came in, and his wife had admonished him for looking at his phone while they were there to identify their daughter's body, and to fill out the paperwork that would allow them to bring Marta home. The contempt he felt for his wife in that moment was entirely new, and Javier didn't even bother responding to her reprimand. He looked at her with mild disgust, and returned his attention to his screen.

You are not free until I am free, he typed back. Return her to me.

"*Ay, no,*" Lydia says out loud beneath the rosewood tree. "No."

The phone battery is almost full, but there's only one bar of a signal. Lydia holds it up overhead and swings it around. She emerges from beneath the tree, steps over Lorenzo's body, and scrambles up the rock wall beside him with his phone. Here. Two bars, three bars. Before she can stop herself, she opens the contact for El Él and hits the video call button. Already it's ringing. Lydia knows the ringtone. It's Pavarotti singing "Nessun Dorma." Ridiculous. Pretentious. Pedestrian. He thought he was aristocratic because he wrote shitty poetry and listened to opera. He's a murderer. He's a scumbag. He's bourgeois. But she is in his pocket, now. She knows. She is on top of a cave in the middle of the Sonoran Desert. She is standing over the dead body of his assassin, and now she has the upper hand, and he will not follow her into this next life. He will not haunt her, and she will not be afraid, no. She and Luca will be free. It ends here.

She hears his voice before she sees him.

"*Dime,*" he says. Anxious for news of her death.

"Tell you what? That I am dead? That my son is dead?"

"*Dios mío,* Lydia." He says her name. *Lydia.* And it sounds the same way it has always sounded coming out of his mouth. *Lydia.*

"I'm sorry to disappoint you, but we are alive. *Estamos vivos.*"

"Lydia," he says it again, and it's so confusing. Because her hatred of him is enormous. It's the biggest feeling she has ever felt. It's stronger even than the love she felt for Sebastián, the day they held hands and kissed in front of the altar at the Nuestra Señora de la Soledad cathedral. It's deeper than the colossal, unnameable thing she felt the day she pushed Luca out of her body and into the world. It's darker than the hole her *papi* left behind when he died without saying goodbye. Her hatred is a living succubus, vast enough and quick enough and wicked enough to crest up from her heart and take wing, to expand across the hundreds of miles between them, to engulf the whole city of Acapulco, to veil the room in which he's standing, to overshadow him and overcome him, to slip into his mouth and choke him from the inside out. She hates him so much she can murder him from sixteen hundred miles away, just by wishing for it. But he is saying her name. "Lydia."

His face is haggard. Skeletal.

"I never wished for your death," he says. "Surely you know that, Lydia. If I wanted you dead, you'd be dead."

She blinks. Pulls the camera away from her face. She closes her mouth and surveys the desert landscape. And suddenly she knows what he's saying to be exactly true. All this time, all her planning, all her strategy and self-congratulations, it was all an illusion.

"I could never harm you, Lydia."

Her mouth opens with an incredulous gasp. "Harm! You could never harm me? You have harmed me, señor. You have tortured me. You have destroyed my whole world, everything."

"No, Lydia. I never meant—"

"*¡Cállate la boca!*" she shouts over him. "Do you think I care what you *meant*? Or how you justify your monstrosities? I'm calling only to tell you that this is over. Do you understand? It's over."

Javier sighs delicately on the other end of the phone. She sees him do this. A familiar mannerism, once beloved. And it tilts her psyche like a fun house.

"But it can never be over, Lydia," he says sadly. "We have both lost everything."

No.

"That is horseshit, Javier. You have lost one thing. One!"

He pauses, lifting his wet eyes. "The only thing."

Lydia's heartbeat feels like a club, but her voice is lower. "The most important thing," she concedes. "But that gave you no right! No right!"

He's in a comfortable sunbeam in Acapulco, in her homeplace. There's a cup of espresso at his elbow. She is filthy and penniless and homeless and widowed and orphaned in the desert. He props his phone somewhere in front of him so his image becomes steady on her screen. He removes his glasses, cleans the lenses. His mouth is an impossible frown. "I don't know, I don't know," he says, blinking rapidly.

"I will survive," she says. "Because I still have Luca. I have Luca."

His mouth is a gash.

"This has to be over now," she says.

Javier places the glasses back on his face, pushes them up his nose.

"I killed the *sicario* you sent."

"You what?"

"Yes. He's dead. Look." Lydia scrambles to the edge of the little ridge and points her phone down at Lorenzo. Later she might feel guilt about this, about using his body to advance her own purpose, about celebrating Lorenzo's death, even in pretense. Later she might ask herself why Javier's last seven text messages had gone unanswered, unread. She might even wonder about Lorenzo's extinguished potential for redemption. But not right now. She points the phone back to her own face. "So we can be finished now, yes? Or should we keep on killing people?"

Javier unleashes a noise that's half sob and half laughter. He wants to plead not guilty by reason of grief. She knows grief is a kind of insanity. She knows.

Lydia is a beacon on that ridge.

The disgust in her mouth has a taste like bile. "Goodbye, Javier."

She doesn't bother hanging up. She tosses the cell phone into the dirt, and the camera yawns up at the vacant sky.

In front of the cave, in the hot height of the desert afternoon, three hours before they should safely set out with the dropping sun, the others are moving quickly down the slope and away into the valley below. Luca, with Rebeca, is waiting for her. Lydia takes his hand.

CHAPTER THIRTY-SIX

It's not far. El Chacal keeps telling them it's not far. It's mostly downhill, he tells them. Two miles. Less, even.

"Come on, you can do it," he says. "We're almost there."

But it's not the terrain or the distance. It's the heat. There's a reason migrants move through the desert mostly at night, in the waxing and waning hours, and it's not for cover of darkness. After all, *la migra* in *el norte* have helicopters, motion-sensing cameras, searchlights, all the nightgear. *La migra* have infrared goggles here, come on. It's the murderous sun. There can be no more rationing of water, because their bodies need it, their bodies will not continue without it. They drink their provisions, and it's not enough. The water pours through them, and out through their skin. It soaks their clothes, their necks, their hair. Beto keeps stopping to lean over, to breathe. It's an extra labor, an extra tax. He's dizzy, and he starts to cough. El Chacal swears under his breath. It's only two more miles. They've come so far, they're almost there. *Carajo, come on.* Their progress is too slow. It's a nightmare.

This is the worst crossing the coyote has made in years. He knew he shouldn't have brought a kid. Two kids. Four women. He knew there'd be problems. But then again, he admits to himself, those six have been the ones to survive this trek so far. They're stronger than he gave them credit for, even the asthmatic one. *Dammit,* El Chacal would never have agreed to bring that kid if he'd known about the asthma. Sneaky *pendejito*. He'd like to wring the kid's neck. But first he has to get them to shade, to water.

"Come on! Pick it up!" he says. There's no time to lose.

He really tries, but Beto cannot move. He cannot *pick it up*. He coughs and splutters, and shakes his head and leans on his knees, and the sun beats down on the back of his head. His black hair eats and swallows the heat from the sun, and his head is so hot, and his neck is burning, and Beto wants to make a joke. He tries to think of a joke he can make without using words, without spending precious breath. It hurts. It's so scary. Enormous pressure on his chest, *gigante*. An elephant, a hippo, the gargantuan, double-wide tires of a Mack truck, crushing trash in *el dompe*. It mashes down on his lungs. An avalanche of garbage. He cannot breathe. *I cannot breathe*. There are no jokes.

Marisol rubs his back and murmurs into his ear, because she's seen this before. Her daughter Daisy had asthma when she was younger. Not this bad, but still, Marisol is familiar. Daisy'd been croupy as a baby, and as she grew into a toddler, she and Rogelio had her tested for allergies. Dogs, cats, pollen. They had to be careful with her, because whenever something triggered her, she struggled for days. They'd have to take her to the emergency room for albuterol treatments. Once, she had an asthma attack on a playdate, and it was terrifying, because Marisol was sitting in the kitchen with the other mom, drinking tea, and Daisy didn't come to her until it was too late. She was already in trouble. Marisol dug frantically through her purse and came up empty-handed. The inhaler was on the bathroom counter at home. They raced out of there so fast, Marisol didn't even buckle her seat belt. When she pulled out, she backed into the bumper of a car parked at the edge of the driveway, and she didn't even stop to leave a note. At home, she turned on the hot shower to steam up the bathroom, and gave Daisy three puffs from the inhaler. Then a fourth. Daisy sat on the closed lid of the toilet, and Marisol stood in the steam, clutching her phone, ready to dial 911. It was tense and frightening, but within minutes, the sucking sounds in Daisy's little chest subsided. The whistling loosened. She breathed.

Beto worsens. Gone is the loose, gurgling cough he's had all week. Gone is the previous wheeze. He hacks, dry and tight.

Marisol raises her voice over the sounds of his distress. "Stay calm. Breathe slowly." But her own heartbeat is quick as a rabbit's.

There's no shade here. El Chacal turns in circles, combing the landscape for a better spot, some minor refuge from the sun. If they have to take a break, they need to break in shade. Every minute here saps the water tables of their bodies that much lower. But there's nothing nearby, and the kid cannot move.

"Try to stand up straight," Marisol tells him.

He tries, he unfolds himself. But this time, when he coughs on the exhale, there's no breathing in again. His eyes are round with panic, his hands fly up to his throat, and the skin on his neck sucks in. Then the tiniest honk of a wheeze, and he coughs again. And again, he cannot inhale. And now his lips are turning blue. Beto's fingernails are turning blue. It happens so fast. He flaps his hands near his neck.

Marisol snatches the inhaler from him, and shakes it, and puts it in his mouth, and squeezes it, but it's empty like the sky, barren. There's nothing. Beto falls back on his bottom, and it's almost comical because he's such a *payaso* and he's always making everybody laugh, so it's almost funny, because he falls down on his butt like a diapered baby with his legs extended, but it's not funny at all, because he's writhing now, and even that desiccant cough has ceased. They're all gathered around him now, they're all terrified, they're breathless, but there's nothing they can do, even though six miles away, as the crow flies, in a brightly painted orange building on Frontage Road in the tiny community of Río Rico, Arizona, there's a pharmacy. Behind the counter in that pharmacy, there's a bin containing four brand-new albuterol inhalers. Of course, there are nonprescription alternatives as well, and steroids for when symptoms are acute. When Beto passes out, Nicolás starts chest compressions. He doesn't know if that's the right thing to do, but he can't do nothing, so Marisol joins him, tips Beto's head back, pinches his nose, and breathes into his mouth. She blows with all her might, but she can't get his little chest to rise.

They're on their knees in the desert, all of them. The migrants pray while Marisol and Nicolás work on Beto. They stay that way for a long time, much longer than it would be reasonable to expect that their efforts might bear fruit. No one wants to acknowledge the passage of time. No one wants to be the one to call it, not even El Chacal. They feel a critical danger to their immortal souls, to be the one to admit: Beto is gone. Soledad and Rebeca are both crying, Lydia's crying, Luca is crying. But there are no tears, with all that crying. There's no water left in their bodies to make tears. El Chacal puts his hand at last on Nicolás's shoulder.

"*Basta,*" he says.

Nicolás finishes his compressions, but then stops Marisol from leaning down again, from trying another breath. He reaches across Beto and puts his hands on her shoulders. They lean toward each other with the boy between them. They make a tent with their bodies.

"No," Marisol says. She puts her hands on him, on his forehead, on the stillness of his heart. She reaches for his hands, brings them in front of him, still supple.

He is so small.

The other deaths. Or other losses. They were excruciating.

But they felt . . . rational. They felt somehow honest: there was risk undertaken. And risk sometimes results in the collection of an unjust payment.

But this. Jesus.

Marisol crumples over him, all the breaths he couldn't take. She gulps them, she squeezes them in her fists. "*Papá Dios.*" She cries over him until, at last, El Chacal pulls her away.

One by one, he pulls them each away. He puts his body between theirs and Beto's. He touches their arms or their shoulders, and releases them. Slim and David stand beside the grim-faced coyote, each with one hand on the other's shoulder.

"We will carry him," Slim says.

El Chacal looks up at him. He considers the angle of the sun, their deficit of water, the fatigue of their depleted bodies.

"No." He shakes his head. He takes the painted sheet from his pack and, to Slim, says, "Help me wrap him."

Then El Chacal takes a phone from his pack, powers it on, and drops a pin to mark the location. "I'll come back for him."

They all stare at him, but no one moves.

"I promise," he says. "We have to go now."

This time, Luca doesn't look back.

In a remote campsite at the end of an unnamed road that's traveled not infrequently by the green and white trucks of the US Border Patrol, two RVs are waiting. The RVs have been parked there for two days, with tarps stretched from poles out front, and coolers full of beer and food nearby. There are lawn chairs set around a central campfire, and country music on an old-fashioned radio with a retractable antenna and a knob on one side. The men sitting at that campsite each day have made sure to nod and wave at the passing Border Patrol agents when they come. The men in those lawn chairs have done the pleasant, casual work of making themselves and their vehicles familiar. The agents stopped by one day and talked to them for maybe ten minutes. The men allowed the agents to look inside their RVs. They had nothing to hide.

When El Chacal and his ten remaining migrants walk into that camp two and a half hours early, the waiting men aren't ready for them. The Border Patrol checkpoint on Route 19 is still open. They can't leave for at least three more hours. What if someone comes by before then? Where are they going to hide eleven people in the middle of nowhere? It's too hot to sit inside the RVs. There's not enough gas to run the air conditioners while they wait.

El Chacal shrugs. "We had no choice" is all he says.

It's a comfortable, tucked-in little campsite, and they're relatively protected here from the noise of the relentless wind. So they turn off the radio and sit in silence, hoping they'll hear the engine of any approaching vehicle before it appears. None does. The migrants drink water and water and blessed water. They sit in the shade of the RVs and drink Gatorade too. Marisol cries abundantly, unblinkingly, as soon as her body's hydrated enough to make tears. She doesn't beckon the tears, but they come. They stream down her face unregulated, like tributaries. They gather in glistening puddles on her hands. Luca and Lydia keep their eyes and mouths closed.

No one speaks.

At 5:15 p.m., the two men begin packing up the campsite and ushering the migrants inside. Marisol and the two sisters board first. Lydia wants to say something to El Chacal. Something to convey her gratitude, and to allay his wounded conscience. There's nothing. She puts one hand briefly on his arm, and he stares at the ground beneath the tires. He nods once, focusing on the clumps of wild grass, the glinting pebbles in the dirt. Lydia climbs into the RV. Luca is on the bottom step behind her, but he doesn't follow. He stops with El Chacal as well.

"He needs a sky-blue cross," Luca says.

The coyote nods once, and there are tears that stand in his eyes. They are the first of their kind. "A sky-blue cross," he repeats.

Luca nods.

"I'll make sure of it, *mijo*," the coyote says.

And then Luca leans close and whispers something in the coyote's ear. And the man reaches up and takes Luca in his arms, and Luca folds himself around the coyote's neck, and they embrace for a long moment, and then they turn away from each other quickly, and Luca ascends the steps. Lydia watches through the window as El Chacal lifts his pack from one of the lawn chairs, hoists his replenished water supplies, and heads back into the desert.

"What did you say to him?" Lydia asks Luca when he sits down on the bench seat beside her.

Luca shrugs. "I told him he was a good man for bringing us here."

There are hollow compartments beneath the benches and the beds, the men show them. They have to climb into those compartments, squeeze and fold themselves up. Soledad has heard stories of other coyotes forcing migrants to strip naked at this stage of the journey, so no one will cause problems. Taking the migrants' clothes is a kind of insurance policy, so no one will try to escape before the coyote is ready to set them free. She's heard that sometimes the coyotes make those naked migrants wear diapers, too, so they can stay hidden in the dark for hours. She rubs her hands down her thighs and feels grateful for her denim armor. In the second RV, the driver scrutinizes Slim and David, and asks, "Think you can fit?"

Slim nods. "We'll make it work."

"It's only forty-five minutes, right?" David asks.

"Thereabouts," the driver says.

David tries out a yanqui phrase he's been saving. "Piece of cake."

Luca's heart thuds in his chest. They hear the engine start up, feel the rumble of vibrating machinery. The driver pulls on the steering wheel and tugs the curtain across behind his head.

"Next stop, Tucson!" the driver says loudly.

The drive is slow. Painfully slow. There are deep potholes and sharp bends and the road is wide enough for only one vehicle at a time, so in the event of oncoming traffic, the RVs must pull up and wait for the approaching car to pass. At length they turn onto a slightly wider road, and a short time later the man in the driver's seat calls out quietly, "Border Patrol. Nobody move." The driver waves at the agents in the approaching vehicle, and they recognize him as one of the campers who's been staying way out, south of the Lobo Tank these last few days. The agents' names are Ramirez and Castro, and they think about pulling the guy over, checking his RV for wets. But he's a white guy with a cowboy hat and a mustache that looks like it's been growing on his face since before they became ironic. Besides, their shift is almost over. Nobody wants to do paperwork during happy hour. They salute him, and squeeze their Chevy Tahoe past the RV with inches to spare. In back, the migrants hold their breath as they hear the tires of the passing vehicle crunch by just outside their window, and then the *click click* of the steering wheel when the driver centers the RV on the road again. And now they're rolling.

"All good," the driver calls.

Luca pins himself in next to Mami in a small dark place. He curls into her even though there's enough room, pressing against Mami as if his life depends on her proximity, because now that they're here, now that it's this close, now that they're minutes away from starting their new life, he doesn't want to. In some primal way, he knows that once they're safe, the monsters he's so far managed to repel will come crashing in, and now there will be new monsters with them. A horde. He can feel them clawing at the door. But not yet.

He squeezes into her. Mami folds her arm around him and tucks the fingers of her hand beneath his rump. She fits him in there and makes herself his shield once more. She pulls his small hand toward her in the darkness and uncurls his fingers. She slips the loose gold halo of Papi's ring around his outstretched pinky. The road beneath them dips and rolls. They cross the startling rumble of a cattle guard, and Luca presses his head against her chest. She wraps her hand around his forehead and closes her eyes. One final jolt of the ungainly RV, and suddenly there's the level promise of pavement beneath their tires.

The Border Patrol checkpoint is closed, as anticipated. They roll through without stopping, and the twin RVs gather speed as they strike north through the gathering dusk. Soledad and Rebeca nearby tip their heads together, and lace their fingers together, and cast their breath together. They are motionless and moving at once. They each have secrets now. And yet, despite everything they've suffered, at this moment together, they're full of something bigger than hope.

Lydia can't see it from the dark place where she is, but she can sense it. She knows it's that perfect time of day out there in the desert. She imagines the colors making a show of themselves outside. The glittering gray pavement, the aching red land. The colors streaking flamboyantly across the sky. When she closes her eyes she can see them, the paint in the firmament. Dazzling. Purple, yellow, orange, pink, and blue. She can see those perfect colors, hot and bright, a feathered headdress. Beneath, the landscape stretches out its arms.

EPILOGUE

Fifty-three days, 2,645 miles from the site of the massacre.

It's not the little adobe house in the desert Lydia imagined. But there is the yellow school bus, and Luca does board it every morning with a clean backpack and a new pair of sneakers. He doesn't wear Papi's hat anymore because it's too special. It's taken on a museum quality. It stays on top of his blue dresser along with his other treasures: Abuela's rosary and an eraser shaped like a dragon that Rebeca got him. Luca's hair is neatly cut and shampooed to smell like Papi's now, with a trace of mint. The bus comes to the end of their tree-lined block, and when Luca gets on it, he does so with two Honduran children, an Ecuadorian girl, a Somali boy, and three *estadounidenses*. Lydia slips her finger inside Sebastián's ring every morning when that bus pulls away. *Today will not be the last day I ever see our child.*

She has work cleaning houses. Her mother would have thought this the greatest irony. Lydia, whose house was never quite clean enough. The money's not good, but it's a start. They live with the girls' cousin César and his girlfriend. The girlfriend's *tía* lives here, too, and everyone contributes what they can. They take turns shopping and cooking.

Lydia's English is a help, but there are many different languages in *el norte*. There are codes Lydia hasn't yet learned to decipher, subtle differences between words that mean almost, but not quite the same thing:

migrant, immigrant, illegal alien. She learns that there are flags people use here, and those flags may be a warning or a welcome. She is learning. Bookstores, invariably, are a refuge. There's one in the town where they live, and the first time Lydia ventures in, it takes her breath away. She has to steady herself against a shelf. The smell of coffee and paper and ink. It's nothing like her little shop back home. It's stocked mostly with religious books, and instead of calendars and toys, they carry rosaries, Buddha figurines, yarmulkes. Still, the upright spines of the books are bedrock. Steady. There's an international poetry section. Hafiz. Heaney. Neruda. Lydia flips past the twenty love poems and reads "The Song of Despair." She reads it desperately, hungrily, bent over the book in the aisle of the quiet shop. Her fingers ready the next page while she devours the words. The book is water in the desert. It costs twelve dollars, but Lydia buys it anyway. She keeps it tucked into the waistband of her pants where she can feel it against her skin.

Lydia tries not to feel jealous when they wake up together and Luca tells her, his eyes still sticky with sleep, that Papi visited him in his dreams again last night. Lydia curls around him as if she can absorb the visit with her body.

"What did he say?" she asks Luca.

"He never says anything. He just sits with me. Or we walk together."

Lydia's body throbs with longing. "That's good, *mijo*."

It's almost a mile to the library, and they walk there together on Saturday mornings. On their third visit, the librarian invites them to apply for library cards, and when Lydia declines, the woman switches to Spanish and tells her there's no danger to them, that they're entitled to them regardless of their immigration status. Lydia is dubious at first, but if you can't trust a librarian, who can you trust? She and Luca both get cards, and it's miraculous, restorative, life changing. Rebeca comes with them sometimes, but Soledad never does.

The sisters are enrolled in school now, too, and it's difficult for them. Not because their English is so minimal, or even because their schooling at home was rudimentary. They're both smart, quick to learn. But their lives have been so expansive, their traumas so adult. They are young women, and now they're meant to clip themselves into a three-ring binder each day. They're meant to hang their jackets in lockers and flirt with boys in the hallways. They're supposed to regress into shapes that were never familiar to them. They don't understand the teenage expectations of *el norte*.

Lydia is coming home from work one day when a boy seated in front of her stands up to pull the stop-cord on the bus. As he reaches overhead, his wrist emerges slightly from his sleeve and Lydia notes the presence of a tattoo there in the shape of an X: a sickle and spade. The stop-cord dings, the bus slows. Lydia quails in her seat. As the bus hisses and lurches, accelerating away from the boy, she watches through the window while he pulls his hoodie over his head. Most days Lydia struggles to accept how peripheral her life has become; today, she's grateful to feel invisible. It's impossible not to wonder about Javier then. Usually she locks him out of her mind, but there are moments when he slips in through the keyhole. She wonders if he's sorry for what he did to her. If he feels justified. She wonders if he feels anything now, or if he's shut it all down, if Marta's death was too much for him, so he found a loophole, a way to opt out of humanity. She is stronger than he is; she feels every molecule of her loss and she endures it. She is not diluted, but amplified. Her love for Luca is bigger, louder. Lydia is vivid with life.

At school, Lydia meets with the principal, who wants to talk about Luca's aptitude for geography.

"There's an annual geography bee," the woman had said on the phone. "I think we should enroll him."

Lydia goes to fill in the paperwork. She sits in a comfortable chair across the desk from the principal, a woman about her own age. In the distance she hears a bell ring, and suddenly the view from the window is filled with swarming children. They shriek and run and climb and swing, and all that beautiful, happy noise is a strange backdrop to what the principal is saying.

"I didn't realize your son was undocumented." The woman swivels the chair beneath her, straining to get the words out. Lydia can tell this is uncomfortable for her. "I'm sorry; he won't be eligible to win the prize."

It's absurd, Lydia knows, to feel crushed over a geography bee. It should mean nothing when weighed against the meaningful recent traumas of their life. She gazes out the window at the squealing children. The principal joins her momentarily in her reverie, and then speaks quietly in the room, crossing a line she's not supposed to cross. It's a border she's disregarded many times before.

"My parents were undocumented immigrants from the Philippines," she says to Lydia. "They brought me here when I was younger than Luca."

Lydia doesn't know how to respond. Is this a kind of solidarity? Should she feel encouraged? What she feels is exhausted. Itchy. Her hands are chapped.

"I know some good immigration attorneys if you need help."

In the fenced back garden of their little home on the tree-lined street, they bury eighteen painted stones. Beto's is sky blue. Adrián's is a *balón de fútbol*. Luca visits Papi's buried stone every day after school. He tells his father's buried stone about his new life in Maryland, how much he likes sharing a room with Mami. How he loves Rebeca more than he loves Soledad, and sometimes he feels bad about that, but not too bad, because the whole rest of the world loves Soledad. She doesn't need his love like Rebeca does. He tells Papi about his teacher and the games he plays with his new friend Eric at recess. Kickball. Four square. Luca cries often. But he also talks, he laughs, he reads. He lives. Soledad and Rebeca visit their father's stone less frequently, but slowly they're beginning to spend time out there. Last week when Lydia was weeding, she found a playing card, the king of hearts, leaning against the base of their father's cross. Once in a while when Lydia stands at the kitchen window washing dishes, she sees one of the girls sitting quietly out there in the grass. Sometimes they move their lips as if in prayer.

They still sleep with the lights on, or Luca does. Lydia mostly doesn't sleep. She sits up in bed beside him, Luca now occupying the space where Sebastián once slept. She rubs his hair with one hand and hopes he's dreaming again of his *papi*. She hopes that one night soon, Sebastián might slip out of their son's dream and into her own, as if he's a physical presence, atoms and particles in the room that can migrate from Luca's brain into hers, ear to ear. *Una frontera santificada.* Late into the night she reads, and the lamplight falls in a soft circle across her tented knees, across the warm blankets, across Luca's casting breath. In their new home, Lydia rereads *Amor en los tiempos del cólera,* first in Spanish, then again in English. No one can take this from her. This book is hers alone.

AUTHOR'S NOTE

In 2017, a migrant died every twenty-one hours along the United States–
Mexico border. That number does not include the many migrants who
simply disappear each year. Worldwide in 2017, as I was finishing this
novel, a migrant died every ninety minutes, in the Mediterranean, in Central America, in the horn of Africa. Every hour and a half. So sixteen
migrant deaths for each night I tuck my children into bed. When I first
began my research in 2013, these estimates were difficult to find because
no one was keeping track. Even now, the International Organization for
Migration warns that the available statistics are "likely only a fraction
of the real number of deaths" because so many migrants who vanish are
never accounted for in the first place. So maybe the number is more like
two hundred deaths for each load of laundry I do. There are currently
around forty thousand people reported missing across Mexico, and in-
vestigators routinely find mass graves containing dozens, sometimes hundreds, of bodies.

It's also true that in 2017, Mexico was the deadliest country in the
world to be a journalist. The nationwide murder rate was the highest on
record, and the overwhelming majority of those murders go unsolved, no
matter if victims are migrants, priests, reporters, children, mayors, activ-
ists. The cartels operate with impunity. There's no recourse for victims
of violence.

I am a US citizen. Like many people in this country, I come from a family of mixed cultures and ethnicities. In 2005, I married an undocumented immigrant. We dated for five years before we got married, and one reason for our prolonged courtship was that he wanted to get his green card before he proposed. My husband is one of the smartest, hardest-working, most principled people I've ever met. He's a college graduate who owns a successful business, pays taxes, and spends a fortune on health insurance. Yet, after years of trying, we found there was no legal route available for him to get his green card until we got married. All the years we were dating, we lived in fear that he could be deported at a moment's notice. Once, on Route 70 outside Baltimore, a policeman pulled us over for driving with a broken taillight. The minutes that followed while we waited for that officer to return to our vehicle were some of the most excruciating of my life. We held hands in the dark front seat of the car. I thought I would lose him.

So you could say I have a dog in the fight.

But the truth of my personal interest in this story is more complicated than that.

There are two other factors that were probably more responsible than my husband's immigration status in piquing my interest in this subject. The first is this: When I was sixteen, two of my cousins were brutally raped by four strangers and thrown off a bridge in St. Louis, Missouri. My brother was beaten and also forced off the bridge. I wrote about that horrible crime in my first book, my memoir, *A Rip in Heaven*. Because that crime and the subsequent writing of the book were both formative experiences in my life, I became a person who is always, automatically, more interested in stories about victims than perpetrators. I'm interested in characters who suffer inconceivable hardship, in people who manage to triumph over extraordinary trauma. Characters like Lydia and Soledad. I'm less interested in the violent, macho stories of gangsters and law enforcement. Or in any case, I think the world has enough stories like those. Some fiction set in the world of the cartels and *narcotraficantes* is compelling and important—I read much of it during my early research. Those novels provide readers with an understanding of the origins of some of the violence to our south. But the depiction of that violence can feed into the worst stereotypes about Mexico. So I saw an opening for a novel that would press a little more intimately into those stories, to imagine the people on the flip side of that prevailing narrative. Regular people like me. How would I manage if I lived in a place that began to collapse around me? If my children were in danger, how far would I go to save them? I wanted to write about women, whose stories are often overlooked.

Which brings me to the final, most significant factor that influenced my decision to tackle this subject. It took me four years to research and write this novel, so I began long before talk about migrant caravans and building a wall entered the national zeitgeist. But even then I was frustrated by the tenor of the public discourse surrounding immigration in this country. The conversation always seemed to turn around policy issues, to the absolute exclusion of moral or humanitarian concerns. I was appalled at the way Latino migrants, even five years ago—and it has gotten exponentially worse since then—were characterized within that public discourse. At worst, we perceive them as an invading mob of resource-draining criminals, and, at best, a sort of helpless, impoverished, faceless brown mass, clamoring for help at our doorstep. We seldom think of them as our fellow human beings. People with the agency to make their own decisions, people who can contribute to their own bright futures, and to ours, as so many generations of oft-reviled immigrants have done before them.

When my grandmother came to the States from Puerto Rico in the 1940s, she was a beautiful, glamorous woman from a wealthy family in the capital city, and the young bride of a dashing naval officer. She expected to be received as such. Instead, she found that people here had a very reductionist view of what it meant to be Puerto Rican, of what it meant to be Latinx. Everything about her confused her new neighbors: her skin tone, her hair, her accent, her notions. She wasn't what they expected a *boricua* to be.

My grandmother spent much of her adult life in the States but didn't always feel welcome here. She resented the perpetual gringo misconceptions about her. She never got past that resentment, and the echoes of her indignation still have some peculiar manifestations in my family today. One of the symptoms is me. Always raging against a perceived slight, always fighting against ignorance in mainstream ideas about ethnicity and culture. I'm acutely aware that the people coming to our southern border are not one faceless brown mass but singular individuals, with stories and backgrounds and reasons for coming that are unique. I feel this awareness in my spine, in my DNA.

So I hoped to present one of those unique personal stories—a work of fiction—as a way to honor the hundreds of thousands of stories we may never get to hear. And in so doing, I hope to create a pause where the reader may begin to individuate. When we see migrants on the news, we may remember: these people are people.

So those were my reasons. And yet, when I decided to write this book, I worried that my privilege would make me blind to certain truths, that I'd get things wrong, as I may well have. I worried that, as a nonmigrant and non-Mexican, I had no business writing a book set almost entirely in Mexico, set entirely among migrants. I wished someone slightly browner than me would write it. But then, I thought, *If you're a person who has the capacity to be a bridge, why not be a bridge?* So I began.

In the early days of my research, before I'd fully convinced myself that I should undertake the telling of this story, I was interviewing a very generous scholar, a remarkable woman who was chair of the Chicana and Chicano Studies Department at San Diego State University. Her name is Norma Iglesias Prieto, and I mentioned my doubts to her. I told her I felt compelled, but unqualified, to write this book. She said, "Jeanine. We need as many voices as we can get, telling this story." Her encouragement sustained me for the next four years.

I was careful and deliberate in my research. I traveled extensively on both sides of the border and learned as much as I could about Mexico and migrants, about people living throughout the borderlands. The statistics in this book are all true, and though I changed some names, most of the places are real, too. But the characters, while representative of the folks I met during my travels, are fictional. There is no cartel called Los Jardineros, nor is that fictional organization based on a specific cartel, though it does reflect the general nature and composition of the cartels I encountered in my research. La Lechuza is not a real person.

One thing I had to learn while doing research for this book was to strangle the word *American* out of my own vocabulary. Elsewhere in the Western Hemisphere there's some exasperation that the United States has co-opted that word, when in fact the American continents contain multitudes of cultures and peoples who consider themselves American, without the hijacked cultural connotations. In my conversations with Mexican people, I seldom heard the word *American* used to describe a citizen of this country—instead they use a word we don't even have in English: *estadounidense,* United States–ian. As I traveled and researched, even the notion of the American dream began to feel proprietary. There's a wonderful piece of graffiti on the border wall in Tijuana that became, for me, the engine of this whole endeavor. I photographed it and made it my computer wallpaper. Anytime I faltered or felt discouraged, I clicked back to my desktop and looked at it: TAMBIÉN DE ESTE LADO HAY SUEÑOS.

On this side, too, there are dreams.

ACKNOWLEDGMENTS

I'm grateful to so many people for helping this story become a book.

For reading early drafts of this novel and being honest about how bad it was: Carolyn Turgeon, Mary Beth Keane, Mary McMyne. For reading later drafts of this novel and encouraging me in the right directions: Pedro Ríos, Bryant Tenorio, Reynaldo Frías, Alma Ruiz. For reading almost-finished drafts of this novel and sharing invaluable expertise: Bob Belmont, Jenifer A. Santiago, Alejandro Duarte.

For allowing me to observe their important work, and patiently teaching me things about Mexico and immigration I never would've understood without their insight: Pedro Ríos (again, a thousand times) from American Friends Service Committee, Laura Hunter from Water Stations, Elizabeth Camarena from Casa Cornelia, Robert Vivar from Unified US Deported Veterans, Norma Iglesias Prieto from San Diego State University and the Colegio de la Frontera Norte, Sister Adelia Contini from Instituto Madre Asunta Esmeralda Siu Márquez from Coalición Pro Defensa del Migrante, Joanne Macri from the NYS Office of Indigent Legal Services, Enrique Morones from Border Angels, Cesar Uribe from Rancho el Milagro, Padre Óscar Torres from the Desayunador Salesiano Padre Chava, Misael Moreles Quezada from Rancho San Juan Bosco, Father Pat Murphy, Andrew Blakely, Kate Kissling Blakely, and all the staff at the Casa del Migrante in Tijuana, Padre Dermot Rodgers and friends, from Saint Peter of Rome Roman Catholic Mission. Thank you to Gilberto Martínez for showing me around Tijuana and sharing cultural insight with me. Thank you to Alex Renteria from the US Border Patrol for answering my questions. Thank you to all the brave men and women I met in different stages of their journeys who talked to me about their experiences.

I'm grateful to the following writers, whose work you should read if you want to learn more about Mexico and the realities of compulsory migration: Luis Alberto Urrea, Óscar Martínez, Sonia Nazario, Jennifer Clement, Aída Silva Hernández, Rafael Alarcón, Valeria Luiselli, and Reyna Grande.

I'm super grateful to my agent, Doug Stewart, for his friendship, enthusiasm, and perfect pitch. I'm indebted to Amy Einhorn for loving this novel, and for not settling when it was good enough. Thank you to Mary-Anne Harrington for being absolutely devoted to this book. Thanks to my foreign rights team, Szilvia Molnar and Danielle Bukowski. Thank you to Caspian Dennis at Abner Stein. Thank you to everyone at Flatiron for their passion and brilliance, especially Nancy Trypuc, Marlena Bittner, Conor Mintzer, Bob Miller, Cristina Gilbert, Katherine Turro, Keith Hayes, Emily Walters, Vincent Stanley, and Don Weisberg. Thank you to Cecilia Molinari for elevating this book with a precise, sensitive, and perfectly bilingual copyedit. Thank you for all the global support from the team at Tinder Press and Hachette Australia. Also, to all the publishing people who aren't working on this book, but believed in it, and support it even though it's not their job: Megan Lynch, Sonya Cheuse, Libby Burton, Carole Baron, Emily Griffin, Asya Muchnick. To Rich Green at The Gotham Group, and to Bradley Thomas at Imperative Entertainment, thank you.

To my first family, Mom, Tom, and Kathy, for their enduring love and support. To Joe, thank you for not insisting I get a job at a bank; thank you for worrying about me and encouraging me anyway. Aoife and Clodagh, I could not be prouder of the people you are, and who you're becoming, so full of compassion and grit. Never mind moving mountains; you girls will move planets. *Mi querido hermano, Padre Reynaldo, por la resucitación de mi fe rota durante el peor momento de mi vida.* And to my dad, who died a week before our forty-fifth president was elected, and whose sudden absence from my life made the grief crater that became this book.

ABOUT THE AUTHOR

Jeanine Cummins is the author of three books: the novels *The Outside Boy* and *The Crooked Branch* and the bestselling memoir *A Rip in Heaven*. She lives in New York with her husband and two children.

www.AmericanDirtBook.com

www.JeanineCummins.com

Recommend *American Dirt* for your next book club!
Reading Group Guide available at
www.readinggroupgold.com